"MR. CUNNINGHAM HAS A VIVID STYLE."

—*The New Yorker*

"MR. CUNNINGHAM KNOWS THE SECRET POWER OF THE NOVEL AND USES IT BEAUTIFULLY, not only to follow the rational thought of his characters but also their private feelings."

—Richard S. Wheeler,
author of
BADLANDS, FOOL'S COACH,
and *SKYE'S WEST*

"MR. CUNNINGHAM'S NOVEL APPROACHES GREAT-NESS for several reasons including those of skilled writing, sensitivity to human emotions, COMPELLING DRAMA, EXCELLENT PLOTTING AND RARE, EVEN RIOTOUS HUMOR. But most of all his novel approaches greatness because of his refreshing deviation from unimaginitively phony character types."

—*The Sarasota Herald-Tribune*

Tor Books by
John Cunningham

Rainbow Runner
Starfall
Warhorse

STARFALL

JOHN CUNNINGHAM

A TOM DOHERTY ASSOCIATES BOOK
NEW YORK

STARFALL

Cover art by Darrell Sweet

A Tor Book
Published by Tom Doherty Associates, Inc.
175 Fifth Avenue
New York, N.Y. 10010

Tor ® is a registered trademark of Tom Doherty Associates, Inc.

ISBN: 0-812-51361-4

First Tor edition: January 1993

Printed in the United States of America

0 9 8 7 6 5 4 3 2 1

FOREWORD

MANY YEARS AGO a man wrote me a letter, telling me this story. His letter began this way:

Sometime, if you like to ride through those mountains, the Gilas, east of San Vicente in New Mexico, you will run across a little lake, or pool, overshadowed by heavy pines, and you will be impressed by its quiet, its perfect stillness. If it should be a Saturday, you might find a man there, sitting by the pool, looking at it, thinking. He generally goes up there with his five boys, and you can hear them off in the woods hollering; but he sits quiet. He is thin, gray-headed, with a face that is half bitter and just half dumb with patience and longtime resignation; a man sitting without question, like a lifer humbly enduring time.

His right leg is stiff as a board, locked at the knee, sticking straight out, but he can mount a horse all right. He isn't uncivil; he will exchange a few of the easy remarks everybody passes the time of day with; but he won't really talk. And after a while you will decide it would be more worth your while to ride along and enjoy those grand woods and mountains, and you will, and you'll most likely forget him.

What you won't know is what he is thinking about—three things at the bottom of the pool: an old rifle, a locket, and a star, that were thrown in a long time ago, when he was young.

This is the story about that rifle, the locket, and the star. And why he sits, and looks that way, thinking.

ONE

BILL GORHAM STOOD on the lip of the big boulder that blocked the canyon and formed the pool. He looked down toward San Vicente and felt nothing of homecoming. Behind him, his men, easing themselves under the trees by the pool after the long day's ride, were talking the usual senseless talk.

Out on the plains, San Vicente lay, as always, white in the late sun, like a promise, a jewel in the hand. Empty promise, paste jewel, like all the other towns. There was no home for Gorham, unless it was Pepe's friendship—Pepe, the little brown man who always sat quiet, listening with a faint, amused smile to the wandering gabble of wandering minds. Pepe and the forest, they were home.

He drew a deep breath. Maybe, after this one last raid in San Vicente, when he could see the boys off with some cash, he and Pepe could forget the robbery end of it, and go back to the mountains and just live as they had lived before the gang was formed—

1

hunters, killing what they ate, nothing more; selling a few furs; the rest of the time just living up there in the high country, watching the animals play, the jays fight, living that life without time or pressure, from day to night and day again, not even knowing what month it was. A life of seasons, wherein time was measured by leaf-color, by the changing depths of the trout in the holes, by the mating time of animals, the feel of the sun. In the winter, south into Mexico with the first flights of geese; in the summer, roving north. One day, a long day's hunt; the next, just lying in the sun or curing a skin; the next, maybe hunting berries, when they would watch a bear eating ants and forget the berries. Or maybe a whole day fishing, when they would see a she-bear with her cubs, scooping fish out of the stream, and maybe whapping a cub end over heels for a lesson.

He was sick of thieving, tired of the responsibility of leading irresponsible men, tired of campaigning and using his brains; and above all, sick of the failure they had just escaped from. Freedom was what he had wanted when he ran away, from everything—his father, the school, even his girl Allie, now so dimly sweet in recollection. But a thief was never free—fighting the law was the closest and worst contact with their lousy society. What he wanted was freedom, pure and simple. He had found it, Pepe had given it to him, and now he wanted it back, the way it had been, three years ago. He would lead one more raid, steal just a few more cows in San Vicente. That was all. Then he would be through.

"I got a girl down there," Harvey said, looking down the long canyon between the spurs of the mountain.

"Home," Ollie said, turning to where Burt was scraping fly-eggs off the last of their beef, "and your old woman. Why don't you settle down and get married, Burt?" The mood of the sunset was on them. A time to be sentimental, even if they did smell like coyotes. What was the difference? They had got out of Mexico safe, after all, and within sight of money again, and Bill would lead them to it. Easy money, once again.

"She says she won't marry a thief," Burt said.

"Who, her? Well, you could reform," Ollie said. The old dream. About once every six months they would lie around the fire and talk about reforming.

"I'll reform as soon as I get enough dough," Burt said. That was the answer, the great secret.

Bill and Pepe kept their mouths shut. To Pepe, towns were no home either, and Bill had already had money, once.

"Dough," Ollie said. "I gotta get dough to get my teeth fixed. I wonder if that dentist is still there. First thing, steal some cows so I can pay for the teeth. First thing."

"In town," Pepe said, "is nothing but trouble."

They ignored him.

The others wanted people; Pepe didn't. They wanted noise, and liquor and whores, fights, arguments, all that; but Pepe didn't. He had run away from home when he was twelve, and had grown up, not wild, but solitary, working in Mexico as a sheepherder until he was twenty-six; then as an outlaw, when he had been arrested as a rebel, which he had not been. If he had been a liar, he could have managed to be on both sides, successively; but he had difficulty lying—he was too simple in his outlook. He simply did not care who was president of Mexico; but Benito Juarez could not conceive that any man could ignore his existence to the extent of not caring what he was, and the rebels couldn't either, so both sides assumed he was a traitor. Once marked as a wolf, he was forced into outlawry because it was then impossible to hold even a sheepherder's job, and so he had stolen what he was not able to earn.

When he was six, he had seen for the first time that when people drank too much of anything, either pulque or tequila, they made fools of themselves. He had seen his mother get drunk, and his father get drunk and beat up his mother and then Pepe too. So he had concluded that there was a kind of devil in the booze, who got into people. Bottled devils.

Life in the village was dirty, cruel and dull, but mostly dull. There was nothing in it, aside from the two women potters, who made little clay animals and gods, that had any interest at all for him, except for what became his dominant preoccupation: the priest, the church, and the tales the priest told the children. These tales had to do with people, not feathered serpents. He would sit and listen to the stories about the saints, and about God Himself, and at the age of five had distinguished easily between the clay gods of the potters and the God of the church, simply because the One God was kind, and the clay gods were either animals, or, obviously, devils, and none of them good. The clay gods were like the police, who were evil and had to be bribed; but the other God was kind, and He Himself paid the way and bought off the devils and, incidentally, the police.

The priest and the police were always at odds, and evidently one could not be friends with both. When Pepe learned that the priest's God had stolen corn from the fields to feed his friends, he had fallen in love with this God, and that was the beginning of a long, odd friendship.

His mother died when he was eleven. The house always had strange women in it after that, one after the other, so he slept in the chicken hovel—not that he didn't prefer it. There had been no outright fight with his father, unless one counted the beatings as fights. Pepe had just gone, and finally disappeared, living in the alleys, visiting the priest, listening to the stories about the saints and other remarkable people. And, of course, enjoying the priest's food, which he occasionally shared. There was another world, it was quite apparent, than the village.

This contact ended when his father, finding that Pepe was evidently working for the priest, and presumably bringing him money, went to the police and accused the priest of immorality with children.

The police jailed the priest in order to undermine his popularity and bought Pepe's father a bottle of tequila.

The police did not want to hear Pepe's denials of the charges, so Pepe smeared dog dung all over the door of the police station, went to the church to say goodbye to his Friend there, and left the village forever.

Harvey said, "I could get a job in the dry goods store. My girl's dad runs it."

"You ought to get rid of them pimples, Harvey," Ollie said, "if you're going to get married to that girl."

"It don't matter," Burt said quietly. "She's got them too. How else did you think she could stand Harvey?"

"Lay off," Bill said. "What about money? You all want to try selling a few to Nulty?"

"If Nulty's still alive, why not?" Ollie said. "It's been three years. Maybe Nulty's dead."

"There's always another Nulty somewheres," Burt said. "I'll ask my widow woman what the lay of the land is."

"Hell, I know that," Ollie said. "*She* is. The lay of the land. The whole land."

"Ah, shut up," Burt said. "She'll know about Nulty, anyway."

Bill said, "Burt, cut some steaks off that hunk of beef, and let's eat. What about the Captain?" He turned around and looked across the fire at the Captain of Rurales, who was sitting with his back against a tree, looking glumly at the flames. "We going to drag him down there with us?"

"I'm going to kick his head off after dinner," Ollie said. "I'm going to turn him loose afoot with the handcuffs on and let the owls eat him alive."

"I heard," Bill said quietly, "there was an amnesty." He hadn't been listening to the others talk. That kind of chatter went on for hours, and after a while you just didn't hear it.

"What the hell is that?" Ollie asked.

"The Governor has issued a pardon to every outlaw, on condition he comes in and settles down. Last chance."

They all believed him. They looked at him with serious faces, in the firelight. He hadn't believed it himself; and yet these men believed him absolutely. It made him happy, and it made him sad, because it proved he was their leader, and it proved that they were children; and what the hell kind of an orphanage was this to be the head of?

"Just a rumor," Bill said. "Probably just some wild tale."

"You mean," Burt said, "just walk right into San Vicente and not get arrested? Bygones be bygones?"

"If it's true," Bill said.

"You mean start over?" Harvey asked. "No more warrants waiting around for you?"

"I guess so," Bill said, suddenly feeling irritated.

"Think of that," Harvey said, awed, staring into the growing dark. "I could get married and everything. Even in church. I could really get a job in her old man's store. For God's sake."

"Yeah, for God's sake, for God's sake," Ollie said, suddenly mean. "You want to turn honest or something, you mealy little fleabag? Is that it? Whatta we got here, an honest man among decent people? I always suspected you of undecent notions, Harvey. I always thought there was something fishy about you—turning honest. What the hell for?"

"Listen," Bill said patiently. "Don't get in an uproar just over some rumor."

They were quieter than usual that evening, while they ate and got their horses hobbled out for the night, and their bedrolls laid out comfortable.

"The thing is," Burt said, in the middle of a silence, "it would be nice not being chased all the time. That's all. I'm getting tired of being chased."

Nobody said anything. They were all tired of being chased.

"It would be nice to go to bed in a bed with my old woman, instead of some alley, and not think maybe Murphy would come stomping down there in the night and arrest me," Burt said. "Nice to get up in the morning and go for a stroll down to the cantina for a beer in the broad daylight. The funny thing is—" He stopped.

"The funny thing is what?" Ollie asked.

Burt shook his head.

"Go on and say it!" Ollie yelled. "Whatta we got, a lotta goddamn secrets around here? What are you, a goddamn school girl? Say it!"

"Well, all right," Burt said, getting sore himself. "I just thought the crazy thought—that would be being free. That's all I thought. That would be being free."

"Whattaya mean, free?" Ollie said. "We're free now. Damn sight freer than anybody down in San Vincente. All them respectable sons of bitches chained in bed with their sniggering wives." He laughed.

"Free," Burt said, suddenly very bitter. "It sure is free, we got to live in the mountain, we got to wait out here like a bunch o' wolves till we get the word it's all right, or Murphy's dead, or they forgot. That's sure free."

"We're free," Pepe said quietly. "And we're going to Wyoming. Remember? Plenty wild country up there."

"Boys," Bill said, "maybe it's just a rumor. We'll find out tomorrow. Now listen, let's get to bed. We got to steal some cattle tomorrow night, we got to find out who's the easiest, we got to sound out Nulty if he'll buy them. That's a lot of work. So let's get some sleep."

A silent evening. All bedded down, fireglow sinking, they lay around, then Harvey said, "If I was working in that dry-goods store, I wouldn't have to lift a finger. Just sell ribbons to the old ladies and smile and take in the cash. What a life."

"The soul of a pimp," Ollie said. "That's you, Pimples." He sat up suddenly and looked at the Captain, who was lying down now, still handcuffed. He'd been handcuffed for three days. "I forgot to kick your head off," Ollie said. "Tomorrow morning, I'm going to kick out your teeth, Captain. Just like you shot up my choppers. You comprenderay? I'm going to cut you in pieces and send you back to your wife in separate packages. You comprenderay? Think it over, you dirty bastard. Think about it, good." He lay back and went to sleep.

The Captain, in the silence, lay and thought it over. He had been thinking about it for three whole days.

After a long while, Pepe whispered to Bill: "I got a bad feeling, Bill."

Bill looked at Pepe. Pepe was not given to feelings. He looked sick with anxiety now.

"You and me, Bill," Pepe whispered. "We could leave, go north."

"Break up the gang?" Bill said.

"Yes," Pepe answered. "It's breaking anyway. You heard Harvey. He always was a coward. Now he's a tired coward."

Bill looked away. "I can't go yet. I can't leave the boys until I see where they're going."

"What are you, their papa? They're going to get killed, Bill."

"How the hell do you know?"

"Listen," Pepe said. "We had a good life before we ever joined this gang. We could go back to it, Bill. You and me. Hunting. You know the life we had."

"All right," Bill said. "I will. But first I got to see what the boys are going to do."

"The big leader," Pepe said. "A very responsible fellow. You got the swelled head, Bill."

It was the first time he'd heard Pepe bitter, Bill thought.

"A day or two won't matter," he said.

"We better don't go down to San Vicente," Pepe said.

"What are you? Some kind of witch doctor? What the hell do you know about it?" It was a rude thing to say to him, and Bill was sorry he had said it as soon as he did.

It wasn't till half an hour later that he knew why he had said it at all. He was angry with Pepe because—well, because Burt was right. The bitter thing was that they weren't free at all. Unless you were like Pepe, who didn't have a home and didn't want one.

If you were like most men, the wandering, the back trails after a while got like an iron ball hanging inside you from your heart, heavy as death. They were all caught in a forked stick, all of them, wanting something, and unwilling, almost unable, to pay the price. Bill lay on his back and looked at the stars. What was the answer, in this world? If you hated to be cooped up, hated their rules, hated regularity, and rebelled, you got freedom; but then another part of you, an older part, got sick and tired of it, and freedom turned into slavery; and you looked back on your old slavery, and remembered the chains with love. What was a man, that he was made like this? To be a man, in the end, was nothing but torture.

He turned his face away from the stars and went to sleep.

About four, he and Pepe waked up with the cold, and Bill put some wood on the fire to keep the others asleep. Bill lay thinking about the Captain. What were they going to do with him?

Overhead, that black velvet sky with its million diamonds aglitter, and nothing left of the fire but the smoking new logs on the old coals. Overhead the pine boughs held themselves out over the pool. Silence as deep as the still water itself, black, motionless.

Ollie asleep, his face ruddy in the fireglow, all the temper and irascibility withdrawn inward, leaving a face oddly childlike—the harsh creases and bold juttings of that hill-billy pan now folded and crumpled into a stubborn pout, as though Ollie were locked inside in some endless personal wrangle with himself. Maybe in sleep the man dissolved, the child emerged, Bill thought, looking at Ollie.

And Burt, as humble, as simple, as patient as a priest, lying on his back, his bald head ringed with black like a tonsure—like the white granite of some frosty peak rising above a timberline of defeated hair.

Patient, silent, he seemed to work so hard at the simplest tasks of life that he had no mind left for talk; like an ox leaning with dumb docility against his yoke, pulling stupidity through eternity. He made his way through petty crime with the same quiet, softly stubborn persistence that a saint might devote to self-perfection. He gave the appearance of perfect, absolute dedication to a career that was actually nothing more than a chance succession of lucky breaks, exactly like the life of a buzzard.

And yet in Burt's eyes there was always a sort of innocence. Burt wasn't stupid; he belied his appearance.

"In all the heavens, a million stars," Pepe whispered. "They shine so, they wink. The same, always the same. Who put them there? Look, they go around, around, but always the same places. All in a pattern. But who are the falling stars? You see them?"

And for a moment they watched the starfall—strange lights winking into the world of the heavens, streaking bright across the night sky and then, like an internal blink, winking out again—always in arcs, sailing across the serenity of the other order. Hundreds a night, the disordered armies of some galactic rout, broken out of some far, unmeaning pageant across the farthest curve of some other, stranger universe; the refugees of some alien disaster, entering a city of peace.

"Like the devils falling from heaven," Pepe whispered. "And all the others are like the angels. I remember the priest he told us. They would not serve."

Silence—the fire, is it still awake? A coal falls, and slumbers under its blanket of ash. Beyond the pool, Bill could see the top of the great, flat boulder, gray in the starlight, that formed the lip of the dam that held the pool at the head of the canyon. The water went over the edge, to the left, in a tiny trickle. A perfect camp. Behind them, wilderness; and one man, lying on that flat boulder with a rifle, shooting down the canyon, could hold off a dozen.

"I'm afraid Ollie will hurt that Captain," Bill said. "If we let him go, it will look like he escaped. Then we wouldn't have any trouble in the morning. We can't drag him all the way to Wyoming, we can't take him down to San Vincente."

"We should not have taken him hostage in the first place," Pepe said. "That was a cowardly act. Treachery."

"Ollie only did it because he was broke. It drives him wild."

"I know, I know." Pepe sighed suddenly, with a terrible sadness. "So much has gone wrong. Now we have no home, no place to run to."

"I know. All a mistake," Bill said. "The Rurales will never forget us. Unless—we might give the Captain a handsome present."

"Their honor is never worth less than a hundred dollars—for a captain."

Bill threw back his blankets. "Come on. Let's let him go."

"If you were a star," Pepe said quietly, still lying there looking up at the heavens, "which would you be? One of those good, serene, patient stars, always in their place—or one of those wild ones, always breaking loose and flying away?"

"Come on," Bill said.

Pepe got up quietly and went around the fire to the hostage, beyond Ollie and Burt, in the dark. The hostage lay quiet, looking up at them, his eyes dull with sorrow, and yet with an aloofness he had always been careful to preserve.

Pepe beckoned the prisoner to his feet with one finger. He led him away, with Bill following, into the trees. Up they went, single file, to the mountain meadow where the horses were hobbled. One of the horses, vague in the starlight, raised his head, alert.

Pepe unlocked the Captain's handcuffs and handed key and cuffs to the Captain.

The Captain sucked in his breath sharply; and then, all of a sudden, his fortitude collapsed, he shrank, a huddle of wrinkles, and stood there like an exhausted old beggar. Pepe waited. Slowly the Captain pulled himself upright and raised his eyebrows again in his characteristic, aloof expression.

He said, five hundred miles from help, "I warn you: you had better kill me."

Pepe said, "To kill you would be to add only one more onion to a stew which already has too many onions. *Hasta la vista, señor.*"

"You broke a truce. You will be shot, without trial."

Pepe said, "My friend Ollie did not know what he was doing when he kidnapped you. He thinks with his bowels."

"One suffers for such friends," the Captain said.

"One suffers for all friends," Pepe said. "Take the worst horse, if you please, *señor*. You can write to your mother for a new one. I am sorry, we have no stamps."

In the starlight, like some improbable ghost, the Captain roped, caught up and saddled the nag they had stolen in Durango. He went east, up the meadow, toward the paling sky, back the way they had come. It was a long way back through the Mimbres Mountains, a long way down to Deming and the border, and his people.

"I don't think the Captain is going south yet," Pepe said calmly. The Captain had disappeared into the trees. "He will circle around and go down to San Vicente and report that we are here—to the law, Murphy, whoever is sheriff now."

"You mean," Bill said, his voice tight with anger, "you knew he would go on down there, and yet you let him go? Are you trying to get us all killed?"

"Do you think it would have improved things to kill that man? After we broke our own word, our own honor, by breaking that truce and taking him hostage? Do you?"

Bill looked at the ground.

"Answer me. Are you a murderer?"

Bill looked up slowly. "No," he said.

"We pay," Pepe said. "For everything."

He followed Pepe back to the fire. The ashes were pale now with the lightening of the eastern heavens. He lay down again in his blankets. He was dead tired, and to a weary man, this time of dawn was the worst—light bringing an end to peace. In a moment the first light, the first tip of pink on the mountains would make his bones ache with an old slave's sorrow for the passing of night.

"Which kind of star would you be, Bill?" Pepe whispered.

He was back on it again. "I'm too tired," Bill said. Pepe and his endless speculations. What does a buzzard feel like? Would you like to be a buzzard—just for a while?

"I think," Pepe whispered suddenly, "it is a picture of those angels, to remind us. The good ones keep their place and serve. The others rebel, they want to be free—and fall from heaven. Which are you, Bill?"

He looked at Bill and saw him sleeping. He smiled gently.

TWO

OLLIE WAS THE last to wake up. The others sat there waiting for him in the brightening day, in the cool shade of the pines by the pool. Again, Burt was idly scraping fly-eggs of the hunk of beef they had killed in Hillsboro, neatly slicing steaks half an inch thick.

There was an ache in Bill's back, from apprehension of what Ollie would do when he found out about the Captain; and, again, about what the Captain would do when he got down to San Vicente. And yet in his heart there was a lightness and happiness that had no base in reason. He was home, the air was warming, the long shadow of the mountain, as the sun rose, was slowly shrinking into the mountain again, like a child against its father. Down there in San Vicente, now sparkling white in the pink plain far below, there was American bourbon, American fried eggs and American girls, and even if you might get shot in the next two days, these things made the heart light. Even the American law was a relief—a bunch of voted-in nobodies you could argue with, not a lot of noble savages like the Mexicans, with their delicately cruel Aztec instincts just glossed over with a smattering of Roman civil law and emperor worship.

One shot, hard, cracking the ears, from down the canyon. All alert now—stiff and listening—Ollie, wide awake, lying quietly in his blanket.

A second shot, the echoes billowing and rolling upward, slapping off the cliffs like laughter. They looked at each other. Ollie sat up slowly, chewing at his cheeks with his gums.

"Hunters," he said, and that relaxed them, true or not. He got his silver tooth-box out from under his blanket, and opened it, and took out his teeth. A look of misery and pain crossed his pink face as he regarded the smashed dentures. The upper front teeth were gone. He stuck the plates in his mouth and looked around at the Captain's bed.

"Now I'm gonna kick the— Where is he?"

"Gone," Pepe said.

"I let him go," Bill said.

Ollie jumped up. "*You* let him go! Who the hell are you?" And then the fury broke, and he was running, charging like a bull, off through the trees toward the horses in the meadow. All four men got up quickly and ran after him. They stopped at the edge of the meadow and watched him going hand over hand up the rope to the gray he had just caught.

Pepe said, "He's been gone four hours, Ollie. You'll never get him."

"You dirty little greaser!" Ollie shouted. "He was mine, I caught him!" The gray kept rearing and wheeling away, and all of a sudden Ollie's temper flew out of him like a wildcat and he jumped and hung on the gray's ears, screaming curses at it. He was beating its head with his fist. The gray shook him off and wheeled, and Ollie, falling, grabbed the rope as it sailed by and the rope yanked him clear around, spinning him cartwheeled onto the grass.

Off went the gray, down the meadow, rope trailing. Ollie sat in the grass, mumbling curses, pulling up the grass by the handful and throwing it around like a baby, lost in a helpless rage.

Then they all heard the hooves crashing and scrabbling on the rocks down the slope in the trees, the soft pummel of unshod hooves, coming fast up through the pines, and then they came, three, seven, ten wild horses, heads down, lunging off up the hill, out across the grass, the tame ones scattering away. As they gained the level, they reached out and flew, their tails and manes streaming behind, mouths open, gasping, reaching for ground, loins humping like running dogs—horses that had never been shod or saddled, as wild as cougars. The four men stood and watched them as they ran, and Ollie watched from the grass.

They disappeared into the pines at the upper end of the meadow, and as they did, another one came out of the trees, but moving slow and hard. There was a cloud of bloody froth on its nose and mouth, and they could hear its breath coming in great grunts as it galloped slowly across the grass, each breath coming as though it were kicked out with a boot, loud, tearing, coughing grunts. It stumbled in the middle of the meadow, fifteen feet from where Ollie sat—fell, rolled on its side, and then suddenly sat up, braced on its spread forelegs, halfway risen.

It looked at Ollie, and Ollie looked back—the two of them sitting in the grass. Slowly the horse's head swung back, and for a moment its eyes, soft, wide, innocent, took them all in, one after the other; then, rolling, it fell back, its forelegs giving, and it lay still on its side.

Silence in the meadow, the tame horses standing and staring at the dying one. Up above, that wide, empty blue of the high mountains. And slowly, the five men converged on the horse. They stood and watched it die. No movement except a flicker of its belly, the last of its breathing. In its side, a small, wet hole.

"For God's sake," Ollie said. "Some son of a bitch killed a wild horse. For God's sake, why?"

There was a bitter look on Pepe's face. "We better go," he said. "This is bad country now. We better go north. Now."

Ollie turned slowly. Summer lightning, that was all he was, furious display coming and leaving, moods like wind on water. "We got to get some money. Nulty will buy something. We can't go north broke."

Pepe hunched his shoulders, looking suddenly cold, as though in an invisible shadow; he looked around quickly, as though for the shadow of a cloud.

"Sh, be quiet. Listen. Do you hear anything?" Pepe was listening. Nothing in the forest. Nothing, but far off, in the summer haze, a jay.

"What the hell's got into you?" Ollie said. And now Ollie looked around the meadow, timid, perplexed, looking for something to be afraid of.

"It's some lunatic loose in the woods," Burt said. "Nobody else would shoot a wild horse. Let's get out of here."

"Go north," Pepe said woodenly. "Right now."

"The hell with you," Ollie yelled, "you little bastard, you let my captain go—it was you that had the key, not Bill—he was my man, I caught him myself—"

"Shut up," Bill said. "Keep your damn trap shut."

Pepe, smiling, waved the abuse aside. "It's all right."

"Like hell it's all right," Bill said. And then it all came out on a tide of their anger, and he and Ollie were shouting at each other. "You pulled a lousy trick down there when you took that captain. You broke—"

"It got us out of there, didn't it?" Ollie shouted. "Where the hell would you be now, if I hadn't of broke that truce and took him hostage? How the hell would you have got out of that house?"

"I don't know and I don't give a damn. The fact is you wrecked us south of the line, Ollie. We can't go back, now, not ever again."

"You would rather just be shot up, or spend the rest of your life in some Mexican jail, is that it?" Ollie cried. "Big noble hero, you're noble all right now I got you out safe. How would you of got out of there? With them nigger bastards all around? They would of brought up a cannon and blowed us out of there the next day. And you got the nerve to bawl me out because I waved the flag and trapped that son of a bitch, that dog meat. Sure, you walked out like the King of Prussia, and now you got the nerve—" He turned away, anger all broken down into bitter sadness. "Talk about your crummy gratitude!"

Bill went over to him and put his hand lightly on Ollie's shoulder. Ollie, stubborn, head down, turned away, full of grief. "Ollie," Bill said, "we couldn't drag him any farther. The guy probably had a family. Three or four little kids. You wouldn't want to kill their daddy, would you?"

They stood in the sun. Out of nowhere the big fat blowflies had come and settled on the horse.

"Oh, hell," Ollie said at last, heavily, turning around, ignoring Bill in a way that meant that Bill had won completely, "let the poor greasy bastard go."

He looked at Pepe. "I'm sorry, Pepe. I didn't mean to call you a greaser. You ain't a Mexican anyway. You're just a sunbaked Canadian." His mouth suddenly widened into a big, freckled grin, with a black hole in the middle where his store teeth had been shot away. He had been smiling that way when the slug had hit him crossways. "Let's go down to San Vicente and get drunk."

"Better go north," Pepe said, looking at the dead horse.

"Tell you what," Bill said. "We'll compromise. We'll go down and see old Lawson and find out where we can pick up some cows; and then, tomorrow, we'll go north. If we see the Captain, we'll just have to duck. All right, Pepe? Fair enough?"

They caught up the horses and in twenty minutes were on their way down the canyon toward Lawson's place.

The dead horse lay in the sun in the summer meadow, with the flies; and presently the first of the black messengers appeared in the sky, sailing slowly over, the shadow of death passing quickly and skillfully over the flowering grass.

Half a mile down they saw Lawson's cabin and its corrals, squatting in the shade like an old blind woman with her hand out, the dead begging. A miser's smoke trickled out of the stone chimney, a sparrow's fire. They came across the roan first, lying on its side, legs still outstretched as in running, but dead.

"Look at his tail," Pepe said.

There was no tail, just the red stump.

"For God's sake," Ollie said quietly. "What the hell is going on around here?"

They went on down, and they found the chestnut

in the creek. It must have been drinking, for it had fallen in a heap, its head in the water. Again, no tail.

"I'd like to catch the son of a bitch that did that," Bill said. He shook out his rope. "Get your rope, Ollie, let's drag it out of Lawson's water."

Ollie's face was cold. He was looking down at Lawson's cabin. "The hell with Lawson's water," he said, and then the others saw, on the rough side of the shack, the five horse tails, hanging in a row.

"It can't be Lawson," Burt said.

"I'd like to see this man," Ollie said. He rode out ahead.

"Don't make trouble for nothing," Burt said. "We got to get some money, Ollie. We ain't staying here."

Ollie said nothing. They pulled up in front of the shack and sat there in a row. Nothing left of the cherry trees; all had died halfway back, had sprung out again, and had died further back, for good. Nothing left of the bed of asters that even three years after the old woman died still bloomed stubbornly. Manure piled against the open barn doors two feet high, and grass growing out of the manure itself—the barn hadn't held stock for over a year. Decay, defeat, sleep, everything slowly sinking back toward the earth.

A man came out of the cabin door, shutting it slowly and firmly behind him, and stood there holding a Winchester—gray hair over cold, unsmiling gray eyes, no sadder than a stone, no gayer, either. Bill looked at the Winchester. Brand new.

"You got anything to say, Lawson?" Ollie said.

"Yes," Lawson said. "Get out."

They looked at him in silence. Then Ollie said, "What's wrong with us? We got the measles or something? That's a hell of a thing to say to an old friend, Ed."

"Listen," Lawson said. One of his eyes walled out

slightly with nervousness. "I don't want any trouble. I don't want any thieves around my place."

"Listen, Ed," Ollie said mildly, swinging up his leg to dismount. "Have you—"

"Don't get down!" Lawson said loudly, and Ollie stopped. Ollie settled back on his horse and asked, "Have you got religion or something, Ed?"

"I've reformed," Lawson said.

Ollie burst out laughing, and Burt began to smile.

"You?" Ollie shouted and began slapping his leg. "That is the silliest thing I've heard in years. I've reformed, he says. What for? Oh, Ed, don't stand there and say things like that—with that face—you got no idea, honest to God, the way you look." He raised his hand to slap his leg again, and suddenly stopped short. "Them tails," Ollie said quietly. "You shot them horses?"

Lawson's eyes, hard as rocks, suddenly unfroze and grew big. "And what if it was?" he cried.

"Why shoot a horse? Are you crazy?" Ollie asked. "You reformed. Where'd you steal that rifle? And shooting wild horses. What *for*? *Nobody* hurts the wild ones. What *for*?"

Lawson's mouth softened a little. "You been away a long time," he said. "Them horse tails is worth five bucks apiece."

"What for? Witch doctors? Them Navajos got some new mumbo jumbo?"

"You been gone a long time, Ollie. They got cattle in the mountains now, you boys. The horses eat too much grass. They eat what a cow would eat. That's what the big boys figure. The stock companies."

"What stock companies?"

"You boys been to the moon, I reckon," Lawson said. "You heard about the Lincoln County War?"

"What's that?"

"You heard about Governor Wallace?"

"Who the hell is Governor Wallace?"

Lawson smiled. "You poor, dumb sons of a bitches. I feel sorry for you. Come in, boys. You can't stay long, but come in. I got some coffee."

"Up your coffee," Ollie said. "You take them tails off your house before I come in."

"Now, listen," Bill said, seeing the pink come up in Lawson's face. "Don't mind him, Ed. You know Ollie's crazy."

"A man can only do what he can," Ed said. "I'm a bounty hunter. Lions, wolves, horses, I don't give a damn. But I got to eat."

Ollie swung down and came over, his long legs skinny as a heron's. "It just kills me to see a man turn honest. You see what happens, Bill? You used to be a pretty good guy, Ed." He went past Ed into the shack.

Inside, they sat silent, sipping coffee from empty tin cans. There hadn't been a cup in the house since the old woman kicked off.

"I don't taste much dead horse in this coffee," Burt said, trying some polite conversation to break the silence, "but it'll be coming down the creek damn soon. What do you do with the carcasses, Ed? Sell 'em for sausage?"

"Leave 'em lay," Ed said sourly. "Wolves, buzzards. Ki-yotes." He looked glum. "It ain't no cinch, being honest. I wish I knew how to do something besides shoot."

"No more weaners?" Bill asked. "Seemed to me that was always a kind of respectable kind of thievery. Nothing rough—run off a man's cow with a calf, and just wean off the calf and keep it—even give the man his cow back. Nothing rough about that."

"I told you," Lawson said, "the mountains are full

of cattle now. No place left to hide a weaner pen.''
He looked up. ''You boys better get wise.'' He was
serious, now, and they knew it, and sat silent, looking at him.

''A lot of new outfits in the valley now. A lot of
English money come in. They been bearing down awful hard on the old bunch. Here we was, going along
like always, stealing back from each other what your
friends stole behind your back, good friends and everything, just the custom, you know how it was, and
here all of a sudden these rich bastards start acting
like rustling was a crime. Of course, they got the law
on their side, they had to bring that up. You wouldn't
believe the things that've happened in San Vicente.
Tom Slattery. *He* was killed.''

''Tom?'' Burt asked, with real shock.

''Ed Robinson. Killed. You know, they didn't even
try to arrest him, they just shot him 'cause he had a
running iron in his hand.''

''Why, that's outright murder,'' Ollie said.

''Listen,'' Lawson said, ''things been getting awful
tough the three years you was gone. Forming new
counties all over. The buggering government's getting so serious about things. The big new outfits hire
these crooks, they's the ones killed poor Tom, pure
strangers they was, and the big money protected
them. I never seen so many crooks, and Murphy
couldn't handle 'em, so he hired 'em for deputies.''

''Aw, knock it off. Murphy's the biggest crook of
them all.''

''Yeah, but Murphy had to look good to keep his
job. He had to try. Crooks all over New Mexico. They
drove 'em out of Texas and even Oklahoma, for God's
sake, and it ain't only that—'' Lawson stopped and
looked down.

''Well, like me,'' he went on, his voice lower and

sad. "I never was a big crook. But hell, you see, with these new companies and so many cattle, and everybody stealing, the big money jumped on Murphy, and he had to side with them; and since he couldn't arrest their men, why hell, he just naturally had to pick on us little guys. They're just naturally shoving the independent crooks out of business. Damn it, I lived here twenty years, boys, my old woman's dead in the hill there and the boy gone to sea. All the old people know me, Choate, Rincon, all of them, you know, we all stole together. I steal theirs, they steal them back, nobody cares much. But now there's too many cows, boys, killing off the mustangs to save grass, and they getting mad at the rustlers. Them sons of bitches, they're so cheap they like to count every stem of grass from here to Magdalena, and then killing poor Tom just for rustling. You know how many times old Choate had Murphy arrest poor Tom in the old days. It got to be a game, never could prove nothing, never hoped to."

He paused for a long time, and licked his lips. His eyes were getting old, Bill thought, lower lids beginning to sag. Summer sun cut down through the dirty back window. Must be warm on old bones, Bill thought.

"So the big outfits and the little ones fighting like cats and dogs, all crooks together. One gang gets hold o' the Sheriff and makes out they were honest, and calls the outsiders crooks—why they was *all* crooks. So then the Governor declared this amnesty, he had to. They had this war up in Lincoln County, dozens of people killed, plain hell, I think they even killed a woman. So the Governor said, You boys lay down your guns and come on in and we'll forget the warrants and tear them up, and start out afresh. And he sent Moore, you remember Moore, sent him down

here from Santa Fe as a marshal and put him in
charge. You remember old Moore, the only peace officer west of the river a man could trust.''

"Sure, I remember Moore," Ollie said. "Put up bail
for me once out of his own pocket.''

Lawson smiled. "You'd be surprised how many of
the boys took him up and came on in. Because they
trusted Moore. That bastard Murphy, when the first
men come in to sign, he tried to arrest 'em on old
warrants, and Moore arrested *him* for breaking the
amnesty.'' Lawson slowly shook his head. "Had to
let Murphy go. But it sure threw a wrench into him,
and it made the boys believe this amnesty, the whole
thing. Him and Moore been fighting like cats and dogs
ever since. Plenty boys came in. Me too.''

"What's the matter with Murphy?" Bill asked. "He
always was a lying sneak, but he didn't used to be so
damned mean.''

"Fisher," Lawson said, frowning. "Fisher owns
him. Buys the elections. And you know Fisher. He's
got a score against damn near ever'body in the territory.'' He looked up at Bill. "You better watch out,
Bill. Fisher's trying to make this amnesty into a trap,
to settle old scores. Some men come in, Fisher gets
Murphy to hound 'em till they vamoose, and then
they call that breaking the amnesty, and haul out the
old warrants again. He always did hate your guts,
Bill, he's been laying for you. On account of that time.
The four-bit piece you threw down in front of Annie.''

"That's all she was worth," Bill said.

"But it made people laugh at her," Burt said.
"That's what got to him. You can't laugh at a pimp's
wife, Bill, even if she is a dirty old whore.''

"If you're going to hang around San Vicente,"
Lawson said, "you better sign up. If you don't, Fish-

er'll get you sure. Not himself, maybe—but Murphy will.'' He sat up straighter and sighed. ''You got back just in time, boys. The amnesty's up Sunday noon. You got today, Saturday and up to Sunday noon to come on in.''

''And suppose we don't?'' Bill asked.

Lawson shrugged. ''They get out all the old warrants and start hunting you down. They got an army detachment down in San Vicente, waiting for the deadline. And a pack of hounds.''

''How you tell the difference?''

''By the ears,'' Burt said. ''The soldiers' ears is longer. What's the hounds for, Ed?''

''For tracking. You. They got four Papago trackers. Indians by day, hounds by night, they'll run the tail right off you, Ollie.''

''We won't be here Sunday noon,'' Ollie said. ''We're going to Montana or someplace, where it's still civilized and they don't hang nobody.''

''All right,'' Lawson said, shrugging.

''Nulty still as crooked as ever?'' Bill asked.

Lawson looked at him without expression.

''I said, is Nulty still selling stolen beef to the Indian agents?''

''And I said, I've reformed,'' Lawson said. ''Do what you please, you'll get no help out of me. That's conspiracy.''

''A lawyer,'' Ollie said.

''I know the score,'' Lawson said. ''Moore read it out to me. Seven of us went in together. Moore told us if we helped any crooks we'd catch it. Moore's fair. And I ain't helping you.''

''Listen,'' Bill said, ''all you got to do is tell us if Nulty is still buying stolen cattle.''

''No,'' Lawson said. ''Joe Ferguson come and signed and he got a job working at the Pringle ranch and he sold a gun to some guy on the run and they jailed him. He lost his—''

''Did you say Pringle?'' Bill asked.

''Pringle. New people.''

''From Texas?'' Bill asked. ''A colonel and a pretty girl?''

''Yeah,'' Lawson said. ''Lot of Texas people moved out here the last three years. Lotta money.''

''Well, I'll tell you what,'' Ollie said, standing up and setting his coffee can on the stove, ''you can tell the Governor to go fly a kite, and you can shoot all the poor damn horses you want. I'm going to see Nulty and work up a deal, and if the rest of you birds wants to reform and live the good, starving life, why, hell, go ahead. I'm leaving.''

He turned and opened the shack door and took one step outside.

''Good morning,'' a man said, holding a shotgun so it pointed at Ollie's stomach. ''No, don't go back in, Ollie, and keep your hand away from that gun.''

Ollie stood still.

THREE

BILL LOOKED OUT, coffee can in hand. "Why, good morning, Murphy. It's consoling to see a public servant so fond of his duty. I must say, you're the last man I expected to see out of bed this early."

"There's three deputies behind the house covering the other door. I ain't arresting anybody, Bill. Just a confab."

"Sure," Bill said, looking at the shotgun. "Just social."

"Safety first, Bill," Murphy said. "You boys come out and lay your guns down on the porch." He was a fattish man, forty-five, hair ungrayed, or well-dyed black, a sociable type, full of joy of life and of this neat coup.

"You are mighty quick, Sheriff," Bill said, coming out. "I didn't think that captain would get to you till noon. Not knowing the country, and all."

"What captain?" Murphy asked.

"Never mind."

"We had a wire from Hillsboro that five men killed a cow. Heading this way. The way they was described, I thought they might be you boys. And I guessed you'd go see Lawson—him being an old crook and all, and on the way." He smiled. "And so you did. Lay down your gun, Bill. You too, Ollie."

One of Murphy's deputies came around the corner of the house, rifle at his hip. Ollie and Bill watched him. He went over to the five horses they had left groundhitched, gathered the reins in his hand and stood there. He had quite a handful, ten reins.

"I guess I got all your rifles with them horses, now," Murphy said. "Everybody come out and lay your pistols on the porch."

"It seems like all those guns kind of go to your head," Bill said, and finished his coffee. "Suppose I don't come out. Who you going to shoot first, me or Ollie?" He turned his head and asked inside the house, "Burt, you see anybody more up there?"

"Yeah. Two more of Murphy's hound-dogging sons of bitches. One behind the woodpile and the other by the hog pen."

"Pepe," Bill said, standing in the door and talking so Murphy could hear him, "if Murphy shoots, will you please shoot him back? Just use the window."

Pepe smiled and said nothing. Harvey said, the sweat coming out, "This is beginning to remind me of those Rurales."

"All right, Sheriff," Bill said, casually. "Now what?"

"Lay down your arms," Murphy said. The sparkle had gone out of his eye, and his face looked as though he had bitten into a rotten apple. "You boys don't know it, but things have changed. The law's respected around here now, and I'm still the law. Lay down your arms."

"Lay down your arms, lay down your arms," Ollie said, flapping his hands. "What are you, Murphy, a bugging parrot? Lay down your own damn arms."

Murphy's face turned dead white.

"Go on and shoot me," Ollie said. "You damn fool. You ain't got a warrant for nothing and even if you had, you couldn't shoot me for cow stealing."

"Like hell I ain't got a warrant," Murphy shouted, suddenly reddening. "I got half a dozen warrants on you bastards. Lay down them guns."

"Lay down them guns," Bill said. "Lay down them guns. Why don't you put it to music, Murphy?"

"Go take a running jump at your Aunt Fanny," Ollie said calmly. "By the way, where is your old Aunt Fanny working these days? Still flat on her back down at Madam Fisher's?" He made a gesture with one hand. "You still in business with Nulty selling stolen beef to the agents? 'Cause if you are, I know where I can get fifty prime head for you quick and cheap."

"You'll be sorry for this," Murphy bawled. "You wait."

"You used to be the biggest thief in Grant County, Murphy," Ollie said, "and you know it. Many's the deal I've done with you and many's the cow I've run on your own orders, and you know it."

"Tell that crock-faced deputy," Bill said, "to let go of our horses. Our horses don't like the smell of hound-dog on their reins."

The deputy's eyes opened wide and blue. He had pretty eyelashes, black and long, and the corners of his jaws stuck out like the ends of a snowplow.

"Who, a-who, a-who you callin' hound-dog, mister?"

"What the hell are you, an owl?" Ollie said. "Who, a-who, a-who."

"What you looking for with that cheap badge?" Bill asked. "Respectability?" He moved to the edge of the porch.

"Don't start nothing, Bill," Ollie said. "Let Moore settle it."

"Stay back," Murphy said, gripping the shotgun.

Bill unbuckled his gunbelt and let it fall on the porch. He walked up to Murphy and pushed his thin belly against the muzzle of the barrels, shoving Murphy back.

"Go on and shoot," Bill said. "Look at him bat his eyes, Ollie. Beautiful." He turned, smiling, and moved toward the deputy. The deputy stared at him out of his blue eyes. His buck teeth shone in his innocent, country face.

"Respectability," Bill said. "That's it. A combination of respectability and easy pickings. Old buzzard Murphy and the three crows, out picking fees off the widows and orphans. Born in a washtub, wasn't you, sonny? Back in the hills, and your father was a Bible salesman and pimped on the side. Born in a washtub and now you're respectable, and safe, and the law can't kick you around because you *are* the law, now." He grinned at the deputy. "Drop those reins, you horse thief. You've got a hold of my property."

"Don't you do it, Shep," Murphy said, rigid.

"Drop 'em," Bill said.

Shep, with one fist full of reins, hefted the Winchester, and then he got it—four knuckles right in the buck teeth, fast. He dropped everything, reins, rifle and all. He made a grab for his pistol and Bill kicked him square in the crotch. With a terrible, dying howl, Shep sank down clutching himself and lay curled up like a baby, mewing.

Bill looked down at him and smiled. "Safety," he said softly. "You sure got it. Drawing on an unarmed man. Sure is safe, isn't it, Shep?'' He kicked him again, in the kidneys, and smiled as Shep let out another shriek.

Bill reached for the reins of the horses, his back toward Murphy, and Murphy swung the shotgun. At the same time, Ollie leaped, and as Murphy fired, Ollie rammed him with his shoulder, bucking him right in the pot. They both went down. Ollie got up. The Sheriff lay and gagged, trying to get his wind back.

Bill went over and picked up the shotgun. He leaned the muzzle against the porch and put the butt down on the ground, and jumped on the barrels till they bent like an elbow. He picked up the wrecked gun and threw it at the Sheriff as he lay gasping on the ground.

''Now shoot it, you old son of a bitch,'' Bill said, and laughed. He looked at Ollie, and Ollie laughed. ''Did you ever see such a hang-dog outfit? By God, they sure asked for it. Disarming free men.''

The two other deputies came around the corner of the shack.

''Shoot 'em!'' Murphy shouted, all his wind back.

At the same time as the deputies brought up their Winchesters, a pistol barrel smashed though one of the windows and held on Murphy, and Pepe said, through the hole, ''Don't nobody shoot, Murphy, or you're dead. Burt, you and Harvey go out there and take the guns off those two deputies.'' The voice was so quiet, so calm, so everyday, that they all knew he would do exactly what he said. Slowly, Murphy and the deputies raised their hands.

Up at the hog pen, there was one more man— Fisher, squatting on his heels, smoking the last quarter inch of a cigarette. He was about Murphy's age, but much more compact. His face had an indoor pallor, and what he had left of a lot of youthful muscle had turned flat and flabby. There was still plenty left; but what was more impressive was the tight, hard whiteness of his face, the intensity of expression that came from constant repression of temper. It was temper restrained by greed—an educated wolfishness, a feral appetite which had learned the indirect approach. No matter how tight, strained and compressed the mouth, the ferocity still showed in the black eyes: they had an impact of their own, and men like Murphy, when Fisher looked at them in a certain way, had a feeling of having been physically struck.

He could hear the voices from below well enough. He could imagine what had happened. Gorham had laughed—a bad sign—and he had sent the two deputies down. Then the smash of glass, and now Gorham laughed again. He saw Burt and Harvey leave the window, which could only mean that somehow Gorham and the others all felt safe. Leave it to Murphy to clown up a simple situation.

He looked around at the mountains. Nobody else nearby. Nobody left to help anybody, except himself. The situation was all his, with Gorham right in the middle, where he wanted him.

He stubbed out the cigarette and got up, pulling his gun deliberately. A long time since he had squatted anywhere; he knew he was soft from sitting at a desk, but he wasn't afraid—he never had been. The one thing Fisher was sure of was that no matter how bad the odds, he would live to win a fight eventually because he had a quality most men lacked—a perfect, eager willingness to hurt and kill. He had never pulled a punch in his life, and never forgotten an injury, and half-measures never entered his mind. In the old days, when he had been a pimp in Phoenix, he had preferred a two-by-four to anything else—the sheer clumsiness of it gave a peculiar satisfaction to his brutality. Nowadays he was reduced to the effeminacy of a pistol.

He went on down the slope, gambling calmly that they were all either outside, beyond the cabin, or looking out the front windows. He was right—only Pepe was inside, squatting by the front window, his gun covering the men in front.

Close to the back wall, hidden from Pepe's view should he turn around, he stopped and calmly took off his laced city shoes, and in his stockings, stepped silently through the back door. He looked at the floor, saw by the worn nail-heads where the joists were, and stepped along a joist toward Pepe without a squeak. He did not hesitate, he swung as he was taking the last, silent step, and whipped the barrel of his gun across the side of Pepe's head.

Pepe folded up forward; glass tinkled; Fisher grabbed him by the hair and held him up, and as Bill, outside, swung around at the sound of glass and raised his gun, Fisher smiled at him through the window and put the muzzle of his own gun into Pepe's ear. Bill saw it and froze, turning pale.

"Drop it," Fisher said.

No move outside—all of them stiff as statues.

"I'll give you five," Fisher said. "If there's a battle here, we'll win it, Gorham. We got the odds. We got the law. All we got to do is claim you ambushed us, and believe me, none of you will say any different."

Inside himself, Bill was quiet as a grave. The heart-knocking and the shakes always came later. He looked at Pepe's mouth, hanging open as Fisher held his head up by a fistful of hair.

Suddenly the bottom dropped out of him. Fisher would do it. The very brutality of the hair-hold told him—Fisher was holding up Pepe like so much meat. There wasn't a thing to do. In a shootout, Pepe would be the first one dead.

He dropped his gun on the ground and backed away from it. Fisher nodded.

"Now you others," Fisher said. The guns fell like leaves, and the sighs came out of Murphy and his men like autumn wind. They bent and picked up their own guns, and swelled up with confidence. Fisher let Pepe fall. Fisher went out and got his shoes.

He came back and stood looking around with his calm smile, and then centered on Murphy. "You buggering idiot," he said, "what are you good for?"

Murphy's face clouded with pink and he looked at the ground.

Fisher looked around at the hills. Quiet, peace, perfect peace. All his. "What now, Murphy?" he asked. Murphy shut his eyes helplessly, and blinked them open again. He knew what Fisher had in mind, he could feel it, and he turned sick.

"Shep, you're the toughest," Fisher said. "Go drag that Mexican out here and put a gun in his ear."

He stepped down off the porch and went up to Bill. "I told you if I ever saw you again, I'd kill you. Didn't I?"

Bill stood quiet and watched Shep drag Pepe out. The same old hair-hold. His eyes blurred with anger, and the anger was stabbed helpless by something like tears. The gun was against Pepe's ear.

"Four bits," Fisher said to Bill. He picked his watch out of his vest and swung the chain free. On the end of the chain was a half-dollar. "This is it," Fisher said. "I've been saving it. Three years. You remember. She was walking up the street and met you and said good morning and you tossed this at her feet and went on."

"I wasn't interested," Bill said quietly.

Fisher's eyes got that gun-look, the ferocity coming out from behind some internal shield. "She said to you, good morning. A civil greeting from a lady to a gentleman at ten in the morning."

"You got it wrong," Bill said. "What she said was, 'How about it, Sonny?' At ten o'clock in the morning. That's what she said."

Fisher's teeth suddenly showed—he slashed the chain across Bill's face. The four-bit piece hit him in the ear. The stinging pain, and then the slow, warm trickle of blood dribbling down the side of his neck.

"Four bits," Fisher said. "Annie said good morning, the civil greeting of a lady. Shep, if this son of a bitch makes one move, you shoot the Mexican's head off. I know they're buddies—old buggering buddies, mountain girls, sheep lovers."

Bill drew a long breath. The next time, the four-bit piece might hit him in the eyes. "She said, 'How about it, Sonny?' She got in my way. I had to stand there. I said no thanks. I guess she thought it was a good joke. I guess she knew I don't play around with whores. So she said it again. I dropped her four bits to get her off my back. And it worked. That's the point, Fisher. She picked it up off the sidewalk."

He was meeting the wide-open hate in Fisher's eyes, looking right into a total lack of limitation. That was the thing about Fisher—all his restraints were outside, self-imposed; there was nothing in the man's nature, pulling from within, to restrain him. He would go all the way, any time, leap into any violence, like a crazy wolf. The only thing that held him back was money, which had to be got by cannier means.

"You tell these men how it was," Fisher said. "How she said good morning and you insulted her just for a joke. Tell them and then get the hell out of here, go back to Mexico. If you don't—'' He looked at Murphy. ''You got the guts to kill these sons of bitches?''

Murphy groaned.

''You better get the guts,'' Fisher said. ''When they're dead, you'll have to tell it my way.''

Bill met Fisher's eyes. ''I'll tell you something, Fisher. You knock us off like this, and you won't last a week. There's a hundred men I know will shoot you in bed. You bought the law, but you haven't bought my friends.''

''I'll give you five,'' Fisher said. ''Tell them how it really happened.''

''Like I said, Fisher. She was a whore on the make, that's all. Just like you're a pimp on the make, no matter how many banks you run or how respectable you try to get. Take it or leave it. Now hit me again, you son of a bitch, but if you hurt my friend, we'll pull your stinking guts out of you and—''

Fisher hit him in the side of the mouth. He was old, but he was fast, and Bill couldn't even get an arm up. He lay on the ground, blinking at the fog. Fisher moved in to kick.

''Somebody's coming,'' Murphy squawked. ''My God, it's Moore.''

Fisher didn't even hear him. He swung a leg, it caught Bill on the back of the thigh as he rolled, instead of in the crotch.

''Moore's coming,'' Murphy hollered. Fisher looked up at Murphy, his eyes totally abstracted with his intentness on the job of kicking Bill to death. He heard hooves suddenly, and then found himself looking at the side of a mule, between himself and Bill. He looked at the boot in the stirrup, on up the leg to a face, and saw Moore looking down at him quietly.

Fisher backed a step and rubbed his eyes. Ollie yelled with pure delight and jumped up and down.

"I been watching you all from up the hill," Moore said slowly. He was a big man, gray, with a big, calm, sad face. He sat the mule like an old king, with great dignity and peace of mind. "Quite a show." He looked at Murphy. "Quite a parade. Quite a campaign. I never saw a legal ambushing with so many angles." He turned his head and said to Shep, "Young man, you better put that gun away. Under the circumstances, it would be murder." He looked back to Fisher. "You have no status here. I know you own Murphy, but you have no legal status—except as the defendant in a battery case. Get on your horse and go."

Fisher stood, fists tight, stupefied with the setback.

"If you don't leave peaceably," Moore said slowly, "I'll arrest you and take you back to town on your horse on a lead rope."

"You can't do that," Murphy said. "I'm the Sheriff."

"I can do anything I want until Sunday noon," Moore said. "Until Sunday noon, I am, as marshal, the complete and absolute law in this county, and if I get trouble, I'll sic the soldiers on you. Is that clear?"

Fisher looked at Bill. He still had the watch, chain and four-bit piece in his hand. He said nothing, but Bill read the look. Slowly, Fisher put the watch and chain back into his vest. Without a word, he turned and went back up the hill for his horse.

Bill stood with his head and face aching. Pepe was sitting on the steps, holding his head. Moore turned to Murphy. "If I were you, I would take your men and go on back down to San Vicente and leave me to tell these boys what the score is. You've done enough damage."

Murphy stood glaring at Moore. "You're a crook yourself, Moore, siding with these outlaws."

"If you defy me, I will arrest you here and now and arraign you in the Federal Court."

Murphy glared some more.

"I heard about that telegram you got," Moore said. "I guessed where you went. If you wanted to see these men, it should have been a peaceful conference, in the spirit the Governor intended. Instead of that, you tried to disarm men who are not in a settlement and who are not under indictment."

"I got seven warrants on these birds," Murphy shouted. He pulled a handful of dirty papers out of his inside pocket and waved them around.

"Suspended," Moore said calmly, "until Sunday noon. You precipitated that fight. I won't speculate on your motives. Now, as I said, you had better go on home. I'll do the talking."

"What about my man Shep?" Murphy cried. "Gorham kicked him in the crotch. Ain't that battery? What about it?"

"He was healthy enough to hold a gun in Pepe's ear," Bill said. "They're all liars. You don't know what they do, Moore. They live off fees and fines. Fee for this, fee for that. Fee to jail you, fee to let you out, fee to spit. They got in with the county assessor ten years ago and upped the assessments on all the Mexican property in town. So when the poor bastards couldn't pay the taxes, the county foreclosed and Murphy evicted them, and Murphy and the assessor bought up the stuff at an auction they held on top of a mountain at midnight. Now Murphy owns more town lots than anybody but Fisher. Guess what Fisher was when they had the auction. Bet you can't. You'd never imagine. The assessor."

"That's a lot of hearsay," Murphy said. "You wasn't even in town then."

"Who owns Madam Fisher's whorehouse, Murphy? You or Fisher? You used to rent it out, but maybe you sold it to him."

Murphy felt old, he was sick. The truth came out, simple and deadly. "You better leave town," he said. "While you can." He was sick to kill somebody. It was so obvious that Moore had to turn his back on him.

"Under the amnesty," Moore said to Bill and Ollie, "you have a right to come in and sign the agreement, and settle down. The old scores are to be forgotten. And I mean to see this put through fair. This thing, this morning, wasn't your fault. You were here, peaceful, and Murphy started the fight. The report is going to the Governor."

Murphy smiled, sick to kill. "Make your report," he said in a quiet little voice. "I know what happens to reports."

He turned and picked up his ruined shotgun, looked at it and threw it languidly into the grass. He turned toward his two uninjured deputies. "Get the horses."

He turned once more to Bill and Ollie. He said, still smiling, "I'll be here long after Moore has gone." He walked away, his deputy lagging behind him.

"You take that kind of Irishman," Bill said as they watched the four men go, "and scrape off all the poetry and good-natured blarney, right down to the bone, and you always get the same thing."

"What?" Ollie said.

"A traitor."

"He's sly," Burt said. "Very sly."

"He can't touch you," Moore said. "Not if you come in. Unless you commit some new felony."

"You know," Pepe said from the background, "the old days have gone, we are all washed up."

Nobody paid any attention.

"You boys come in the house," Moore said, "and I'll tell you what to expect. I got the signatures of seventeen men in Grant County alone. I can get you jobs, if you sign up. Come on."

They looked at each other, and all but Pepe followed Moore inside the house. Pepe looked back toward the mountain. The buzzards had followed them, and circled high over the two dead horses. The free things were passing, the wild horses that had fled through the forests were being killed off. It was not just the grass they ate—they were hated because they could not be harnessed.

What made Murphy so confident? Something had happened, in three years. The wilderness was no longer wilderness.

"Pepe," Bill said from the door, looking out at his small friend. "Come on inside. You had better hear Moore out." He turned back into the shack, and Pepe got up and followed. And behind him the buzzards came down a little closer, like soot circling in the wind, falling inevitably, like wreckage descending in a whirlpool.

Moore sat among them, casual, at ease. He knew they were all bums, chaff, rubbish, and the county would be better off if they were dead. He knew this, but he did not feel it. Because he was such a big man, outlaws and outlawry did not frighten him the way they frightened Murphy. The way Moore felt, these men were like crazy children. They were equal to children by virtue of their defects.

He could feel what was lacking in Ollie, the balance wheel that most people had; he could feel something missing in Burt—some kind of focus that most people had, the lack of which left Burt just slogging along without any purpose at all, like an ox. Not stupid, just purposeless.

He sat a long time with his coffee, trying to think of how to put it. It was hard to be simple.

"It's just this," Moore said finally. "New Mexico is closing in. It used to be wild, plenty of free space where you boys could run off to. It was the last wild place in the country. But now it's settling down, and there's no place left for you to go. Do you believe it? Or not?"

He looked around. Five pairs of eyes. They believed him, but not it.

"You either got to learn to fit in, boys, or you're going to be run down, run over and run under. There's no leeway left."

No comment.

"You going to find out the hard way?" Moore asked. "You going to get killed learning?"

No answer, no expression. Warm sun slanting down through the dirty window. Back in Virginia, when he was a child, in a mountain shack something like this one, there had been this still, deep peace, the perfect tranquillity of sun shafting down golden on a small, warm brown pine chest of drawers, with an apple, red as a heart, upon it; and the small, grave child, studying, absorbing the knowledge and the love of peace; gold motes dancing like angels in the shaft of light, and the apple, red and beautiful as blood, the light upon it like the love that came out of his mother in that soft, constant, invisible stream. Moore loved peace. "Listen, boys, if you don't come in, there ain't going to be any mercy." He looked around from face to face. They listened, intent. For once they were getting the truth, and they knew it.

"The Governor's a good man," Moore said, and they believed him.

"Why don't he get rid of Murphy, then?" Burt asked.

Moore sighed. "A county election is county business. You're stuck with Murphy. There's always crooks in high places. They get inside the law, they're protected, but they're still crooks. And they hang guys like you, outside the law, that are crooks. And they're still crooks, living off the fat of the land. Don't talk to me about justice."

"That's what Murphy would do to us," Bill said. "Because we're competition." He smiled faintly. "In short, if you're not Murphy's man, you don't get a license to rustle cattle, not in Grant county."

Ollie looked at Bill. "We better move on."

"Where?" Moore asked.

"Montana."

"The vigilantes have cleaned it all up," Moore said.

"Nevada."

"Not enough people to rob," Moore said. "And they'd spot you in a minute." Moore put down his cup. "This amnesty is a real chance for you boys. The last one. If you turn it down, it's like telling the cattlemen, go ahead and shoot. I mean it. They got eight lion dogs waiting for Sunday noon, and Murphy has got all his old warrants ready. Old Simon Shaw told Murphy to go to hell last Tuesday. Shaw will never come in. And they're going to kill him, boys. I talked to him, he's old and stubborn, there's nothing I can do. He's living up in the mountains and he thinks he's safe."

He looked around at the blank faces.

"Shaw is first on the list. Sunday noon, they start out with the pack from Colonel Pringle's place, and they'll run down Shaw, and he'll resist, or run, and

they'll kill him like an animal. He had his chance."
A long pause. "What you boys going to do?"

Silence.

"Burt, you were a meat cutter once, weren't you,
down in Port Arthur? I can get you in with Braun.
Pepe, I can get you a job in the livery. Ollie, you can
get a job with Johanssen. Harvey, your girl's been
looking for you for a coon's age. Her old man will
give you a chance."

"The hell with Johanssen and the carpenter business," Ollie said. "I could get a job riding."

"That's the one job you can't get. The first steer
that's missing, you'd be blamed. That's out. You got
to work in town, where Murphy can't frame you and
you can't get tempted."

Moore stood up. "Well, all right. You decide. You
want to take me up, come on in. Nobody'll bother
you in town now. You're free as birds." He put down
his coffee can, got up and walked out. They followed
him out onto the porch and stood watching him get
on his mule and move down the old rut road.

"It's a good deal," Harvey said, his eyes bright. "I
could get that job in the dry-goods store."

"How about it, boys?" Ollie said. "One last job.
Get us some money to tide us over. Then if we want
to we can take the jobs." He grinned at them.

"All right," Burt said.

"Bill?"

"All right." He was looking down the valley toward the little town. "Maybe Moore's right. We're all
fed up with running. We could try it, couldn't we?"

"After this one last job," Ollie said. "I ain't going
to town broke."

"All right, you go fix up something safe with
Nulty," Bill said. "I got to pay a friend a visit."

Pepe looked at him and Bill felt the look. "What's

the matter with that? Can't a man go see an old friend?''

''Who?'' Ollie said. ''Them Pringles? Hell, Bill, you could get to know that lieutenant. Find out his plans. Poison his dogs. Thousand things you could do. We'll meet you in town in three-four hours. Red Dog Saloon, if it's still standing.''

''You mean,'' Burt said slowly, ''we can ride right into town, in the broad daylight? And nobody will arrest us?''

''That's what he said, didn't he?'' Ollie cried. He laughed and started for the horses. ''Thirty bucks a head, we get fifteen, twenty head for old Nulty, that'll set us up for a celebration. Then we settle down and become decent citizens, and line up a bank robbery. Come on, boys.''

Burt and Harvey followed him. Bill and Pepe stood alone on the porch. ''You think about the old life,'' Pepe said quietly. ''How it is to sit in a velvet chair. Smoke a cigar. Women like mothers, not whores. You think I don't read your face, Bill? You're hungry all over.''

''I haven't seen them for four years,'' Bill said in a small, cold, tight voice. ''Sure, I'd like to see them. Why not?''

''Sure, that's right, Bill. You go ahead.''

''Listen, Pepe, whatever happens, remember this,'' Bill said. ''You and I are partners. You been the best friend any man ever had. I'd rather have you for my friend than all the Pringles that ever lived. I haven't said I was going to sign up. Maybe I will, maybe I won't. I don't have to decide for two days yet. You understand that?''

Bill got on his horse and rode away at a canter, passing the others. They all disappeared around the hill. Pepe stood on the porch, alone with Lawson. His horse nickered impatiently.

"Thank you for the coffee, Ed," Pepe said. "You are a generous man. As you see, we are about to steal some cows. I know you won't tell anybody. But first, get a rope together and we will pull the dead horse out of your little creek."

Lawson grinned. "Pepe, why don't you stay here with me? You're the best mountain man there ever was. What you want with that Bill for a partner? You and me, we could make a killing, here with these wild horses and the lions and all."

"Thank you," Pepe said, going to his horse. "I don't want to make a killing. But I will help you drag yours out of your drinking water."

Lawson's grin died and his face closed up. Pepe set his teeth in his tongue and bit down on it. Why did he say things like that? Why couldn't he just keep his mouth shut? Lawson had been a friend.

FOUR

THE ROAD TO San Vicente had changed a lot in three years—it was rutted now with wagon tracks, where before had been mostly hoof prints. Bill passed one brand new outfit—new house, new barns, new corrals, white paint and raw poles shining with sap in the sun, neat as a gallows. Alfalfa in a big patch, far away by the river—slowly it all sank home together, fences, alfalfa, new barns and everything.

Once you could look down on San Vicente and see nothing but the long, high grass, and you could ride anywhere, anywhere at all, go like a bird across the sky, with nothing to stop you. You would see the cattle trails coming into water from all over, and the old game trails, all mixed together, cattle and game both wild, and the horsemen came and went like hawks, leaving no paths, following their own will. But now you rode down a raw, rutted ugly road between wires.

Before, you could look out across all that yellow

grass, and it was true, in those days, that you were lord of what you surveyed—for no matter what the law said, all men always owned the land that was under the soles of their boots, and if a man could go anywhere, he carried his two little kingdoms with him. But now the wire cut him off. Somebody had title, and wherever he went, he would be walking in another man's shadow. Three years ago, the range had been open; now it was being closed in, and in five years it would be dead in a wire coffin.

Two miles down was Murphy's ranch, at the head of the five-mile slope down into town. He went into Murphy's, just for the hell of it, and had a look around. Nobody home but the cook, with his apron on, watching two hands at work in a corral.

Bill rode up and the cook turned around from where the two men were shoeing a Hereford Bull. It was Ed Stafford. He had been in a gang working down by the border, robbing mule trains coming up from Sonora; and here he was in an apron—probably signed up.

"Howdy," Ed said, and winked at Bill with the eye on the side of his face turned away from the two cowhands. That wink said a lot: "Welcome home, friend—watch out for these two bastards."

"The Sheriff around?" Bill asked. "I had something to report to him, I thought it my lawful duty."

"Maybe he's in town," Ed said.

The two hands looked up from the bull.

"Meet Joe and Jeff," Ed said. "They're twins."

They didn't even nod. New blood in the county, flat-faced fellows who could double for Murphy either as deputies or horse thieves.

"Tell him I heard that Bill Gorham's gang is back," Bill said. "He'd better watch out for cow stealing."

Ed winked again, enjoying himself.

"You know where the Pringle outfit is?" Bill asked.

"Sure. Little outfit. But rich. Just south of town, on the river. Want a cup of coffee, stranger?" Another wink.

"No thanks, friend. No time." Bill turned and headed for the road. The twins squatted perfectly quiet by the bull, watching him like a couple of hawks. They knew it was fishy.

There was wire all over Murphy's place. There were about twenty-five head of Herefords in a holding pasture, behind some trees, a mile down the road. Herefords in this country were brand new imports—they stuck out among the skinny old longhorn stock like English lords at a Texas barn-dance.

He rode through San Vicente slowly, taking it all in. On a Friday morning, nobody would be around, ordinarily. But the place was full now, full of people from out of town, men from the woods and from little back-country ranches who only got off the place once every two months. It looked as though the fair was on, but there was no fair. And then he saw the main attraction, in the middle of the dusty little plaza—a small encampment of soldiers. Down by the flagpole, on the east side of the plaza, where the cheapest bars were—the river side, the railroad side.

Three Sibley tents and two wall tents, one probably for the Headquarters, the other for the mess, with a big canvas fly on one side—and behind all this, in one long row, the picket line with its rope and stakes and horses. They must have been there more than a week—the grass was gone and the straw was scattered all over.

In front of the HQ tent there was a small field piece, aimed at the open eastern sky. Young men hung around the fronts of the east-side saloons, sneering at the military. The rest was like the usual Saturday crowd, with a little more noise than usual because the kids were all in town.

"Hi, Bill," a long man said softly as Bill sat his horse watching. "You coming in?" He was smiling faintly.

"Don't know," Bill said. "You?"

"Don't know either," the other said. "Lotta boys don't know. We're just watching. You know what they're gonna do with them soldiers?"

"I heard," Bill said.

"They're getting awful serious," the long man said, in his quiet, drawling voice. "Maybe it's time to quit fooling around. They's other kinds of fun."

"You trying to talk me into it?" Bill asked, "or you trying to talk yourself into it?"

The other smiled. "There's a lot of the boys in town, Bill. We all figure it's a chance to square up that we won't get again."

Bill nodded his head and turned his horse away.

In peacetime it was a sleepy town, a lovely town, the buildings of humble shape and soft colors, mostly white, but some light blue, some pink, a few gray. Even the bank was dobie, but it had four wooden pilasters in front, painted to look like marble. There were a few red-brick houses in the upper part of town, with steep slate roofs and tall, narrow windows—rich spinsters.

Inside the bank would be Fisher, the master pimp, the ex-assessor, sitting in the cool shade of a thousand-dollar bill. It was a long time since Fisher had been head bouncer at Madam Fisher's emporium of joy in Phoenix, and few remembered it.

Cottonwoods waving in the little breeze, sounds of the plaza fading out behind as his horse walked slowly down the dusty street. Sleepy town by the happy river, little wooden clapboard houses on the

side streets, sometimes boardwalks and picket fences,
but mostly just dust with the prints of children's bare
feet running around.

It wasn't only a cattle town. Back in the mountains
were some silver and gold mines and some lumber
mills, even a sash-and-door company. Something new
was an ice company, with a cooling tower sticking up
on the edge of town, down by the railroad.

Pringle's house lay in a bend of the river, a short
mile south, rather isolated on a point of land, and he
had a long ranch road running off the highway to
Silver City. All his land lay along the river—it was a
choice spot, though not large. In front of the clapboard house—one-storied, green-shuttered, white
paint faded to bone-gray—there was a turnaround that
had been pounded bare of lawn and bushes into a
little plaza. Chickens about, some old hound-dogs;
out to the side, in between the small barn and the
orchard, the ranch-hand houses, two dobies, and by
the barn, a common bunkhouse. It had a comfortable,
rundown look, and around it bent the silver San
Francisco River, like the arm of a mother.

He knocked on the door, and after a while a Mexican woman opened it. An old woman with a dusting
cloth around her hair; her eyes were bright with the
red wrath of tequila kept in old kerosene cans, and
under them hung purple bags, like dead prunes.

"Who you wanna see?"

"The Colonel."

"The Colonel he is slipping."

All this time he could see the Colonel at the end of
the long, straight hall, in a far, silver-lighted room,
and she knew it.

"You don't have to lie to me, reverend mother,"
he said. "I'm not a policeman."

She scowled, lifted her lip, and said a horrible word

in Spanish. She went back into the parlor, where she began beating dust off the furniture in a blind rage.

The Colonel came down the long, dark passage, like a train down a tunnel, growing bigger and bigger.

"Hello, Bill," he said as he came out of the tunnel into the gray light from the open door. "I've been expecting you. Murphy's men have been going the rounds like Paul Revere." He put out a hand and shook Bill's hand hard, smiling.

"I judge that his motive is revenge," the Colonel said, smoothing his moustache and turning back up the hall. "For something you did to one of his men up in the mountains. Not that it matters. Come on back, my boy. I've still got plenty to drink."

"So has your housekeeper," Bill said, following.

"Don't mind Serafina. Murphy jailed her husband last night. Claimed Manuel was intoxicated. Murphy is getting too big for his britches."

"I wish somebody's horse would step on Murphy's head," Bill said. "I can hear it popping now. Like an egg."

"You haven't changed a bit," the Colonel said, leading him out into the far-off sitting room. Windows on three sides, looking out over the bend of the river, across it to the yellow, rolling country, up to the farther western mountains. "Have you?"

"I don't know," Bill said.

"No, I don't think so. Beneath all the uproar and deliberate camouflage of poorly assumed ill breeding, you still have a solid core of—pure inconstancy." He poured two glasses of whisky and lifted one. "Here's to change."

Bill looked down at his glass. "If I drink this, I'm giving Murphy an advantage."

"One more or less won't matter. Besides, Murphy

won't come on my property." The Colonel smiled, looking out the window. "After he arrested Manuel last night, Serafina went into town and threw a bottle through his office window. He came out here to arrest her too. I wouldn't let him. I am, in fact, already harboring one fugitive from justice—if you can call it that."

He took a sip of his whisky. "Murphy doesn't harass me. I have too much money." He looked at Bill, smiling. "That's what you need, Bill. It takes lots of money to live the feudal life. Oh, the beauty of democracy! Everybody with an equal chance to become an aristocrat."

"You used to insist on personal honor—the sole need."

"That was when I had a job and social position— before our beloved war. Destitution is an eye-opener, Bill. I made a lot of money after you ran away from Pembleton's."

"Dice?"

"Hogs. We had ten thousand Poland Chinas up on the Edwards Plateau." The Colonel sat down in a wicker chair, which creaked luxuriously. "All you have to do is put the males and females together in pens, and then they do all the work, and have all the fun too, for that matter. They say the hog is a very cleanly beast, if you give it a chance. I never did. A wonderful business. Now I am raising thoroughbred bulls. Fantastic profits; everybody is trying to upgrade their cattle. If you want to steal cattle, please don't steal mine, they're much too valuable to eat." He smiled. "Sold all my unregistered Herefords to Murphy last week. The damn fool thought he had a bargain."

Bill looked at his drink, still afraid of it.

"What an anachronism," the Colonel said.

"Huh?"

"You. There are no more noble bands of outlaws roaming the western plains. The successful outlaws have become inlaws, like Murphy. But you—the classic rebel, Lucifer and Garibaldi, you're all outdated. Watch out, Bill, you're headed for a mighty fall. If I remember Milton—'thrown by angry Jove sheer o'er the crystal battlements.' " He drank. " 'From morn to noon he fell, from noon to dewy eve, a summer's day; and with the setting sun dropp'd from the Zenith, like a falling star.' That's you, my boy. Too many angry Joves around nowadays—including the Federal government."

Bill took a tiny sip of his drink.

"You make me tired," the Colonel said, "standing up like that. Sit down."

Bill let himself down in another wicker chair.

"The wild ones," the Colonel said, "always looking for freedom. You, Lucifer and Jefferson Davis, and assorted angry Joves, including that end-man Lincoln. I know exactly how you felt about Pembleton's school, and I understood exactly how you felt about your father. On the other hand, you and Allie—I had grown fond of that idea. But I didn't blame you for running off."

"Why did you come to San Vicente?" Bill asked quietly.

The Colonel looked at him directly, with a quiet smile in his eyes. "I didn't mind the Edwards Plateau being full of hogs, but when San Antonio started filling up with retired Union Army Poland China pigs, I decided to leave. I never cared much for the Union Army, even when they trounced me at Chattanooga, but when they started soliciting my approval socially—well, I had to secede from Texas, in the end. So here I am, in the beloved wilderness."

"Where is Allie?"

The Colonel looked at him for a moment. "I don't think you could make her happy. Not the way you are going."

"I just asked, for God's sake, where she was. Is she dead? Is she alive? I haven't seen her for five years. Is that a terrible thing to ask? Just where she is?"

"It all comes back, doesn't it? You forget it, with distance, and then you come back, and it all returns. You see that bookcase yonder, the same one we had in the Houston Street house, and that old rocking chair, and the sideboard, and it all comes back. A thousand miles, across all those deserts, home again. I wonder what old Chippendale would have said, if he could have seen that sideboard trundling along across the Llano Estacado, ninety miles from water."

"He probably would have asked, 'Where is Mrs. Chippendale?' "

"Allie is out riding with an Army lieutenant. The Army has one peacetime use, at any rate—it scatters eligible bachelors around the country in the most hopeless places."

Bill looked at his drink and sank back into his chair. "Are they engaged?"

"Possibly. I haven't been told." The Colonel looked down at Bill, seeing him slump, noting the vacant look.

"I'd like a bath," Bill said.

"Does this herald a return to polite society?"

Bill suddenly smiled. "Is that an invitation?"

"I never wanted to see you leave. Bill, I had a terrible time in San Antonio. Everybody suddenly shabby genteel—holding up their pants with their eyebrows. When I went into hogs, I let down the South, you see, betrayed my shabby friends. I made

money, and I was lost. Oh, thank God for hogs. I
say, God bless all hogs, I love them, every one. Bill,
only the rich are free.''

"Is—does Allie—like this Army fellow? Is that it?''

"Your mind is not only single-tracked, but narrow-
gauge. Can't we talk about anything but my daughter?'' He paused. "Well, I hope not.''

"Is he a West Pointer?''

"Yes. There is absolutely nothing wrong with him.
He is a good, good man, an excellent man. But he is
hard to talk to.'' The Colonel's face was sad.

"I wish I had a bath,'' Bill said nervously. "I
haven't had a bath in three weeks. When is Allie getting back?''

"Oh, any time.''

"How about a bath? And could I borrow some clean
clothes?''

"Suddenly mad for a bath! Why, of course you can
borrow some clothes. I even brought my old copper
tub, the one my father brought from Greensboro.''
He stood up. "My grandmother had that tub made
the year Washington retired. She always said that after the War of 1812 the solder was never the same.
I'll have Serafina heat some water—if she feels up to
it.''

"They told me this lieutenant was living here,'' Bill
said.

"Not true. He is keeping his dogs here, that'll be
all, thanks.''

"*His* dogs?''

"Well, no, they belong to the trainer, a lion hunter
from Colorado. But I say 'his dogs' because they're
officially with his detachment. I suppose you know
what they're for? Serafina!'' he shouted.

"Yes, I heard.''

"Just like *Uncle Tom's Cabin*,'' the Colonel said.

"Life is extraordinary. Of course, *Uncle Tom's Cabin* was not life—a preposterous tale, as you know. Serafina!"

"*Sí, sí,*" she shouted in a fury. "Whatta you want?"

"Heat six cans of water," the Colonel shouted back through the house, "and put them in my copper tub."

"Oh, *puta*!" Serafina shouted, at the limits of exasperation.

"She has quite a vocabulary," Bill said.

"I am very fond of Serafina," the Colonel said. "She has a very solid core—of pure irascibility."

For the first time, Bill sat back in the chair and let himself smile. "There's a bunch of thieves—my friends—out somewhere arranging a robbery I am supposed to take part in. It seems like another world, from here."

The Colonel looked at him. "Too bad for you it's not," he said. "Nobody is more demanding than an outgrown friend."

"I haven't outgrown them," Bill said. "Let's go look at the dogs while we're waiting for the water. I'd kind of like to see what kind of animal I may have chasing me on Sunday."

FIVE

DOWN THE ROAD, around the foot of the hill out of sight of Lawson's cabin, Murphy and his three deputies stopped. Murphy looked at Shep. "How you feel? You up to riding cross country yet?"

Shep was riding straight up, standing in his stirrups. "I want to go home."

"You all go down to town then. You keep an eye on that bunch when they come in. They'll probably go to the Red Dog, so you get George to pass on what they say. And Harvey might just go in to see Judge Quires on account of that girl he used to run around with. You warn Quires to keep his ears open."

The three deputies went on down the road. Murphy turned his horse up the back of the hill, clambering up through the pines to the top. Hidden in the trees, he watched Pepe and Lawson out in the meadow, dragging the dead horse out of the creek. He waited till Pepe had left and then kicked his horse down the slope, back to Lawson's.

Down the road, Pepe saw the tracks where Murphy
had turned off, and he too turned off up the hill. He
climbed halfway up, left his horse, and taking his rifle
from its boot, went upward on foot. In a minute he
was lying down watching the cabin. He saw Murphy's bay standing before it. He settled down in the
pine needles and waited.

Inside the cabin, Murphy stood facing Lawson, and
Lawson, sitting, looked at the floor.

"They must have said something," Murphy said.

"Not while I was in the room," Lawson said stubbornly. "I got five tails, Sheriff. You want to pay me
and take 'em now? Save me a trip down to town."

Murphy smiled faintly. "You signed that agreement. You got to report any crimes."

"I don't know any crimes," Ed said stubbornly.

"You got to aid the law. They're planning something. They got to be. They're broke. What did they
say?"

Lawson couldn't remember a thing of the conver-
sation except that they had talked about going to see
Nulty and stealing some cows. "They talked about
Mexico, mostly."

"That's a lie," Murphy said calmly. Only the best
got by Murphy. He knew his own. "They come to
you to get a steer to some business. What they got in
mind? Nulty?"

The hit was so precise that Lawson flinched out-
wardly.

"Listen, Ed," Murphy said, pulling out his wallet,
"I'm the one where the money comes from." He
pulled out five ones and held them, fanned, in his
hand. Lawson looked at them.

"Tell me, Ed. You don't want to lose out by protecting those bastards."

Lawson sat slumped, looking stubbornly at the floor. "You gonna pay me? Five tails."

"Maybe you got a partner in Deming—buys tails at the slaughterhouse. Comes up here with half a gross at a time. I can't tell a wild tail from a tame one. Can you?"

Fatigue came over Lawson's face. He licked his lips as though he were thirsty. His eyes roamed the dark cabin walls.

"Did they mention Nulty?" Murphy asked, very softly.

Lawson said, shutting his eyes, "Yes, they did mention Nulty once or twice."

"Like they was going to visit him?"

Lawson said, "They asked me if he was still buying stolen cattle."

"Well, now," Murphy said, in a motherly way, "that don't hurt anybody, does it? What did you say?"

Lawson's face firmed, his eyes shot directly at Murphy's. "I didn't say nothing."

"Good for you," Murphy said. He held out the money.

Lawson took it. Sun from the window hit it, a hot, bright green. "I ain't selling out any old friends, Murphy, law or no law, amnesty or not. Keep that in mind."

Murphy smiled. "Ed, anybody calls you a traitor, I'll hit him in the mouth, myself." He put his wallet away and left, closing the cabin door behind him.

Lawson stood in the room with the bills in his hand, listening to Murphy's horse go down the road, away. He sat down, slowly, and looked at the empty chairs where the gang had sat, looked at the coffee cans, scattered about where they had put them down, and for a moment it was as though he heard their voices, the voices of ghosts. He stared at the money as though it were his enemy, and in him a hollowness grew, as all around him the silence deepened.

Pepe let Murphy get well ahead and then he caught up his horse and followed the dim trail through the pine litter. He already had a suspicion of what Murphy was doing: cutting south, through the foothills, he would go around the town, and go down from the hills secretly, to Nulty's, which lay south on the highway to Silver City. He could only have gone back to Lawson's to pump him.

As for Lawson, Pepe knew well enough that it didn't take ten minutes' talk for a man to keep his mouth shut. Pepe felt no anger at Lawson; he understood him too well. There was bound to be a certain lack of sensitivity in a man who would chop the tail off a dead horse.

He reached Nulty's twenty minutes after Murphy did, hid in a ditch behind a row of poplars, and waited again.

The wind sighed through the shingles of Nulty's roof, and heavy gray clouds came over; the light inside, already gloomy, dimmed further. Cold drafts came and went around Murphy's legs as he stood waiting while Nulty unlocked the door of his little office. Nulty stood there in the doorway, a giant rat, with his long, pendulous and bulbous nose like a dangling section of well-blocked bowel. He had a sparse gray moustache which grew, or spurted, straight outward from each side, as though the frantic hairs were desperately fleeing from the nose. When he smiled, as he was smiling now, his little mouth grew pursed and crawled up under the nose, and his little eyes twinkled like phosphorescence in a cess-pool.

He almost always wore an old tweed cap, and con-stantly sported a pair of leather puttees. The girls at Maddy's said there was nothing worse on earth than the sight of old Nulty, crawling around on the floor half drunk, with nothing on but his cap and his put-tees, which, to him, were the incontrovertible badges of gentility and which he never took off, even in somebody else's bed.

"Hurry up," Murphy said. "I ain't far ahead of Ollie now. You got a place where I could hide?"

Nulty smiled with mellow malice—he was old, and had learned that other people's troubles should be squeezed slowly and gently for the fullest enjoyment.

"Hairing vats is empty," Nulty said. "You could squat down in one of them, Sheriff. If Ollie seen you he'd just take you for an old scalded sow, most likely."

"You're funny as hell," Murphy said, shivering.

The packing shed was big and full of old death. The scalding tubs where they dunked the dead pigs were cold and empty. All over the dirt floor there was the black stain of old blood where the white, indecent carcasses were hung on iron hooks to bleed.

Murphy had a delicate side; this was certainly not his favorite spot for a picnic. He had been involved in several slaughters, mostly of people, but he'd never got over his early qualms. He was one of those hu-manitarians who have outgrown humanity, and will run down three or four old men to avoid hurting a dog.

Life was hard for Murphy, in lots of ways nobody would ever guess. He knew women like Maddy, down at Madam Fisher's, didn't like him, and this hurt, even if Maddy was only a high-class whore.

Many's the time he went down there with Fisher, throwing his money around like a big shot, making a real sacrifice for good fellowship, and the dirty bitches didn't even appreciate it. They tolerated him, and he knew they laughed at him, behind his back. Why? He would never, never know: actually, it was because of the mute, sad shape of his forlorn behind.

Murphy saw himself as astute, alert, sensitive to the winds of politics and opportunity, riding the thin, dangerous line between serving the big cattle men on the one hand and robbing the not-so-big on the other. People said he was so sharp he had stolen his mother's milk behind her back, he was that fast. Once he had become sheriff, he had Nulty under his thumb, and Nulty could do no less than bribe Murphy by offering his channels of trade, which were far better than Murphy's had ever been. Why, Nulty, as the local cattle inspector, had even shipped his stolen beef in officially sealed cars.

And in a sense, Murphy was doing Nulty a favor, because if Nulty and he stole together, Nulty would feel safe from him, and after all, Nulty did have a lot of money in Fisher's bank, and was very good friends with Fisher. It did not pay to become deadly enemies with anybody who could swing such weight with Fisher, because after all, Fisher held the notes of the cattlemen, and the cattlemen elected the sheriff. So Murphy extorted from Nulty and Nulty bribed Murphy and it was impossible for anybody but their Creator to tell where the extortion left off and the bribery began.

Nulty finally got his office door open—his office being a sort of large box, standing alone in the packing shed, which he kept locked because of the safe in it— and Murphy went in, grateful for the warmth of the iron stove, and for escape from the mournful sigh of the wind in the building which surrounded them.

Murphy sometimes had faint inklings of life after death. Not just sleep—or some Dantesque abyss—but a dark place like Nulty's, full of the real, terrible horrors of a new universe—smells and screams which no man could endure alive.

He would have said that life on the globe, within the comfortable dominion of a beneficent sun, and all the obedient customs of men, was a screen behind which abided a world of night, unseen, but hinted at. Even at night, the promise of tomorrow's light held at bay a multitude of terrible creatures which might pounce on him, some day. These thoughts he fled as fast as he could, and he regarded these fits of depression as hangovers from childhood fairy tales and the ogreish fancies of religion, rather than—possibly— shrewd premonitions which some vague Irish gift was according him. Poor Murphy, he had no real malice; he lived in perpetual flight on the edge between two worlds, fleeing between law and crime.

He sat down, now, with the warm stove on his left, managing to forget the souvenirs of carnage which surrounded him; Nulty, back against his paper-crammed desk, was looking crafty, cosy and warm in the red firelight from the open stove door.

"They're back, you know," Murphy said. Faintly the wind sighed, a paper stirred; remotely, something howled in the stovepipe, reminders of the other world. He shivered.

"Gorham's gang," Nulty said, twinkling.

"They're coming down here to make a deal," Murphy said.

"That's nice," Nulty said. A rat crawled out of a corner, looked speculatively at Murphy, drooled appreciatively, and crawled on.

"Give it to them," Murphy said. "Find out who they're going to hit and let me know. I want to be laying for them."

"You weren't always the one for shooting," Nulty said gently. "Suppose I arrange something with them and they manage to get by you, and come here with the beasts. What am I supposed to do? Tell them it was all a plot, and go home?"

"You talk like I was a fool," Murphy said, his face setting with anger. "Find out where Gorham will hit, and I'll get him."

"Speaking of fools," Nulty said, "I heard that Pringle sold you twenty-five head of Hereford grades that you had took for purebreds."

"Never mind that." Murphy leaned forward. "All right, you work it out with Gorham to hit Pringle. That'll pay me back. Twenty-five head of Pringle's best breeding stock. We could sell them somewhere, and split it. After I get Gorham."

Nulty looked bored. "Without pedigree papers, Pringle's bulls are dog food, Murphy. With papers, I could go to jail. So they're dog food." He turned toward his desk and picked up a paper, blinked, yawned, and patted his little mouth. Murphy sat still. A long silence, in which Murphy fought with his suspicions, his greed and his better judgment.

"All right," he said finally. "We can turn the bulls loose in the woods and just run the ass off them. Blame it on Gorham. That'll fix Pringle's wagon." He paused, and then tried to look casual—a sickly attempt. "You want the twenty-five grades he cheated me on?"

"Why don't you breed with 'em?" Nulty asked. "Make a million dollars on fees alone."

Murphy reddened.

"Mighty fine beef," Nulty said, turning his paper

over. "Seems a pity to let 'em go just as Indian canners."

"Indian canners!"

"After what you paid Pringle. Sell 'em to somebody—surely you ain't the only fool in the county."

Murphy bottled up. His fists clenched and his mouth pinched.

"You should stick to being Sheriff," Nulty said, "where you can make ignorance like yours show a profit."

"Not as canners," Murphy said, retreating another ditch. "They're prime beef."

"Eight a head."

"That's plain damn thievery!" Murphy yelled.

"They're a drug on the market," Nulty said affably.

"Nine bucks," Murphy said desperately. "Write me a check."

"Show me a cow."

"Listen, I'll have the twins drive them down at five o'clock. Give me a pen for a bill of sale."

They scratched away for a minute and swapped papers. Murphy stood up to go.

Nulty said, "You going to Maddy's tonight?" There was hunger in his eyes.

"I thought, out of respect for Mrs. Fisher—" Murphy was tired, he sagged inside, the last thing he wanted was a night of fun with those inexhaustible girls.

"Oh, can that. Fisher's going. I'm going. All that respect stuff, all right, all right, it's all right. But we're going to Maddy's." Eyes shining bright as money in a puddle. "After all, the old lady never gave a damn what Fisher did when she was alive, why should she care when she's dead?"

"All right. I'll be there." Late, he promised himself.

"Big party," Nulty said in a sly voice. Almost a whisper.

"I'll be there," Murphy said, like it was his mother's hanging, and left, closing the door behind him. Nulty and his secrets, he thought. Not a soul in the world that cared what Nulty did, but he still had to have a secret. From who? From the wife he had never had to betray, maybe. Murphy was adept at seeing the faults in others, particularly if they were his own.

Murphy went out through the empty, smelly packing house, hurrying. In the shadows it seemed as though there hung the bodies of murdered widows. Just imagination, Murphy knew—and yet did he not just now recall some dream of this place? On that table there, was not that where the devils had slaughtered men and women, and hacked them bone from bone? And a bloody, picked corpse, eaten by birds, hanging against a dirty wall. A dream? Or a prophecy?

Suddenly, instinctively, as though he were to be answered, he jammed his hands over his ears and rushed out. Outside, there was nothing, just the wind, the high, gray clouds. He stood, watching the wind bend the line of poplars across a field. Straw blew through the empty, desolate corrals, where the beasts had been herded like the damned waiting judgment.

Nulty came out behind him, smiling around a cigar, and leaned his torpid gray length against the door jamb. Murphy went down and mounted his horse. The dead grass sighed, and Nulty smiled as Murphy rode away, hunched in his saddle.

Pepe watched them, from the trees.

SIX

SHEP, MURPHY'S DEPUTY, rode down the main street
of San Vicente through the crowds and stopped in
front of Quires' Dry Goods and Notions Emporium.
Quires was the Justice of the Peace, but on the
grounds that the meek would inherit the earth, he
refused to be called Judge during business hours; indeed the profits of this humility were largely in real
estate. Mr. Quires was in, smiling humbly over ten
cents' worth of No. 14 needles at one of the town's
first ladies, a Mrs. Bentley. Behind him, his daughter,
fondly known to her many friends as Pimples, stood
and watched Mrs. Bentley. She loved Mrs. Bentley.
Mr. Bentley owned the sash-and-door company and
Mrs. Bentley was always elegantly dressed, even more
so than the wooden mannequin in the front window,
which Pimples fixed up monthly in the latest frills
from Kansas City, via Santa Fe.

Her parents called her Euphobia—a name which her
mother had derived not from any fear of beauty, but

from a seed catalogue. In the catalogue had been represented a certain species of Euphorbia commonly called Snow-on-the-Mountains—a very virginal and pure thought if Mrs. Quires had ever had one. Somewhere between Kansas and Albuquerque, Mrs. Quires had dropped the ''r.'' Nobody had ever missed it.

With such a cultivated name, Euphobia was a dead cinch to excel in school plays and classical tableaux. She was especially fine as a Greek goddess, and had even appeared once, in an emergency substitution, as Zeus. Her career as Chief Goddess was, of course, helped immensely by the fact that her father furnished all the gauze for the goddesses' costumes at a very handsome discount to the school board, which still left him a fantastic margin of profit, since it was next to worthless. It was the same kind of gauze which Quires sold to Nulty for wrapping the hams down at the packing house.

Mrs. Bentley left, graciously, as Shep came in. ''Good morning,'' Shep said, taking off his black hat and smiling at Pimples. ''I have a duty to warn you, Mr. Quires, that Bill Gorham's gang is back in town.'' He looked at Pimples. He knew very well that she and Harvey had been old pals. Pimples' face turned bright red and her eyes dropped. ''Harvey Muntin is still with them.''

Pimples raised her face and squeezed out a smile for Shep. It had to be done. Shep, feeling slightly better, bowed and left.

Father and daughter looked fondly at each other for a long moment.

''Well,'' Quires asked, ''are you going to make a jackass out of yourself all over again?''

She looked up, and her eyes had a glint in them. ''Harvey has come back to me.''

''Broke.''

"You could give him the job, like I asked you before, and you wouldn't. He *would* have been respectable, if you'd helped."

"A thief. Shep's respectable."

"Shep's stupid. Harvey is smart, and you know it. Harvey would make money for you. He's just adventurous. Besides, it was Harvey that thought up the sewing machine franchise, and you know it. Daddy, you can't say Harvey is dumb."

"I never said Harvey was dumb," Quires said, thinking of the sewing machine sales.

"Then you'll let him come around?"

Mr. Quires looked steadily at his daughter. "On one condition. He signs the amnesty. I can't have anybody unrespectable around you or my house, or my business either—especially since the biggest banker in Grant County has a mortgage on it and is my best friend besides—even if he was a pimp."

"Don't you worry, Daddy," Pimples said, smiling. "I'll make Harvey sign up. I'll make him get a deputy's badge, even. That'll show 'em."

Shep drifted into the Red Dog. The place was cool and dark, the floor was still wet from the daily swamping. George, the owner, was finishing his third beer of the day, and was just barely sociable.

"Bill Gorham's gang is back, George," Shep said with great weight, as George carefully poured him a bribe. "They'll come in here. You remember everything they say, and let me know where they'll be going, where they'll be staying, what they plan to do."

"Martha," George shouted. His wife came waddling out of the back room, holding a laundry list in her hand, at arm's length, frowning fixedly. "Those lousy chinks," she said, "they oughtta ship them back where they come from. Where the hell *do* they come from, anyway?''

''Nunnaya business,'' George said. ''Bill Gorham's gang is coming in here. You set your big old butt over there and keep your ears open. You hear where they're going, you trot over to Murphy and tell him.''

''Don't slip up,'' Shep said, downing a second bribe. ''A feller from Silver City come in yesterday and offered me five hundred for a license to open a place across the street.''

George looked bitter. Shep patted him on the shoulder. ''Don't worry, George. You and me are friends.'' He flapped out through the swing doors and George looked bleakly at a puddle of beer. He looked at Martha, for a moment, sitting with the laundry list and counting on her fingers. Then he simply shut his eyes and stood there, thinking of crime after crime.

A lot of people greeted Ollie as he and Burt and Harvey came down into town. Good old Ollie, sloppy in the saddle, on that gangling horse, smiled his wide, loose smile, raising a hand to this one and that one, men he hadn't seen for years.

He saw plenty of faces he knew among the people coming and going on the boardwalks, but the strangest part of it was the number of thieves he knew, standing around, right out in the open. There was a tension in the air; women of the decent sort, housewives shopping, the merchants, all had the same grim, patient expression.

He passed the encampment on the plaza, and seeing the cannon, he almost laughed. Good humor came and went in him, enjoyment of the breeze, of the faces of his friends, the flicker of sun and leaf, the whipping of the bright flag. He had time, and a good plan.

Once in the Red Dog, they stood in a row in front of George's bar, Ollie grinning, Burt smiling and Harvey with an alert, youthful expression on his face.

"Set 'em up, George," Ollie said, his grin spreading his freckles apart. "Good old George. By God, George, you're looking good. Good, that is, for a married man. Ha, ha, look at old Martha's face."

"Where did *you* crawl out of?" Martha said.

"Like I said, George, if Maddy's as hospitable as she used to was, we'll be down in there tonight—how about ditching the old woman and coming down for a ride on the merry-go-round, like we used to? Huh?"

George's face was a little pinched. Martha got up and left, pushing her stomach through the swinging doors. George grinned at Ollie, an empty, toothy grin. "Ha, ha," he said. "Them days is gone, Ollie." A couple of drops fell from the mouth of the bottle as he finished measuring out Burt's shotglass. George carefully corked the bottle and with a rueful expression wiped up the two wasted drops. "Got any money, Ollie?"

Ollie's grin settled a little. "Not a dime, George. Why? You want to borrow some?"

"I just wondered how you was doing, that's all," George said, glancing at the doorway.

"I'll be loaded tomorrow," Ollie said.

George glanced at him quickly. "Listen, Ollie, don't flap your mouth around too much. Things ain't like they used to."

Ollie's grin was still there, but his blue eyes were cool and watchful. He looked carefully around the saloon, using the big mirror. Three or four men were doctoring hangovers in the shadows. "It's beginning to dawn," he said.

"You going to sign up with Moore?"

Ollie leaned forward a little. "Why is that so important to everybody? And what the hell you so nervous about?''

''Hell, drink your drink. Go on, drink up. Have another.''

''You act like there was somebody waiting out that door with a shotgun to blow my head off. If there is, why don't you tell me? If there ain't, why don't you relax? Have I got any money, says you. Like I was going to drop dead.''

''Now, don't get wound up, Ollie,'' George said. The hangovers in the back were watching dully.

''You scared you ain't going to collect? You telling me I'm a thief?'' Ollie leaned farther forward. ''You trying to insult me, George? Or what the hell is this?''

George stood with his hands on the edge of the bar; his mouth was tight, his face pale. ''Ollie, for cripes sake, simmer down. This is a respectable bar.''

The doors swung open and two big men came in. The three at the bar watched them in the mirror. Very neat men, big and ponderous, but part of the ponderosity was fat. Their hats were in the hundred-dollar class; their pants hung smooth, their shirts were clean, their vests unspotted, their neckerchiefs dainty, and their bland faces were such a smooth, plump pink it was hard to tell whether they had been to a barber or a taxidermist.

They smiled at George without saying a word, and looked all around without seeming to see anybody. Ollie, Burt and Harvey, dirty, ragged and with their hair hanging over their ears, watched them with simple awe.

The big men drank one drink each. Then one of them, still without a word, but smiling his faint smile, his eyes far off behind George, paid; the two walked slowly, ponderously, out.

''Well, who the hell was all that?'' Ollie said.

"Cannon brothers," George said, dropping his money in the till. "Rich as Fisher himself."

"Never heard of them," Ollie said.

"They never heard of you," George said. "But they own half the county up around Reserve. Come from Texas last year. Fisher was scared to death they'd open another bank, but they went into cows."

"I never seen anybody so clean," Burt said. "It makes me kind of sad."

"Strangers," Ollie said. "Never heard of them."

George looked at him boldly. "Ollie, wake up. It's you that's the strangers. Things have changed. It's men like them own the country now. We ain't had a shooting in town for eighteen months. This is a business town now, Ollie. Those big boys come in here to do business. I got to be respectable."

Ollie's grin came back and slowly widened. "Oh, yeah?" He slammed his palm flat down on the bar. George jumped. The hangovers sat bolt upright. "I'll pay you your money after I rob somebody, and if you want to, go tell Murphy I said so. Come on, boys, let's go someplace where it stinks like home sweet home."

He slammed out the doors and swung up on his horse, spat on the sidewalk in front of the saloon, and shambled off down the street, north toward the plaza.

"What about Nulty's?" Burt asked, hurrying after him. "We better get down there, Ollie."

"I gotta get my teeth fixed first," Ollie said. "I can't pull no job without my teeth. If I can get that dentist working on them now, we can pull it tonight and leave tomorrow. You all wait for me in the plaza."

Ollie passed Fisher's bank on the corner of the plaza, and cutting across the main street, hitched up in front of the Higsby Building, which was a two-story adobe decorated with a blue wooden cornice.

Downstairs were two stores; upstairs, reached by a wide central staircase directly from the street, was a long, open-ended hallway, and down this hall there were two offices on each side, a doctor, a dentist and two lawyers. At the other end of the open hall, a flight of stairs led directly into the alley running through the middle of the block. A constant draft of air flowed down this hall, making the whole building delightfully cool in summer—especially enjoyed by stray dogs which would come in to relieve themselves against the door jambs, or haul in quantities of old bones and sheep-heads to gnaw on in comfort; leaving them scattered about for the tenants to turn their ankles on. The tenants stacked firewood in cord lots along one side of the hall—it was all very informal and convenient.

Ollie went up the creaking wooden stairs and down the oiled floor of the hallway, kicking his way through the old bones, dogs, and chunks of stovewood. Everything creaked, the floor sprang and swayed like a foundering frigate. Calsomine flaked from the old adobe walls; the doorframes rattled, where the adobe had slowly dusted away, like teeth in an old skull.

Cameron's office was in the front. Ollie went in and looked around the six-by-six waiting room. He still wore his grin, a permanent reflex to any situation that called for enterprise. He grinned at the dusty little palm tree, its tips gray with drought, he grinned at the horse prints on the walls, and at the *Harper's* magazines stacked neatly on the small table.

Beyond the frosted-glass door to the inner office, through whose pane seeped a dim and careworn light, Dr. Cameron's foot thumped as he built up speed on his drill. Ollie sat down, pulled out his teeth and looked at them. As he thought of his plates, repaired, shining in renewed perfection, a slow warmth grew in his heart.

Ollie's teeth were all that he had to be proud of. He had never had anything that called a look of envy to anybody's face, except these teeth, and many an old Indian, mourning the wooden pegs in his jaw, had looked at Ollie's teeth and thought nostalgically of murder. Ollie had not even worn shoes until he had been baptized. On that fateful day he had put on his mother's field-shoes, which she had got from his father only after his father had managed to steal the boots off a corpse after a lynching; he had staggered proudly into the river where the preacher dumped a dishpan full of water over his scraggly head. But nowadays everybody had boots just as everybody had guns, and they were nothing to be proud of.

But nobody had a complete, perfect set of artificial teeth like his. Certainly they were better than the ones he had been born with—small, yellow, and so soft that they'd started to rot full of holes almost as soon as they came in. He could remember a time, before his teeth had begun to pain and shame him, when he was wholly happy. Dawn in East Texas, lying beside his lovely, warm mother, watching the eastern sky turn pink beyond the mossy trees, watching the slow flap of white cranes rising across the sky, their feathers too a delicate pink. That was the happy time, peaceful and slow as the flying white cranes; but then the teeth began to hurt. He had hated his teeth, and when the last abscess was pulled he would have been happy again except everybody began laughing at his empty gums.

The store teeth made him a man—even a kind of superman. After his own teeth, he knew that anything artificial was bound to be better than something natural. With his own teeth he had always felt just like little Oliver Trevillian, a scrag-headed nobody that just got kicked around. But with his store teeth, his mouth had a better shape, his tongue felt more comfortable, and the teeth themselves closed on each other neatly, so that he faced the world more handsome and more poised.

From the day he had got them, he had felt better toward the world, and he was, in fact, a better man. He could meet people better, knowing that when he grinned, he would be beautiful. He smiled more often, so people liked him better. Or he could just sit, quiet and poised, while somebody haggled or badgered at him, calmly aware of the perfection which he carried in his mouth. He could even talk better. He could shoot better, because he was more confident and relaxed. And he could think better, because, having more of value in himself, he could face extraneous losses with more composure.

So he loved his teeth, and beyond their esthetic and practical value to him, they had gradually acquired the identity of a special god—they were a talisman. Without them, he was lost.

The inner door opened, and an elderly lady, her black satin all awry, staggered out, smiling and blind as a bat. She bumped into the door jamb and reeled out. Doped to the eyes.

Dr. Cameron removed the stub of the drill he had just broken off in the old lady's penultimate fang, and threw it into a corner. He saw Ollie, through the sanctum doorway.

"Yes?" Dr. Cameron asked, smiling invitingly. His teeth were actually his own, but they were naturally so white and regular that they looked handmade, and everybody thought they were, so he made the most of it by using them to demonstrate the fit of his plates—by tugging hard at his own teeth, which, of course, never came out.

"My teeth is busted," Ollie said, handing Dr. Cameron his tooth-box, in which lay his treasures.

The Doctor looked at them thoughtfully and stuck out his lower lip. "You really ought to have a new plate," he said, as, indeed, he always did.

Ollie's proud smile died slowly. "Don't start that," he said. "There's only four teeth missing."

"My dear sir," Cameron said, smiling in a friendly way that made Ollie feel like a miserable fool, "as you can see, the upper plate is badly cracked. I'm afraid if we merely put in new teeth, it won't be a week before the whole thing—"

"How much?" Ollie asked.

"For the plate, eighty-five dollars," Cameron said.

"For the teeth, damn it," Ollie said.

The doctor looked at him. There was a small, hot light in Ollie's eyes, and even more evident, a tension in him that came out to the doctor in waves. The doctor felt very uncomfortable. "For the teeth alone, ten each. Forty dollars."

The light in Ollie's eyes burned finer and hotter. "Forty bucks for four teeth and eighty-five for a whole damn new plate? What the hell kind of a deal is that?"

"My dear man," Dr. Cameron began, out of habit, and then stopped. This was not a dear man. "Are you, ah, by any chance one of the *new* men in town? May I ask?"

"Twenty dollars," Ollie said.

"Thirty-two-fifty in advance," Dr. Cameron said.

"In advance," Ollie said, beginning to tremble. Without his teeth, composure was impossible. "How do I know you won't fall over dead, and then where's my teeth and my money too?"

"Otherwise forty dollars when you pick them up,"

Cameron said, noting Ollie's nerves and regaining his own calm as a result.

"I'll take the damn things to El Paso," Ollie said, his jaws rigid with rage.

Dr. Cameron languidly handed the teeth back. Ollie stood there, his hands at his sides, looking at the teeth in the outstretched hand. His fists clenched.

After a moment, his fists loosened. "All right," Ollie said in a low voice, "forty dollars. What time tomorrow can I pick them up?"

"In a week," Cameron said. "Not sooner. I'm busy."

"A week!" Ollie cried. "I got to have them tomorrow morning. I won't be here a week. I'm leaving tomorrow."

"I could work tonight," the Doctor said, reposing his coils calmly around his victim a little more tightly. "It would be seventy-five dollars, for that kind of rush emergency work."

Ollie wanted to call him a dirty bastard, the words were right on his tongue. He looked at the doctor and locked up tight; his eyes bulged, he got red in the face; he clamped his arms tight to his sides, straight down.

"All right," Ollie said after a long moment. "Sixty dollars, and I get 'em tomorrow morning at nine sharp."

The doctor looked tired. He looked out of the window and laid the teeth down on his instrument cabinet. "Seventy-five," he said wearily. "It'll take me till midnight."

"All right," Ollie said, glaring at the floor. "*All right.*" He looked at Dr. Cameron for a moment, thinking how he would look dead, and turned and went out. He slammed the hall door as hard as he could. Dust and calsomine flew from around the loose doorframe. He rattled down the steps to the street.

Burt and Harvey were coming toward him. He looked at the town around the plaza. In his mind's eye, he could see it in flames, flattened to the ground, the people dead in heaps.

He looked at Fisher's bank, on the corner across from him, and suddenly the thought leaped up out of the sea of his rage. "Rob Fisher's bank," came the thought. Here he was, beat to the ground by a lousy dentist because he had no money. There was money in Fisher's bank, stacks of it. Why fool with cows?

The thought awed him. It was too big for him, and he shrank, and his anger died. Robbing a bank was life and death, you might get killed, you might kill somebody else, and that meant hanging. No, stealing cattle was Ollie's line—a trade that was poorly paid, but still better than working, and pretty safe. He turned up the walk as Burt came alongside.

"Seventy-five bucks," he said. "We got to get enough off Nulty to make it split down to that for me, say a hundred apiece. How we gonna grab five hundred bucks worth of cows in one night?"

"Borrow it from Maddy," Burt said. Burt was full of a warm calm. Nothing ever seemed to bother Burt much, and his bland placidity always soothed Ollie.

"I ain't no stinking pimp," Ollie said, looking at Fisher's bank and unhitching his horse. "Come on, let's get down to Nulty's. Back way, down the river."

SEVEN

THEY CAME DOWN in the water, horses mincing along and stumbling a little on the gravelly bottom—Ollie, Burt and Harvey, single file, their tracks whirled away in the glittering, tumbling stream.

Pepe, hidden in the willows, watched them. He had come secretly down from Nulty's, winding in and out through the pens, across the single line of weed-grown tracks, past one empty cattle car, and then down the long lane between the two big fenced pastures that led down to the river.

Pepe came out of the willows and beckoned. They turned their horses and crossed the twenty feet of water to the wide, dry-rock-and-gravel flood-bed. They sat their horses there in the shade with the tall cottonwoods and willows all around them. The horses blew, bowed their heads, and flicked their tails at the drowsy summer flies.

"It's all off," Pepe said.

Ollie's smile died. "Oh, yeah? Why? You tell me why."

"Murphy was just up there," Pepe said quietly. "Ten minutes—talking. Enemies don't talk so long."

Ollie took that quietly; a slight pinching of the lips, a tiny narrowing of the eyes. They sat in silence while Ollie thought.

Then Ollie said, "Nobody else is sure."

Pepe said, with a look at Ollie that seemed mere stubbornness, "Three years ago, Nulty was sure. He isn't sure now, not if he talks to Murphy so long." He shook his head. "They were friends. The way Nulty stood in the door, when Murphy rode away. Leaning there smiling, the way a friend would. Maybe if he was Murphy's enemy, he would smile at Murphy's face, but not at Murphy's back."

"You tell me this," Ollie said, his face sharpening, his voice harder, "did Murphy act suspicious? Did he look all around? Did he come in secret? Huh? Was he scared of being seen?"

Pepe shook his head.

"Then I tell you what," Ollie said, positively, "he came down there just to find out if we'd been to see Nulty yet. Murphy knows we'll try some kind of a job somewhere, he knows we used to work with Nulty. So why wouldn't Murphy come down and try to pump the old bastard?"

"Maybe Lawson told him," Burt said quietly.

"I think he did," Pepe said.

"Harvey," Ollie said, "ride up behind the sheds where you ain't likely to be seen, and get the old goat to come here. Tell him it's us. Tell him we got a deal."

Harvey moved his horse off through the willows.

"What deal?" Burt asked.

"Them Herefords we saw, up the river. It's a setup."

"Hell, Ollie, you must be losing your mind," Burt said. "Driving Herefords through longhorn country."

"How the hell you going to see a red cow at midnight?" Ollie said.

"Pringle's cattle," Pepe said. "Bill's friend."

"Yeah? Well, Pringle won't miss twenty head in one night. We seen a hundred and fifty in the medders west of the river."

"They're too fat," Pepe said. "Won't drive good."

"What the hell's the matter with you today?" Ollie asked. "What's got into you, Pepe?"

Pepe smiled suddenly, trying to put a good face on it. "I am sick of San Vicente. It is going wrong. I wish I was in Mexico, hunting deer in the pine forests. Where it's safe."

"Not after that captain," Burt said.

"So you're stuck with us," Ollie said. "You better take a deep breath, pal, and resign yourself to it. Nobody can do nothing without some cash. Hell, we're damn near out of cartridges." He eyed Pepe's gunbelt. "You got the most left. How about sparing a few? In case we get in a fight tonight."

"No fight," Pepe said. "I don't fight anybody over cows."

Nulty came out of the willows, following Harvey. He came across the open flood-bed, tall, loose in the saddle, his tweed cap pulled down over his narrow little eyes.

"Make him sit down-wind," Ollie said. They bunched up, tails upstream, against the breeze, and waited.

Nulty rode up and sat there—tiny warts on the backs of his hands like nipples on a mother rat, liver spots like drops of bat-blood, while his sharp little eyes peeped out from alongside his long, limp nose, from under the visor of his cap. The puttees hadn't been shined for ten years. Still, there was something remotely fashionable about Nulty. The little mouth puckered up in a smile and Nulty said, "What you got, boys?"

Ollie said, "Murphy was in to see you just now. What about?"

The twinkle of Nulty's eyes, hiding back there in the dark like rats in their holes, was brighter and more friendly. "You mean, are him and I friends? Is that what you mean? Well, I tell you, Ollie, if I was Murphy's friend, any more than I used to be, would I be down here now, talking to you?"

They sat and looked at each other, and nobody but Nulty realized clearly that he had said absolutely nothing. The sun shone warm, and the leaf shadows danced on the gray gravel and stones. Nulty waited. He knew what Ollie was doing—trying to justify an unjustified trust. In the back of his mind, Nulty thought about Maddy. Maddy was his favorite girl; Ollie and Maddy used to be mighty good friends; and he was wondering if it would make any difference, now, with Ollie back here again. It was just possible that Maddy might be taken off the market. That was as close to a disappointment in love as Nulty would ever get. That, or have the price raised to ten bucks. That would really break his heart. His final thought was that Ollie would look good with a hole in the front of his head.

Pepe watched Nulty without expression, and without seeming to. Pepe knew Nulty. One never trusted people like Nulty at all, because Nulty was obviously a dirty old man, and all cattle traders were liars. The idea of his probity was ridiculous.

"All right," Ollie said out of nothing. He had made his decision on one, solitary basis—he would trust

Nulty because he needed his teeth back; and if Nulty crossed them, he would kill him. "I got twenty Herefords up the river. Or will have."

"That's good," Nulty said. 'I was going to suggest you clip that herd. It ain't never been touched, and it ought to be touched. Right next door, it looks like I was laying off on purpose, and that makes people suspicion me. You know how it is. Only amateurs rob their neighbors; well, I could stand to be known as an amateur. Nobody would think I was fool enough to steal from Pringle, which is exactly why it's a good idea."

He smiled with a hard, complacent bitterness. "And if you hit Pringle, it might look like Murphy done it, him operating mostly up the other end of the valley. Only I can't hold 'em. You'll have to drive 'em a day west toward the Agency."

"No," Ollie said. "We drive 'em over in the next valley west, and your boys take over from there. We get 'em off Pringle's range and over in the clear, and that's all."

"For that, I can't pay more'n eight a head."

"Why, damn it, Nulty, that's less'n we got three years ago, and the market's up." Ollie's face was red, as Nulty had foreseen.

"Can't help it," Nulty said, mouth tight, eyes averted.

"Why, we're taking the risk, we're running on Pringle's range, we're the ones get caught in the act, not your boys. I give you the phony bill of sale, that puts you in the clear. Damn it, Nulty, twelve bucks." Ollie was desperate. Even at twelve bucks it would only mean two hundred and forty dollars split down to fifty dollars apiece.

"Ten bucks," Nulty said. He didn't give a damn.

He picked his teeth with his tongue, looked around at the tree tops. "Think it's going to rain?"

"I don't give a damn if it pees," Ollie shouted. "You gimme ten bucks and take *thirty* head, then."

Nulty smiled. "All right," he said. "Ten bucks and thirty head, I can't handle more, in the next valley." They'd never even get off Pringle's range.

"Pay off here," Ollie said.

Nulty shook his head. "In my office."

"I don't want to get near your office. Murphy might be hanging around."

Nulty shook his head. "I don't carry no three hundred bucks around in the dark. You guys rob me, and then come up and claim I welched. Has been done. But not on me."

"What's the difference?" Burt asked. "If we get took in Nulty's office, he gets took too for receiving stolen goods."

"What time?"

"About two-three o'clock," Ollie said.

"Too late. Got a big party that night. Make it eleven."

"With everybody still up?"

"What's the odds? It'll be a surprise. I got this party," Nulty insisted. He watched Ollie expectantly, looking for a sign of anger. "At Maddy's."

"Oh," Ollie said, "you play it up at Maddy's, do you?"

For the first time, Nulty smiled so that his teeth showed—little teeth, like popcorn kernels, pale, yellowish-white in red and bloody-looking gums. "Maddy's sure a pretty girl."

He watched closely, coldly, through the smile. Ollie's face just got shrewd. Nulty decided to say nothing more about Maddy. It was a funny thing, that some men, like Ollie, could actually be fond of a whore. Nulty, even while he cavorted, maintained an attitude of complete moral contempt for such women. Fisher felt the same way. It was the only way a man should feel. They were creatures to be abused, by invitation. But men like Ollie, these daft buggers from the uplands, had no sense of values. They treated such women as humans. They even married them.

"All right," Ollie said, gathering his reins up. "You have your boys waiting over across the mountain by nine. Two boys will do. We'll leave one to hold the cows, and bring one of your boys back for a witness that we delivered, and collect from you at eleven. All right?"

"Fair enough," Nulty said. He almost smiled—a witness to the delivery was one thing he would not be in need of, providing Murphy could get close enough to Ollie to kill him.

None of the gang knew why they felt so gloomy, when they should have felt gay. Then, as they walked their horses back toward town through the water, upstream, Pepe realized the reason and said, "Murphy and Nulty. They're partners."

"Why?" Ollie cried out, exasperated. "What's the matter with you, anyway?"

Patient, calm, Pepe said, "Nulty should have arranged for the witness to the delivery. He shouldn't have left it to you."

"Pepe, what are you, a lousy Pinkerton agent? You got a screw loose?"

"Nulty just don't expect any delivery at all," Pepe said. "That's the only possible reason he slipped up. It's going to be a trap, Ollie."

"Look," Ollie said, halting his horse in midstream. "You listen to me," They were nearing the end of the trees that covered the river like a tunnel, nearing the last slope of the big hill that had cast its shadow over

Nulty's pens, coming out into the rolling country where Pringle's red cows grazed. "You don't want to go along, Pepe, you just say so. You can have out any time."

Pepe looked at him in silence.

"What do you say, Harvey?" Ollie asked. "Do we go through with it or not?"

Harvey looked at Pepe quietly for a moment, and then answered. "I say go ahead, but be careful."

"What do you say, Burt?"

"I got a mind to get my old woman and clear the hell out."

Ollie's face suddenly brightened. "That's an idea. I'll get Maddy and we'll go the hell west somewheres where it's like the old times." He grinned, and turned back to Pepe. "Four against you, Pepe."

"Bill hasn't voted yet."

"I need the money," Ollie said. "If Nulty crosses us, I'll kill the old son of a bitch. We're going ahead."

"To steal thirty head of cows we maybe got to kill a man?"

"Damn it," Ollie said, "I got to have the money."

"Listen," Pepe said quietly, "everything is wrong, and you think you can change it back by killing somebody. Don't you see where you are heading, what will happen? Don't you know when to quit?"

"Sure. Tomorrow. I'll get my teeth and take Maddy with me."

"Ollie, you are going to get yourself killed. And not just you. You'll drag Burt into it. And Harvey. But not Bill. I won't let you drag Bill into it. You can count him out too."

"You go to hell," Ollie said, and turned his horse away.

They left Pepe there in the middle of the river, and he sat and watched them go.

He watched them, and felt nothing but pity for them. He knew they were simpler men than he was, more easily moved to more predictable ends. He could have left them then, turned his horse out of the water, and gone on, left them all, including Bill. But he could not leave Bill, and for a moment his heart twisted that Bill was now at the Colonel's place, and not here, where they could have made some decision. And yet, how could he blame Bill for being where he was? Those people were in Bill's past, they could not be escaped. So he sat there, unable to move or decide, waiting for his friend.

How many years had it been since he had found him? Five years, so long, so full of things, since he had seen that bundle of a body in the alley in El Paso. A night of rare, heavy rain, with the water pouring off the roofs, and rushing across the dry ground, too dry to soak any up; muddy brown water sluicing along down the alley, soaking the bundle lying there in the corner between the adobe wall and the dirt of the alleyway.

Why had he stopped? Some compunction, some inability to pass by, he who had for years traveled completely alone. Some recollection of the priest's voice. He had sat there on his horse, beside the bundle, and it had reproached him, or its angel had spoken for it. Why are you there, while I am here? it said. Who are you, that you should be on the horse, while I lie here drunk in the mud? If it were not for God's goodness to you, you would be here, and I there, and you know it.

In the end, it was his innocence, his own purity, that led him to get down. For if he had gone on the way, he would have forgotten such things as the priest and his stories, he would have had to have been hardened over with drunkenness and whores and his own crimes against the recollection of his mother, lying beaten on the dirt floor. But he had lived by himself in the wilderness for years, with nothing but the animals, and had stayed out of the way of self-desolation.

How could he have left that man lying in the rain? His clothes soaking up the wet, gradually turning sodden, while he slept, dead drunk, his mouth open, the water falling on the white, haggard, bearded face—endless, dead-cold water running cross the cheek, into the mouth, to dribble out the other side.

First he got down from the horse, and stood there, wondering what to do. He knelt. He put his hand on the forehead, and felt its heat. If only the man had merely been drunk, it would have been simple—Pepe could have found a dry place for him in a stable, covered him in some stall with straw, so that he would keep warm. But if he were sick, what could he do? He rented a room among the Mexican hovels.

He had paid a week's rent, planning to leave him there—but once the sick man was in bed, unconscious, he could not leave him to die. He had waited, day after day, sitting beside the bed.

But then, instead of dying, the stranger began to recover, and life, like a little seed, again began to grow; and day by day, slowly feeding stuff back into this corpse, a little soup, a little bread, Pepe watched this little tree of life very slowly growing again, unfolding one leaf after another, and it suddenly became fascinating. Intent, he watched, listening to almost every breath; and when he was absolutely sure that this stranger would not, suddenly, turn around again and go off back into death, suddenly he realized that it was he who had brought back this individual life, that in some way he now owned him. And so Bill had become a permanent responsibility.

This was the way it had gradually unfolded to Pepe. And now he sat his horse in the river, and could not move. Because Bill was at his old friend's house, and he could not leave until he knew what would happen to Bill.

Looking after the other three, going up the river, he might have hated them, but he was too old to take any consolation in hatred. He understood now well enough why his mother had stayed with his father, suffering the beatings, until she died. Even while she was being beaten, she knew she was dealing with a helpless infant, she knew that the child in his father depended on her and loved her, and the man in his father hated the child in him and her both, for its dependence, and so he beat her, and could escape neither. So she stayed. And so Pepe stayed, against his better judgment, simply because of love. So Pepe watched his other three children go on up the river; and he picked up his reins and slowly followed them, keeping to his obscurity, in the shadows.

EIGHT

PEPE WAS THE only one who didn't drink, so when
the others banged in through the swing doors of the
Red Dog, he sat down on the bench outside in the
shade of the covered boardwalk. He could see Murphy across the street, sitting in his office.

Inside the saloon, Martha again took up her listening post; she hustled across to Murphy's. Murphy
came out, got on his horse, and rode away.

Pepe, at a safe distance, followed on his own
horse—along the creek down through town, under
the railroad, cutting across lots. Maddy's house, at
the south end of town, sat among the cottonwoods
beside the creek. Pepe hid his horse in the creek bottom, farther up from where Murphy had hidden his
near the house. He settled himself in the brush, and
again waited.

Back at the Red Dog, Harvey was standing quietly
looking at his drink, his face very thoughtful. There

were half a dozen men drinking at the bar now. Ollie was talking loudly with one of them.

"Mrs. Fisher?" Ollie cried. "She died?" It was a profound shock. "What of? The D.T.'s?"

George leaned across the bar. "Listen, Ollie, Mrs. Fisher was one of our most prominent citizens. Have a little regard for other people's feelings."

"Yeah," Ollie said, "she was prominent, all right. The biggest butt in Phoenix. Pour me another, George, and lay off the fancy airs. Whatta you think you're running, the Palace Hotel in San Francisco?"

"Listen," George hissed, his eyes flicking up and down the bar looking for a respectable citizen to be afraid of, "if you don't shut up—"

"Poor old George," Ollie bawled. "Don't you know that the whole, entire prosperity of San Vicente is based on that one thing? Annie's bottom? Why, Buck Fisher married Annie on account of her rear. When they built that west wing on the whorehouse in Phoenix, they put up Annie's butt as collateral—all the bankers knew it was good." He looked up and down the bar and lifted his drink. "Anybody mind if I drink a toast to the hind end of Annie Fisher?" Nobody said anything. "Here's to Annie's butt," he cried, "the great white hope of New Mexico, the proudest boast of San Vicente. God knows it was big enough to support the town—it supported Phoenix for years, Buck and all the rest of the pimps." He gulped down his shot.

"I'll have to ask you to leave," George said, his face red.

"'S a pleasure," Ollie said. "Leaving this place will be one of the brightest memories of my life. Let's go, boys. Time we went to see the girls."

"Euphobia might not like for me to be in a whore-house," Harvey said soberly.

"Euphobia?" Ollie asked. "What's that? A new kind of clap?"

"Euphobia is my girl friend," Harvey said, his face reddening. "I said she might not like me to be in a whorehouse."

"Euphobia," Ollie said quietly. "My God."

Harvey blushed to the hairline and rushed out the door.

Outside, he turned up the boardwalk and headed for Quires'. It had suddenly dawned on him that Ollie was not refined. Ollie was almost repugnant. It was the thought of Euphobia that had suddenly refined Harvey. He stopped in front of the Emporium and looked at the window display, and it all came back, his old ambitions to be a merchant, before he got mixed up with Trevillian, whom he had thought daring in the old days. The wooden mannequin he had persuaded Quires to buy three years before was short of paint on the face, and one arm, broken probably by Euphobia while dressing it, had been crudely tacked together. He shook his head sadly. He went inside and stood blinking in the dusk.

"Harvey," Euphobia said from the rear, and ran forward. She stopped suddenly, six feet away from him, and stood abashed. Mr. Quires looked stiffly at Harvey.

"Euphobia," Harvey said softly, looking at Pimples.

"You have returned, Harvey," Euphobia said.

"Yes, I have returned," he said solemnly.

"You got any money?" Mr. Quires asked in a small, rasping voice.

"I got ambition, sir," Harvey said. "I've learned a lot, on the road. I'm gonna get—I've got about a hundred dollars."

"Let's get one thing straight," Quires said. "I ain't

going to have Euphobia wrastling around in the back room with no good-for-nothing bum tramp, much less a thief.''

''Those are hard words, Mr. Quires,'' Harvey said smoothly, ''to say to a young man who has returned to what was almost his home. How is Mrs. Quires? She was like a mother to me.''

''That's all very well,'' Quires said, softening to the malarky even while he saw through it, and so raising his voice sharply. ''You answer my question.''

''Will you give me a job here?'' Harvey asked.

''Well, now,'' Quires said, out of habit making things difficult for the young. ''Well, now.''

''I got ideas for improvements already,'' Harvey said. ''That mannequin. You ought to send it down to Johanssen and have him fix that arm right and paint up the face. You need a skylight. Bigger windows. Customers can't half see the merchandise. How you expect to sell stuff,'' he said aggressively, gesturing at the tables of ribbons, pins, thread, gloves, stockings, corsets, and so on, ''if people can't even see what it is? It looks dead. You got to make it look alive.''

Quires liked all this. He recognized a kindred talent. His eyes brightened. ''You ain't changed, Harvey. We been selling a lot of sewing machines lately. You got a head on you, Harvey. Only thing is, you ain't respectable. That young deputy, Shep, he's been coming around seeing Euphobia a lot, and he's a comer. He'll be Sheriff one of these days.''

Harvey's eyes narrowed. ''Yeah. So he gets to be a rich crook. And how does that get *you* any money? But with me in here, working with you—you retire, you still own the business. With me, you won't be begging for cigar money, Judge.'' He smiled.

The Judge was sold. "Harvey, you come in the stockroom a minute. Euphie, you stay out here."

He led Harvey back into the deeper gloom and pulled up a chair in front of his desk, which was between the shoe-boxes. "Listen, Harvey," Quires said in a low, confiding voice, "I'm really glad to see you back, son. It's just that Murphy still has those warrants on you. You'll have to sign up with Moore and then they'll be forgotten."

"Uh-huh," Harvey said.

"That ain't quite all," Quires said. "You got to do something outstanding to prove you've completely changed. The ladies will go for you if they think you're a reformed crook, but they won't really appreciate you unless you look like a saint. You ought to have a badge, like that Shep. Can you do anything for Murphy?"

"Like what?" Harvey asked blankly.

"You're not stupid, Harvey. Murphy could use some help. He's got it in for that gang of yours. Shep told me. He wants to arrest you for something. If he can, you lose the amnesty rights, and you're outside the law for good."

"So what?" Harvey said.

"It all ties in together." Quires leaned forward. "Suppose Murphy could catch them other guys stealing cattle. Suppose you gave the information to Murphy, as a good, reformed citizen. That would clean you up, Harve. Get rid of your old ties, get rid of the warrants on you, prove your good faith—I could even talk Murphy into making you a deputy. That would really clean you up."

Harvey sat silent, stunned, his mouth open.

"I got the capital," the little voice went nibbling along. "You got the ideas. You'd inherit it all, boy."

"Listen," Harvey said. "You ain't going to ask me to turn in my old friends."

"Friends?" Quires asked. He shook his head slowly, smiling. "I'm your friend, Harve. Mr. Fisher's your friend. We're all friends together in this good little town, Harve. We're getting a good class of steady people in here now, good, patient, dumb suckers, the kind that can be taken for years on end and never get a squawk—that's where the real money comes from, Harve, not robbing banks. I learned that from Fisher. The rough stuff is gone. You got to make the right kind of friends—and you can't have both."

They sat in silence. Up front, the door slammed, the bell tinkled, they heard Euphobia talking to a customer.

"The thing to do," Quires said, "is to hit Murphy up for a job as deputy. Sell him something. He'll think you're crazy at first, but not if you give him some information he can use. You get that badge on for six, seven months, Harve, and nobody'll ever remember you went off the rails. That's what I want."

Harvey just sat there, staring into space. Quires left him, went softly up front and said to Euphobia, "Daughter, go back and give Harvey a nice, big kiss. I'll stay up here. Show him what a woman's comfort can be. Not everything, of course."

"Yes, Pa," Pimples said. Her eyes shone with happiness. She turned and quickly, eagerly, glided away behind the counter, toward the stockroom.

After a while, when the sound of tumbling shoeboxes had died, Harvey came out. He looked a little tousled and his face had a soft, addled look, like a half-poached egg. "Mr. Quires, I'd like to have the honor of marrying your daughter."

Quires beamed. "She's a fine girl, Harve, all wool

and a yard wide. You just get a badge for her, son, as a wedding present.''

"Listen," Harvey said in a low voice as his brains began to operate again, "why don't you have Murphy to dinner tonight? That ain't my fault, is it, if I just happen to drop in by accident, and kind of make his acquaintance?''

Pepe had waited fifteen minutes when Murphy came out of the back door. As Murphy got to the willows beside the creek where his horse was hidden, Nulty came out of the bushes and they talked together. Then the two of them disappeared into the brushy bottom. Pepe followed them.

Ten minutes later, Ollie and Burt came past Pepe's hideout, invisible beyond the willow suckers, Ollie gangling, slumped, knees spraddled, like a stork on a camel, red hair sticking out between his hat and his collar, the hat pulled down over his ears, and his head pulled down into his shoulders. They went around to the back of the house.

Burt's old woman was in the kitchen, peeling potatoes. Ollie and Burt stood there looking at her. She looked at them, against the light from the doorway, out of some private, slow potato world of her own. She didn't know them.

"Where's Maddy?" Ollie said.

"In the parlor," she said, and then frowned with the pain of thought. "But you're awful early, ain't you?''

"Good God." Ollie said, and whipped through the inner door, slamming it after him. Burt could hear him, running away down the hall toward the front of the house.

"Gracie," Burt asked, "don't you know me?''

She looked up again, against the light, squinted and

shaded her eyes. Her brownish, wooden face suddenly came alive with a smile. She put up her hands to cover it, dropping the paring knife; took them away, smiled in an agony of shyness at Burt, and covered her face again. Her brown hair stood out in wisps, and she had the same kind of dumpy figure that Burt had. He just stood there, looking at her, a feeling of depression rising in him. There was something about his old widow woman that always filled him with sadness. But the old magic was back, he felt it: in some strange way, she was making him feel respectable. It was her one great gift. He looked no different around her, but he always felt that he stood up straighter when she was smiling at him—that goofy, snag-toothed miserable smile that made him feel, at times, so depressed that he wanted to cry.

One day Ollie had said, "She is absolutely the most ugly, miserable thing in the whole creation."

"I know that," Burt had said, humbly.

She got up, as he stood there looking down at her, and the potato pan fell off her lap and the potatoes rolled all over the floor. She clasped her hands together, not even aware of the potatoes, and grinned at Burt, her soft eyes wet and bright with affection, the intensity of her happiness expressing itself in the twisting of her hands. "Burt," she said.

"You dropped the potatoes," he said.

"Potatoes?" She smiled, her head tilted, beaming with adoration.

He looked at her hopelessly. "Never mind, Gracie. Just take it easy, Gracie. I'm home. Don't get all in a sweat." He got down on his knees, heavily, and began collecting the potatoes. She stood beside him and gently patted his bald head.

"Oh, Burt," she said softly. "My good, good Burt."

Locked in the parlor, far from the potato heaven in the kitchen, Ollie had found his girl. Lord, what a difference from Gracie—how could they stand each other? the beauty and the clod. Maddy had red hair, and Maddy was a beauty: green eyes, slanty and sly-looking; pale, very fine skin; and delicate freckles.

"For God's sake," she said. "You."

"Sure, kid," Ollie said. "Old ugly, back again."

She ran over to him and his long, gangling arms closed around her. They forgot about Gracie and Burt in the kitchen; they forgot about the whole world. On the pale linoleum floor, the long leaves of a bay tree danced in shadows and the wind blew dust along the window sills. Outside, the air was full of the rustling of leaves, but inside, nothing but the silence and the wild glitter of the leaf-shadows on the floor.

He put a forefinger up, touched it gently to the hair just in front of her ear, that soft, silky, red-gold hair, and ran the tip of his finger very gently, slowly, down along her wide jaw, over the fine white skin, as soft as a child's.

"Murphy's after you," she said quietly. "He was by here just a while ago."

"What did he want?" Ollie didn't care much. He was sleepy. He watched the slanty green eyes with affection and amusement.

"He wanted me to tell him what you was going to do. Tell me something, Ollie. Anything, so I can tell him."

"Why you got to tell him anything?"

"He'll close me down if I don't. I got to pay forty dollars a week now."

"The son of a bitch."

"Running a whorehouse has got awful expensive since the town got respectable. I'd move along, Ollie, only I don't know where to go. It ain't like when I was working in Dodge—then you could choose the whole country.'' She smiled sadly.

''Tell him we're going to Wyoming. Say we're going to hold up Fisher's bank tonight.''

''Oh, Ollie, he wouldn't believe that.''

''He's such a liar, he'd believe anything.''

''You wouldn't hold up a bank, Ollie. That's serious. You might kill somebody.''

''I know. I wouldn't kill nobody, Maddy. But he don't know that. You tell him that. That'll keep him from bothering you.''

''You really going to Wyoming, Ollie? She was wistful. ''Why don't you stay here, Ollie? Be my bouncer. Why you got to be always flying like the wind?''

''You come with me, green-eyes.''

''You work for me, Ollie. I'll keep you. You can stay here, cosy as you please. As long as you love me. You be my little pet, Ollie. My little pet. Oh, you're so ugly,'' she laughed, her mouth on his scrawny neck, ''I just love you, my poor, poor duckling.''

He held her gently, smiling. ''Suppose I got some money. Real money. Maybe you'd come then. I'm getting kind of tired of cutting around. It's getting so I'm going in circles. I tell you what, Maddy, when I was a kid I thought I was going somewhere. I thought there was a where to go to, but now I see it's just circles. But I wish I had someone with me. I used to think maybe there was something else—but it's all like clouds and hawks in the sky, Maddy, I look up, and I get lost. Maybe there ain't nothing, but just a woman.''

She kissed his neck very slowly.

''Suppose I got some really big money,'' he said softly, ''and we got married.''

She started, and then looked at him carefully.

"Go north," Ollie said, "and you could get in business again. Me the bouncer. Just like Buck and Annie Fisher. Maybe someday I'd be a banker too."

Looking at her, he was suddenly confused. There was something in her eyes, an intensity, he didn't understand, somber and almost angry.

"How much money?" she asked.

"Maybe a thousand." He had thought of it as a kind of joke; certainly a thousand dollars was a joke, to a man like him.

She looked at him for a long moment. "You really mean this?"

He looked back at her for another long moment. He was beginning to tremble, his head was full of blood and confusion because of her eyes, almost glaring at him, wide and forceful.

The joke in him was floundering around, he was trying for his sense of humor, and then some remnant of the truth in him came up out of some forgotten corner, and he said, "You're a beautiful girl, Maddy. I always did love the hell out of you. And I'm ugly." He fought for the humor. "We oughta go good together."

"Married?" she said.

He lost his voice. "Yes," he whispered.

"All right," she said. "I will."

He sat there stupefied, and his arms began to tremble. "I thought you'd laugh," he said. "I said it as a joke."

"I know," she said. "I know you pretty good, Ollie. But I said yes. And I don't mean it as a joke."

He looked at her, and his wide, ugly face turned soft. He smiled, and the trembling stopped. "All right," he said.

"There's just two things I ask," she said. She

looked down at the floor, serious and quiet. "I meant it about the thousand bucks. Without that, you're just another whore. Rent, bribes, food, clothes, booze, you got to keep a stock, I need the capital."

He didn't feel like smiling, but he did. A thousand bucks was a lot of money, a lot of cows, he knew he'd never make it on cows alone. "Okay," he said.

"And the other thing is your teeth, Ollie. Get your teeth."

Out back, Burt sat watching the serene, happy smile on Gracie's face as she finished the potatoes. He didn't know how to say it. "Listen, Gracie," he said. "We're going north. Ollie and me. You want to come along?"

She looked up, steady, simple and serene, the odd brown of her skin just flushed with pink. It was peculiar how even the most horrible looking women could, at times, become perfectly beautiful; there was something inside them that flowered out, that made a man forget what they really looked like.

"Sure," Gracie said. "All I ever done was wait for you, Burt."

"I guess," he said, looking desperately at her hand, "I'd better put a ring on you."

The beauty fled. "I'm not good enough, Burt," she whispered. "A hoor can't get married. Somebody told me."

"Like hell you can't," Burt said. "You're a woman, ain't you?"

NINE

BILL WAS BUTTONING the top button of one of the Colonel's big, loose white shirts when they heard the hooves coming down the long drive. The Colonel was standing by the corner window, looking out at the mountains. The copper tub and its copper cans shone in the light of the lamp.

"It's Allie and the Lieutenant," the Colonel said, and waited for some reaction. There was none. Bill's face was quiet. He had been thinking of Allie, as she had been, the recollection lost in lethargy. How far away the past seemed, looking back—a tiny scene, back in Texas, with tiny images moving through remote concerns, clear as in an eagle's eye, and yet, with all the intervening abrasion of the last few years, reduced to a children's play, voices too far off to be heard distinctly, words too old to be remembered; passions, comforts and diseases as clearly ephemeral as the agonies of some woman of whom there is nothing left but a lock of hair in the back of a drawer.

And yet, how many times he had remembered the warmth of rooms similar to this, the dull tones of drapes, furniture and customs made round and cosy by generations of human acceptance; how many times, at night, lying cold among the rocks of some Mexican canyon, he had remembered just this scene, this comfort, this security, and exactly this same scent of the Colonel's cigar, that strong, sweet pungency alive in his head again, itself the perfect summation of all those lost civilities. How many times he had remembered her.

The sound of hooves was a little closer. There was not the slightest excitement in him, nothing left of all that passion, that love like perpetual music, an inexhaustible spring of life. All those things had eroded into shadows, and then, slowly, even the shadows had disappeared. If he had forgotten her, what was there that he could not forget?

"Quite a handsome couple," the Colonel said, leaning against the window frame. "Picturesque. Exactly the kind of picture one would want in a novel—very promising, the elegant young lady, the handsome officer. It will all end in organ music, and the genteel difficulties their love will suffer will only prove its verity. We even have an aging father, wringing his hands in concern, lest the Lieutenant escape. You can imagine how happy the old man is to see his only daughter, in a lovely green velvet riding habit, parading alongside a male animal who is, above all, safe. Within the cast-iron confines of that uniform there beats not the slightest possibility of personal initiative; the fellow is bound to die poor, but of course, highly honored for the slight stupidity which has made him the best of risks. Forgive me if I bore you." Bill now had the complete picture, the Colonel thought: let him react as he will.

"You don't bore me," Bill said. He had sat down suddenly on a stool, slumped over, suddenly heavy with insight. If you started out a rebel, seeking the impossible, throwing aside all the normal restraints which most young men accepted; if you sought perfect freedom, despising civilized life which was nothing but a vast compound of compromises between liberty and slavery, then inevitably you ran afoul of the law and your whole life became simply a search for something to eat, and pure freedom became the perfect slavery, the slavery of a man to his stomach.

He felt, above his solid, immovable depression, like laughing; and yet he fought off the laughter, because if one laughed, it meant that one resorted to cynicism, and the cynic was the most futile of cowards, merely confessing the inadequacy of his former ideals. Burt was right—in some way, by some incalculable alchemy, the fight for freedom in the end became the worst of tyrannies. But what else? Freedom was an illusion: one could always strike a bargain with one's stomach, settle down into the common mold, and thus attain obliteration with pleasure if not honor. Like everybody else, he could trade the eagle's wings for five decades of successful carnality and two of prostate trouble, and die at home instead of in jail.

"There's nothing worse than a philosophic thief," Bill said. There was a certain humor in the human situation; and certainly he was not alone—he could console himself that behind all these social façades about him, these human masks, each composed or contorted somehow to meet their worlds, there existed other little internal worlds like his own, no less mysterious; strange little universes, or stars, wandering for a space of time across his own course, winking out quite as soon.

"Don't fool yourself," the Colonel said, letting out

a mouthful of rich smoke. "You're no philosopher. Nobody born south of the Mason-Dixon line could ever be truly philosophic. Philosophy is the art of seeing what there is instead of imagining what you want. Appomattox was not so much the end of the war as the end of a dream." He pulled slowly on the cigar. "How hard it is to accept God's providence—it so often smells like a hog."

"God provided you with the hogs in the same way he provided Eliza with the ice."

"What do you expect? An assortment of fancy-house girls? The greatest gain a man can make is to find peace."

"Peace with ordinary existence? Merely to exist?"

"What else? Existence, under certain select circumstances, is a pleasure. Not yours, I know. The problem is to make the pleasure greater than the pain, and the solution is money."

"You go through all this juggling for what? In the end you face nothing. It's incredible. If you had any courage, you'd shoot yourself in the head."

The Colonel smiled, a little falsely. "My boy, let's not get too deeply into the matter."

"Then you admit there is a depth—that you avoid it."

"I feel I have reached a satisfactory compromise—based on a sufficiency of money. I won't go so far as to say that I believe money is the answer, but it is a pretty good substitute for an answer."

"All right," Bill said. "But I haven't found any compromise. Any man with an ounce of common sense knows it's not worth the candle. For the simple reason that in the end, you die. You are garbage. If the effect is garbage, the cause is garbage."

"Don't use old, dead thoughts to rationalize bad habits."

"I'm not. But Moore is insisting that we come in. I am not going to submit to his damned society of Murphies unless I have a reason."

"Isn't she a handsome girl?"

Bill turned and looked down at the little plaza beneath the window. It was just as the Colonel had said—an ideal picture.

"She was sixteen when you ran off," the Colonel said. "She's quite a young woman, now." He looked at his cigar for a moment. "What it comes down to is that you either find your answer by Sunday noon, or you will have to run for the hills like an animal, Bill. Let me suggest one line of thought. What you need is a sort of tolerance for what the human race has learned is a certain basic necessity. Conformity. Not absolute conformity, not perfect conformity. One needn't think society is perfect, or even desirable. But what would you have? Riots and murder in the street? Conform in public, escape in private. That's the formula."

"Enjoyment is your touchstone," Bill said. "Not mine. I see no reason for coming in, for that." He smiled at the Colonel. "Your society is like a huddle of sheep in a snowstorm, all conforming to each other. Sheep without a leader, waiting to die. Enjoy that if you can."

The Colonel looked at his cigar, and saw it suddenly as a mere fabrication of weeds, a primitive folly. To what tribe of savages did he himself belong? Lo and behold, men picked leaves off trees and tried to put themselves to sleep. *Ecce homo sapiens*, a kind of crazy, animate tree with leaves of hair, a trunk and four broken sticks attached, stumbling and staggering in a fun-house world. Occasionally, with Bill around, he saw life as a total mystery, plastered with a tatter of clichés.

Down below, Manuel was taking the horses by the bridles, holding them while the young lady and the young gentleman dismounted.

"I'd better go down and warn Allie you are here," the Colonel said. He dropped his cigar in a water can and went out.

Bill looked down through the window. He saw Allie, and suddenly excitement rose; it all became alive again, that old memory, the old impossible thing that he had given up, the old, happy simple thing between them: love.

Downstairs, the Colonel met Allie coming down the hall, peeling off a glove. She stopped, facing him.

He said, "I have an unpleasant surprise for you." He said it so soberly that she stopped peeling the glove and prepared herself with an internal steeling for whatever unpleasantness her father had been unable to preclude.

"Yes?" she asked. Then, calmly, she removed the other glove.

"An old friend of yours has turned up," her father said. "Bill Gorham is in town."

Inside herself, she began to rise, as a bird starts up; immediately, her habit of sorrow clamped down on it, the sadness she had acquired after he had left, then a smooth control took over. There was nothing one could do about the heart—the heart, amid all the confusion, entanglements and stultifications of adult emotion, was forever a child, simple and clear.

"In fact," her father said, "he's upstairs. Shall I ask him to stay for dinner?"

She said, "You like him still, don't you." She hadn't meant to add anything, but the words came anyway. "Erratic. Willful. Selfish." She waited. He said nothing. "You'd like to have him around, wouldn't you," she said. "Simply because you enjoy

him." Words had a quality of building upon themselves, and angry words produced anger, and anger
produced angrier words.

He looked up, smiling faintly, at the wallpaper.
Handsome stuff, long gold stripes running vertically
on an ornate maroon background. "As a matter of
fact, I believe he is planning a robbery for later this
evening. So I doubt if he would stay long."

It startled her out of her anger, and she too smiled,
just barely. And then she killed the smile, it reminded
her too much of an earlier self. "Let's not make a
policy of being amused by Bill Gorham. Let's not be
like indulgent relatives. He has all the social feelings
of a stone."

"He seems to have given you quite an edge."

"I'm twenty-one," she said. "People like Bill are
useful in one way—they make other people grow up.
Yes, invite him to dinner. I won't have Dick. Dick will
wait. Dick is able to wait. Thank God for people like
Dick."

"The salt of the earth," the Colonel said gloomily,
and went out the front door.

As the Colonel came out, Manuel took the lieutenant's horse and stood there while the Lieutenant, in
his turn, removed his gloves—but slowly and precisely, not peeling, but taking each glove-finger by
the tip in turn.

"*Señor*," Manuel said to the Colonel. Short, fat and
brown; patient, humble and stubborn; unshaved, red-
eyed with tequila, and emanating waves of garlic,
Manuel lifted a hand in the direction of the long drive
in a gesture of tragic resignation—restrained, simple
and profound. "Behold—*Señor* Murphy."

The Colonel looked around with a start, and saw
Murphy far down the drive, approaching. The im-

mediate problem was to keep him away from the house and Bill.

"Come on, Dick," he said to the Lieutenant, and moved casually forward along the drive toward Murphy. "Let us meet the gallant Sheriff. He came last night for Manuel and Serafina, and now he is coming again. Indefatigable buzzard. I never saw a man more assiduous in the pursuit of the helpless." He quickened his long stride and the Lieutenant could not help falling behind, without the indignity of running.

Seeing them coming, Murphy pulled up and waited, and it pleased him to confront the Colonel from the back of his horse. The three of them stood facing each other between two cypresses, one on each side of the drive, and all of them smiled.

"Good evening, Sheriff," the Colonel said. "A pity I can't invite you in for a drink, but the fact is, I am having the house done over and the wallpaper is all down on the floor. A terrible mess." His smile was wider and more friendly than ever.

So was Murphy's. "I understand you have a young man, a William Gorham, visiting with you."

"If you would like to pay your respects to Gorham, why don't you try us Sunday, around four? We'll be having tea about then."

Anger began to boil in Murphy. Not that the Colonel was so smart, not that what he said was nettling; in fact, the Colonel only made himself a fool with his prissy airs and womanly speeches—and yet, somehow, hatred rose, hot and red, and Murphy could not keep up the mask of civility he always promised himself to maintain.

"This man Gorham," he said in a voice still low, but quite harsh, "is the head of a gang which I happen to know is planning to steal thirty head of your cattle tonight. At eleven."

The Colonel raised his eyebrows. "Indeed. With so much detail, one would almost guess that you were going to buy them."

Murphy leaned forward in the saddle. "They saw Nulty. Nulty told me. I want your help, Colonel, in arresting these men." Murphy sat there in silence. The Colonel waited. "And of course," Murphy went on, "you won't tell Gorham that I know, even if he is your guest, will you, Colonel?"

The Colonel's smile disappeared. He stood looking at the dark bulk of the cypresses. "I beg your pardon," he said gravely.

"For what?" Murphy asked suspiciously.

"For supposing that you were a fool," the Colonel said. "You can depend on us, Sheriff, not to give you away. We will be waiting for you at eleven o'clock. Or whenever you say." He was looking steadily at a small pebble in the drive, at the feet of Murphy's horse. "However, you won't object if the Lieutenant brings along three or four of his men, will you?"

"My men can handle Gorham's gang."

"A precautionary measure," the Colonel said. "You may meet more surprises than you think. Lieutenant, since this will be, if it occurs, a felony taking place during the amnesty, you as representing the Federal government will be involved. Bring four men."

"I don't see why he will be involved," Murphy said.

"Are you protesting against extra help?"

Murphy said nothing.

"Or possible interference? We wouldn't want this to degenerate into a personal brawl between you and Gorham—like the one you had this morning."

"I am only doing my duty," Murphy said.

The Colonel said, "The Sheriff's duty reminds me

of charity in the number of things it can cover. Farewell, my good and noble Sheriff. May flights of angels sing thee to thy rest."

Murphy's mouth tightened. He turned his horse with a rough yank and left. The Colonel looked at the younger man. "It's all lies about Bill," he said. "I think you had better meet him."

TEN

ALLIE HEARD FOOTSTEPS overhead, and the closing of a door; then the footsteps going down the upstairs hall, on the stairs. She braced herself, and then, as the steps came down the stairs, she knew that the place was all wrong, she needed some occupation. She could not talk to him, face to face, without something to prove her indifference. It was the old girlhood horror of not knowing what to do with her hands. Why was he able to do this to her, to undermine her in this way, to strip her of everything she had gained? What possible justice was there in this? She opened the front parlor door, stepped quickly inside, and closed it just in time.

She heard the steps come down the hall, she heard them approach the door, and in her nervousness, she coughed. The steps stopped outside. She almost died at the thought that he might take the cough as an invitation. She could feel him, beyond the door, and out of her helpless anger at her own helplessness against herself, there simply rose the old affection, out of the indefatigable, ineducable, incorrigibly recalcitrant and nonchalantly idiotic heart. But he owed her something—a great deal—and he would have to pay it, love or not.

Outside, passing the closed door, Bill had heard the cough. He stopped. Nothing could be more anonymous—and yet he knew it was Allie—in his mind he could see her bend slightly, handkerchief held with delicacy to mouth, the gesture suggesting somehow not that it was needed, but rather that it was totally unnecessary.

Nothing between them but a thin door and four years; and how easily those years fell away into nothing, how little they must have contained, if he could feel this peculiar dizziness, fullness of the head, as though they had parted only an hour before, as though nothing had happened. If this was love, then love was not part of him, but almost like another person, sleeping inside him, waiting, dismissing and ignoring the petty agonies of any other experience; and then, when suddenly, by accident, their orbits neared again, rising like a woman out of her sleep, simply taking up again its existence where it had been cut off. He neither willed it nor unwilled it; there it was, all by itself.

He knew then, that love was superior to the rest of it: it had a simpler, more complete existence, less dependent on other things. Time had almost erased his memory of her, but that was another failure, an erosion of images, and not a failure of love, which had merely been waiting, complete and final as ever.

She was there, inside—not waiting, but there. A tap, very gentle, and slowly she would open the door, and stand there, a mystery still, with five years of strangeness—but behind all that, still the same, the

same warm, sweet Allie. A knock would begin it
again.

He raised a hand toward the door, and something
stopped it. He stood there, wondering at it. Something else in him had moved; another, invisible and
unknown hand had reached out of his mind, taken
his wrist, and held it. A caution coming from the
wilder side, the new side. He looked at the warning,
surprised, almost amused. He felt again the warmth
in himself, her warmth beyond the door, and with a
smile, raised his hand again to knock. But again the
same steel caution locked him; and he was again
aware of the wariness in himself. He looked at the
door, and suddenly, in the silence, the blank panel
became a danger, and he recognized in his feeling the
sense of warily sniffing out a canyon for a box-end,
the suspicion of the alley that might turn blind. The
room was simply, a trap.

He looked dumbly at the thought. His thought? He
remembered her, not here, but removed in mind from
all circumstances, and the same old fatal affinity arose
in him, inevitable, warm and lovely. But he could not
knock—even though now in pain, he could not force
it, he would not; for he had learned a fearful respect
for the animal warnings of experience. And all the
time, his reason and his love knew this was absur-
dity, and scoffed.

He dropped the hand and stood appalled at the
confusion of personalities this simple door had faced
him with. Which one was he to believe? And then he
understood it clearly enough—he had grown a second
self: he saw it now with bitter understanding. The
wildness of impulse with which he had fled five years
ago had compacted into an instinctual canniness, a
cool razor-edge of guardedness and caution, so habit-
ual now as to be utterly uncontrollable.

And he didn't want it—not now—he could see this self within himself like a dirty brown animal, isolated and repugnant. He wanted to go in, he wanted to see her—or part of him did. But the other part, that was tied to the mountain tops, that never moved ahead without a planned retreat in mind, that evaded enemies by dissolving into an infinite forest, that knew the wilderness was its true home, and the towns merely a temptation and a dangerous luxury—this part stifled action even when the old, warm self would have surrendered blindly to any trap of circumstances, as long as it contained Allie.

Wait, was what the wild fox said inside—sniff around, make sure, better to leave it alone than risk a snare. And yet he saw, with his more human mind, the folly of such caution—love asked for, demanded commitment; caution was absurd, granted love. He saw it, he ridiculed it, yet the move to knock filled him with actual fear to the point of suffocation. See her, touch her, his brain said, and the fear will dissolve. But he could not force it.

He took a slow step back from the door. Not goodbye, no, never goodbye—but just a little longer. Wait. He knew he would see her sometime, or at least he promised this to his love. On the road, in the woods walking, when there would be freedom at hand, where the friendly forest was nearby. But not here, not now, not yet.

The door. It was the fault of the door and the trap of a room beyond. The door, the damned, damned door, with its flat, smiling face, like a policeman—and its lock.

You are a fool, a real fool, he said to himself; a nerve-shot, helpless fool. He stood, waiting for a miracle of change. But the door stood there, blank, imponderable and fatal. He turned suddenly and walked, as quickly as he could, toward the open, out, away from the house.

The Colonel, coming back down the drive with the Lieutenant, raised a hand to Bill as he came out of the house, and the three came together. The Colonel's face bore the special mask of pleasant impassivity which he intended to assume while lying exposed in his casket—a situation which was, to the Colonel's mind, roughly the equivalent of going to bed in the middle of the street, and one which required great poise. He had long been preparing his face for this event; in the meantime, the expression did very well for introducing people unlikely to prove friends.

"Lieutenant Aberforth, Bill Gorham."

"How do you do, Lieutenant," Bill said, putting forth a hand.

"How do you do, Mr. Gorham," the Lieutenant said, taking it.

"Mr. Gorham is thinking of coming into the cattle breeding business with me," the Colonel said blandly, looking at Bill with his coffin smile. "I have made him an offer as my manager. Mr. Gorham is something of an expert on cattle selection." All this, though news to Bill, was no surprise: the Colonel evidently had merely reached that point in his mental cycles at which he believed things were going along too smoothly. On the theory that society could not long stand success, the Colonel greeted an excess of peace with a spirit of helpful disruptiveness—he misdirected all strangers, added up his deposit slips wrong on purpose, took the wrong horse from the hitchrail, and returned most of his mail to the senders, marked "Deceased."

"A fascinating business, I am sure," Aberforth said. Aberforth's light blue eyes, set in his nice, square face, bore very little expression at all. He might have been watching something on the horizon—possibly a distant fistfight between two of his second cousins—just that amount of faint concern. "A fascinating business, cattle. One sees so many different kinds—black, white, red. Tremendous variety."

Bill was relieved. He would like Aberforth. Conversation, with Aberforth, could never end in tears. "I hear you have a good pack of dogs with you, Lieutenant. Been doing some hunting?"

"Well, no, not exactly. You see, I—that is, this assignment. As a matter of fact—" Dead stop. They waited; but if they wanted more than this Delphic information, evidently they were going to have to make out with a handful of chicken guts, as the Lieutenant had finished his thought, whatever it was.

"I understand," the Colonel said, "that Sellers' pack is one of the best in the west, is that right, Dick?"

"Yes," Aberforth said mildly, as they sauntered toward the barns. "Recommended because of some very fine work he did on some convicts out of Canon City."

"Oh, is that so?" Bill said. "I didn't know you could mix the, uh, quarries. I mean, lions and people."

"Don't know much about it," Aberforth said, looking down into the pens by the barn. "It's the bloodhounds that do the business on people—smelling, I mean. They never bite anybody."

"How nice," Bill said, looking down in the pen.

The bloodhounds had a small private pen to themselves, and two large dogs, mostly mastiff, had another pen to themselves. The rest of the dogs, the mutts, were in one large pen, carrying on a furious barking and leaping at the shaky fence of poles. The two bloodhounds looked sad and very sleepy in their pen. The mutts looked like a happy lot, and it was hard to imagine them biting anybody either. The two mastiffs, however, simply lay there, staring at the men with primitive yellow eyes.

"Man's best friend," Bill said. "At least, until recently. I suppose they regard it as a matter of duty."

This was too much at once for Aberforth. "Duty?" he asked, and then smiled. "Oh, I don't see how a dog could entertain the concept of duty. And man's best friend? I thought that was his mother."

Bill smiled. "Figures of speech are often confusing."

"Oh, to be sure," Aberforth said, evidently recalling his English Lit classes at West Point with difficulty. "Figures of speech," he mumbled, "of course."

"Those big ones," the Colonel said, "look as though they could pull down a man easily enough."

"Yes," Aberforth said quietly, a little absently, "I suppose they could." The Lieutenant rose, once, very slightly, on his toes, and settled down again. His hands were behind his back, as at parade rest. "I'll be glad when it's over," he said. "This really is a kind of police duty."

He looked pleasantly at Bill, the light blue eyes perfectly matter-of-fact. "These things, the troops, the dogs, the cannon, all that—seems like overdoing it, don't you think?"

"What cannon?" Bill asked.

"Tell him about the cannon, Dick," the Colonel said.

"Just a small field piece," Aberforth said, smiling. "Makes us seem more dangerous—I hope. I really don't like the idea of chasing down people. Of course, Indians aren't people."

"Certainly," the Colonel said. "Perfectly natural."

"That Simon Shaw," Aberforth said, his face saddening a little. He shook his head.

"You'll have to go for him?" the Colonel asked, and looked at Bill.

"Yes, I'm afraid so. Such a dignified old character—reminds me of some old line officer, in fact. It's hard to believe that these men are really criminals."

"Rather like political criminals," Bill said, watching the mutts as they barked and leaped. "They are criminals, and your line officers are gentlemen, by definition; as we stand in the United States rather than in Mexico, by definition. Not much actual difference."

"What's that?" Aberforth asked politely.

"I mean, the land is the same," Bill said, knowing perfectly well that he and Aberforth were beginning, slowly, to separate, as a ship slowly widens from the shore, "and the men, fundamentally, are the same."

"A figure of speech," the Colonel said.

"Oh, oh, I see," Aberforth said, smiling suddenly. "Interesting. Fascinating. I don't quite get the reference to Mexico and the United States?" he asked. "Something new? Deportation?"

"No, no," the Colonel said, helping things along. "I believe Bill is making some kind of literary reference to the Treaty of Guadalupe Hidalgo."

"Literary," Aberforth said glumly. "Yes. I certainly had a bellyful of books at West Point."

Manuel approached the pens with a bucket full of raw beef.

"I haven't had to read a single thing for three years, thank God," Aberforth said.

The mutts threw themselves on the chunks of beef as Manuel tossed them in. The bloodhounds ambled slowly over to their dinner. Manuel, his face serious, advanced toward the mastiffs' pen, picking out a huge slab of meat, and hefted it to throw.

"Makes a man think twice about coming in under the amnesty, doesn't it, Lieutenant?" Bill said.

"I hope so," Aberforth said sincerely. "It brings it home, I imagine, that the government is seriously bent on cleaning up—"

With a roar, the mastiffs threw themselves furiously at the fence. The whole pen shuddered under the crashing weight of the huge bodies. Manuel staggered back, tripping in terror. The great dogs, making horrible roaring growls, lunged and leaped at the top of the fence. Manuel got to his feet. His face was a dead, dark gray.

"Manuel," the Colonel said sharply, "go in the barn."

Manuel turned and hurried away, leaving the bucket of beef.

The three men stood there, watching the mastiffs throw themselves at the fence again; their faces were pale, and their mouths tight, their eyes held steady on the shaking fence.

Bill walked over to the bucket and deliberately threw the rest of the beef into the mastiffs' pen. They stared at him with wide yellow eyes for a moment as their rage died, and then turned and lunged at the beef. They gulped it down with huge, snake-like thrustings of their heads.

The Lieutenant drew a sudden, deep breath, as though he hadn't had a good one for minutes. "Good thing that fence held. I don't know how we could have held them off that Mexican if they'd got out."

"It's the color," Bill said quietly. "They don't seem to like the dark skin."

The Colonel looked at Aberforth. "Brutal Mexican keepers?"

"I haven't heard of any," Aberforth said.

"Maybe those convicts were Mexicans," Bill said.

He sighed. "And there are cannons, too, you say." The mastiffs, full of raw beef, were lying down again, their yellow eyes growing sleepy.

"Oh, yes, that cannon," Aberforth said. "Worth its weight in gold. I mean, if old Shaw, for example, holes up in some sort of natural fort in the mountains, he might very well pick off several of us, and we simply can't have that. Hence the dogs *and* the cannon."

Bill smiled slowly. "I have to get back to the house," he said. He held out his hand. "I'll look forward to seeing you again. We might do a little hunting—when you have time."

"A pleasure, Mr. Gorham," Aberforth said, taking Bill's hand and shaking it slowly. "I come around every day to go riding with Miss Pringle and see the dogs. Why don't you join us?"

"If I'm still here," Bill said, bowed slightly and walked away toward the house.

In Aberforth's eyes, the Colonel saw something strange to that plain, honest face—the sad dawn of cynicism.

"The damnedest liar I ever saw," Aberforth said quietly, looking at the mastiffs. "One would almost think he had never heard of cow stealing."

"Best not to be too hasty," the Colonel said. "Bill's no liar. He simply doesn't know about this particular plan Murphy's heard of. He's not the kind to repay my hospitality by stealing my cattle. It's not his brand of humor."

"These literary people," Aberforth said glumly.

"He's not literary," the Colonel said, and the young man looked at him blankly.

"Why," Aberforth said, "he made several literary references. Figures of speech and so on."

"Ah, I see what you mean." Suddenly the Colonel realized that he was learning to know Aberforth much better, and that he would have to be handled carefully. Aberforth had got the notion that Bill was a literary fellow, possibly even a writer, from one of Bill's silly allusions, and now the idea would never come out, and if the Colonel persisted in denying the idea, Aberforth would merely conclude that the Colonel was a fool. Where else was it possible for Aberforth to go wrong?

Aberforth told him. "You say," Aberforth said, "that Gorham is an old friend of yours? Let me caution you, Colonel—he may have changed since you last knew him."

From somewhere, the devil put a knife in the Colonel's hand. "Allie used to be *very* fond of him," the Colonel said pleasantly, slipping the knife home, and then watched the Lieutenant's face to see what would happen.

For a moment, nothing, while the thought percolated through the Lieutenant's reflexes. Then the jaw muscles flicked under the skin. Without perceptibly moving, the face had become hard.

Instantly, the Colonel felt compunction. "But of course, Allie is older now. Maturer judgment."

The Lieutenant's look of relief struck him to the heart. God bless you, Aberforth, he thought, so young, so honest, and so stupid. Not much choice between a scoundrel and a dolt, but on the whole, I'd rather have the scoundrel.

And in a flash, reflected from the serene countenance of the younger officer, the Colonel saw himself, an old, nicked rapier lost in an armory storeroom of old sabers. Considering the number of honest enemies his devil had made for him, he was lucky to have become a Colonel, even in an Army that was full of them. The Colonel looked at the ground, and behind that pleasant, impassive face, he suddenly ground his teeth in an agony of frustration. He had to make a choice—if he chose to favor either of these men, without a doubt, Allie would end up married to that one. He wanted Bill; but he knew that Aberforth was without a doubt the better man. And yet Bill could come around and outshine Aberforth four to one, if he chose to try. If only Bill would come around, if only Bill would suddenly, out of nowhere, grow a spine.

To favor Aberforth was so much like going back into the hog business—and so much less promising. He could not, for the life of him, decide whether his instinct for safety was prudence or sheer cowardice.

"I had better be getting along," Aberforth said. "I'll have to round up Moore and my men. For tonight."

Aberforth looked at the Colonel, and in the failing light, the Colonel could just read his eyes, the unspoken thought. Like Murphy, Aberforth was wondering if the Colonel would tell Gorham about the trap. And seeing this, the Colonel realized that he had witnessed the birth of an enemy, for such thoughts do not occur to friends, at least not coldly. Something in the Lieutenant had changed; from somewhere in the Lieutenant's orderly mind, a simple clearcut mistake had risen: the suspicion that the Colonel too, like Gorham, might be a liar—and possibly literary as well.

Certainly, the Colonel was all too quick, a fault that betokened too much reading. And besides that, the Colonel was only a V. M. I. man.

The Lieutenant bowed, and turned. A girl like Allie really ought to be taken away from such influences, and given a new start in life. Poor girl, she had never known anybody but Southerners.

Fat, humble and stubborn, Manuel was waiting quietly among the bushes beside the path. "*Perdone,*

señor,'' he said as Bill walked back toward the house.
Bill stopped.

"Thank you for feeding those dogs," Manuel said.

"Don't mention it," Bill said.

"There is a man by the name of Pepe waiting to see
you in the barn. He says it is urgently necessary."

Bill took the side path past the house and in the
gathering dusk went down toward the corrals. Pepe
came out of the barn to meet him, and for a moment,
Bill saw him as a stranger—a small, nondescript Mexican, like a million others, waiting patiently in the
half-dark.

Out of nothing, irritation arose, and he wondered
at it. And then, as he came closer, and saw Pepe's
face, this peculiar feeling vanished, and he felt easy
for the first time during the day. Pepe was like peace
itself—very gentle, reserved, never familiar, yet always friendly, that was Pepe. He sat there now, an
old friend, reliable and staunch, proven not merely
many times, but constantly, and still he was reserved,
friendly, polite. His delicacy was most evident in his
fingers—his small, thin, competent hands.

"Ollie is planning to rob your friend tonight," Pepe
said in a low voice, conversationally. "Thirty head of
red cows. I tried to talk him out of it, but he wants
the money. Nulty is to buy them for three hundred,
but I am sure Murphy is in with him, I am sure it is
a trap."

"Why the Colonel's cattle?" Bill asked.

Pepe shrugged. "Perhaps a joke. Ollie's like that."

"We better stop him," Bill said.

"You can't stop him," Pepe said. "He is bitter and
stubborn, he wants to believe I am mistaken about
Nulty. He has begun to hate me, ever since we let the
Captain go." Pepe shrugged.

They sat in the growing dark, silent. In the barn,

the horses made their soft noises, rustling the straw, pulling down hay from the cribs.

Bill said, "I am going to stop Ollie this one last time, and then I am through. We'll break up. He isn't safe any more."

"That's good," Pepe said, and sighed.

"We'll get somebody else's cattle for him," Bill said.

"It is all a trap," Pepe said.

"You go and tell Ollie I have thought of a better idea. I'll come along and talk him out of it."

"All right," Pepe said, and stood up.

"Where is he?"

"At Maddy's house." He moved away, his feet making no sound, and disappeared up the path.

Bill could still remember it, in the center of his mind, that single, muffled cough—a nothing, an accident, and yet, for some reason, speaking more loudly to him than anything he had heard for years.

ELEVEN

THROUGH THE FRONT window, Allie had watched
Aberforth and Gorham outside, and recognized
something she would never have guessed, five years
before: it was possible to love somebody who bored
you, and possible to hate somebody you loved.

She let them go away. She stood there, in the half-
dark of the room, her head bowed, and thought. The
pain of it lay in one's helplessness. You could not
help it if a certain curvature of bone, say, on the tem-
ple, had a particularly intense meaning to you, a
wordless meaning which you alone could understand. It was as though his actual shape, his attitude,
his mind, had a certain language which she alone understood—conformation and posture and attitude, all
a silent language of gesture far more profound than
what skipped off the educated tongue. She understood, without mind, what he meant, what he was
meant to mean, and she knew that she was the only
one who had been meant to understand.

Very well, granted that there were things in her own nature which she could not alter, still, she had a certain dignity to maintain. She had no control after marriage; all her control lay in her choice. And it was not a simple alternative, either, wild horse or none. She had Dick, already, now; and furthermore, Dick was the kind of man who could be sacrificed. If she chose otherwise, he would be saddened, but not lost.

A new thought appeared in her mind, and she looked up, suddenly, down the path where they had gone. Suddenly her mind had widened clearly, and she knew intuitively that she had, in an instant, fully grown up. The last time she had lost Gorham for herself; but this time, if she lost him again, he might be lost absolutely, totally, in himself, as the wild might always vanish into their own wilderness. Love was consecrated in responsibility; this was what she saw, from a new clarity. When she finally met him, it was after dinner, in the first dark of evening. Quite aware of the oddity of her actions, she had told her father that she was ill, and had then, secretly, gone down to Manuel's house and had dinner with him and Serafina; and then had come back, while Manuel served dinner in the big house, and watched her father and Bill, sitting at the table, through a window. She felt quite mad, and yet it was all perfectly rational, in a feminine way. She didn't know exactly what she was doing, and yet she knew that everything she did was necessary, as an oriole has a vague notion that the mess it is making will turn out eventually to be a cozy nest.

The wind blew about her in the garden, the broken clouds came and went over the moon, and a little rose bush, like an impatient child, continually plucked at her skirt as the wind moved it.

When he came through the door into the garden,

she had already begun to move away, slowly, down
one of the paths, in the moonlight, and he had to
lengthen his step to come up with her.

"Allie," he said.

She turned as he approached, and faced him, and
they stood there silent, about six feet apart, looking
at each other. She let her face say nothing, and
watched him.

She was still all that she had been, to him, the same
Allie, he could feel that across the wind, as she stood
there, her skirt moving, her hair moving. He had forgotten her scent; time and again he had tried to remember it, and could not; but now it came, her own,
too sweet, too naive, to be an artifact.

"It's so dark," he said, "I can hardly see you."
Moon-shadow, cloud-shadow, racing swift as ships
eastward, the rout of some storm, light of the moon
that was more like a shadow of light, that suggested
what he remembered.

She wanted to say: You could come closer. Instead
she said, "The moonlight *is* deceiving, isn't it? Those
roses are really a dark red; and yet now they look
black. It's all like a photograph."

He looked at her, a little taken aback by her causal
tone. He had thought they were better friends.

"How did you like Dick?" she asked.

The question put him back even further.

"Do you approve of him?" she asked.

"Approve?" he asked. Was he to take the attitude
of a brother? "You've changed," he said.

She had got under his skin, she could hear it in his
hesitancy, and now in that accusation.

"Very likely," she said. "So have you, I suppose."

They stood in silence. The wind died.

"I was going down to the barn, to look at the

horses," she said. "You may come along if you wish."

Her manner, her indifference, stung him. She went on down the path, and did not look back, and part of him, angry, would gladly have let her go; and yet under the pique, there leaped up a genuine concern for her; instinctively, he understood what she had been saying all along: You have hurt me. Delicate, controlled, she was going away, and nothing in her would turn back. What he felt was what she had never understood: that he simply understood her. The movement of her moods, as he saw them, moved in him too, echoed in him as they sounded in her. She understood him, in her mysterious fashion; and he comprehended her in a way she never even guessed; not that he could foresee what she might do, but that everything she did was perfectly understandable, and even when unexpected, perfectly logical. It was as though, behind his mind, unseen, there existed a perfect knowledge of her, by which he recognized her perfectly as she revealed herself to him, little by little; and yet he could not imagine or calculate what she had not yet revealed. They understood each other's language; only when they insisted on conversation did they ever misunderstand each other.

"Allie, wait for me," he said, almost by calculation, to give her a means of conferring a favor. But she did not stop. So he followed her, as, of course, she had known he would.

In the barn, she lighted two lanterns, and hanging them on nails, looked at the horses. Bill came into the barn after her, and stood behind her, looking at the long heads of the horses as they swung out of the loose-boxes over the half-doors. Wisps of hay stuck out of their gray-black, whiskery lips, large eyes under the lanterns shone brilliantly. Deep chuckling in

throats, full of contentment, the whole barn was busy
with the sound of horse-dinners, full of the rustling
of feet in straw, soft knocking of hooves and hocks
on wooden walls; blowing of noses, clink of chain,
coughing, and everywhere the myriad whisper of
chewing.

"If you shut your eyes," he said, "they sound just
like people in a hotel. Except they don't talk."

She smiled inside herself. She would have liked to
have turned, smiling, and welcomed him back again.

"When are you going?" she asked. It was the rud-
est thing she could think of.

"I hadn't thought. I suppose I could stay."

"You know about the amnesty," she said, still
looking at the horses, her back to him.

"Yes," he said. "A kind of funny situation."

"Hilarious."

"I meant, odd."

"Opportunities I suppose always seem odd, to the
inept."

It glanced off; apparently he didn't even feel it.
"Like your father's hogs. I come back, and find you
and an amnesty. I didn't know you were here, you
know."

"I wondered," she said. "You could have said,
you heard I was here, and you came a thousand miles
to find me."

"I didn't think you had forgotten me that much.
Why should I tell you a lie? Just to impress you? We
were friends, Allie."

She turned around, and now the lamplight showed
her face as he remembered it, but a little fuller, more
the woman.

"How could I have stayed?" he asked. "Seventeen
years old. Not a dime. And him for a father, an impossible future. What could I plan for you?"

"I know," she said. "If you had asked me, I would not have demanded much. Where did you go?"

"El Paso. I caught pneumonia."

"When was that?"

"Right after I ran away from Pembleton's school. What did they all say? I suppose that I was a coward, couldn't face the music, and all that."

"Yes, that is the kind of thing they were expected to say, so they said it. They didn't try to understand, and, after all, why should they?"

"Well, I didn't ask them to understand, or care if they didn't," he said. "Did you expect me to stand up to some imitation court martial for socking Pembleton?"

"I? I don't know. I simply watched you. Without thinking. Military schools always seemed silly to me, anyway. I think they seem silly to most women, and after all, I was not exactly a child. What went on in Pembleton's was all silly enough, all the time. Parades. Soldiers. Surely you don't think I liked you because you were rational. That is not the reason women like men." She smiled. "But it would have been more amusing if you hadn't been so serious." The smile died. "But then, men are always so serious—that's what makes them so silly."

"I wouldn't have been so serious if I had understood my father better. The passed-over soldier. Aberforth would have delighted my father."

"Nobody but your father would have delighted your father," she said. "Himself as a major general instead of just a major. If he hadn't been passed over so many times, you might merely have amused him. As it was, you enraged him. At least that's what my father says."

"How have you been, Allie? Have you been well?"

She could hear it in his voice, calling to her, suddenly clear, across all those years; how are you, my beloved? Have you been well? Has nothing changed? Are you still you? Am I the same, in you? How are you? As though the question, the reiterated concern, were a constant caress.

She wanted to cry. Love could make love, as anger could make anger.

"I couldn't come back," he said. "I thought, I used to dream, how I would get hold of lots of money, and come back for you."

"You could have written."

In the silence, he looked past her. "I didn't say I thought I would get any money—I said, I used to dream it. What I had, in El Paso, I gambled. What I won, I drank, so I ended up in the gutter. You'd be surprised how comfortable a nice, dry gutter can be. Just fits the human corpse." He smiled. It was the same smile, she thought, but sharper, harder. His whole face was more angular, all the child, that had lingered into youth, was now completely gone. And as he spoke, his eyes seemed so far away, remembering many things.

"And now," she said, "you're just a thief."

He looked at her, looking for condemnation. He said nothing.

"You steal for a living," she said, as though he hadn't heard. "You still haven't grown up," she said.

"The peculiar thing about women," he said, "is that they reach a kind of wizened, dried-out state of mind that they think is maturity, and from this knee-high eminence proceed to look down upon—Oh, the hell with it."

She turned away, heavy with sudden fatigue. Nothing had advanced, here they were still arguing about a situation that had been dead for five years. If he had changed at all, could this be possible? Was he still lost in that silly situation, or the memories of it? The same old quirk of picking on all womankind just because he was angry with her.

"All I wanted," he said, "was to be free to try to live a reasonable life. You don't seem to understand how important that was. You couldn't, unless you'd lived under a father like mine. I used to love him, and you don't know how I admired him, how I sweated to please him. But it wasn't only that he demanded perfection in everything—he didn't even recognize it when you performed it, nothing, nothing, ever pleased him, nothing was ever enough. Because he wanted me to fail, I guess, at least that's the only way I can understand it. As long as I wasn't quite good enough he could keep whipping me on, but if I got to the top he hated me, because he himself was a failure, or at least he thought he was. That's what happened that last year at Pembleton's. Do you know, when I became battalion commander that last year, and took all the horsemanship prizes and got the straight A's for the whole year, my father went to Pembleton and accused him of getting slack? Nothing would be perfect—but when I gave him what he asked for, he couldn't stand to see me at the top, it couldn't be true that I too had passed him over, so it had to be that the whole school was slipping. He even complained to the state Board of Education about the degenerate standards of Pembleton's Academy. And when I accused him of it, it all came out. He didn't want me to succeed, he just wanted someone to drive, and when I started to look better than he did, he couldn't stand it. Well, how can you live in a situation like that? It was crazy."

He looked at the ground. "So I took a good look at the whole setup. After all, when you tell your father to go to hell, there isn't much left." He looked away, his eyes sad. "A lot of things you do in anger, you wish you hadn't done, but I used to admire him so much, I had to hate him when I finally saw through him. And there he is, an old, fuddled old man, a poor, poor old man, who had nothing, never got anywhere, and that's all he wanted to do—get somewhere."

"Can't you forget it?" she asked, after a pause.

"What do you mean? I forgot it a long time ago. It was you who brought it all up again. As you said, I am a professional thief, I have other things to worry about."

"And you just wander."

"Yes, we wander here and there. Mexico. Up north."

"And that's all. You'll never have anything. And someday soon you'll be caught, and go to prison. And after that, more prison."

"I served several years in school, and didn't know it. Every man is in some kind of prison; what I wanted was the greatest possible freedom, and I've got it, and I pay for it. And I will keep it until I find a reason for surrendering it."

They stood in silence, looking at each other.

"You're beautiful, Allie," he said. "Right now. I never thought much about how you looked, before, I just loved you. But now I know you're beautiful."

"You're lonely," she said. "Naturally. Bumming around with a pack of thieves. You see me again and you think I am beautiful. It doesn't really matter. Freedom is the thing."

"For God's sake, will you please quit playing the superior female?" he cried, and then was sorry. "I'm sorry. You are superior, Allie. Highly superior. Go on and act superior."

She had the upper hand—not quite what she had wanted.

"Aberforth would make you a fine husband," Bill said. "He's a good man."

This was not what she had wanted, either. Noble renunciation.

They stood in the lantern light and watched each other's eyes. "There's only one thing," he said at last, "that would ever make me change. I don't give a damn for their lousy world and their lousy standards. There's only one thing I love enough to quit for, and that's you. Just you. The only reason I'd ever come in, would be to take care of you. I never could, as a thief."

"That's not good enough," she said coldly. "You've got to have a better reason than a woman."

He looked down at the barn floor. "Do I?" After a moment, "Is that really true, or just something you read in a book or heard in a pulpit?" He looked up at her. "You mean, before I can do something for a woman, I've got to have a principle for doing it? So that I'd be doing it for the principle, rather than for you?"

She said nothing, just looked at him.

"You know that's a lie," he said. "It's not true. Men don't do things on principle. Principle is what makes men refuse to do things. When they do things, it's always for love, of women, or God, or something. Marry me, Alice."

This was what she wanted, so she said, "You are simply fantastic," and backed away a step. She was not being coy—she was cutting him down to the roots.

He looked down at her, his eyes hard and his face cold. "You marry me, Alice. You marry me, and I'll tear down that stinking little town and build it up again, the way you want it."

"You're hard and cruel, Bill. You've changed a great deal."

"One thing hasn't changed. I love you."

"It all comes back to you, doesn't it—you see me again, it reminds you of all those times we had; after five years of silence, it all comes back, and you see me, and you say you want to marry me."

"I never thought it was possible to marry you," he said. "But now there's this amnesty. How did I know you were here? I thought you'd probably married somebody else."

"And now all you have to do is ask me. Or rather, tell me."

"All right, I was crazy. I've been crazy for years."

"I don't like proposals by bandits, empty proposals with nothing to back them up. I'm too old. I don't intend to live the life of a camp-follower. If I ever married you, it would be because you proved something. Proved it with your life, maybe, but proved it. I'm not a fool, Bill. Not enough to marry you, no matter how much I loved you—"

"You said, you said—"

"I didn't mean to," she said sharply.

Vaguely, distantly, the mastiffs began barking, their deep, fierce roars.

"You couldn't stand it," she said. "The daily life, the dull grind of it, having to get along with men you don't like, people you looked down on, that had differences of opinion. You're weak, Bill. We'd be happy for a year, and then it would begin to get on your nerves, and you'd start drinking again. I know you very well."

"Marry me, Alice."

"No. Not as you are. It takes more than love, Bill, much more. At least the kind of love we had. It takes a lot of courage. Putting up with the same dirty life, day after day; I know, I watched my father in the hog pens, wading around in all that filth. We never thought it would come to an end, and if it did, it was just luck, the market went up so high. And another thing, I don't want brains. I want character. And you haven't got any.''

''That's a damn lie,'' he said. ''I'll show you if it's the last thing I ever do.''

''I don't think you've got the guts,'' she said. ''And it's too bad, Bill, because I do love you. But I'll never marry you, Bill. I would rather live here with my father, alone, until he dies, than live in a constant hell of rebellion with you.''

''All right,'' he said. ''I'm coming in on the amnesty.''

''Bill,'' somebody said from the door. They both turned. It was Pepe.

''You better come,'' Pepe said. ''Ollie is getting ready to go.'' He looked at Allie for a moment, and smiled. He took off his hat and bowed slightly, and then disappeared into the dark. In a moment the roaring of the mastiffs began again, savage, and they could hear the huge bodies smashing against the poles as Pepe went back the way he had come.

''You see,'' she said, ''you have other responsibilities. Other friends. It's not half as easy as you think.''

He looked out at the dark for a long moment. ''Maybe not,'' he said quietly. ''We'll see. We'll have to wait, and see.'' without looking at her again, he went on out into the night, following Pepe.

Twelve

LIEUTENANT ABERFORTH, HAVING rounded up his enlisted men and arranged with Moore to meet them at Colonel Pringle's at ten o'clock, had decided that he should arrive earlier.

Riding down the Colonel's drive again, about eight, he met Bill on his way out to see Ollie, and the Colonel's remark that Allie had once been fond of this man, which had been growing darkly in his mind, like some evil wasp, arose now, at the sight of Bill's smiling face, and stung him with a kind of pain against which he had no defense.

Somehow, the smile on Bill's face, which actually was the barest civility, seemed to Aberforth not merely a token of success, of conquest with Allie and indeed repletion, but far more, a barefaced profession of total superiority, which was only enraging because it was so complacently confident. Aberforth had been deeply stabbed by the Colonel. Moreover, his grades in English Lit had been none too good, he had always preferred surveying, and figures of speech were an irritant the more harassing for their subtlety. He was one of those people who are not quite simple enough to be innocently happy with simplicity, and not quite intelligent enough to be able to focus on their short-comings sufficiently to know what they are. Most of all, he distrusted literature because it was concerned with things which could not be reduced to whole figures. That part of man which could not be triangulated, he felt, should be strangled. The worst of it was that he was becoming painfully aware that such a part existed in himself—had it been anybody else, he would have dispatched it with a field piece. That was what field pieces were for.

He would not have resented Gorham, if Gorham had merely pretended to be superior; what galled him was that Gorham actually seemed to believe that he *was* superior—the simple sincerity of the assumption was maddening because it was so obviously wrong. Or was it? Did Gorham *have* something? Could it possibly be literature? Whatever it was that Gorham had, it threatened all Aberforth's values.

Allie had become the proof of who was the better man, by some fantastic piece of illogic that gamboled through the Lieutenant's mind. Whoever finally gained Allie was the better, and hence gaining Allie would vindicate all Aberforth's values. For had not the Colonel said that she had been very fond of Gorham? And assumed that she might still be? But how could this be possible, with Aberforth around?

In short, he was bound to get Allie not only by his own admiration of her, his love and decent senti-ments, but, finally, in the ultimate pinch, by his de-votion to the traditions of West Point, a place of learning established by the wishes of George Wash-ington, the father of his country. No West Pointer could come off second in a contest with a miserable thief—moreover, a literary thief.

Thus the Lieutenant's wish to take Allie into his arms could only be construed as an act of patriotism and devotion to George Washington, in the final analysis, and if he should, by some strange circumstance, be shot in his marriage bed, it could only be said, by way of epitaph, that he had died for his country. Aberforth's mental position was perfectly impregnable, and as a result, like all such positions, totally sterile: where nothing could get in, nothing could get out.

He had once been shot in the buttocks by a Piute, but that was nothing to the agony that now seized his stomach and twisted it. He loved Allie, or thought he did. As he rode toward the house, he sank in the saddle, cold, shriveling within himself, aware of a forest of suspicions arising around him. Which thought should he believe? Had Allie's old flame sprung to life again? He fought them off, those vague, inchoate forms dancing in his bedeviled imagination—impossible visions of Gorham kissing her, holding her hand, and so on.

He knocked on the door and Serafina let him in; and then he was in the living room, with its soft glow of light, and she was there, at last, solid, real and alone. A sudden paradise of certainty—all the horrors vanished. Everything was so simple and obvious he could have photographed it.

"You're early," she said, smiling.

"Yes," he said, "I suppose I am," and was suddenly seized with a feeling of guilt. He would not have been early if he had not been suspicious of what she might be doing. Was she, in fact, rebuking him? The paradise of certainty vanished, the horrors returned. There was a stiffness about him which he disliked, and yet he could not ease it. He wanted to ask her, Was *he* here? What did you two do?

And suddenly, he knew in his heart that he hated Gorham, not for what Gorham was, but simply as an irritant. If Gorham had never come, had he not been an old friend, this insecurity, this anxiety, would never have begun. He could, even now, remember the perfect, happy peace of that afternoon's ride. Had anything ever been less complicated?

"Would you like to go riding tomorrow?" he asked. He had to be sure.

The question surprised her. Why had Aberforth interrupted their pleasant, easy-going relationship with this rather formal request? Now, she didn't even know if she really wanted to go riding with him.

In his face there was a peculiar mixture of pleading and command, the suggestion of a child and the shadow of an ogre. To him, it seemed suddenly that he must look like a fool—it had, indeed, been a silly question. To himself, he seemed to be crawling, and he never knew that the stick, in his unconscious hand, was quite visible to her in his manner. The small coal of rage in him, barely discernible to himself, was rage at her, that she should dare to set him aside this quickly, but he was unaware of this. To him, it seemed like anger at Gorham, for intrusion on their happiness.

"Riding," Allie said, and could not keep a sort of sadness from making her voice not quite enthusiastic.

Her lack of enthusiasm fell on him like wet plaster from a rotten ceiling; the roof of his paradise was leaking badly. And yet he was forced to smile a constricted, unpleasant smile.

Then he went one step further. "A fine fellow, Gorham." He was surprised to hear himself saying it. It did not seem like a lie, a hypocrisy. To him it seemed like a posy, handed to her, a veritable delicacy of tact. "An old friend, your father tells me."

And suddenly she understood him, it dawned. Aberforth was jealous. Instantly, a whole roil of mixed thoughts and feelings arose in her. She knew immediately that Aberforth could not possibly really love her, if he was jealous. And she was sorry for Aberforth.

At the same time, she was overcome with an elated realization that she could spit in his face if she wanted, and it would only make him more stubborn. She could use him, and this too pleased her, instinctively, for she naturally had a part of her that reveled in trampling on the faces of the poor, a pleasure which is usually most poignantly enjoyed by the destitute, rather than the rich. And yet her better self was sad.

She would not encourage Aberforth—that would be dishonest in her, disastrous to him, and unnecessary to the situation. Aberforth already had a sort of stubbornness that needed no encouragement, which would, if led on, actually give him certain rights which he now merely presumed to have, or was attempting to usurp. Somehow, she saw, he had got the idea, in the last three weeks, that they had a certain kind of relationship which entailed rights, and she understood now that he was reacting to Gorham on the basis of this fiction.

She realized that it would be extremely difficult to dissuade him of this fiction. She could feel Aberforth's hidden anger; and resented it. What right had he to anger? He had no right at all.

It was an act of pride, of presumption, and deep in her heart, she knew that presumption implied condescension, and hence contempt. Who, after all, was this Aberforth? The Colonel in her stiffened, and his voice echoed in her head. A paltry sprout of the

U. S. Military Academy—a mediocre institution designed to produce flunkeys for the politicians rather than leaders for the people. Granted that George Washington had, by vague references and strained implications, founded the place, he himself would never have attended it. He himself would, of course, have gone to V.M.I.

"Riding?" Allie asked again. "Why, I suppose so."

How reluctant she was, he thought. He had almost had her, had been on the verge of proposing, and she had understood that, and allowed it, at least allowed him to think it; she was still here and as long as she was unhad, he stood in the shadow of defeat. He never saw that it was not conquest he loved, but defeat that he hated, because he was not big enough to absorb it. To his mind, the strategy seemed to be patience.

"Gorham seems to be somewhat of a literary fellow," he said, starting out with an intent to concede and ending with a rather visible sneer, which invited company. He couldn't help it.

"Really? I hadn't noticed that about him," she said, as though it were a disease. "I suppose he *has* read a good deal."

"Exactly!" the Lieutenant cried. "That's what I meant."

She looked at him, for a moment amazed, and all thought of Aberforth-as-Husband instantly vanished.

Conversation was a slide which was leading them rapidly down toward enmity, pure and simple. Aberforth could not find anything to say except comments about the diet of the dogs, the condition of the men's horses, the heaves, cannibalism in swine, thrush, the temperamental quality of his men, the pathetic incompetence of enlisted men in general, and so on and so on, all of which he knew was acutely boring to her, but which he could not restrain because these petty complaints gave vent to his deeper grievance.

Helpless herself, she let him struggle in his own morass, and then she suddenly, by inspiration, took refuge in the grand strategy of all beleaguered women—she led him to talk about himself, which is the tactical equivalent of blowing up the enemy's ammunition dumps.

"Tell me about your home, Dick," she said, desperately.

His color rose. Immediately he felt comfortable, easy, and happy. Didn't this prove that she was interested in him? He rambled on about his horses, his dogs and his mother, in that order, infinitely content; while outside, the black wasps waited.

She thought of Gorham, the surface of her attention barely following Aberforth's sincere and heartfelt self-accolade. Outside, in the dark, somewhere, her own beloved fool was running wild. In her heart lay sadness, and not much hope; but she held it in abeyance patiently.

THIRTEEN

IT WAS GRACIE who opened the back door to Bill's knock. They were sitting in the kitchen, around the table—Ollie, Maddy, Burt and Gracie. It was a nice, clean kitchen, with white oilcloth on the table, the kind that had an imitation damask design embossed on it, flowers and whatnot, and yellow curtains on the window; the top of the stove shone like bright steel all over where Gracie polished it every day that she was sober.

"Have a seat," Ollie said, waving a hand at a chair. Half a bologna on the table, bread, jam, a bottle of whisky, four empties of beer, crumbs all over.

"Where's Harvey?" Bill asked.

"Up at his girl's," Ollie said. "I reckon." He took a mouthful of rat cheese and gummed at it.

"Where're your teeth?"

Ollie's eyes came to points, he gummed away in silence, trying to get the cheese down so he could talk.

"Don't talk about his teeth," Maddy said. "He left them up at the dentist's and he's short twenty-six bucks to get them back."

Bill cleared his throat. "Listen, Ollie, I don't want to bring this up. But Pepe told me you were going to steal some of Pringle's cattle."

"Yeah?" Ollie asked. "What's wrong with that?"

"Pringle's my friend."

"That damn Pepe. He said you wouldn't like it."

"Listen," Bill said, "the whole thing smells like a doublecross. You can count me out. From now on."

"All right," Ollie said quietly. "You're out. Pepe too. That leaves Burt and Harvey and me. A hundred apiece." Ollie's eyes were cold. "That's more like it, anyway. Only don't come around me looking for cigarette money. I don't like people backing out when we need hands the most."

"Lay off Pringle's cattle," Bill said quietly.

"I got this all set up," Ollie said. He was trying to sound calm and reasonable. "It's all arranged with Nulty. Nulty wants the Herefords. It's too late to change."

"It's a crazy setup," Bill said. "Nulty wants red cows. Why? Because Pringle's got the only red cows in the county. So why red cows? Because they want to set up a trap and catch you with the goods. You'll die running, Ollie."

Maddy's face dulled. "Maybe he's got a point."

"You shut up," Ollie said. He leaned forward, stiff, his face sharp and set. "Then where the hell do we get the three hundred bucks? Maddy ain't leaving without dough."

"I ain't leaving if you get killed, either," Maddy said.

Ollie looked at her and shoved his chair away from the table. "All right, stay here. Stay here and pay off

Murphy forty bucks a week." He looked up at Bill. "You got three hundred bucks to buy me off this Pringle?"

"You already took one hostage too many, Ollie," Bill said. "You'd better get out of the habit."

"You show me some other red cattle that Nulty can't tell from Pringle's, and I'll take them instead."

"I saw about twenty-five head," Bill said, remembering that morning, "up at Murphy's."

"Murphy's?" Ollie smiled. "Wouldn't that be a laugh? Selling Murphy's cows to Nulty." He began to laugh. "Where?"

"Off in a big pasture, fenced, down behind some trees. You can go up there with fence cutters and get them out on the road and bring them right down to Nulty's, and in the dark nobody'll know. I'm handing you this, Ollie."

"All right," Ollie said, "I'll take it, too. Maybe they have got a trap at Pringle's. Thanks for the idea. What if Murphy's got dogs? What about dogs?"

"You want me to cut the fence for you, too?"

"All right, all right, but what if some other reason? Listen, Bill, there's ways I can get Pringle's cattle, and you know it."

"I know it. Ways to get men killed, too."

"I don't mean a shoot-out," Ollie said. "I mean, start a raid up at the town end of his range to draw off Murphy's people, if it is an ambush. Then two of us cut out our cows down at Nulty's end. Plenty of ways to do it. Set fire to his barn."

Bill stood up. "I can see you're bent on trouble. But take it from me, Ollie, lay off Pringle. As for me, I'm through. What you do will be blamed on me, because you've been part of my outfit. So I'm going to start building myself an alibi, right now, in the Red Dog. As of now, I'm seeking company. If you hit Pringle's

I'll have to make good for him. I'll have to catch you, Ollie. Otherwise, the old man'll never believe I wasn't in on it.''

Ollie was staring at Bill, eyes steady, bright and hard. "I don't like being pushed around," he said.

Bill went to the door. "So long, boy. Be careful."

"I'm sorry you're counting yourself out," Burt said soberly.

He meant it, Bill could see—the ox-eyes were really sad.

"Things have changed, Burt," Bill said. He closed the door behind him and went back to his horse, in the dark. He headed for the Red Dog, and Pepe fell in beside him.

The lights were on in town and the Red Dog was full. Murphy sat in his office and watched Bill go through the batwings. He turned to Moore and said, "Marshal Moore, meet Captain Mora."

Moore put out his hand, and the Captain bowed his head and smiled, taking it. He had had his uniform brushed and pressed since that morning; he had shaved, and trimmed his moustache; but he still had no hat.

"Captain Mora has a story," Murphy said. "He and his men surrounded Gorham's gang down in some little village near Durango, and when Gorham waved a white flag for a truce and the Captain went in, they kidnapped him."

Moore's face showed mild surprise. "Didn't know Gorham went in for things like that," he said.

"Men change," Murphy said. "They were surrounded. Anyway, the Captain wants them all back. He wants to extradite them. How about it, Marshal? I'd give them to him like a shot except for this amnesty thing. I can't serve the old warrants."

"What do you intend to do with them?" Moore asked the Captain.

The Captain smiled his easy, genial smile and cleared his throat. "We were attempting to arrest them for stealing horses," he said. "Also we had reports that they had been stealing cattle and running them north—into this country. There were three charges of cattle stealing. There is now the matter of resisting arrest and firing on and wounding members of the arresting party, as well as kidnaping myself."

"A hundred and eighty years each," Moore said.

"Approximately," the Captain said, bowing slightly.

"Far cheaper to execute them," Moore said.

"By far," the Captain said. "They might even prefer it."

"Of course," Murphy said, "we could simply deport them. On the basis of being immoral characters."

"Not if they are American citizens," Moore said.

"One of them is a Mexican citizen," the Captain said. "The one called Pepe."

"I am not sure of that," Moore said. "You would have to prove that, Captain."

"I am positive he is a Mexican," the Captain replied, coloring a little in spite of himself.

"I don't doubt that you are sure," Moore said, "but it is a question of paper proof. Please don't take all this as meaning that I do not want to cooperate, Captain. I want to do everything I can to help you."

"How," the Captain asked, taking a deep breath, "can he be anything but a Mexican citizen? He speaks broken English, only Spanish fluently. He has been known for years in Mexico, on the police records. He lived five years in Guadalajara."

"Yes, yes," Moore said calmly, "most probable, but

we must be sure. You could provide us with certified copies of the baptismal record in Guadalajara, or wherever he was born. It would probably not take more than four months for a representative from our legation in Mexico City to make a personal inspection of the records—assuming that they are still there, have not been destroyed in some revolution. Another year or so for it to go through the State Department in Washington, besides another three or four months in Santa Fe—the Spanish Americans in Santa Fe are sometimes obstructionist in these matters, but I think it is safe to say we could manage the extradition in, say, three years or so.''

''If it weren't for the amnesty I could arrest them now,'' Murphy said.

''And when is the amnesty over?'' the Captain asked.

''Sunday noon,'' Murphy said.

''Well, that is not long to wait,'' the Captain said. ''A day and a half more.''

Moore said, ''If these men come in under the amnesty, they are safe, Murphy.''

''From my warrants,'' Murphy said. ''But the amnesty says nothing about foreign warrants against an alien.''

''If this Pepe is cleared of United States warrants,'' Moore said, ''he could apply for first papers as an American citizen.''

Murphy raised his hand and with all his might smashed it down, flat on his desk. That was all. His hand coiled together into a fist, and he sat there looking out the window at the Red Dog.

''Supposing,'' the Captain said gently, ''these men committed a new felony? And a new warrant were issued?''

Murphy suddenly relaxed. He began to smile. ''If

they do that, they lose the Government's good will, Moore loses jurisdiction, and I can arrest them on a county warrant—they lose the amnesty rights automatically." He looked at Moore. "Is that right, Marshal?"

Moore said, "That is right—assuming you got a conviction."

"Let the convictions take care of themselves," Murphy said. "What time will you meet us at the Colonel's, Marshal? The raid is supposed to come off before eleven. I thought we might meet at nine-thirty and post ourselves on the Colonel's range."

"As I told Lieutenant Aberforth," Moore said, rising and shifting the weight of his heavy gunbelt, "I will be at the Colonel's at nine. Goodbye, Captain, I will see you then."

"*Adios, Señor,*" the Captain said, smiling.

Murphy, the Captain and the deputies watched Moore cross the street to the Red Dog.

"A formidable man," the Captain said.

"If we catch them tonight," Murphy said, "I can turn them directly over to you, Captain. I don't have a technical mind."

"Excellent," the Captain said.

"Come on," Murphy said, getting up. "Shep and I are going out to dinner. At the Judge's. You come along with us."

"I would not be intruding?"

"You are my guest," Murphy said. "Besides, there is somebody there who is going to talk to us—so I am told. One of the gang. The one named Harvey."

Across the street, in the Red Dog, Moore found Bill sitting at a back table with Simon Shaw and Ed Stafford. "You boys better stay clean tonight," he said quietly to Bill. "That's all I'm telling you, just what I'd tell my own sons." He passed on.

FOURTEEN

THE CAPTAIN MADE himself decently charming to Mrs.
Quires—a lady with a long upper lip and shrewd, kind
eyes who, having gone down with all hands under
twenty years of marriage to Quires, felt a pleasant
tingle at being mistaken for a woman by a rather
handsome, dark-skinned stranger.

She had often dreamed of running off with a gypsy,
but unfortunately, she had never met one. Mexicans
were something like gypsies, in her esteem. Now,
talking to the charming Captain, she liked them more
than ever, especially since she was smart enough to
know that the Captain was being nice to her not because she was attractive, but because she wasn't.

She had one great talent, in which, like many lonely
people, she took refuge, pride and comfort—she was
an expert seamstress. Her acknowledged master-
piece, until her present effort, had been a burial gown
in black satin for an ancient crone named Robbins.
The pity of it was that all Mrs. Quire's best work got

buried with her clients. As Quires often said, in the privacy of their bed, what was the use of all that yard goods in the ground? It wouldn't grow. Mrs. Quires couldn't understand why her best work went into the ground either, but of course, it was because she had the true tragedian's instinct—there is no end like a dead stop. One simply could not put one's best into a dress if one were continually envisaging all the assorted garbage that would, through the happy years of use, eventually land upon the bodice—a perennial drizzle of hair tonic, face powder, and cat hairs, mashed potato and chicken drippings, heaviest on national holidays. Far better that her dresses went—as she had not the sense to go—virgin to the grave.

Mr. Fisher had chosen, for the gown in which Annie Fisher would be buried, a wine-purple velvet, which, in a way, perfectly epitomized Mrs. Fisher's status as a reformed whore; the effect, now complete, was magnificent.

Mrs. Quires was supposed to put it on Mrs. Fisher down in Johanssen's cabinet shop, Johanssen being a combined carpenter and mortician. The butcher shop next door to Johanssen's had of course a large ice room, and by a private arrangement with the butcher, Johanssen had installed a door connecting his "farewell room" with the ice box. There had been no difficulty on how to handle Mrs. Fisher to make her keep over until Sunday—they had simply put her on a shelf in the ice room, as they always did. If Johanssen's casket for her was not finished before the gown was, they would simply put the gown on Mrs. Fisher, wrap her in butcher paper to keep the sawdust off, and put her back in the ice-box with a tag marked "Annie" so the butcher wouldn't get her mixed up with the fresh meat.

Mrs. Fisher had died, unexpectedly, on Wednesday, in the act of frying an egg. Nobody knew what of, for she had seemed in the prime of health. Some people said she drank too much, but this, of course, was nothing but a damned lie. There were a few malicious souls who said that she had so much alcohol in her system that Wednesday morning, when she opened the stove to blow on the fire, her breath touched off in a blue flame and she exploded.

The Captain thought the gown was magnificent, and said so. Mrs. Quires gently beamed out of her shrewd, kind eyes; the clock banged out half past eight. The time allotted for the usual incivilities of light conversation after dinner had passed, and Quires glanced at his wife in a penetrating, malevolent way which he used when he wanted her to leave the room; Mrs. Quires humbly beckoned Euphobia from the corner, where Harvey had been nudging one knee and Shep the other. Euphobia, in a daze because of these attentions, rose and followed her mother out of the room, and immediately Murphy turned to Harvey. Harvey glanced from one face to another. He was a little pale.

"All right, Harvey," Quires said, digging a piece of beef out of a tooth and enjoying it once more, "I told the Sheriff the setup, what you want, what I want. The Sheriff is always willing to help a young fellow get a start. Go on."

Dead-pan on Shep; the kind of cynical dead-pan behind which lives a great store of facile malice. He regarded Harvey with a look that would have been heavy if it had not been so self-confident.

"Okay," Harvey said, returning the look as a competent wolf would return the look of a competent wolfhound, "I want a badge."

"They ain't easy to come by," Murphy said, mastering an impulse to laugh in his face.

"Information ain't easy to come by either," Harvey said. "Like who's stealing what."

"So who is stealing what?" Shep asked.

"Do I get the badge?" Harvey asked.

"Listen," Murphy said, "you want to do me a favor, or you want to sell me a life insurance policy? I ain't got all night."

"All right," Harvey said, coloring a little, "in about two hours, Bill Gorham, Ollie Trevillian and the guy named Burt are stealing thirty head of Pringle's beef."

"I know all that," Murphy said.

Harvey's face seemed to get fuller. He leaned forward, his eyes mean. "That's too easy," he said.

"You watch your attitude with me, young feller," Murphy said.

"Now, see here, Murphy," Quires said, his face shocked, "you can't do this. This was a bona fide proposition. It's not fair."

"I tell you, I knew all this this morning," Murphy said, turning on Quires. "Nulty told me."

Shep smiled. The rest of them sat in silence. The clock ticked. "Son of a bitch," Harvey said, his anger rapidly fading out.

"So you got nothing," Shep said. "You sold out your friends for a mahogany veneered knothole." He laughed. "What'll they do to you when they hear?"

"If they come after me, boy, I'm coming after you."

Murphy glanced at the Captain and stood up. "Time to go."

Harvey walked over to him and laid a hand on his arm. "Listen, you going to arrest them tonight?"

"That's the idea."

"I got to be in on it with them. If I ain't, and you take 'em, they'll wise up to me."

"Fall down and break your leg," Shep said. "That'll do it."

"Listen, Sheriff," Harvey said, "I'll find out other things. I'll stay in the gang and keep my ears open."

"There ain't going to be no gang after tonight," Murphy said. He started to turn away.

Harvey's fingers tightened and held him. "Listen, I can talk them into something bigger. You'd like to hang 'em with something bigger, wouldn't you?"

"Will you kindly let the hell go of my arm?" Murphy said. "I don't need nothing bigger than a cow stealing with ten witnesses. Come on, Shep."

"But what about me?" Harvey cried out. "I gotta show up. If I don't, they'll think I crossed them. Suppose I talked 'em into holding up a train? Huh? How about that?"

"Like I said," Shep remarked, as Murphy went out on the porch, "go break a leg somewhere. That'll put you in the clear all the way around." He carefully stepped on Harvey's foot as he passed, laughed gaily and ambled away.

Behind Quires and Harvey, left staring from the door, Euphobia came softly up and laid a hand on Harvey's shoulder. "Did you get the badge, sweetheart?" she asked softly.

"No, I did not get the badge," Harvey said. "All I got is my tail in a sling—and the sling's too tight." Without even kissing her, he turned and went for his horse.

Five minutes later, he was down at Maddy's. Ollie was alone with a bottle of beer, at the kitchen table. He was rubbing some of the dust out of his gun with a rag dipped in kerosene.

"Hello, Pimples," Ollie said. "Sit down and have a shot of coal oil."

"Listen, Ollie," Harvey said, "I got an idea. We're a bunch of fools to be stealing these cows. Why don't we really make some big money?"

"Like how?" Ollie asked cynically.

"Like robbing Fisher's bank."

The idea shocked Ollie; here it was again, stabbing at him when he had already put it out of his mind twice. He smiled quickly. "Boy, you're a hot one. Whyn't you think of something easy, like robbing a train in the middle of a trestle?"

"Listen," Harvey said, his face intent, leaning forward. "We could do it Sunday morning, when they're burying Mrs. Fisher. It's going to be the biggest damn funeral in San Vicente, ever. The minister is going to make a big speech. They ain't even holding church. Everybody'll be out there at the cemetery."

Ollie looked at him quietly, his face as blank as a child's.

"The cemetery's a mile from town," Harvey said. "We could blow out the vault and be on our way before they got back even if they heard the blast."

Ollie blinked. "How much money you reckon is in that bank?"

"It says half a million on the window."

"I mean in paper money," Ollie said slowly. "Over Sunday."

"Hell, I don't know. We can find out tomorrow. Maybe fifty, hundred thousand. Old man Quires would know. How about it, Oll? Forget this job tonight. To hell with Nulty and his peanut money. I'm out of it. As of now. I can tell you that. For the same risk, we could knock off the whole damn bank. Less risk."

Ollie looked at Harvey's tight, intent face. "Nobody ever got hanged for stealing a cow, Harvey."

"All right," Harvey said. "But I'll be damned if I'll stick my neck out on Nulty's scheme."

Ollie shrugged and smiled. "Okay by me. I guess

Burt and I can handle it if we're careful. That makes a cut of a hundred and fifty each, and I can get my teeth out of hock easy.''

At half past nine, Murphy's party had spread itself out over that part of Pringle's range which lay on the house side of the river, and two of them were watching Nulty's packing house itself from behind the row of poplar trees.

They couldn't miss. Wherever Gorham's men might strike on their side of the river, one of Murphy's people would be bound to see or hear them, and the others were close enough to come to his aid at the first shot.

Murphy had quite a team. Himself, his three deputies, the Colonel, Captain Mora, Moore, Aberforth and the four enlisted men of Aberforth's command.

There was no moon, but the starlight was enough. Murphy had given two sets of orders—he had told his own men to fire on sight, if they saw anybody moving cattle, and to keep on firing. If any of the Colonel's or Aberforth's party got shot up in the confusion, so much the worse for them; it could always be blamed on Gorham.

At nine-thirty, Ollie and Burt left Maddy's and rode out through town back the way they had come that morning, making no effort at quiet until they got within a quarter of a mile of Murphy's ranch. When they saw the lights of the house, they stopped and Ollie took stock, sitting in his saddle and listening.

In the back of Ollie's mind, there was a bleak, stale realization that nothing was going as he had anticipated. Nothing except Maddy. As he and Burt sat in the road, listening for sounds from Murphy's house, he was full of a dull disgust. He took out his package

of ground meat and held it while he dismounted and
Burt tied the horses to the fence.

There were plenty of reasons why he should go
ahead—the need of money being the biggest, the need
to assert himself on the lousy town the second. And
yet it was all dust in his mouth, there was no hunger
in him, no force, no drive, not even the prospect of
amusement. Ollie was tired—just as they all were,
tired of kicking around; yet there was nothing to do
but keep on, stealing what he had to steal to live.

And inside him, invisible behind his mind, there
was a kind of argument going on, because of the kidnaping. At the time it had seemed brilliantly logical,
and yet he was constantly running up against criti-
cism. What he could not understand was why it was
held against him. Everybody had accepted it at the
time, nobody had refused to escape; if it had been the
wrong thing to do, why had they followed him out
of that house?

But in his heart, he too knew it had been the wrong
thing, though he was unwilling to admit it. The kidnaping had led from one misfortune to another. Because of it, the mountains of Mexico had risen up in
a dark wall against him, forbidding him, locking him
out.

What he really wanted was to crawl into bed with
Maddy, just for a while, to be warm in bed with a
nice girl, to wait there for as long as it took until it all
came back to him, his drive, his purpose. It was losing Mexico that hurt him worst, as it had hurt them
all. Mexico was a place you could always hide in. In
bed with Mother.

Maddy was a hell of a mother, but that was what
Ollie wanted—very vaguely he felt it, the ancient sen-
sation of being a child, climbing into bed with Mother,
big, smooth, soft and warm, once again, and lying

there watching the sun come in the window. And all he had was dust in the mouth, and hate. The thing he would like to do would simply be to go over to Murphy's and set fire to the bastard's barn. Stealing cows was cold, brainy stuff.

He got his club untied from the saddle, and when Burt had his, they went quietly up the dark road, meat in one hand, club in the other. There were lights in the bunkhouse, and a light in the main house kitchen, and that was all. Burt and Ollie stood in the weeds that covered an old kitchen garden. The cold night air drifted down on them from the mountains up Lawson's canyon, bringing a wry whiff of woodsmoke, and very faintly, just a hint of the forest. The place was full of peace. In the dark, images of peace crossed Ollie's mind—wagon tongues leaning down on the ground, exhausted; a bit of wool, caught on a splinter of a shed door where the sheep had passed, now stuck forever in sun and rain, wavering in the winds; ancient leather hanging on dark walls, sleeping, dry and dusty; old tools in the dusty corners of silent barns; the long, grass-polished teeth of buck rakes, their worn rust a shiny brown, teeth dug into the earth like the fangs of dead dogs.

Somewhere in the buildings a dog barked, and then another, and then Ollie and Burt saw the two of them, mutts, standing in the light, facing them, sniffing, barking, sniffing the wind again.

Ollie unwrapped the ground meat and dug an egg-sized hunk out of it with his fingers. He lifted his head and barked like a dog, and the dogs darted forward at the challenge, furious.

They came out past the house, back into the dead garden, and then they saw Ollie and Burt and bayed them; as their voices rose hysterically at the sight of men on foot, Ollie tossed a meatball the fifty feet between them.

They saw the arm throw, thought it was a rock, and dodged; and then as the beef smell hit them, they both shut up. Ollie whistled very softly, a love whistle, sweet and wheedling, and he knew that the dogs knew then that they had a friend. A heaven-sent friend who was throwing them free dinners.

Ollie laid out a track of meat, up to his feet, and the dogs came. When they got to him they were growling, but they were wagging their tails too. Ollie could guess what their expressions were, looking at each other with that foolish, soft-faced look of fellow-conspirators, half ashamed, half mischievous, gone over to the enemy and the hell with it. A couple of Benedict Arnolds. He patted them and made friends.

"We ought to knock their heads in," Ollie said sadly. "You take one and I'll take the other."

"Better not," Burt said. "Miss one, and we're through. They're quiet. Keep 'em friendly."

Ollie began dropping more meat around. Gradually he and Burt worked the dogs back down the road; Ollie played and gamboled with them in the starlight while Burt cut the wire and opened the fence. The wire sprang back.

They mounted their horses, and the dogs, now firm friends, trotted along with them, looking up expectantly. They went across one meadow, cut their way through the second line of fence, and brushed through the bunch of trees into the hidden meadow.

Nothing. Nowhere. Just dark, and grass and wind and vacant pasture in the starlight. Ollie looked carefully along the fence, around the whole pasture. Anger began to fill his head, slowly tightening. Anger, dismay, disbelief.

Burt had got down, he was feeling a cowpie. Over

near the water tank, which gleamed dully in the starlight, he found the mud full of fairly fresh prints.

He came back to Ollie. "They ain't been gone three hours. Some of them cowpies is still warm."

Ollie sat solid and tight in his saddle, his head bursting. "That bugging Gorham," he said in a low, thick voice. "Let's go get him. He's at the Red Dog." He turned and kicked his horse to a canter, blind through the dark, back through the trees. Burt ran for his horse, and followed.

"Wait, Ollie," he panted, riding alongside. "For God's sake, cool down."

"Come on," Ollie said. "He's going to pay. The son of a bitch." He jogged out through the road fence.

"Listen," Burt pleaded, "ain't we going to button up those fences again?"

"The hell with it," Ollie said. His eyes moved from side to side in painful rage, looking for something, anything to lay his hands on. "I gotta get cattle," he said. "I gotta get hold of some cattle, Burt, we gotta get that money." Burt looked at his partner silently. Ollie's voice was far too desperate for the situation. Why couldn't he shrug it off? Ollie had lost all calm, all proportion. Burt was slowly becoming alarmed.

In Ollie there was a desperate sense of grasping at straws. It was as though the ground had fallen away from him, he was suddenly lost. All his expectations had vanished, and now this crazy trick, this peculiar betrayal, had put a sense of curse on him; he was full of anger and confused fear. He was too much of a gambler not to see signs and portents in everything that happened, and these signs and portents he could not fathom, except to see that they were all disastrous, from the dead horses to these disappearing cattle.

It was already ten o'clock. He knew he wasn't going to make it to Nulty's with any cattle at all, this late. But he had to get the money. His hand was still on his stick, but in his mind, his hand had seized his pistol. It was up to Gorham. This was Gorham's fault, and Gorham was going to have to help make up enough hands for a raid on Pringle.

He threw his stick away into the ditch grass, and one of the dogs ran and picked it up and brought it back. They stood there in the road, panting, eager, expectant.

The poor bastards, Ollie thought, they look just like that son of a bitch captain, when he came in that door, thinking he had won. And then the aspect of the grinning dogs suddenly changed, and the cold of fear entered him. They were laughing at him, like ghosts and images of the Captain he had betrayed. He turned his horse and beat it into a hard run.

FIFTEEN

"So you're coming in," Ed Stafford said to Bill, lifting a shot of saloon hooch with satisfaction.

"Don't look so damn smug," Bill said. "You remind me of Murphy's ranch cook."

"I am Murphy's ranch cook," Stafford said complacently, "and I ain't forgetting it."

"You can leave your lousy apron at home," Bill said, "when you're drinking with free men. I haven't signed any papers yet." Allie was far away, and he was getting nervous. Where the hell was Pepe? He drank, and suddenly the mountains came back, full in his mind, a lovely wilderness of wildflowers and animal innocence, full of clean life and sudden death.

This place stank. The saloon was full of men, town men and ranch men in on business; and in addition, another sort of man, stiff and uncomfortable, reserved and sober—outlaws on their good behavior. They gave the big room the air of a convention, and added a rumble of sober conversation to the usual chatter.

Old Simon Shaw, sitting opposite Bill at the round table in the back of the saloon, lifted his shotglass to his lips and tipped the stuff in. He swallowed it without a quiver, without a tear, and looked past Bill at some distant scene, beyond the wall.

"When you packing out?" Bill asked.

"Don't you worry about me, son," Simon said. "I got plenty of time. I ain't had a chance to set in town like this for fifteen years, and I'm enjoying it." His old gray eyes with their sagging, red-edged lids shifted to Bill. He grinned, teeth like a wolverine, one solid gold one, in front, shining in the light. "You shoulda been around twenty years ago, Bill. You was born too late."

"Maybe you were born too late yourself," Bill said. "Twenty years earlier and I wouldn't have had to look at you at all."

Shaw's eyes opened with surprise, and then he smiled. Then he laughed. "You amuse me, boy. A whipper-snapper." He kept on chuckling. It really tickled him, being insulted by a squirt like Bill, not even a third his age. "Bill, you're just another maverick. You won't last. You'll sign up, and sweat it out for a year and then you'll get drunk and shoot somebody. You'd be better off in the mountains, with Pepe and me."

"I'm getting married," Bill said, lifting his drink.

Shaw's eyes narrowed and he leaned forward half an inch, intent. "You? Married?" He paused and licked his lips. "To a *woman*?"

"Not to a damn sheep, like you, Simon," Ed said. "Bill's a human being. Did you know, Bill, that one time Mr. Shaw here went through a full wedding ceremony with a seven-year-old ewe, up in Idaho?"

"She was a lovely creature," Shaw said, pouring himself another shot. "Pure white, she was, with the sweetest little yellow eyes you ever saw. And all she could say was Baa. God, what a relief. I once lived with a Chockahominy squaw. God, what a chatterbox. Christmas come around, ever damn time, it's Merry Christmas, Merry Christmas! Wait all year, she would, to get that off her chest. Then a week later, out it comes again. Happy New Year, Happy New Year! And I'd know the next year it would be the same damned thing, more talking. So I traded her off for a packhorse and went south." He looked carefully at Bill with his dead, lying eyes. "That's a woman for you. Always jabbering. You'll be sorry."

Bill sat in silence, smiling. Nothing else to do. Just take it. Stafford and Shaw looked at him. The three listened to the rumble of talk all around them, slowly sobering, and the present slowly coming back.

Shaw sighed. "Sunday noon, and we go back to murder as usual. Then I got to be gone. I was kind of hoping I could make it for Annie Fisher's funeral, but I don't know." He shook his head once. "Kind of cutting it short."

Bill looked up in surprise. "You aren't leaving till Sunday?"

Shaw raised his own eyes, equally surprised. "No. What's the rush? Come to that, I might even stay on next week—plenty people would hide old Simon Shaw in their house. Let that Murphy chase the wind in the mountains."

"They got you first on the list," Bill said. "With those dogs, and that cannon."

"You shouldn't have told him that," Stafford said. "Ain't playing fair with Murphy."

"I haven't signed up yet," Bill said.

"And when you do," Shaw said, "then you'll be

the all white boy. You'll do just what they say. Just what Murphy says. If you know where I am, you'll tell them, Bill. Just stand up straight and speak out, like a little man.''

Bill flushed.

''What else you going to do?'' Stafford said, ''if you sign up?''

''Look who's talking,'' Bill said. ''Murphy's cook.''

''Don't worry about me,'' Ed said. ''I got it all figured out. I'll lie like a trooper.''

''And they'll know,'' Bill said.

''So they won't ask me in the first place,'' Ed said. ''But you, Bill. You're getting married. That's different. You can't lie to your friends.''

Stafford and Shaw sat and looked at him.

After a long moment, Shaw said quietly, ''You're going to have to sell me out, boy. You've going to have to, if you sign up. You can't ride the fence in this, you can't be on both sides, after Sunday noon.'' No resentment. Just a statement of fact.

''You know,'' Shaw said, ''that's what I hate about the law most. It makes men enemies, it turns them against each other. You think, now, how it was in the old days, when we was all trapping around here. Apaches didn't bother us none, we used to go down to their councils and sit in and smoke with them. Down where Silver City is, where the spring used to be. And us white men, most of us were friends.''

''Nobody ever got drunk and shot anybody,'' Bill said.

''Sure they got shot. But the thing was, you trusted people. Until they proved different. Then you settled things yourself.'' He looked past Bill at the wall. ''Now they got all this law, and all the stuff written in books, you can't look in a man's eye and know how he feels about you, you got to read a book, a law book, and find out in court. And the end is that no-body knows anybody else. Everybody got his nose in a lawbook and everybody is strangers.''

"Simon, the country has changed," Ed said. "It's a damn shame, I know, but it's happening. In a while you'll see the ladies going on picnics up where you used to fight bears."

"It ain't changed that much yet," Shaw said. "And besides, I'm getting pretty old, be seventy or so pretty soon, I guess. I won't last much longer, and as long as I do, I'd rather live with the beavers, what's left. I always liked animals. They're so much more human than people."

"You hate people," Bill said.

Shaw looked up. "No," he said, "Just crowds."

Behind Shaw, against the multicolored crowd of men and lights, Bill suddenly saw Ollie's face, set and pale behind the freckles. Ollie came up behind Shaw and stood there, his hand tight on the back of Shaw's chair.

"What's the matter?" Bill asked.

Very slowly, Ollie sat down. He wanted to shout it out, but he didn't dare, not in this room. He leaned forward and said in a low voice, "Them cattle wasn't there." He was so mad he was almost crying. Shaw blinked and straightened up.

"I'm Murphy's cook," Ed said. "I like you fine, Ollie, but right at the moment, I better not be seen with you."

"Go to hell," Ollie said, staring fixedly at Bill.

Stafford got up and moved away from the table.

"Let's go outside," Ollie said. "I've lost my chance. You got to make it up."

"Don't talk to Bill," Shaw said, looking at his drink. "Bill's going to get married. He's got future friends all over this room."

"Those cows were there this morning," Bill said.

"Yeah?" Ollie said. "Well, they ain't now, and you was the one said they was. I ain't saying what I think, but you know it anyway. You get on your horse, Gorham, and help me and Burt cut out thirty head of Pringle's cows. Right now. I did what you said. Now you help me and Burt, and the hell with your new friends."

Bill looked at him quietly. "Take it easy, Ollie. Have a drink and I'll help you think of something else."

"Listen," Ollie said, still leaning forward, his eyes bright and hot on Bill's. "If you won't help us, there's only one thing left. Go on down and take the cash off Nulty with a gun."

"They got men all over, waiting by their horses," Pepe said. "I just went down there. Colonel Pringle is there too."

"The hell with them," Ollie said. "I'm going." He started to get up. Shaw's arm moved like a snake and his fingers dug into Ollie's arm.

"You set still," Shaw said in a low voice. "You go for Nulty and you'll hang. You'll end up killing somebody sure as hell."

"That old son of a bitch!" Ollie cried. "I'll just scare—"

"Shut up," Shaw said, digging his fingers in. "You're a fool."

"All right, I'm a fool," Ollie said. "And I don't give a damn if I do kill somebody." He yanked his arm free and stood up. "So long, you bastards," he said. "In the nose." He turned and moved off, straight and fast, through the crowd.

Shaw and Bill looked at each other. "You going to let him get hanged, Bill?"

Bill's face twisted. "The lousy bastard. I told him I was out."

"You better do something," Shaw said. "He's like a kid. He was damn near crying."

Bill sat there, unable to move, thinking of Allie's face, as he had talked to her. Just walk out, he had said, sign a paper. Just announce that you are through, and it is all over.

And then some addle-headed son of a bitch like Ollie goes haywire because he can't get his teeth out of hock. And suddenly he saw Ollie, racing away through the dark, saw him in his mind, that wild, skinny figure, all knees and elbows, hair sticking out from under his hat, and he heard the Captain of Rurales, saying in the moonlight, to Pepe, "One suffers for such friends." And Pepe, saying, "One suffers for all friends."

It had sounded so Spanish, so operatic, the way they always seemed with that specious nobility, and their exalted emotions.

"That son of a bitch," Bill said, and Shaw relaxed, easing at the new sound in Bill's voice, the sound of sadness and trouble. All was well again, Shaw thought, as he lifted his drink.

Bill stood up. "Come on, Pepe. We'll have to stop the idiot some way."

They caught up with Ollie and Burt halfway down to the Pringle place. Ollie wouldn't stop, wouldn't even talk. Bill harangued him for a quarter of a mile and then gave up; he and Pepe fell behind, but still hung on. There were plenty of people camped outside of town. Bill and Pepe could see the faces around the heart of a fire, the vague shape of a wagon top. Occasional riders went back and forth between the camps and the saloons in town, passing on the road with a clopping of hooves and broken conversation. Everybody moved carelessly. With the amnesty, they had suspended hostilities.

On Pringle's side of the road, opposite the far-scattered fires of the camps, there was pure dark, because the place was fenced.

"Wait a minute, Ollie," Pepe said. "I can see Murphy's men."

That stopped Ollie. He could see nothing in the dark except the dark shape of a cow, here and there.

"Listen," Pepe whispered. "Once in a while you can hear a bit clink." Campers singing, distant clopping of hooves, along the road. "They are standing by their horses," Pepe said. They could see nothing. "You can tell the horses from the cattle, the way they move. Listen for the bits."

Ollie said nothing, but he was sobered.

"Come on back, Ollie," Bill whispered. "Let's go back."

"Nulty sold us out," Ollie said.

"I told you he would," Pepe said.

"You're so smart," Ollie said. "If this is a trap, Nulty'll be down there—with the money. He's the bait."

"There's two men in the poplars," Pepe said. "There's bound to be others inside the packing house, covering Nulty."

"Anything wrong with going to see my old friend Nulty in the middle of the night?" Ollie asked. "Come on, Burt, let's give it a try, maybe we can catch him with his pants down."

They turned their horses away. Bill and Pepe watched them go.

"He's going to kill him," Bill said. "He'll scout the place to see if they got men on it, and if he can, he'll kill Nulty."

"Maybe," Pepe said. Ollie had changed—something had broken down, some basic cheer, the humor that had saved him.

"We could knock him on the head," Bill said. "Burt would be easy to handle. Drag Ollie back to town."

"The trouble with knocking on the head is that it doesn't stop with that," Pepe said quietly. "You start it, you don't know where it ends. Somebody gets killed."

"I'm putting it to you, which is worse, to let Ollie kill Nulty, or knock Ollie on the head?"

"All right," Pepe said, gathering his reins. They went on down the road after Ollie, moving into a fast trot. They got halfway down Nulty's road to the packing house when suddenly a light speared out of the building and they saw Ollie and Burt, standing in an open doorway. The door started to close, but Ollie stuck his foot in it, and a moment later, they had gone inside and the darkness came back. Nothing alarming or hurried. Just a couple of friends calling in the middle of the night, one of them holding a gun where the guards couldn't see it.

Then, from the row of poplars, a bit clinked and Bill caught the barely audible hissing of whispers from the guards. A squeak of leather, and then, with a quick, muffled pound of hooves, two riders were gone toward Pringle's.

"They know something's wrong," Bill said, "but they're afraid to tackle it alone. Gone for help. I give them ten minutes." Very carefully, he crept up the steps and stood by the office door, listening. Talk. A quiet fight, and if it was quiet, it was because Ollie had a gun in his hand, pointing it at Nulty. Bill got off the porch. He was beginning to sweat.

"I can't just leave him. The poor damn fool doesn't even know he's been spotted." Then he heard riders coming up from the pens by the river. Two horses.

"Get in the poplars where those guards were," Pepe said. They rode over to the trees and took up the vacant posts. The two riders from below came along quietly, straight up to Bill and Pepe and one of them whispered through the dark, "Shep?"

Bill didn't answer.

"Shep, that you?"

Bill got his breath going again and said, "Yeah, yeah, what the hell do you want?"

"When the hell we quit this, Shep? Nobody's coming." The other one spoke. "We ain't even et yet. You didn't say we was going to have to stay down here all night. All you said was for us to drive down Murphy's red cows, they was sold to Nulty; you didn't say nothing about no rustlers, Shep, and it don't seem fair, no dinner, nothing."

It suddenly dawned on Bill that they were Murphy's twins. They had driven Murphy's cows down here; that was the reason Ollie hadn't been able to find them. Those cows were somewhere in Nulty's pens. Anything to get rid of the bastards. "All right," he whispered to the twins, "you go on into town and get something to eat." He faked it up a little stronger. "You be back in an hour. I'll take the rap if Murphy finds out. Beat it."

The horses turned in the dark and were gone. "Come on," Bill said to Pepe, and led him down toward the river. "We got us some cattle, boy, Murphy's cattle." They found the grades in a back pen, hardly visible in the starlight.

"What you going to do?" Pepe asked.

Bill laughed. "Bail Ollie out. Let's move them up to the slaughter pen." The cows ambled along, nose following tail through the starlight, drifting up to the slaughter gate.

They left them there and went into the shed, through the slaughter-pen chute, and stopped in the foul, deep dark. Cracks of light beamed out from Nul-

ty's little office. The voices were louder. Bill knocked
on the office door and said, "Ollie, it's Bill. We got
the cattle in the pen outside."

The door kicked open and there was Ollie, his face
mean and white, and Nulty sitting backed into his
chair with Burt's gun pointed at his eye.

"It's all right, Nulty," Bill said calmly. "Ollie insisted on having his little joke with you, while we
were working. Ollie, we got the Herefords right outside, kid. Nulty, you got the three hundred?"

"What Herefords?" Nulty asked, his little eyes
trying to get wide open. "Where'd you get any Herefords?"

"Why, right off Pringle's range, like you told us,"
Bill said patiently. "Come on out and count them."

"Why, you couldn't—" Nulty began, and stopped
himself.

"Come on and count them, Nulty," Bill said, not
smiling any more. "We got your Herefords, and we
want the money, and in a damn big hurry, too."

Nulty sat there, his lower lip trembling, his eyes
blinking.

"Get on your feet, you old son of a bitch," Bill
said. "You agreed to buy, the cattle are here. Count
'em and pay off. And you're receiving stolen property, so if we go up, you go up too. I know darn well
you sold us out to Murphy, but with the cattle here,
delivered, Murphy'll never believe you didn't sell him
out too." He held the front sight of his gun under
Nulty's chin. "Up."

The old man got up and wobbled to the door. "You
couldn't."

"You say that again," Ollie said, "and I'll put a
forty-five slug right up your tail. You sold us out, you
bastard. Murphy's men are all over the country waiting for us."

Nulty blundered out of the shed and stood looking at the cattle in the pen. He counted them, and stood swearing.

"Pay us," Bill said, and the old man turned and wobbled back in. Inside, he knelt in front of his safe and began twirling the knobs, his hands shaking. "I never turned you in, boys," he said huskily, opening the door. "I made a bargain, and I'm mighty glad to get the cattle. If Murphy found out, it wasn't me. I'm a square dealer, boys." He counted money, whispering. He shoved a handful of bills at Ollie, and Ollie counted them over.

"Let's go," Ollie said, and turned toward the door.

Then they heard the horses, a faint rumble, and then a confused rattle in the yard outside, and low voices. The four of them stood quiet in the office, frozen, and slowly hope began to glimmer up in Nulty's pasty face. "You brought stolen cattle, you forced me to buy them," he whispered, and suddenly giggled. "I'm as innocent as a lambkin. Ha, ha, ha."

"All right, you in there," Murphy's voice rose in the night. "We got your horses. You're surrounded. You can't get away. Throw out your guns, Gorham, and come out with your hands up. This ain't no parley this time, this is an arrest, and we'll kill you if you make us."

Bill's knees began shaking uncontrollably, and then he began to curse in a whisper. He shook himself, swearing quietly, and opened the little office door, crossed to the outside building door, and opened it wide.

"I don't know what you were expecting, Sheriff Murphy," he said into the dark, "but we're just concluding a little business deal with Mr. Nulty here. If you want to arrest somebody, wait till we're through, if you don't mind."

"Bill," the Colonel said out of the dark, his voice quiet and serious, "this is no fooling matter."

He saw the rifles, light from the doorway gleaming in long slants from the barrels.

"You come out of there," Murphy said then, in a dead level voice, "with your hands up, or we'll open fire."

"Do you want to kill Nulty too? You gents just come on in, while we finish our business."

"Don't be too hasty, Sheriff," the colonel said. "Maybe he's telling the truth." The Colonel swung down from his horse.

"You going in there?" Murphy cried. "They'll ambush you, Colonel. They'll murder you."

"Melodrama," the Colonel said, and started for the door. Bill turned back into the office.

"Put your guns away," he said to Ollie and Burt.

"We can ambush the sons of bitches," Ollie said, his face hard. "Clean out the safe and beat it."

Bill took one step toward him and grabbed the barrel of Ollie's gun. He jerked it out of his hand. "You keep your trap shut, Ollie. You got us all in this mess. All I can do is try to talk us out of it."

"You bastard," Ollie said. "You're a dirty, rotten traitor."

Bill stood there, all set to slug him.

"You got no right to leave me without my defense," Ollie said.

Boots sounded on the porch steps. Bill shoved the cartridges out of the gun, threw them in the corner, and handed the gun back to Ollie. "You're through pulling guns, Ollie. We don't want anybody dead." Ollie, his face a dead-white, freckled mask, stuck the gun back into his holster.

Bill turned to Nulty. "Get this," he said. "If you don't stand with us, every outlaw in the country will know you sold us out to Murphy. I know twenty men in town that will kill you as a matter of conscience.''

''Oh, God almighty,'' Nulty said, leaning back and swallowing, rolling his little red eyes.

A fist banged on the office door. ''Open up!'' the Colonel said. Bill turned and opened the door. ''Good evening, Colonel,'' he said politely. ''Won't you come in?''

SIXTEEN

As THE COLONEL entered, Murphy pushed past into the center of the room, his gun in his hand. What gave him pause was the calm in his enemies' faces, and the confusion in Nulty's.

"All right, Nulty," Murphy said. "What did they do?"

Nulty feebly waved a hand here and there, raised his little eyes to heaven once, and closed them again.

"They've hurt him," Murphy said. "He can't speak. Gorham, I place you under arrest."

"What's the charge?" Bill asked.

"Stealing cattle," Murphy said.

"On what complaint?" Bill asked. He was still trying to control his trembling; his poise was slowly coming back.

"That you stole off Pringle's range," Murphy said.

"Haven't been on Pringle's range tonight," Bill said.

"Me neither," Ollie said.

"Shut up," Bill said. "We all came down from the Red Dog. Plenty of people saw us up there, not half an hour ago. We didn't have time to steal any cattle, even if we'd wanted to."

Murphy's eyes opened wide. He stared first at Bill, then at Nulty. "Why," he shouted, and stopped. He looked at Nulty with a stupefied glare. "What is this?"

Nulty waved his hand again in a generally comprehensive motion, designed to cover everything.

"They threatened you?" Murphy asked. He looked bewilderedly around the room, and saw the open safe door. "Was this a robbery?" he asked. "Were they holding you up?"

The Colonel said slowly, in a heavy, sad voice, "Bill, I want the truth from you."

Shep came in the door. "There's thirty head of cattle out back." He was smiling. "Herefords. Pringle's brand."

"Come on," Murphy said, waving his gun at the gang. They all pushed out of the office and went through the packing shed. They came out on the back loading porch single file and stood looking at the cattle in the starlight.

"Mr. Nulty," Moore said, "it looks like you have taken over some of the Colonel's cattle. With the safe door open, it looks like some money passed. Is that so, Gorham?"

Bill said, in a small, tight voice, "Yes."

"How much?" Moore asked.

"Three hundred dollars," Bill said.

"Ten bucks a head," Moore said. "That would be a fair price for stolen beef. What about this, Bill? I take it you have threatened Nulty and I can't read his mind."

"We didn't steal any cattle," Bill said quietly.

"That's a damn lie," Murphy said, "with the cattle right there in front of us. Speak up, Nulty, for God's sake."

Nulty opened his mouth wide, and closed it again. Voices rose in the barn, where the soldiers were standing guard.

"You can't pass here," somebody said.

"Like hell I can't," Simon Shaw said. "You get out of the way, sonny, or I'll wrap that rifle around your dirty neck." Shaw came out on the porch and stopped, looking around. "Colonel, your daughter said maybe you'd be here. I come about Ollie. I was sitting in the Red Dog half an hour ago, talking to both Bill Gorham and Trevillian. You can't make a cow stealing out of that." He smiled at Nulty, and Nulty looked quickly away.

"Colonel Pringle," Murphy said, "there's thirty head of your Herefords. I want you to make a complaint. Now."

"Just a minute," the Colonel said. He let himself down into the pen and ran his hand over the cattle's earmarks. He came back out and stood kicking manure off his boots. "No complaint by me," he said. "They aren't my cattle, Murphy."

"Oh yeah?" Murphy cried. "Just because Gorham's your friend don't mean you can get away with—"

"They're yours," the Colonel said. "Your earmarks."

Murphy got down and felt them. He stood there opening and closing his mouth. "Why," Murphy said, "I sold these cattle to Nulty this morning, they was delivered here at five o'clock."

Nulty got his voice back. "Damn you," he

screamed at Ollie, "gimme my money back. You son of a bitch, you sold me my own cattle." He ran at Ollie, lashing furiously with his long arms, and Ollie stumbled backward. The Colonel and Shep grabbed Nulty and held him, panting and glaring at Ollie. One of the deputies began to snigger.

"You keep that smelly old bastard off me," Ollie said, backing into a gun and stopping.

"Gimme back my money," Nulty shouted, oblivious to everything. "He tricked me. It's a fraud, a dirty, lousy fraud."

"Oh, come, now, Mr. Nulty," Bill said. "You're all mixed up. All we did was move your cattle from one pen to another, doing our job, and all you did was give us a week's wages in advance. Surely you don't want Murphy to arrest you for receiving stolen property, do you? Why don't you just tell the Sheriff that you hired us to run cattle for you, and we did. We ran them from one pen to the other, by God, and we came to collect our pay in advance because we were broke. Isn't that right?"

"Yeah," Simon Shaw said, looking at Nulty, "ain't that right?"

Nulty ground his teeth and clenched his fists. He did everything but throw up. "Yes," he said, "that's right."

"You stinking liar," Murphy shouted, "you know damn well we had it all fixed up, you know damn well they came to you, and you agreed—"

"Shut up, shut up," Nulty shouted, trying to drown him out. "I didn't receive no stolen cattle, they didn't sell me no stolen cattle, and they ain't even stolen cattle at all, they are just working for me, that's all, and I paid them wages. Hell, I love these boys here, I'm going to adopt them. Now, you stupid Irish bastard, get the hell off my place. All of you, get out, get out."

Shaw began to laugh, a slow, incredibly harsh sound, deep in his chest.

"For God's sake," Nulty shrieked, his long arms rising into the air, fists clenched helplessly, "Won't somebody shut that man up?"

"I suggest," Moore said in his big, soft voice, "that we go some place where there's more light. I would like to be able to see people's faces while we thrash this out."

"Come to my house," the Colonel said. "You had better come too, Mr. Shaw, since you're alibi-ing these men."

"I ain't going," Nulty said. "I ain't leaving my property. I'm staying here with my gun, that's all. And anybody coming around," he said, eyeing Shaw, "had better be bloody careful."

Shaw smiled. "There's plenty of time for everything, Nulty," he said pleasantly. "Come on, Lieutenant. I want to see those dogs you're going to chase us with."

The Lieutenant was embarrassed by this old man. He stood there dumb, looking down at Shaw. Shaw smiled up at him with a warm, fatherly expression.

"There's going to be some killing, Lieutenant," he said with great charm. "There may be plenty dead by Sunday night. Dead dogs. Dead soldiers. Dead Shaw, even. And maybe a dead lieutenant, too." His stumpy old teeth showed in the starlight as he smiled benevolently.

"Let's go and look at those dogs, Lieutenant," he said softly, "and think over together a while how it feels to be dead." He took the Lieutenant by the elbow and ushered him carefully through the doorway, as though the Lieutenant were rather fragile. Almost in a trance, the Lieutenant let himself be led by the kindly old man who was smiling so pleasantly at him, talking quietly about killing him on Sunday.

SEVENTEEN

"UNLESS I AM mistaken," Captain Mora said, as he sat at ease in one of the Colonel's wing chairs, smoking one of the Colonel's cigars, "these men were going to steal some cattle and sell them to *Señor* Nulty tonight—and then be taken in the trap. Am I correct?" He looked at Murphy.

They were all sitting around the Colonel's living room—the gang by the door, standing, while Mora, Murphy, Moore and the Colonel sat in the North Carolina furniture and Judge Quires and Shep sat on the wicker chairs. The Cannon brothers had come in with the Judge, and they sat in the back of the room, side by side in monumental silence, with Allie, who, working on a small piece of embroidery, was inconspicuously ignoring the fact that this was no place for a woman. Simon Shaw sat in a corner. Aberforth stood at the door to the corridor. His men and the deputies were out in front with the horses.

"You are correct," Murphy said. He looked at

Shaw and grinned. "Poor old Nulty." He looked at the end of his cigar and suddenly laughed, with his mouth open, and tears of immense enjoyment squeezed out of his eyes. "Boy, is he up the creek. He's as good as dead. You know that."

The Colonel looked at him, appalled.

"Well, it happened, anyway," Murphy said. "I couldn't help it." He calmed down and looked at Quires. "The fact is, the reason I got you here for a warrant, is because Gorham actually stole Nulty's own cattle out of one pen and moved them into another, and deceived Nulty into thinking that they were Pringle's. So that's fraud, isn't it?"

"It was a mixed-up deal," Bill said. "Kind of a joke, kind of wages, kind of a sale. I don't know. I'm still confused. We all got to playing around with Nulty down there, seemed kind of funny—we all had a good laugh. Didn't we, boys? Shucks, Judge, it's getting so a fellow can't have any fun at all."

"Where's Nulty?" Quires asked.

"Scared to death, holed up in his office with a shot-gun." Murphy smiled. "Judge, I make the charge. I want a warrant for these men, you issue one. The people versus Gorham et al."

They all sat there looking at the Judge. He sat there looking at nothing, straight ahead.

"Where's Harvey Muntin?" he asked suddenly.

"Safe," Bill said. "He didn't come along."

"Ain't nothing to it," one of the Cannon brothers said suddenly, his big, slow voice rumbling and filling the room. "If you say they's sufficient evidence for a warrant, then Murphy can arrest him, Judge. If not, he don't get no warrant. What's the trouble you can't make up your mind?"

They all listened with respect; they all nodded, and waited for Quires' answer.

Quires drew back his head and blinked. They had thrown it right at him. He started a glance at Murphy, but controlled it. The Cannons, the big, bland bastards, knew well enough what the trouble was: there was too much confusion in the evidence for a warrant, but Murphy and Fisher wanted the warrant, and Quires was Fisher's man—as why not? Somebody had to get the Judge his election, a judge had to owe something to somebody, to be a judge. If the big bastards wanted him, why hadn't they got him the election instead of Fisher? But there he sat, Fisher's man, and they all knew it, and he knew they all knew he knew they knew. Perfect communion, especially in the bland mockery in the Cannons' eyes. Quires sweated inside, his guts tightened, but nothing showed: he was a practised judge.

He looked at the Cannons with real pain; the silence in the room was getting thicker and hotter by the second. He wanted to shout: Damn you, why hate me? Just 'cause you don't like Fisher? Then why didn't you buy me instead, you big, ignorant slobs? He sighed heavily and blinked, anger dying in the trap. Behind it all was this fear: the Cannons were powerful—if they put their cows into cash, they might even be able to bust Fisher, open a bank or something. And if they did?

The Cannons smiled at him with bland irony, reading the sweat on his upper lip, and he had to nod, he had to agree. They were enemies, and he couldn't afford any. But nobody lasts forever, not even Fisher, and a man had to foresee, and prepare for possible changes. But how to do it gracefully?

The Colonel smiled, also noticing the sweat. He took no pleasure in pinned worms—far better to ease the pain. ''The trouble, is'' the Colonel said quietly,

"You ought to have a strong case against them to sign a warrant."

"He ain't the prosecuting attorney," Murphy said peevishly.

"Bound to look funny to an appeals court," the Colonel said, "not even a complaining witness, and all that. Gorham might even get Nulty on the stand to contradict the charge itself. Appeals court would throw it out even if you got a conviction. You got a big future, Judge. With us behind you."

The sweat broke out on Quires' forehead. He looked sideways at Murphy. "I told you before, you got to have an open-shut case on cattle stealing, Murphy. You got to have eye-witnesses to make it stick. Now, in this, you ain't even got a complaint. You see how it is."

"Yeah, yeah, I see how it is, all right," Murphy said bitterly. He looked at the floor. For a moment, the Colonel almost liked Murphy. He was always getting battered around, and yet he always came back up, asking for more. Pigheaded and misguided, as crooked as they came, still, he had some sort of guts.

"Just one thing," Murphy said, lifting his head and looking at the gang. "You took three hundred dollars off Nulty. And I claim that you took it at the point of a gun. You saw them draw a gun when they went in, didn't you, Shep?"

"Why, fellow," Bill said quietly, "you don't think Ollie was serious with that gun, do you? It was all a joke, wasn't it, Ollie? Show them the gun you held on Nulty for our little old joke, Ollie boy." He stuck out a hand and Ollie put his gun in it. Bill tossed it to Murphy.

Murphy turned the cylinder of the gun and sighed wearily.

"Is it empty?" Quires asked.

"Yes," Murphy said dully. "It's empty."

"Just for insurance," Bill said, "I unloaded it. Safety precaution. We didn't want just a joke to blow up in our faces."

"Give me the gun," the Colonel said. He inspected it and passed it to Moore.

"You through with me for tonight, Murphy?" Quires asked, getting up. "You want any more warrants today?"

Murphy said nothing, and Quires left the room.

"You got three hundred dollars," Murphy said to Bill. "Hand it over. A joke's a joke, but it shouldn't cost Nulty three hundred dollars. I guess you're planning to give it back to him, but I'll see that he gets it. Who's got it?"

"Ollie," Bill said.

Murphy stood up. "Give it," he said, his hand out to Ollie.

Ollie frowned and backed a step.

"Ollie," Moore said quietly. "Give it up. Fun's fun."

Ollie stuck his face out. "Where's my money, then? How do I get my teeth?"

"Shut up, you bloody idiot," Bill said, "and give it up."

Ollie's face burned, but his eyes dropped, hiding. He dug into his pocket and came out with the roll of bills. He handed them to Murphy.

"And now," Murphy said, "I arrest the whole damn bunch of you for vagrancy, and I don't need no damn warrant for that. You're all dead broke and you got no means of support."

Mora smiled. "The one there, the Pepe," he said. "He is a Mexican fugitive. If you would like, I can take him in my custody now."

Murphy had them all back against the wall.

"I never heard of anything so outrageous," Allie said, her voice coming clear and competent from the back of the room. "Mr. Gorham is our new ranch manager. Didn't you know, Mr. Murphy? And all the others are signing up with Marshal Moore and he has jobs for them. Isn't that so, Marshal?"

"Yes," Moore said.

"Moore's right," Bill said to Murphy. "We were going to sign up all along, weren't we, boys?"

Ollie was seething, speechless, breathing deep and fast as though he wanted to shout something.

"You take these jobs," Moore said, "or I'll have to let Murphy take you in as vagrants. If he takes you in, God knows what will happen. You'll probably be in Mexico by tomorrow noon."

"Yeah," Ollie said at last, "I got a job. Johanssen's."

"Yeah, me too," Burt said. "I'm working for the butcher, what's-his-name."

Pepe smiled slowly, his eyes amused on Mora's face.

"That one," Mora said, his face darkening. "I want him."

"He's working for me," Bill said. "Here on the ranch."

Murphy looked at them all, one after the other. "This puts an end to it," he said finally. "The end of talking. The next time, it'll be different." He turned and left the room, marching down the long hall. Mora rose, put out his cigar calmly, and bowing to the Colonel, followed Murphy.

The rest of them stood silent, looking at each other.

Moore said, "You boys know what would have happened if he'd got you in jail, don't you?"

They said nothing.

"He'd have put you in irons, in a wagon, tonight,

and turned you over to Mora." He stood up. "You watch yourselves. I'll expect you in my office at eight in the morning."

"I'll be there," Ollie said. "No two-bit sheriff is going to jail me. When I leave this town, I'll be rich." He turned on Bill. "And as for you, you double-crossing rat, stay out of my way. From now on."

"Just a minute," Allie said, quietly and coolly, putting down her embroidery. She got up without hurry and, brushing past the Cannon brothers, came down to Ollie.

"Mr. Trevillian," she said, facing Ollie's outraged eyes, "Bill went down there tonight to help you, personally. I heard him talking about it to *Señor* Pepe. Mr. Gorham decided this afternoon that he was through with your wild life, that he was settling down. But he risked arrest, just to help you."

The Cannon brothers looked at her doubtfully.

"That's right, Ollie," Shaw said from his corner. "He saved your bacon, boy. Bill was sitting with me in the Red Dog, telling me about his new plans, and you came in with this idea of a—a joke. And he tried to stop you. He's no double-crossing rat."

"Reformed," Ollie said bitterly. He hated them all, but most of all he hated Bill. "The funny thing is, his reforming cost me three hundred bucks. Not him. Me. That was my money. I got it, not him." He stared at Bill, grief and rage in his eyes. He could no longer remember clearly what had happened. All he knew was that Bill had taken his gun; Bill had made him give up the money; Bill was coming out on top, weaseling his way into a soft job on a fat ranch, where he could steal all he wanted. Bill, the educated bastard, was getting it all for himself, and Ollie was getting nothing but a good, swift kick in the head. "How the hell am I gonna get my teeth?"

"You aren't leaving town," Moore said.

"Oh, yeah?" Ollie cried desperately. "Yeah? We'll sure as hell see about that, we'll sure as hell see." He turned and ran away up the long hall. Slowly, Burt picked up his hat, and then slowly turned to Moore. "His gun," Burt said. "He's so crazy, he even forgot his gun."

Moore handed it to him, and Burt stuffed it into his pants. "We'll be good," he said mildly. He turned and walked away down the hall after Ollie.

The room seemed a lot emptier with them gone, and cooler. The freshness, the ease, the peace was coming back. The Cannons got up and moved with their ponderous weight down the room, their big, pink, bland faces gently smiling as usual. They stood smiling down at Bill.

"We haven't had the pleasure, Colonel," one of them said.

"Terry, Alfred, this is Bill Gorham—my new manager."

Terry was the one with the thinner face, the brown eyes that were somewhat amused. Alfred was the truly bland one, with the pale blue eyes. "I'm sure glad you've come in," Terry said.

"Let's have a drink," the Colonel said, and walked off. He came back with a bottle and glasses. "Where's Shaw?"

"I'm right here," Shaw said, out of his corner, and got up. He came waddling over toward them like an old bear.

"Lieutenant," the Colonel said, "join us."

Bill looked around. Pepe was gone. Where, when, he hadn't noticed. Allie, too. Just vanished.

They drank in silence.

Alfred Cannon looked down at Shaw with his blue

eyes. "Mr. Shaw, no use fooling around, you're the first on our list. That right, Lieutenant?"

Aberforth was tired—more, he was weary. He felt Allie's absence like salt in a wound. He cared nothing for these men or these times. He was tired of life, because life had stung him in the depths of his simplicity. The black wasp hovered over him and he did not dare look at Gorham, for fear Gorham would see what was in his mind. How nobly she had defended Gorham, with what coolness and precision she had walked into this circle of men and pinned Murphy down so neatly. She would not have done that, except for love. And there was Gorham, standing there, complete, unwounded, unharmed, scot free, easy before these two ponderous men who held half the wealth in the country. Anybody the Cannons accepted, was in, up and over.

"Here's to happiness," Aberforth said bravely, and raised his glass again. "Yes, Mr. Shaw is first on our list."

"We start from here, on Sunday noon," Alfred Cannon said, his amused brown eyes looking down on Simon Shaw. "I hope to God you won't put us to the test, Mr. Shaw. Might as well have it out. Pork barbecue, isn't it, Colonel? Pork barbecue and beef sandwiches, whisky and bottled beer, and then we take out after the dogs. Why don't you join us, Mr. Shaw?"

"Don't be too cocky, boys," Shaw said quietly. "I've run the britches off many a sheriff before now, and I can run them off you too."

The Cannon brothers laughed, big and hearty.

"Colonel," Shaw said, "let me give you some advice. Don't drink too much water, because a bullet in a full belly can blow you right apart; and keep your dogs on a chain, or they might be taken in snares."

He turned and walked straight away down the hall, the Colonel's bottle of whisky bumping in his coat pocket.

In the silence, Bill said, "Roast pork and beef sandwiches."

"You are with us, then," Alfred Cannon said, looking down blandly at Bill.

"You don't expect me to do any shooting," Bill said.

"No," Alfred Cannon said. "That's the soldiers' job."

"Good enough," Bill said. "I will be on hand, and I'll eat a pork and beef sandwich; and I shall ride with you, as far as you go and as long as you want."

"Be seeing you," Alfred said casually, and waving a hand at the rest, walked out with his brother behind him.

Bill heard Allie talking to them down the hall. "Don't be alarmed, gentlemen," she said gaily, "Manuel has taken your horses to the barn." And then she came back up the hall. She looked around at the men—her father, Bill, the Lieutenant and Moore, standing glumly in silence.

"Why," she said, "you seem depressed. Tired? Had a long, hard day?" There was something very gay about her, Bill thought.

"Your little friend," she said to Bill, slipping up and meekly suppressing her internal good feeling in front of his glum looks, "is going to stay with Manuel. I hope he will stay on here, Bill. I know you're fond of him."

Aberforth was looking at her as though from behind invisible bars. In one afternoon, he seemed to have wasted slightly.

"And you, Dick," she said, turning away from Bill swiftly and sailing up to Aberforth, putting her fin-

gers under his lapels and dusting his cravat lightly
with a swift, intimate and possessive gesture that
made Aberforth suddenly dizzy with reprieve. "Are
you and Bill going to be friends? You are, aren't you?"
The Colonel looked at the wallpaper and smiled.

"You can sleep in the tackroom, Bill," he said.
"There's a couch there."

"Why not Manuel's?" Bill said. He felt very far
away from Pepe, suddenly. It had not occurred to
him that Pepe would have to be relegated to the servants' quarters. "Has Manuel set up a color bar
against Americans, or something?"

"Bill," the Colonel said, "let's not make too much
out of it."

"If I had my way, I'd have him here in the house.
If you want a gentleman, you will hardly find a better
one than Pepe. I'm perfectly happy in the tackroom,
to preserve the morals of the county, but Pepe is—"
He stopped.

"Poor boy," Allie said. "Why can't we fight in the
morning? I have to take your bedding down to the
tackroom now, so if you'll pardon me—" She waved
her fingers at them and ran out.

The Colonel said, "Certainly Pepe understands the
situation as well as we do."

"No doubt," Bill said. He felt like a dog, beginning
to bristle instinctively at the Lieutenant, who had not
said a word. Why was the fellow all ears that way?
"Lieutenant, perhaps you will stay the night and join
me in the tackroom? I'm sure there's room on the
couch for two."

"Certainly," Aberforth said, suddenly wooden.
"I'll say good night, Colonel. Moore, will you ride
along into town with me?"

"I'm going the other way," Moore said, and looked

at Bill in such a way that Gorham's anger died. Aberforth went on down the hall.

"I'll get a new bottle," the Colonel said. "There's nothing like three or four nightcaps." He went out toward the kitchen.

"Just a word, Bill," Moore said. "You're going to have to keep your mouth shut. You understand that, don't you?"

Bill said nothing. He was looking down at the piece of embroidery Allie had left on her chair.

"Don't make it more difficult for Pepe," Moore said. "I like loyalty, but let's play it right. Get the chip off."

Bill stood silent.

"If you're going to sign up with me in the morning you're going to have to change. You're going to have to eat crow for a good many years. Keep your mouth shut and your head down."

"Thanks," Bill said, "for the advice."

"I'm thinking about Pepe," Moore said. "I don't give a damn about you. You're a lucky little upstart who's got two good friends willing to gamble on him. Pepe's got nothing. He hates this town. I can't understand why he doesn't hate the people, but he doesn't. He just hates the town, it's like death to him, to bow his head and take it, here. Don't make him an issue. Spare him that. Don't parade around as a friend of the poor, and end up having your enemies throw rocks at him because they're sick of you."

They stood looking at each other in silence.

"The way I hear it," Moore said in his big, quiet voice, "is that Pepe picked you up somewhere half dead and put you on your feet. I don't know exactly why. Do you?"

"No," Bill said.

"You aren't the only bum he's picked out of the gutter," Moore said. "Just the biggest."

"Are you looking for trouble?"

"Go ahead," Moore said. "Get sore. But keep your mouth shut and don't lose your temper. You understand?" All this was quiet, but the words came like fists, big and heavy.

Bill said nothing. He was too angry to trust himself to speak.

"Knuckle under, Gorham," Moore said. "Take it. No more running away. You understand?"

Bill lifted his face. "Who the hell do you think you are?"

"I'm your friend," Moore said. "You think this is tough to take, wait till one of your enemies gets to you."

Moore turned and went out down the hall, moving quietly.

When Allie got down to the barn with her armful of blankets, it was empty. She made Bill's bed on the couch, her heart warm and happy. She did not see Pepe quietly enter the barn; but she did see Aberforth through the window, a moment later. Then she heard Aberforth's voice through the wall of the tackroom.

"Get my horse," Aberforth said to Pepe, drawing on his gloves. The lanterns gleamed in the barn, and the soft light came back from the whites of horses' eyes along the stalls. Pepe was sitting on a bale of hay. He had been waiting for Bill. He continued to sit, now, looking at the Lieutenant's feet.

"I said, get my horse and tighten up the girth," the Lieutenant ordered, his voice calm.

"Pardon me, *señor*," Pepe said, his eyes still on the ground, "but I believe you are mistaking me for Manuel. Manuel is the servant here. I am a guest."

Allie sat quiet, listening to the voices through the wall. She felt a growing coldness of fear. This was an Aberforth she did not know, the calm, strained quality of brutality held in check.

"You are a Mexican, aren't you?" Aberforth asked quietly. "Get out my horse before I report you to the Colonel."

Pepe's face looked pained for a moment. "I do not believe you understand, *señor*," he said. "You see, I am a friend of *Señor* Gorham's. I am just waiting for him."

"Mr. Gorham has no Mexican friends," Aberforth said. "I know you are one of Colonel Pringle's servants, and I know enough about Mexican servants to know how insolent they can be. Now get up off that bale of hay and get out my horse. Or would you rather I reported this to the Colonel tomorrow?"

"You are returning tomorrow, *señor*?" Pepe asked.

"I come here every day," Aberforth said. "Come on, get up."

This was the way it always was, there was no surprise in it, no grief, no hurt, just weariness. This, along with everything else, with the Rurales, the government of Diaz, the beating of his mother, the jailing of the priest, all these mistakes of identity.

"*Señor*," Pepe said, "I would not cause any trouble. I will get your horse. Which one is yours?"

"The bay there," the Lieutenant said, quite calm, fully composed, and complacent at his success.

Pepe got out the bay and tightened up the girth, and held the horse by the bridle while the Lieutenant prepared to mount. The Lieutenant had not asked him for a hand up, at any rate. That was something.

"Give me a hand up, will you?" the Lieutenant asked. Perfectly civil and even in tone. "I'm a little stiff in the legs."

Pepe stood there, suddenly full of an immense fatigue. The Lieutenant would go to the Colonel with his complaint, and it would cause the Colonel embarrassment. Better by far to oblige; because in the end, it would all react on Bill. Bill would get angry and make a great uproar.

All this went through his mind in an instant as he stood patiently looking at the earth, at the straw and manure on the floor. What he had to do was to abide, to endure, until he saw that Gorham was going to fit in again, and not go wild.

"As you say, *señor*," Pepe said quietly. "I am sorry for your stiffness."

He cupped his hands and half-crouched, bracing his forearms on his thighs, and watched distantly while the Lieutenant raised his boot with its clots of manure and straw, and put his foot in the cupped hands. The Lieutenant thus mounted and adjusted himself complacently in the saddle.

Pepe stood back, his hands, wet with filth, hanging at his sides. A good servant would make no move to clean them in the presence of the Lieutenant. A good servant was not supposed to mind such things.

"I am sorry if I have caused the Lieutenant any inconvenience," Pepe said.

"Forget it," Aberforth said generously. If he was any judge of human nature, by tomorrow, this Pepe would be gone, which was what he wanted. If Gorham and the Mexican were so thick, a break between them might be a move to get Gorham off the place. He touched his horse with his heel and moved out into the night.

Pepe stood in the dim, soft light, with the dung on his hands. He thought of an eagle in the sky, of the mountains, of timber, of dead fallen trees, of quiet, of snow, of water in small streams, of alpine flowers.

That, up there, far away from men, was all that was left of the creation of God as He had wished it. Everything else, the cruelty, the shame, the perfidy and the stupidity, was the creation of man, the faithless creature.

He looked down at his hands. The horse, who had made this dung, would not have done what the man had done.

He heard somebody coming down the path and went over quickly to the water trough. He washed his hands quickly and turned to see Moore getting out his horse.

"How is it?" Moore asked.

Pepe shrugged.

"If you get tired of it here, I have the job for you in the livery," Moore said.

"Maybe," Pepe said. "I will think about it."

EIGHTEEN

ALLIE SAT QUIET on the sagging couch, looking at her hands. In the barn, after Moore's departure, no sound but the horses, nothing from the little Mexican.

Why had he taken it? She felt contempt; if he was so servile, so cowardly, as to take that kind of thing from Aberforth, then he deserved what he got.

At the same time, she was furious with Aberforth. She would not have thought Aberforth could be so deliberately, coldly abusive. And then it occurred to her that of course, Aberforth must have known Pepe was not a servant. Aberforth had seen Manuel numbers of times, every day, he knew Serafina, and he knew the Colonel had no other servants. What on earth could have been his reason for abusing Bill's friend? Could it be some incredible reflection of jealousy?

In her mind there was nothing but confusion. She was much like Bill, in that thought translated too quickly into action. At the same time, she was collected enough to wonder why she did not feel more sympathy for Pepe, and then, on the impulse to run away from the answer, she caught herself and quietly forced herself to recognize the reason: she was jealous of Pepe.

All at once all kinds of reasons filled her mind, for abhorring him. It was unbecoming of Bill to have Mexican friends, it lowered her, it lowered her father, it lowered Bill, and yet, in confusion and the beginnings of grief, she saw where this line would end—in the denigration of the very person she loved. It could not be quite true, that Pepe, if he were Bill's best friend, was an ignoble creature.

She took a deep, tired breath and sighed it out, stood up and went to the tackroom door. She opened it and looked out through the barn. Pepe was still sitting there, looking up at her from his bale of hay, genuine surprise on his face.

He stood up and took off his hat. The surprise warmed into a smile.

"Good evening, Miss Pringle," he said, carefully avoiding Spanish. "I was waiting for Bill," he said, assuming the obligation of explanations to relieve the embarrassment which he saw in her face, behind her rather stiff and resolute expression.

"I was making Bill's bed."

"And I was sitting here thinking. If I had known, I would have knocked."

She saw it then, he was assuming responsibility for the situation. What had Bill said? A gentleman. Her hostility subsided. Before such self-effacement, what could one do? And if he had guessed her jealousy, or sensed her enmity, where had he learned this gentle art of heaping coals on one's head?

"You are Bill's friend," she said.

He nodded, smiling. "And you too are his friend," he said.

She could hardly be offended. The kindliness of his manner not only recognized her rights, but even abdicated what was necessary of his own. Why had she been jealous? He had, obviously, already given up. This sort of knowledge ran between them like arrows of thought, intuitive, immediate.

She knew instinctively that he was hostile to her way of life, and that he did not want Bill to stay in it; there was something, a sort of aloofness, reserve, caution, unrelaxing integrity about his posture, which made it quite plain that he was alien and was making no effort to change; and yet, he had given in, provisionally. Hence, no doubt, the precise English, the insistence on being taken for what he was, a man of integrity and intelligence. He was forcing her to accept him as he was. The eyes and the smile were what did it; through them, she became aware of the man behind the conventional disguise, and her liking for him, growing quietly out of his rather formal courtesy of manner and consideration for her embarrassment, suddenly warmed quite full.

"Why did you do it?" she asked. "He was rude to you on purpose. Deliberately."

"Yes," he said. "I realized it too, afterwards. He had something in mind. A purpose."

"You need not have taken it," she said, her eyes a little hot. "I assure you, if I had realized—if Bill had known—if my father had been aware—"

He lifted four fingers of one hand slightly, enough to excuse her from further excuses. "It would be better if Bill did not find out," he said. "Better for Bill. You understand. Bill, he feels too much. He gets angry too easily."

"Thank you," she said, "but I know Bill quite

well." Complaisance from this little man was one thing—advice another. "You're not going to stay. I can see that."

"No, I don't think so," he said. "I am not a Manuel." He gave a long, heavy sigh. "I do not think you can do it," he said, his eyes dropping for the first time. "I do not think any woman can do it."

"You mean," she said, "keep him from blowing up again."

"If he loves you enough, maybe."

She colored a little. "I can take care of him."

He smiled at her. It was a woman's most common and most fatal delusion, that she could take care of a man, as though care solved everything. "You won't mind if I wait until Sunday," he said. "All I want him to do is—"

"Is to be happy," she said, smiling.

His face suddenly died and dulled with heavy fatigue. He looked down. "No, no. To endure. I don't think he will ever be happy. To be happy is to want nothing and to accept misery. He runs away, and he never sees that there is no place to go. He is too healthy. Sometimes a sour stomach is as good as a level head—but he has neither. If he were a cripple, he would have to sit in a chair and face things."

"You are exaggerating, I think," she said coolly. An iciness of sudden, intense dislike, of resentment, thrust out of her. "Perhaps you don't like finding yourself indispensable."

He was suddenly cut off from her. They stood there, strangers. He smiled. "I did not mean to be discourteous." He did not say it, though he knew it: that to pursue an idea in the presence of a woman was the basic insult.

She heard Bill's footsteps coming down the path,

but that was not the reason she did not respond. She looked at Pepe now as a might-have-been friend.

Bill came down into the light, his face set and determined. He saw them standing there and suddenly smiled, surprised.

Pepe turned. He said, before Bill could speak, ''I am going to work in town, Bill.''

Bill said, ''You had better stay with me. This is a good place, Pepe. You won't have any trouble with Murphy here.''

''All the same, Bill,'' Pepe said quietly, ''I think it would be better in town.''

Bill looked at Allie. ''Has anything happened?'' His voice was sharp. ''Has anybody shot off his big fat mouth about greasy Mexicans or something?''

''No, no,'' Pepe said, ''nothing of the kind. I am being careful, Bill, that is all. Besides, you know, I could not stay here forever.''

''The hell you can't,'' Bill said. ''You can stay here for the rest of your life.''

''It is a thought,'' Pepe said, and went to get his horse. ''Until we finally decide, I think I will work in town.''

He pulled up the cinch, mounted, and waving, rode out of the barn into the dark.

Bill stood looking after him.

''Bill,'' she said, smiling at him.

''He can't go, just like that.''

''He's only going to town,'' she said.

He said nothing, looking up the dark drive.

''Bill,'' she said again.

He turned slowly and looked at her.

''Well,'' she said, ''I'm here. And I love you.''

His face changed completely, the set stiffness softening, warmth rising from his heart. ''I'm glad to know it," he said. "That's all I wanted. For us to get married. Maybe that's the answer."

"If you can stand it," she said, smiling, trying to make a joke, trying not to be serious about it.

"I'll stand it, if they don't come any worse than the Cannons."

"Goodbye forests, goodbye mountains," she said. "Goodbye outlaws, goodbye all that. Do you think you can stand peace for a change? Call off the war?"

"Sure," he said. He started to take her in his arms, and in the dark, up the drive, the mastiffs suddenly began roaring with fury and smashing against the fence.

He froze, turning, facing the dark, listening, shocked still with instinctive fear, as the great dogs howled and moaned with helpless rage as Pepe, invisible, went by. And suddenly he knew that there was another dark, invisible, even in the brightest sky, the hottest noon. All hell could stand by, watching, and he would never even know it. He stood silent, looking at the dark around them. What else was there, besides the two great beasts, forgotten, but waiting, always ready—what other beasts?

In the dark, outside, leaning against the front of the barn, just a few feet away from the door, Lieutenant Aberforth waited and listened. What were they doing? He could see nothing.

He could not bear to think of it, that she might be in Gorham's arms. The dogs roared and howled in agony, and his insides contracted in another agony as he fought away the images of what might be going on. Everything inside him was tied into a dreadful, drawing knot, dragging him down. He could not forget that she had been his—or almost, anyway.

They were coming out. He shrank against the

boards, breathless. God help him if they glanced back.
Stuck there against the boards, like an insect, he
trembled with horror.

But they went on, toward the house, and he collapsed with relief. He stood there for a moment,
sweating and limp, exhausted, weak, dried out and
full of loathing. For what? Not himself, but merely for
the world around him. Aberforth was in love, he
thought. Actually, the only thing left that he loved
was the picture of himself as beloved. There were
times, interludes in his anguish, when, like a sufferer
who lies lax and lucid between agonies, he saw it all
for what it was, when he hated not them, or himself,
but simply his situation; when he almost saw that he
was merely the victim of circumstances, like a second-
ary character in a novel. Was he, after all, merely the
victim of a cliché which he had imposed on himself?

He had the kind of mind which was fascinated by
the merely appropriate—lost in the hinterlands of the
West, alone among barbarians, a distinguished and
cultured young officer, happening upon a lonely, attractive and genteel young woman, was it not all too
appropriate that they should fall in love? He could
not escape the simple trammels of the trite. If he had
been posted to some remote camp with one married
superior officer, he would have run all the risks of
adultery simply because it was appropriate to the circumstances.

So he suffered in the grip of a fiction, because he
could not let go of the situation without seeing himself as possibly not the most desirable of men. The
fact was that Aberforth, if he had been less well
brought up, would have been a thorough lecher, because there again, he could not imagine a relationship
between a man and a woman which did not, eventually, end in bed. For him, every story must have a

happy ending, and every hero must be rewarded by the most palpable of goods. In all the operettas he had sat through, he had never once seen a hero take a hearty laugh at himself and give up a woman he did not really half-want; to do so was almost immoral.

Pepe, observing the Lieutenant from the bushes, was dryly amused. He had come across Aberforth's horse—the concealment had been so clumsy that Pepe, accustomed to some subtlety in horse-hiding, had almost tripped over the animal. But as the Lieutenant crept away through the dark, the amusement died and a subtle alarm was born; Pepe saw that at some time recently, in the heart of an over-simple man, duplicity had been born, and there was no telling, once this had happened, where it would end.

Allie and Bill were standing before the front door of the house, in a shaft of light from inside. Aberforth, struck by something in their attitude, paused and watched them. Were they arguing? Could Gorham's gestures possibly be interpreted as desperate pleading? His heart lifted slightly with hope. In any case, Gorham would be coming back to the barn, to sleep, in a moment. Aberforth started to creep away again, and suddenly froze.

Gorham had taken Allie, stiff and resisting, in his arms. He kissed her. In Aberforth there rose an anger he did not know he possessed—a horrible, helpless, swelling mixture of panic and rage. He took a step forward, his fists clenched; and suddenly he saw Allie wilt, and her arms go around Gorham's neck and cling; and into his rage shot a terrible despair.

There they stood, locked together in the light. He stood fixed in terrible confusion of fury. His hands opened and came up in a helpless gesture; and then the two parted. Allie turned abruptly. She went into the house; but the light continued to stream out on Gorham.

Now that Allie was gone, all Aberforth's mind fixed on Gorham in simple hate. A light went on in a room above—Gorham stepped back and looked up smiling, and it seemed to Aberforth that the exposed throat was meant to be a point of aim. He did not think—instinctively he knew that the circumstances were perfect. His own horse was close by, he was thought to have gone long ago; Gorham had a dozen enemies who would be blamed. He simply acted without thought, his hand unconsciously and automatically going to his pistol, pulling it out. He cocked it softly. He raised the gun, aimed and then hesitated—the body of Gorham found on the front steps was all wrong. Better to catch him as he came down the path.

Gorham, smiling in the light, turned, and Aberforth's finger began to tighten on the trigger. Gorham again stopped and looked upward with that infuriating smile of complacent victory. And something touched Aberforth gently on the left ear.

He turned and looked into the muzzle of a pistol, two inches away from his eyes. With the shock, his rage and fury dropped away, leaving a vacuum of fear. Behind the sights of the pistol were the quiet eyes of the little Mexican.

"You had better leave, *señor*," Pepe whispered. No smile—perfect calm. "Your horse is over here." Not a quiver in the pistol. Aberforth had never seen anything so steady. The blood left his face and his eyes blurred; a fit of trembling weakness in his stomach and his knees. He opened his mouth—to speak—nothing came except a rough sigh.

He felt his own pistol leave his hand with a gentle tug. Pepe lowered his. "*Señor*," Pepe said. "I have seen this tonight. I will be careful to tell a few close

friends about it. If anything happens to Gorham, you
will be killed. Do you understand?''

Aberforth looked at him. So simple, so quiet, no
elaboration. And suddenly he imagined others behind the Mexican: Ollie, Shaw, Stafford, Burt, and
fifty others without faces, standing in a silent league.
''Yes,'' he said quietly, ''I understand.''

''Now go away,'' Pepe said, and handed him his
gun and, out of the dark, a set of reins. ''Before you
are seen.''

Aberforth looked at the gun, again in his hand. It
seemed to be a highly dangerous weapon. He put it
quickly back in its holster. ''Yes,'' Aberforth said. He
was cold; his stomach was a stone. As he rode quietly
away, fear of the Mexican behind him crawled up on
his back and settled down permanently.

NINETEEN

"HERE," MADDY SAID, and threw a roll of bills on the table. "Go get your teeth and let's get drunk. I don't know where Murphy and Fisher are. This is their regular night, they got a franchise on the dump, you know? But, hell, if they ain't coming, we may as well have some fun."

Ollie looked at the money without taking it. He was sitting with his elbows on the kitchen table, holding his head up with his hands beside his temples, like blinders on a horse. The light from the single coal-oil lamp shone clean on the fake damask oilcloth. Burt sat opposite him, sideways to the table, one leg crossed over the other, eating potato chips out of a bowl.

"So now I'm a lousy pimp," Ollie said.

"I thought we was going to get married," Maddy said. "You ain't a pimp, you're just a husband."

"Take the money," Burt said. "We got to get out of town. I don't want no job in no butcher shop."

"Shut up," Ollie said. "I ain't a lousy pimp." He looked sick. He got up and began wandering restlessly around the room. "Where's that Harvey? I'm beginning to think he's the only one that's got any brains."

In the front of the house they could hear the three other girls laughing, knocking themselves out with dirty jokes.

"Go on in there," Ollie said to Maddy, jerking his head toward the parlor.

"What're you up to now?"

"Never mind," Ollie said, looking at her in a tough way he had never used before. "What you don't know won't hurt you."

In a way, she felt a new respect for him. He was changing fast. The smile was gone, he looked pinched, and he looked mean. Maybe he was on to something better than cows; if he was, let him go to it. She didn't have much saved besides the money on the table. The way the crummy crooked Sheriff worked it, you had just enough to keep going and no real profits, just a lot of money coming in and all going out. It had taken her a long time to get hold of enough money to set up a house, and she wasn't going to leave it for nothing. The whole difference between living as a decent madam and living as a common hustler was simply a thousand bucks in capital and a little common sense.

"All right, Ollie," she said. "I'll leave this one to you." One thing sure, he was fast. He moved fast, he thought fast and he hardly ever hesitated. That was a good thing, if things were set up right, and if they weren't, it would end you up dead.

She turned and walked out of the room, closing the kitchen door behind her.

The outside screen door whined open, and Harvey stepped in with a match in his mouth.

"Where the hell you been?" Ollie said.

"I was waiting across there by the stable for her to go out," Harvey said. "I can't come in here with one of them around." He nodded at the racket beyond the parlor door.

"You got ideals," Ollie said.

"You sure as hell turned sour," Harvey said.

They sat looking at each other across the table, with Burt shoving potato chips into his mouth, munching along like a cow. "It's his teeth, Harvey," Burt said placidly. "He ain't got the money for his teeth and he won't leave town without them."

"There's forty thousand bucks in that bank, over Sunday and Monday," Harvey said. He spoke in a low voice, and he was sweating. "You give it any thought?"

"I give it plenty thought," Ollie said, his eyes steady, his face thin and cold. "You're right, I turned sour. I cut out the horsecrap, is all. I'm sick of playing around and getting kicked for a fare-thee-well. That bugging Gorham, now he's a manager of a lousy ranch. That stuck-up son of a bitch, that phony. And me and Burt, with an old broken-down saddle apiece to take home and think over. There's one thing for sure, it can't be no harder knocking down a bank than it was getting the cash out of old Nulty tonight. I never seen such a mess. Never. Crime's getting so lousy complicated you might as well turn honest."

"The thing is," Harvey said, "if we bring off a haul like that in the bank, we could sit easy for years."

"Yeah," Ollie said. His eyes were on something beyond the kitchen wall, far away. He had to graduate. The kidding days were over. He looked at Harvey. "What time is the funeral?"

"Eleven. Sunday."

"All right," Ollie said. "We'll knock it over at eleven sharp, when they're all out there listening to the preacher spout off. Where's the money?"

"In the vault," Harvey said, his eyes lowered.

"What's the vault like?"

"It's steel. It's a good one, at least I think so. Got a wheel on the front and those little teeth that come out and stick in the frame, you know what I mean?"

Ollie grinned tightly. "You sure know a hell of a lot about vaults, don't you. Little teeth sticking out."

"Little teeth is all I know. The hell with it."

"Don't get your whatnot hot, Harvey," Burt said, munching along. "I had a friend worked on that vault when they put it in. I know all about it. Two years ago. Name of Mereno. The front is good, it's supposed to be set in the front of a concrete room, but they didn't have no concrete or something, so all it is is just brick. The back of the vault is the same brick wall you can see back on the alley. Same wall."

"You mean just one brick wall? What about a lining?"

"I don't know," Burt said. "Maybe it's got some kind of tin lining, just to fool the customers. I never been in it. Somehow, I don't think so. If there was, Mereno would of said so. He worked on it, building the brick room in the back corner there. So he knows."

Ollie smiled for the first time. "You ever worked with black powder?" he asked Harvey.

"No," Harvey said.

"I did," Burt said. "Simple as blowing yourself up. All you need is a twenty-five-pound can of powder and we can blow the back right offen the building. Hell, it ain't nothing but three rows of bricks and the mortar's so rotten you can pick it out like picking your teeth.''

''Where we going to get the powder?'' Ollie said.

''Steal it, I guess, Saturday night. Powder, and some fuse.''

''Don't forget the matches,'' Burt said calmly, chewing. ''Steal it at the hardware store. Hell, everybody's got black powder.''

''You sure it won't burn the money?'' Ollie asked.

''Never blowed up a bank. But you got to have enough. You ain't going to get in two shots, that's for sure.''

''All right,'' Ollie said, ''Harvey, you go in the hardware store tomorrow and find out where they keep it, fuse and all.''

''Okay,'' Harvey said, his face pale.

''Then me and Burt will sign that lousy agreement in the morning, and go to work tomorrow. Then tomorrow night we steal the powder.'' Ollie watched the thing beyond the wall shrewdly. ''Then we got to have cartridges. Rifle and pistol both. We got to get plenty of them the same time we get the powder. And what else?''

Burt stopped chewing and thought. ''Feed the horses up good tomorrow, plenty oats. Canteens full, plenty food and bedrolls. Where we going? Over to the Blue?''

''Sure,'' Ollie said. ''Roughest country there is. One thing else. We got the soldiers down there to think about. They won't be at the funeral.''

''Suppose we blow up something at the north end of town,'' Burt said, ''something that'll draw them all up there. Something important. like a church. Blow up the Methodist Church, they ain't many Methodists in San Vicente, that way nobody'll get kilt. That'll get all them people out of the plaza.''

"All right," Ollie said. "It'll work, Harvey. It's a cinch."

Harvey tried to smile.

"What's the matter?" Ollie asked. "You scared?"

"Who, me? Hell, no. You sure this thing is going to be exactly at eleven, huh?"

"Right on the nose."

"You let me blow up the church," Harvey said. "Burt, you give me the can of powder all fixed up, and I'll just go up there and light the fuse. Then I meet you at the bank."

"All right," Burt said. "But you better wait near that church in case she don't blow or something. Sometimes them fuses poop out. If it does, you got to shoot it with a rifle."

"All right," Harvey said. "Suits me fine. Then I meet you at the bank."

"Don't you worry about the bank," Ollie said. "As soon as the church blows, the people in the plaza scoot out of there, and we blow the bank. You just be there by the time me and Burt get the dough, boy, because we ain't waiting for nobody."

They sat looking at each other.

"Is that all?" Harvey asked.

"What do you mean, is that all?" Ollie asked. "What the hell more do you want? Another explosion?"

"I mean, it seems so simple."

"It's Annie's funeral," Ollie said. "Any other Sunday, and we'd never get away with it."

Harvey looked kind of sick.

"What's the matter, boy?" Ollie asked. Harvey looked at the table, his face gray.

"I better go see Pimples," he said, and left.

"No guts," Burt said as the door slammed. "Suppose he don't blow the church? Suppose he don't draw off them soldiers? Then we can't blow our end of the town."

"Get a bottle, Burt. Let's take it easy for a change."

"Suppose some bastard shoots us."

"Nobody's going to shoot us," Ollie said, turning up the lamp. "We'll be out of there so quick nobody'll know what happened till we get clear to the mountains. After that, I don't care what they know. There's only one thing worries me, Burt."

"What?"

"My teeth. I can't hit that bank till I get my teeth. I can't leave town without them. That's the one thing I got to do."

Harvey met Sheriff Murphy three blocks up the creek, coming down the road on horseback with two other men. He couldn't make out their faces in the dark, but he could tell Murphy's voice easily enough. "Sheriff Murphy," he said, pulling up.

The other three pulled up short.

"Listen, Sheriff," Harvey said, "who's that with you? I don't want to talk before no strangers."

"This is Shep and this is Mr. Fisher," Murphy said.

"I got some information for you," Harvey said. "Private."

"There's one piece of information I can use," Murphy said. "What's Trevillian going to do? I know he ain't going to stick to that job, it'd kill him. If I knew he was going to skip town, I could arrest him in the act."

"I tell you one thing," Harvey said. "He won't leave town until he's got his teeth, and he's too broke now to get them back from Cameron. But I got something better than that."

Murphy pulled away from the other two, and Harvey went with him under the cottonwoods beside the road.

"How do I know you're not a liar?" Murphy asked when Harvey was through.

"All right," Harvey said, his voice rising in anger. "Let them get away with the money. I don't care."

"What money?" Fisher said, moving his horse closer.

"Your money," Murphy said. "The Gorham gang is planning to bust your bank on Sunday. At eleven."

"The sons of bitches," Fisher said. He was a little tight. "If it wasn't for burying Annie, damn her, I could meet them bastards at the bank and kill them myself. Let's get them now."

"You wait, Buck," Murphy said. "We'll lay for them Sunday morning at eleven. We can sneak back into town and wait."

"That damn, cocky little bastard," Fisher said. "I knew Trevillian in Phoenix, when he was a kid. Always coming around the house raising hell to get in, only fourteen years old, he was. I musta booted him out ten times. And now him, thinking he can bust my bank." He laughed. "Like he used to think he could lay Annie. Where are they, what's-yer-name?"

"Down at Maddy's," Harvey said.

Fisher laughed. "That's a hot one. The only home he ever had. I'll tell you what, Murphy, you let them blow it open, and then gun them down in the street. We got to build a new vault anyway. Let them do the work. And then kill 'em."

"Yeah," Murphy said. "Muntin, I'm mighty suspicious of you. Where you living?"

"In the livery stable. Until you give me that badge. After I get the badge, the Judge will take me in, he says."

"I seen old Simon Shaw bedded down in a stall

there. You got anything to do with him?" Murphy asked suspiciously.

"No, I ain't," Harvey said. "I didn't even know he was there."

"I tell you what," Murphy said, "you turn around and go on back down to Maddy's and tell Trevillian and Burt we're coming. Make 'em stay out of sight. I don't want no trouble with Ollie now. Not till Sunday."

"I ain't going to tell them nothing," Harvey said. "I don't want them to know I talked to you. If this gets out, somebody'll kill me sure as hell. I'll go up by the church and set off the blast in the middle of the street, and run like hell when you shoot them. But don't let on to nobody." He turned and rode off toward town.

"All right," Murphy said. He looked at Shep. "You go on down and tell Ollie to keep clear."

"You know something," Shep said, "I forgot to lock the office."

"Like hell you did," Murphy said. "I can always hear you lying."

"Well, anyway, I got to go back uptown."

"What's the matter?" Fisher asked. "You think you got competition with the Judge's daughter? That pimply little bag. That Muntin must have an in somewhere, if he's going to live there."

Shep laughed. He turned his horse and headed back toward town.

TWENTY

THE CROWD ON the main street was thinning out and the Red Dog was only half full, mostly with far-gone drunks. It was half past two by the time Shep got uptown. The livery was still open. Horses had been shoved out of the barn to make room for people. A dozen men lay in the stalls on clean straw, blankets down, drinking, some of them playing cards.

Shep found old Shaw in the last stall, drinking the last of the Colonel's bottle of whisky all by himself. Shep squatted down and said in a low voice, "I got news for you, Mr. Shaw."

"Uh-huh," Shaw said, not moving a muscle.

"Ollie and Burt are planning a holdup on Sunday. Fisher's bank. Eleven o'clock."

"Uh-huh," Shaw said.

"Harvey Muntin just turned them in to Murphy."

"Is that so," the old man said.

"I thought you'd like to know."

"Why?"

"I thought you and Ollie Trevillian was friends," Shep said.

"So I'm supposed to tell Trevillian?" Shaw asked. "Then what?"

Shep smiled. "So he saves his neck by not pulling the job."

"And then what? Like what are you getting out of it?"

"All right," Shep said, "so they kill Muntin."

"Oh," Shaw said. "That's what you're after. You know what? They're more likely to kill you, or at least Muntin is. When they face Muntin with it, what's going to happen? One way he can prove himself out to them is by shooting the tail off you, son. Ever think of that?"

Shep hadn't. It had seemed logical to him that Shaw would kill Harvey, or tell Ollie.

"I might tell Harvey myself," Shaw said, "that you told on him. Then what?"

The thought was uncomfortable. "Suppose we forget the whole thing," Shep said, standing up.

"I might," Shaw said, "but I'm running out of whisky. For twenty dollars I might just keep my mouth shut."

"Yeah?" Shep said, suddenly getting a mean feeling. "Suppose you go take a flying jump at the moon, you old bastard."

"That'll cost you ten more," Shaw said. "You better be glad I ain't greedy, as old men go. Now, fork over, you son of a bitch, and don't give me no trouble about it. There's a dozen men in town that would hang you with your own guts if you pulled a gun on me, and don't you forget it."

Shep said nothing. He turned on his heel and walked away toward the livery door. As he faced the street and watched men coming and going, he stopped and thought.

The old bastard was telling the truth about his friends. A murderous rage rose in Shep's head. He dug his hand in his jeans and pulled out his whore-money, which he had got from fines taken off four drunks that afternoon. He pulled off thirty dollars and went back to Shaw's stall. Shaw was still sitting there with the bottle.

"I thought you'd get smart," Shaw said, taking the money. He waited till Shep had gone, then got his horse out of the corral, bought a fifth of bourbon at the Red Dog, and rode down to Maddy's. He found Ollie and Burt in the stable. "You ain't got much sense, Ollie," he said, handing him the fifth, "but if you're going to knock over the bank, you better move the time back to ten o'clock. Murphy knows."

Ollie stiffened in his chair, his eyes fixed on Shaw's.

"Don't look so scared," Shaw said. "No harm done."

"Who told him?" Ollie said, standing up.

"Harvey. Least, so Shep says."

"I'll kill that little son of a bitch."

"Which one?"

"Harvey."

"Wouldn't be worth your time," Shaw said.

"For crissake, what for?" Ollie cried. "What's he get that's worth a cut of that bank?"

"The Judge's daughter's tail," Shaw said affably. "That's worth a hundred thousand, over the years, I would guess."

"That's why he was so scared," Burt said stolidly. "Not of the robbery. Of us."

"I'll have to kill him," Ollie whispered.

"Waste of time," Shaw said. "The harm's done. Killing him will do no good at all. Like I told you, just move the time up to ten o'clock. Let the bastards get all set to nab you at eleven. You'll be gone. But if you kill Harvey, you'll just wise Murphy up that you know. Just sit tight, and change the time. That's all.'' He laughed. ''Besides, what do you think Murphy's going to do to Harvey when you get away? Don't get too drunk on that bottle.'' He went out and climbed aboard his horse.

Over in the house, Fisher, sitting in the front parlor, with the two new girls standing opposite him, pulled a small coil of leather thong out of his pocket.

''What's that?'' Murphy said, slightly alarmed. Everything Fisher did alarmed him a little, you never knew what to expect. Fisher shook the thongs out—a three-tailed cat. ''Better than shoelaces,'' Fisher said. ''Nulty would like this.''

Shep came in, and Murphy glanced at him. ''What's the matter with you?''

''Nothing,'' Shep said, his face heavy and sullen. Shaw would blab. The cat was out of the bag—they'd never hit the bank now. And what if it got back to Murphy, who had told? Murphy would kill him. ''I heard a rumor. I heard Ollie was planning to leave town tomorrow. This bank robbery was just a lie, to get us off guard until Sunday. Tomorrow they skip.''

''A rumor?'' Fisher said. ''You keep him in town tomorrow. I want to get him on this bank job. Good. Too crazy to be a rumor.''

''Suppose it is, though,'' Murphy said. ''No robbery.''

''You fix it so we win both ways,'' Fisher said.

''Get his teeth,'' Murphy said. ''Muntin said he wouldn't leave town without those teeth.''

''Get them now,'' Fisher said. ''Then, no matter what he's really planning, we win.''

* * *

Up in his office, Dr. Cameron was working quietly on Ollie's plate, a much easier job than he had let on to Ollie. He enjoyed working late at night, with quiet in the streets, and no movement anywhere in the light of the lamp except that of his own fingers. It was after three, and everybody had gone to bed or passed out. At such times, in the peace of such quiet, he lost himself in his work. It was almost like working in the lab back in Philadelphia once again, back in the drowsy security of Chestnut Street.

Cameron's one mistake had been stealing five hundred dollars' worth of gold from that lab—gold used for crowns and other castings. Just a simple case of long-term opportunity and gradually eroding resistance. New Mexico was almost safe—and almost unbearable.

But laudanum helped. Once in a long while he would put the neck of the laudanum bottle in his mouth and swallow a teaspoonful or so. The beauty of it was that, unlike whisky, it left your brain clear. Peace, safety, security, above all, clarity in a confused and jumbled world.

Heavy steps came up the stairs from the street. He stopped working, and stared at the wall with a faint smile, wondering, without alarm, who that could be at this late hour. Surely not Trevillian?

A fist banged on the door, and he was faintly amused. He got up from his stool, went out into the ante-room, and opened the door into the hall. Sheriff Murphy, a reliable fellow, and one of his fine, up-standing young assistants. They weren't, obviously, going to arrest him. Opium made it quite clear, in the absence of tension, that nobody would ever get out of bed at three in the morning to arrest anybody for

stealing five hundred dollars' worth of gold or anything else.

"Yes, Sheriff?" Cameron asked pleasantly, ushering
them in.

"You got a set of teeth belonging to Ollie Trevillian?" Murphy asked.

Cameron slowly lifted both eyebrows in mild, so-
phisticated surprise—purely rational surprise, without
alarm. He smiled with faint amusement. "Yes, I have.
I'm working on them now."

"You wouldn't mind giving them to me," Murphy
said. "For a few days."

"He's expecting them tomorrow," Cameron said,
completely unmoved. "What would I tell him? How
would I explain?"

"You wouldn't," Murphy said. "You'll go home.
Or out of town, for a few days. That would be safer,
all around. Take a trip to El Paso. Go have a good
time."

Cameron blinked.

"I need the teeth," Murphy said patiently, boring in. "You are going to give me the bloody teeth.
Even if Trevillian shoots you. You know that, don't
you?"

"Yes," Cameron said. "Very well, Sheriff. I will
take a trip, and I suppose El Paso will have to do."
He turned toward the lab. "Since there's no place
else within a thousand miles."

He picked up the plates, put them in a small box,
and handed them to the Sheriff. "He'll be very angry," Cameron said with perfect calm.

"It don't matter," Murphy said, taking the box and
heading for the door. "By the time you get back, he'll
be dead." The door slammed behind them, shaking
dust from the frame.

Cameron, watching the dust settle, picked up the laudanum bottle and took a good belt of it. One had to be careful, though, if one's capacity were to last. Moderation in all things, the via media, the golden mean—and the dream of gigantic poppies nodding forever in a sunny land of peace.

TWENTY-ONE

ON SATURDAY MORNING the crowds in San Vicente started suddenly to thin out. Most of the wild ones got nervous, grabbed their horses and began to make distance while they could. The trouble was that the worst, like Shaw, refused to leave and it looked like trouble on Sunday. Men who had come in a spirit of adventure, bringing their families, decided prudently to pack up and go back home. The town women postponed their Saturday shopping till after the crisis; the town began to have an empty look.

The gang came in and signed up, and Moore took them around to their jobs, all except Bill, who went down to the Red Dog with the Colonel to meet a few of the Colonel's friends who had come into town for the barbecue the next day.

Moore took Pepe across to the livery and introduced him to the owner, who handed him a broom; and Pepe set to work shoving manure across the slimy clay and pitching the old bedding out of the stalls.

Moore took Burt across the street to Braun's Butcher Shop and left him there; and then took Ollie next door to Johanssen's and left him in charge of the old man—not so old, actually, but old-looking because of his pallor, his ringlets of gray hair, and his cynical expression.

"You know anything about butchering?" Braun asked Burt. He nervously jabbed parsley at the lamb chops. He didn't believe in reform. He believed in predestination, although he was decent enough to feel sorry about it.

"Used to kill hogs for my uncle," Burt said, smiling pleasantly.

"Good. I got one hog in the ice box now, the Colonel's hog. Colonel Pringle. He ordered the whole hog special, for the barbecue. The hide's on yet. Do something, Mr. Burt." He gave Burt a lantern and a knife, and Burt went into the ice box, blinking like an owl. He stood in the cold, dark room, peering around.

"Over there!" Braun said. "Watch out for Mrs. Fisher—she is on the bottom shelf on the left, under the sausages. Don't slop nothing on her."

He slammed the door, and Burt jumped. He looked around, not for the hog, but for Mrs. Fisher. It was awesome, being in there with all the bodies hanging around. First he saw the hog, a black and white one not yet reduced to the great anonymous army of the skinned. Beyond the hog, four sides of beef were hanging in the gloom. He half expected to see Mrs. Fisher hanging beside them. He was relieved to find her, wrapped up in a sheet, lying where Braun had said, on her back. At least he supposed it was Mrs. Fisher. The sheet was over her face, too.

He stood there gnawing at his lip, with the lantern in one hand and the knife in the other. An ungovernable curiosity slowly rose in him. This was supposed to be the great Annie Fisher, about whom he had heard so much from Ollie, but was it? Suppose, instead, it was an Unknown Colored Man? He had no way of knowing, unless he looked, and the longer he gnawed at his lip, the more he wanted to look.

He crept over to the shrouded body and leaned over. Very gently, he lifted the end of the sheet, pulled it back, and held the lantern close.

Yes, it was Annie Fisher, red hair and all. And she was looking right at him, with big dead blue eyes and a big, dead red grin on her mouth. Burt shuddered, his eyes rolled up and he turned away in panic. Even in death, she could not lose the habit of invitation. He burst out of the ice room and stood shaking in front of Braun.

"What's the matter?" Braun asked.

Burt swallowed. "It's cold," he said.

"So it's cold, so it's an ice room, so go skin the pig," Braun said reasonably. "I can do it, you can do it." He even smiled. He always felt sorry for the damned.

Burt sighed, turned around and went back in. He stood in the gloom, looking at the pig. One thing for sure, it wasn't going to last long. One day of butchering, and they'd be gone. He went over to the pig, set down the lantern, and began to skin it. He began to dream about spare ribs. His mouth began to water. He remembered seeing some bolognas on the shelf above Annie. He went over and cut himself off a hunk of liverwurst and stood chewing it meditatively, looking down at Annie. Would it be so bad the second time, he wondered? He pulled the sheet back and took another look. There she was, laughing at him. Eyes like strangled oysters. He finished the liverwurst, and suddenly had a pronounced thirst for a shot of

whisky. Johanssen's was next door, just beyond the
big connecting door. Ollie could get him a drink.

He lifted the latch and opened it quietly. He could
hear Ollie and somebody else talking somewhere in
the shop.

From where he stood, peering through the crack,
he could see a casket standing on a couple of trestles,
surrounded by shavings, sawdust and odd sheets of
worn-out garnet paper. Johanssen must have been
finishing it just now—Burt could smell the shellac and
the powerful smell of the alcohol it was cut with. He
waited, but the talking went on and on. Finally, sigh-
ing, he shut the door and went back to the pig. He
slowly worked away, first skinning a little, and then
trying a bit of braunschweiger, then skinning a little,
then a bit of hard salami. It wasn't a bad life. If he
only had a drink, he would have been perfectly
happy. He might even have been singing.

"So you think you want to be a carpenter," Johanssen said to Ollie. "What would you do? There's
a big trade in coffins and you could help build up
business with a line of gibbets."

"Who said I want to be a carpenter?" Ollie asked.

"How long you going to keep this job?" Johanssen
asked.

"You want me to tell you a lie, or the truth?"

"Is that important?" the old man asked.

"All I want is enough money to get my teeth away
from the dentist, and I leave town."

"Usually it's the other way around," Johanssen
said. "He usually keeps the teeth. Oh, you mean false
teeth. Well, how much money?"

"The bastard wants seventy-five dollars."

"How do you know he is a bastard?" the old man
asked.

"I don't know he's a bastard. But he wants seventy-five dollars," Ollie said, a little impatiently.

"If he wanted a hundred, would that make him a son of a bitch?" Johanssen asked.

"What the hell you getting at?"

"Well, for one thing, which, to you, is worse, a bastard or a son of a bitch? I have often wondered. Like you call somebody a bastard, is he just half a son of a bitch, or is he two sons of bitches? What is your theory?"

Ollie said, "All right, it takes two bastards to make one son of a bitch, and four sons of bitches to make one Buck Fisher."

"It only took Annie Fisher," Johanssen said. "The Great She-Bitch. You know where she is now? Annie?"

"She's dead."

"She's dead on the shelf in the icebox over there," Johanssen said, jerking a thumb at the big door beyond the coffin. "Stiff as a salt herring. Cold as a clam. I ain't fixed her up yet. Got to close her eyes and make her look virtuous, you know; every fathead in town will be wanting to look at her for a quick jolt."

"You got any money?" Ollie asked. "How about lending me enough against my pay to get my teeth?"

"Look, son," Johanssen said, "I like you, and all that, you mean well, you'd even mean to pay me back, but it would get to be something you just thought about once in a while, when you felt generous, or got drunk, now, wouldn't it? And I'm getting old. Whyn't you borrow the money from Fisher? He's right over there in the bank, there. He's loaded with the stuff."

Ollie looked out of the window at the bank, and it

suddenly occurred to him that it would be a good excuse for taking a look at the vault.

"Suppose you gave me the time off?"

"Take it," Johanssen said. "It's Saturday. I don't like working Saturday. All I got to do is put one more coat of shellac on the old bag's coffin, and shut up her eyes and powder her face before Mrs. Quires and Mrs. Bennett come down here with the dress. That's five o'clock. I'm going home to lunch, and you do what you please, Mr. Trevillian. Just don't set fire to the place or something. Oh, and one thing. That dummy of Quires over there got to go back sometime this evening." The old man turned and went out the front, leaving Ollie in the dusky shop. Ollie turned around, and saw the big door to the ice room opening slowly. Horror rose in him, and then he saw Burt's smiling face coming out into the light. In one hand Burt was carrying the lantern, in the other, a sausage. "Hi, Ollie," he said. "You got a drink?"

"No," Ollie said. "But I'm going over to the bank. I'll bring a bottle back with me."

Ollie went out and cut across the street toward the bank. He saw Pepe in the door of the livery, holding a horse for a fat old man who was scolding Pepe for not holding it still enough.

He paused one moment at the door of the bank, and stuffed his shirt in; it was a gesture resulting not from his awe of banks in general, but from his memory of the times he had spit on his hands and slicked back his hair at the front door of Annie Fisher's whorehouse in Phoenix. He went on in and stood in the cool, pleasant dimness, blinking and looking around. It wasn't much of a place—open corral in the middle for the suckers, four barred cages like the front of a tomb. He went up to one of the tellers and said, "I want to see Buck Fisher. Tell him it's little Ollie."

The teller looked at him for a moment, took in the big, flopping dirty hat, the red hair sticking out horizontally over the freckled ears and said, "Just one moment," and added, squeezing down, "sir." He went on back, and Ollie stood there, inhaling deeply the sweet smell of money.

"He will see you, sir," the teller said, coming back, and opened a little gate in the corral for Ollie. Ollie went through, nose lifted like a hound to the money-smell. Looking right at him, through the door of a glassed-in cubbyhole, across a new-fangled flat-top desk, was Buck Fisher, smiling. He had a cigar in his teeth, and his eyes were wide, bright and alert. The atmosphere was more like that of a mountain lion's den, just before breakfast. Fisher was alert, all right. He liked Ollie's audacity, if that was what it was. Nothing like having a man call on you the day before he robbed you and case the joint right under your nose.

"What's on your mind, Ollie?" he asked.

"You sure have come up in the world," Ollie said, looking around.

"Oh, I don't know," Fisher said, sitting back and grinning around the butt of his cigar. "We had it pretty good back in Phoenix."

"I can remember you with a white apron," Ollie said, "and a tray of empty steins, standing in the front door telling me to go to hell."

Fisher laughed. "I'll never forget it, Ollie. Nice to hear from old friends. Lot of Annie's old friends coming over from Phoenix for the funeral tomorrow."

"Oh, yeah," Ollie said. "Forgot to say anything about Annie. Sure sorry to hear about that, Buck."

"Yeah," Buck said. "Drank like a horse. Good way to die, though boy. Conked out like an old cow shot through the head. Hit the floor like a ton of bricks, she did, and never even twitched. Easy death, boy. Hope I die that easy.''

"I hope you do too," Ollie said, looking at him earnestly.

Fisher laughed. He was still dark-haired, probably dyed it. Dark-haired and young looking, tough, hard as an anvil, and pale as death. "You mean, you hope I just die."

Ollie smiled. "Never was no getting past you, Buck."

"You never did make it, did you?" Fisher asked.

"There was one thing I always wished I could say, Buck," Ollie said quietly, his voice throttled in a goiter of fury, "and that was that I had slept with Annie Fisher. I guess it's too late now. Unless you're still peddling her, dead."

Fisher leaned forward in his seat, his eyes bulging, gagged, and then sank back again, the grin stuck on his face as though with pins, all his teeth showing around the cigar butt. He kept the grin there, and after a moment, said, in a tiny, faraway voice, like a man who has been kicked in the stomach, and is just getting his first breath back, "You always were a great wit, Ollie. Good to see you haven't lost the old edge."

"But I never got past you, did I?" Ollie said, not smiling, just looking at the other, down across the desk. "I never made it."

Fisher's grin came unpinned; the muscle strain was too intense for him to hold it up. He sat there, slack-faced, looking at Ollie with eyes dull with hate and contempt. There was something about Ollie that made him just want to kick Ollie's face to pieces. It had been there the first time he had seen him, outside the whorehouse door. The cockiness, maybe.

And there was something in Fisher's face that made Ollie just want to kick Fisher's face to pieces. It had been there the first time he had seen Fisher, inside the whorehouse door, the first time Fisher had slammed it in his face. Maybe the confidence, the certainty, the hard aggressiveness.

"Yes, sir," Ollie said, "I sure can remember you in that apron. Stains and all. How many years was you a pimp, Buck, before you got into the real money?"

Fisher hoisted the smile again, with a block and tackle. It weighed a ton, but he managed it. "Just what did you want, pal?" he asked softly.

"I want to borrow a hundred dollars from your bank," Ollie said. "To get my teeth out of hock."

"Yes, you better get those teeth, Ollie. You look terrible without them. A toothless babe."

Ollie flushed and his eyes dropped.

"But no collateral," Fisher said. "Tell you what, Ollie, I'll give it to you as an act of Christian charity. Won't be the first hundred I've handed to a lousy beggar." He took a bill and held it out to Ollie, between two fingers. Ollie looked at it, his face tight.

"Don't feel like a bum, Ollie, don't feel like a lousy tramp that never even could get inside a third-rate whorehouse. Take it."

Ollie looked into Fisher's eyes. "You know something," he said. "I ain't got no pride. I got something better. A gun." He reached out and took the bill. "Thanks." He grinned, and his gums showed red. He turned to go.

"Don't rush off," Fisher said, rising. "Let me show you my vault."

He took Ollie's arm, to Ollie's surprise, and guided him out of the office. He led him over to the open vault door. Ollie peered inside. It was true, the back wall was plain brick. There wasn't even a tin lining. Fisher was a fool, showing anybody this place, just to boast about his money.

Fisher led him in. "Look there," Fisher said, pointing to a stack of bills on top of a big steel file. "And there." More stacks, on the other side. "And there." Four bars of gold, each the size of a hot dog, each worth maybe five thousand bucks. "Fisher money, Ollie. Pimp money. It's nice to be rich, Ollie, it's worth it, being a pimp for fifteen years and having a whore for a wife. Whyn't you get a whore for a wife, Ollie? You marry Maddy down there, so you can get title to her earnings, so she can't run out."

Ollie turned and walked out, blindly, past the tellers, out the front door.

"Hello," Murphy said, suddenly beside him. Ollie looked at him once, saw Shep behind him, and went on across the street to Cameron's office. He shook Cameron's door, and then banged on the panel.

"Nobody home, I guess," Murphy said quietly, standing behind him. He was fingering Ollie's teeth in his pocket.

Ollie was getting scared. Murphy's smile was odd. "Where does Cameron live?"

"He's out of town," Murphy said. "I think he went to El Paso."

Ollie's fists tightened, and then his hands straightened out again. "I got to get my teeth," he said.

"He'll probably be back Monday. Can't you wait?"

There was something terrible about Murphy's smile. "Don't you like your job?" Murphy asked.

"Sure," Ollie said, his face dead, "I love my new job." He shoved past Murphy and left him standing there.

TWENTY-TWO

OLLIE WENT ON down to the Red Dog for a bottle of bourbon, and there was Bill Gorham, leaning against the bar with Pringle, talking to a couple of well-dressed ranchmen, the kind that had so much money they could afford to be honest, at last.

"Why, hello, there, Ollie," Bill said, smiling, and put out a hand.

"Two fifths of bourbon," Ollie said to George, laying the hundred on the bar, and leaving Bill's hand hanging in the air. The bottles and the change slid across the wood, and Ollie turned his back on Gorham and left.

"He thinks I crossed him up last night," Bill said.

"You're just as well off," the Colonel said mildly.

"You're better off," one of the others said, "without that kind of friend, Gorham, now that you've come over to us. After all, you can't keep both kinds."

Gorham turned, and looked at him. He was a young fellow about Bill's age by the name of Burns, and he stood there with his father, cool, confide. smiling a little with complacent self-righteousness.

"I suppose you're right, Harry," Bill said, keeping his voice very smooth and calm.

"Of course Harry's right," the elder Burns said, helpfully insistent. All was well in the world, as long as the Burns ranch stayed in the black. A good man, who got along with his hands, cheated nobody any more, and hoped to die respected. The kind of man Bill would live with and talk to for the rest of his life. Suddenly an appalling loneliness rose in Bill. "Well," he said, "let's have another." He raised his shotglass and smiled with painful effort. There was one thing you could say for booze, it was a great anesthetic.

Across the street, somebody said in a loud, clear voice, "You lousy, stinking son of a bitch, hold that horse still."

Immediately every eye in the saloon went to the door, every man stiffened. It was the tone, choked with rage.

"*Si, señor,*" another voice said mildly and Bill suddenly set down his glass and walked slowly toward the doors. Outside there was the same dead silence.

"Bill," the Colonel said quietly. "Bill." Bill went on, through the door. The Colonel hurried after him. Bill stopped on the porch and looked across at the livery.

Pepe was holding a big gelding, and a man was trying to mount the horse as it danced and shied around. It was Buck Fisher. The horse had too much life, and Fisher was having a hard time getting his foot in the stirrup. His hat fell off, and he stood back from the horse.

"Damn you," he shouted at Pepe. "Hold that horse still."

"Si, señor," Pepe said, in the same, small, clear voice. His face was empty as death.

Bill went slowly down the steps, out into the middle of the street. He was in a kind of hazy dream state, half his brain in a fog, his head tight enough to burst, the rage swelling huge inside him. He was only remotely aware of his movements; everything seemed very clear before him, as he stood in the street, but somehow far away, detached. At the same time, he knew he should do nothing, nothing at all.

Fisher picked up his hat and jammed it on his head, and grabbing the reins again, seized the horn and thrusting his foot in the stirrup, he tried it again. The horse side-stepped, dancing around Pepe's hold, and Fisher hopped after it on one foot. Suddenly Fisher, in a blind rage, swung at the horse and hit it in the neck, and the horse reared, breaking out of Pepe's hold and turning, barged over Fisher, knocking him down in the dust. The horse cantered away down the street.

Fisher got up. He clouted Pepe across the face. Pepe fell back against the front of the building, blood from his nose running over his mouth.

"Damn you to hell," Fisher shouted in the silence, "you let him go on purpose." He swung again, and Bill was not aware that he had moved before he caught Fisher by the shoulder of his coat and swung him around. Fisher stood there, glaring at Bill, blind with rage, and swung at Bill, and Bill hit him in the face as hard as he could. The knuckle of the third finger of his right hand landed on Fisher's left nostril, fitting neatly. Something in Fisher's face crunched, and Fisher went down, stumbling backward and landing on his back. He lay there, dazed. Bill moved in, completely crazy, and began to kick him. He got him once in the ribs and once in the side before hands

grabbed him and dragged him off. He had been going
to kill Fisher, kick him to death with a profound enjoyment.

They dragged him back across the street to the steps
of the Red Dog, and he stood there, with the hands
on him, just looking at Pepe now, and then down at
Fisher.

Nobody moved, except Fisher, slowly getting up,
holding his side painfully. Then plenty of people,
suddenly, ran to help Fisher, the tellers from the bank
and half a dozen others. He dragged himself away,
back toward the bank, not even looking in Bill's direction.

"Come on," the Colonel said, and grabbed Bill's
arm. Burns grabbed the other, and between them they
steered Bill back into the Red Dog. Bill was frozen
blind, nothing left but a vast heaving sea of rage. His
knees shook. He stood with his stomach against the
bar and the Colonel shoved a drink into his hand.

"That was one of Bill's friends," the Colonel said.

"Who?" Burns asked. "You don't mean that little
Mexican?"

"Bill's a good friend to have," Pringle said. "He'll
never let you down."

"I can see that," Burns said, confused.

Outside in the street, Murphy stood with Shep and
looked all around. Everybody had disappeared. One
of the tellers came out of the bank and spoke to him.
Murphy followed the teller back into the bank.

Bill shook off the Colonel's hand and headed for
the doors again. He crossed the street and went into
the dark of the livery barn. He found Pepe out in the
back, leaning against the wall. He went up to him and
said, "Any son of a bitch that lays a hand on you
again, I'll kill him."

"Bill," Pepe said, holding a rag against his nose, "I could do that myself. It is better to go away."

"You go on back to the ranch, Pepe," Bill said. "Keep out of the bastard's way."

"No, no. Listen, Bill, I could have told you this would happen. I am going back to the mountains— that is where I belong." He bent and picked up his saddle and went to where his bridle was hanging on the wall. "They will be after me now. I would be arrested."

He stood up, holding saddle and bridle, and looked at Bill. "And how about you? What next? Do you think he will do nothing about that punch in the face? Now you have an enemy, Bill. A real enemy."

Bill said nothing.

"Do you think you can take it?" Pepe asked. "You didn't take it just now, you got mad. And yet if you thought about it at all, you must have foreseen that something like this would happen, you must have prepared yourself, as I did. If you can't control yourself, you had better come away with me again. You will kill somebody, if you stay here."

"You mean, for me to stand by and let a man like Fisher beat you?"

"You are right," Pepe said, and went out toward the corral. "It isn't possible." He threw his saddle on his horse, bridled it and mounted. He sat there looking down at Bill. "I will wait up there by the pool, up behind Lawson's. You decide, what you should do. I will wait till Sunday night. If you want to come away with me again, come by then. If you don't come by then, I will know you have decided to stay here for good."

"I have decided now," Bill said, and yet he was full of coldness and confusion. "I signed the amnesty. I'm going to get married."

"Yes," Pepe said, knowing these were just words, bluffs against uncertainty. "I will wait, until tomorrow night. Goodbye, Bill. I will say it now, in case you do not come. Goodbye—take care of yourself. If things become too—too much pressure, go away, go hunting, go up in the mountains for a while. Up by the pool, eh? Think things over. I will not forget you. Wherever I go, I will—yes, I will pray for you. I have not for years, but I will, for you."

Bill looked up at him. So suddenly, after five years. "You don't have to go yet."

"No?" Pepe smiled. "I know a man like that—he said I let go the horse, he will send Murphy to arrest me, they will say it was malice. Goodbye, Bill." How would it be—hiding out in the mountains, circling around the town, alone, a visit now and then over the years, to see how Bill was doing, coming down at night, secretly, and slowly, strangeness growing up. He turned his horse and headed it out the back gate of the corral.

Bill stood there for a long time. After a while, he turned and went back to the Red Dog.

"Where are the honorable Burnses?" he asked the Colonel, who was still at the bar.

"He and Harry went over to the hotel for lunch," the Colonel said. "I told them we would join them."

Bill looked at himself in the backbar mirror. He looked perfectly calm, perfectly cool; the trembling was all inside. It was true, he could go away again, rejoin Pepe, before tomorrow night. If the worst came to the worst, he could do that. He thought of Allie, and all her sweetness came over him.

"Don't worry about Fisher," Bill said. "I'll go over and apologize to him in public, right after lunch. I'll tell him I was drunk. Being drunk excuses a lot of things."

"Oh, you'll have lunch, then," the Colonel said, much relieved.

"I'm a civilized human being," Bill said. "Occasionally. George, fill this up, will you?"

The Colonel watched Bill drink it with just the slightest concern. "Fisher's coming to the barbecue tomorrow," the Colonel said. "I wouldn't go into the bank just yet. Let him cool off. Wait till he comes out there. I know he'll come, because he'll ask me to fire you. But if you make a statement right in front of all our friends, and show a little good will, he'll have to show good grace."

"And who is going to apologize to Pepe?"

The Colonel did not attempt an answer.

"Drunkenness is a wonderful excuse," Bill said. "George, fill this up, will you? Don't think I'm going to get drunk, Colonel. I'm not going to get drunk. I just want to relax, that's all. I mean, if we're going to have lunch with the Burns family, I want to feel good and be able to keep the conversation going about Hereford cattle and all that horseapple. I can't do it unless I'm partially unconscious."

"Maybe we'd better go home," the Colonel said, looking suddenly old and tired.

Bill looked up at him. He put his hand on the Colonel's arm. "Listen," he said. "I won't let you down. I won't turn into a drunk on you. I won't even talk too much. I'll use iron control, I'll just ask an intelligent question now and then. I'll do you proud. You understand?"

"Then do me a favor," the Colonel said without expression. "Just leave that one drink on the bar."

"All right," Bill said. "I will. Let that be my sign and symbol—one drink left on the bar. As you say, conform in public, escape in private. Let's go."

He turned and with a wooden face and perfect

steadiness of gait, walked with the Colonel toward the door.

Fisher sat in his office, hunched sideways to ease his ribs, looking at Murphy with cold hatred. Fisher thought he was ruptured; two ribs seemed to have been cracked. The front of his face felt as though he had been kicked by a Shetland pony. He sat, breathing as shallowly as possible in order to prevent any further pain. They were waiting for Shep, who had gone for Lieutenant Aberforth and Judge Quires.

"Arrest that Mexican," Fisher said, "the greasy bastard broke the amnesty, and you can take him and Gorham on assault and battery." He closed his eyes.

Quires came in, followed by Aberforth. "I heard about it," Quires said. "It's a terrible thing, Mr. Fisher."

"I want a warrant for the arrest of William Gorham," Fisher said, still in the flat, low voice. "Assault and battery."

"Pardon me, Mr. Fisher," Quires said. "I hate to say this, but I heard you hit that Mexican first. At the trial—"

"You fathead, there ain't going to be any trial. All I want is them two in jail. Murphy's going to turn them over tonight to that bird Mora. He can take them back to Mexico and shoot them across the line."

"The Mexican's gone," Murphy said.

"Where? Where the hell where?" Fisher cried, shuffling his feet in crazy exasperation.

"Nobody don't know," Murphy said. He always said stupid things around Fisher, because Fisher scared him.

"You mean, they won't tell you, you bugging idiot," Fisher said. He looked at Aberforth. "You're the military. You're responsible for catching these outlaws tomorrow. One assaulted me and has got loose. Why the hell didn't you people finish the Mexican War like you ought to? What are all these bugging Mexicans doing around here, anyway?''

Aberforth drew his heels together. He had been about to tell Fisher that Gorham was having lunch in the hotel right across the street, but the speech about the Mexican War changed his attitude toward Fisher. Furthermore, he would be a damned sight safer if he were not directly connected with these private vendetta arrests. ''Mr. Fisher, to the best of my knowledge, I am not under your orders.''

Fisher screwed his mouth into a horrible leer, a smile in agony. ''I know, General. But you will co-operate, won't you?''

''If you'll allow me,'' Quires said. ''It won't look well, Buck, turning these men over to the Mexican authorities. It could ruin you.''

''Who's bought you up now? Nothing can ruin me but a good, solid bankruptcy.''

''It could ruin you. I venture to say there are twenty men in San Vicente who would shoot you, Mr. Fisher, if you did such a thing. Certainly they would rescue Gorham, who is a Texan. Think of the flagwaving, Buck. American citizens betrayed to the Mexicans, and so on. They'd be calling you Santa Anna.''

Fisher sat quiet, his mouth screwed up in pain and frustration. ''Damn it, then, kill them,'' he said.

Quires glanced at Aberforth. He could see that the Lieutenant didn't like this direct approach. As a matter of fact, Aberforth, who had been thinking hastily, had made up his mind to keep his mouth shut about Gorham's being in the hotel. If Gorham were to be killed as a martyr, nothing would make Allie forget him, or the fact that Aberforth had had something to do with it.

"Do you want the real truth?" Judge Quires asked.
"No," Fisher said. "Yes."

"Nobody would convict Gorham of an assault charge. Defending his poor, downtrodden buddy. You can't charge eight percent interest and not have a great many people delighted when somebody knocks your teeth in. That's the plain truth."

Fisher sat, hot rage cooling as he looked at the men across from him with complete contempt. He lifted his lip at Quires. "All you know is what not to do. What's your advice, you helpless shyster?"

Quires tried to smile; helplessly, he shrugged and looked at Murphy. Murphy looked miserably at Fisher. Fisher turned the sneer on Aberforth, and Aberforth began to blush. "You fatheads, why do I always have to tell you everything? Just let them run. The Mexican's broken the amnesty already by running. On Sunday, we can shoot him legally. Gorham—if we make it hot enough for him, he'll run too." He looked at Murphy. "Go on, you jackass, get out of here, find Gorham, and start riding him."

Murphy stood on the boardwalk beside Aberforth, and looked up and down the street. No Gorham, and Murphy was glad. He had challenged Gorham's gang, and he had begun to wonder why, after all, he had not handled it a little better. It was Fisher who had wanted them disarmed at Lawson's, so he could do what he wanted; if he had not asked for their arms, they would not have fought him. As for himself, what revenge he wanted he had got; now, with the gang broken and trapped, he had had enough. But now Fisher, that madman, was after them all the harder. Gorham, at least, was safe, for the time being. In a way Murphy knew that he too was safe, as long as he didn't catch Gorham—Pringle could be a strong enemy; and then there were, worst of all, the men like Shaw that Bill knew.

The key to his position lay in catching the Mexican, not Gorham. If he could catch Pepe, that would largely appease Fisher, and nobody would mind much if Pepe were shipped off with Mora, or killed, and Aberforth could do the killing, for that matter.

"I knew they were friends," Aberforth said, standing beside him, "but I didn't know they were that much attached. The fighting."

"Oh," Murphy said, "you mean Gorham and the Mexican. I don't suppose you know where the Mexican has gone?"

"How on earth would I know?" Aberforth said.

A wagon creaked down the street. Where on earth had everybody gone?

"Do you know where Gorham is?" Murphy asked.

Aberforth said, cautiously, "I saw him earlier."

Murphy didn't press it. He could tell by Aberforth's calm, deadpan look that he was lying. He decided to try something else. "If Gorham made a break for it, and we had to chase him tomorrow, would you mind killing him? Is he a friend of yours?"

Aberforth was appalled. To kill Gorham would be a disaster of the first order. Let the soldiers do it, or Murphy.

"Duty is duty," Aberforth said.

Murphy knew how little that meant, and washed Aberforth out of his mind. They must be friends. He looked up at the clouds. Fresh, white, clean, with just a touch of gray shadow on the undersides. He thought of rain showers and pinon nuts, for some reason. "Then it will be Shaw tomorrow," he said, making ready to go. Just where would he go? Some place out of the way, where Fisher couldn't find him.

"By all means, Shaw," Aberforth said. He hadn't

been caught trying to murder Shaw. "Nobody loves Shaw."

Murphy looked surprised. He hadn't expected anything so astute, or candid, from Aberforth. Well, if you wanted to eat steaks, you had to kill cows. He stepped off the walk and left Aberforth to himself.

Aberforth's head was full of facts, but they refused to settle into place and kept floating around like leaves in an eddy. Something in his mind wanted to be heard; he kept sniffing for it like a hound. True enough, Gorham was sitting over there in the hotel dining room, chatting with the Colonel; but Aberforth couldn't turn him in, it would be taken as treachery, not duty. If Gorham could have been lifted by the hair and transported by an angel, he would have asked for nothing more. Desire and prudence agreed on that; during the conversation in Fisher's office, Aberforth had realized that Gorham could not be defeated by danger, but only by disgrace.

The thing kept buzzing at the back of his mind, the way to get rid of Gorham, in all this. But he was not used to dealing with these vague drifts of thought, whiffs of suspicion, hints at solutions. The harder he grasped, the less substance it had. Still, the secret lay in or with Pepe somehow.

He stepped down off the walk and crossed the street to the hotel. There was nobody left in the dining room except the Colonel and Gorham, seated against the wall, where the Colonel was talking earnestly. Gorham was looking down at the tablecloth with a tight look around the mouth.

Aberforth went over casually, and they both looked up. He smiled briefly, and noted the somewhat strained courtesy in the Colonel's manner. Evidently he had been in the middle of an important speech.

"I think I had better tell you something, Gorham,"

Aberforth said, and sat down. "Fisher is going to try to get you to run away."

They both looked surprised, and then suddenly friendly. "It's damn nice of you to tell me," Gorham said.

"Fisher's trying to take advantage of the amnesty situation to get you into trouble. I wanted to caution you. If you do nothing, merely sit tight, you'll be all right. They feel they'd be better off not arresting you, unless you break the amnesty." More surprise. "If you broke the amnesty agreement, they'd be after you like a shot."

The Colonel and Bill looked at each other.

"It's too bad your Mexican friend got into that trouble," Aberforth said.

"Yes, it's too bad he felt he had to come to town," Gorham said.

"If they catch him, they'll deport him."

Gorham smiled a little. "They'll have to find him."

"I suppose you know where he is," Aberforth said. "Better be careful not to let it drop." He smiled with perfect candor.

"I won't," Bill said, smiling back.

It hadn't worked, the charm, the friendliness and candor, but Aberforth kept on smiling. Gorham put out a hand. "I had an idea that you were a little hostile, Aberforth," Gorham said. "I beg your pardon. Thanks for your help."

Aberforth shook the hand. And, knowing when enough was enough, he stood up, bowed to the Colonel, and walked out.

TWENTY-THREE

STANDING ON THE porch, Aberforth knew it had been the right thing, even if he hadn't found out where Pepe was. The slowly circling facts were settling. It was all so simple, suddenly, it came to him as a decision that was almost an instinct. If he got at Gorham through the Mexican, nobody could ever blame him for attacking Gorham. What was needed was some attack on the Mexican, to force Gorham to defend him again.

He saw Moore coming down the street on his horse, covered with dust. Moore looked tired. Aberforth waved to him, and Moore came over to the boardwalk.

"Come on up and have a drink," Aberforth said. "Things have been happening."

Moore got down and came up the steps. "Somebody took a shot at Nulty last night," he said. "Bullet hit the safe."

"Why?" Aberforth asked, his face a blank.

"I thought it was obvious," Moore said, pushing through the swing doors to the bar. "They've got Nulty down as a traitor. He'll be lucky to last a month."

"A traitor?" Aberforth asked, leaning against the bar. "Helping the law?"

"A lot of people don't like the law," Moore said, pouring himself a drink.

"Tell me something," Aberforth said. "The men who sign up under the amnesty—are they not obliged to turn in their old friends? For example, if you wanted to know where somebody was, could you ask one of these amnesty people, and force them to tell you?"

Moore put down his drink and looked at Aberforth quietly for a moment. Aberforth, he decided, had tremendous depths of pure ignorance. "It has to be that way, legally," he said, slowly, "it's the form, in the agreement. They have to aid the law in every way they can. Naturally. That would be part of any surrender." He looked down at the bar. "Naturally it's something I would not do."

"For instance," Aberforth said, "take Simon Shaw. We're going to have to ask tomorrow, where he is. What direction he took."

"I would rather wait to be told," Moore said. "Informants."

"I don't quite understand," Aberforth said.

"Suppose you had sworn to uphold the law, and I came and asked you where your outlaw brother was. What would you do?"

"I imagine," Aberforth said slowly, "that I would tell you some lie and pack up my stuff and head for the mountains." He looked at Moore sharply. "But you could force the issue."

"If I were son of a bitch enough," Moore said.

"Thanks for the drink, Lieutenant." Moore lifted a hand and walked out.

Aberforth watched him go. It was perfectly simple. Get somebody to ask Gorham where Pepe was. Gorham evidently knew. He stood watching the clouds beyond the door, his face benign with gratification. If Gorham were put on the spot, then Gorham would be only getting what was coming to him—and the results in terms of good things for Aberforth would be merely incidental to the grand operations of justice and, who knows, possibly even those of Providence. Society would be served, possibly even God. Gorham would not betray his friend—he would have to run away with him again. Aberforth began a careful examination of what was left of his conscience. Was it possibly none of his business, he asked himself? Was he possibly going outside the line of duty? Did his prescribed duty prohibit this action? Or did it, rather, suggest and advise it? Was it a civil matter, or partly military; or, again, was he a quasi-civil officer, in this quasi-military role? If the affair were quasi-military, and he were quasi-civil, it could be construed as an act not partly civil, or partly military, but wholly military-civil. This settled the matter. He was duty-bound.

This satisfied Aberforth's reason as his prurience usually satisfied his moral qualms, simply by stifling them. The only thing left was to satisfy his mother. Would he, by destroying Gorham's position, be protecting his mother? Obviously, Gorham, as a threat to society as a whole, was a threat to Aberforth's mother, and, indeed, to all mothers everywhere. This thought made up Aberforth's mind, finally. Gorham could not be tolerated as long as Gorham remained a threat to motherhood.

Thus, in the end, Aberforth would marry Allie if he

could, only to protect his mother; and by being an assiduous husband, he would thus also prove himself to be a loyal son. What more to ask?

These thoughts did not appear as thoughts to Aberforth—they came and went as instincts, emotional twinges, a kind of informal ballet. He was the master, and yet he danced; imperturbably he had his way, shaping himself into a plausible integrity, perfecting a fall.

He was interrupted by one last little ray of light, one last, tiny suggestion of innocence. A bird flew up and lighted on a window ledge of Fisher's bank, and as Aberforth looked at this bird he felt a memory of childhood—the suggestion of innocence. For a moment this memory held in the center of his mind, and it brought with it such a feeling of relief, of purity, of safety, of simple happiness, that the panorama of his adult concerns suddenly filled him with the beginnings of fatigue—an excellent material substitute for wisdom. But the bird flew away; Aberforth did not seize Providence quickly enough. He looked once more at the door of Fisher's bank, and stepping off the walk, crossed the street toward it.

Fisher, with a bottle on his desk, was feeling better. "What's on your mind, Lieutenant?" he asked.

Aberforth looked at the bottle. "I'm going to ask you to keep this quiet, Mr. Fisher. In complete confidence."

Fisher kicked the door shut.

"If you handle this my way," Aberforth said, "I think we can get both Gorham and the Mexican at the same time."

"What way?" Fisher asked. He was trying not to show interest, as usual, but his eyes, under casual lids, were brighter.

"Tomorrow, when we meet at Colonel Pringle's to start the hunt, I want Murphy to say that we have changed our plan. We are not going to hunt Shaw, we are going to hunt this Mexican. And Murphy will ask Gorham where the Mexican is. I understand that under the amnesty agreement, Gorham is bound by oath to answer."

"And how do you know that Gorham does know?"

"He as good as told me."

Fisher smiled slightly. "Don't worry. Murphy can do the asking, as you say."

Aberforth looked at the floor. "Don't misunderstand me, Fisher," he said. "I am only doing my duty by my country. All I had in mind—"

Fisher's gentle laugh interrupted him.

Aberforth felt cold and empty. "On second thought, I can see that it might be interpreted as a kind of personal treachery, by some people. Instead of a duty."

"Yeah," Fisher said, watching Aberforth squirm. "It might. But I told you, Murphy will do it. Nobody will know."

"I want you to forget it," Aberforth said.

"Don't order me around," Fisher said. "You come in here trying to double-cross a man so you can get a piece of tail out there at Pringle's. You think I can't read?"

Suddenly Aberforth knew that it wasn't going to stop where he had planned it; in Fisher's hands, the whole affair might take a course he had never intended.

"I said I wanted you to forget it," he said again.

"Thanks for the idea, Lieutenant. Nice of you to drop in."

Aberforth slowly got up. He could not look at Fisher. He could not look at the bottle. He could not look directly at anything. He turned and walked awkwardly out of the room.

Across the street, Moore, sitting at the Colonel's table, looked quietly at Bill and asked, "Bill, do you know where Pepe is?" He could see Bill begin to stiffen, and then, almost as imperceptibly, restrain himself and relax.

"At the moment?" Bill asked. "No."

Moore smiled faintly. He did not press the evasion; of itself, it had proved that Bill knew. He looked at the white cloth on the table. His face was sad. It was quite obvious to Moore, now, that Aberforth had asked all those questions for a reason. There had been something in Aberforth's manner, despite his casual words, a touch of speculation and surmise, that smelled of purpose.

There was something about Aberforth that Moore, thinking him over again, didn't like. He hadn't noticed the quality before, in the last three weeks. Something new, something fishy. Moore's hand, lying on the tablecloth, slowly closed into a big fist, and held there for a moment. The Colonel watched the fist, and saw it slowly relax, and he knew that a storm of some size was going through Moore, behind that big, impassive face. All of a sudden, the Colonel knew, with perfect certainty, that something unseen and dangerous was hanging over Bill.

"I want you to stay on the ranch, Bill," Moore said slowly, and the gentle statement was so serious in tone that Bill simply accepted it as an absolute order.

"All right," Bill said, and stood up to go. Outside, the Colonel looked at the bright sky. He would have expected, to match his trepidations, darkening clouds. How clear and bright the surfaces, all full of peace. A shambles, a horror, in the last event, if a man like Moore could be made so concerned, so perturbed.

Half an hour later Fisher had Murphy standing before him. "Gorham won't tell us where the Mexican is," Fisher said. "But we got to know so we can catch him out on a lie, you understand? And if you don't find out where he is, it's going to be your job."

Murphy just melted. His palms turned outward. He knew it was hopeless, trying to find the Mexican in the mountains. "How?" How could you find a man who simply got on his horse and left?

"Get out," Fisher shouted, and Murphy ran.

Outside in the street, Murphy saw Bill and the Colonel, riding away from town. His mind suddenly cleared. He turned and headed back to the office to find Shep. He would have to put somebody on Gorham to watch him, and Shep had more brains than the other town loafers he used for deputies. The idea gave him no satisfaction. He knew it was perfectly logical for Pepe to come to see Gorham, but he also knew that was exactly why it wouldn't work. Logical thoughts were rarely the answer in human affairs. Logic made him tired—it had to be allowed for, but he was too old to have any faith in it. Life was largely a matter of breaks and accidents. He would get a break on this, or he wouldn't. What he really needed was a good informant—a good informant was worth his weight in gold.

Nobody in the office—as usual. He'd have to do it himself—as usual. And then he remembered Harvey. Why not? Harvey was still one of the gang, and he had sold out the rest once already. He found Harvey in Quires', cleaning out the left show window.

"Pepe has left town," Murphy said. "Where would he go?"

"I don't know," Harvey said blankly.

Murphy's jaw set with impatience. Why was Harvey so stupid all of a sudden?

"Anyway, the gang's broke up," Harvey said. "All through."

Murphy spat on the floor. Why couldn't the damn fool be some help? Harvey should have been the break, he should have had the answer. But no, Murphy thought bitterly, that would have been too logical. He walked out of Quires', back to his office. He knew tailing Gorham wouldn't work, either. He sat down and had himself three stiff drinks. He was haunted by a vision of Fisher, snarling at him. He began to swear under his breath, and when Ed Lawson ambled through the doorway, carrying two horse tails, Murphy looked at him with rising nausea. The damn, lying, two-bit horse-killer, here he came with more horse tails for his lousy bounty.

"What the hell do you want now?" Murphy said, trying to strangle his irritation.

"I know where that Mexican Pepe is hiding out. How much you pay me to tell you?"

Murphy didn't laugh with joy, he didn't shout, he didn't jump up and down. He sat still, faking a yawn.

"You and your lousy horse tails," he said, pulling ten bucks out of the drawer where they kept the fine-money.

"I heard you was looking for him," Lawson said doubtfully. "Heard you guys were all out to nail him."

"Huh?" Murphy asked. "Oh, we just had a few questions. All right, ten bucks," he said, holding out the money. "Where is he?"

He would have paid five hundred.

"I saw him when I was coming back down the mountain with these here tails, from hunting," Lawson said, licking his lips and counting over the money again. "He's camped out by the pool up the creek from my place. Up the canyon."

"Camped out?"

"Yeah. He was fishing in the pool. Bed all laid out. Looked like he was set for a couple of days anyway. Damned greasy little bastard."

Murphy's eyes turned sleepy. "Did you speak to him? Does he know you saw him?"

"I ain't speaking to him no more," Lawson said, stuffing the money in his pocket. "He made a snide crack at me, Sheriff. I ast him to go partners horse-hunting and he made me feel like a fool. I didn't speak none to him, coming down, and I ain't speaking to him none, going up. To hell with him."

"Don't go up there no more," Murphy said. "You stay around your cabin."

Lawson went, and Murphy called Shep. That's what it took in human affairs. One enemy, one informer was worth his weight in gold. The hell with detectives.

Half an hour later, Shep left with a packhorse, and that night, after circling around through the mountains, he camped out half a mile up the mountain from the pool, waiting with his rifle. There was only one way east up that canyon into the mountains, and he had orders that if the Mexican rode out that way, he was to be killed. It wouldn't be much of a job. A man riding up the meadow toward the trees would be in the rifle's sights for a hundred yards, the easiest target in the world. One shot would drop him, no matter where it hit.

When Murphy had reported all this, Fisher said, "All right, just sit tight. Tomorrow night, we'll have the whole damn gang."

TWENTY-FOUR

AT FIVE O'CLOCK, Mrs. Quires knocked on the door of Johanssen's shop and Johanssen opened it, bowing solemnly. He was half drunk off the smell of shellac alone. He was holding a can of it in his hand, and he smiled at Mrs. Quires in an unconsciously salacious way. He only meant to be pleasant, but the combination of the leering white teeth and his jiggling gray ringlets, behind the ears, made Mrs. Quires feel quite faint.

Mrs. Quires was not alone, however, and the leer died on Mrs. Bennett, who was carrying the dark wine-colored dress tenderly across both arms, like a dead child. It would not have done for Mrs. Quires to dress a corpse in solitude, let alone with a couple of strange men.

"Where?" Mrs. Bennett asked with a faint, sad smile.

"Where what?" Johanssen asked, putting down the shellac on nothing, in midair. He had meant to put it on the trestle that held up the casket, but the trestle was not there. "Dear, dear."

Mrs. Bennett had not meant to be specific. It seemed to her so much more could be expressed by sighs. But she was forced to be earthly. "Where is our poor, dear, departed friend?"

"In the icebox," Ollie said. Ollie and Burt were sitting in the corner with a fresh fifth of whisky.

"Is that man drinking?" Mrs. Bennett asked.

"My goodness no," Johanssen said, "I never allow drinking on the premises. Especially when there is a Dear Departed lying around. Ollie is mixing shellac for me."

"Oh," Mrs. Bennett said, raising her eyebrows. "Do you mix shellac with whisky?"

"Not ordinarily," Johanssen said, lifting the cover of the casket and letting it slam down. Dust flew, and Mrs. Bennett coughed genteelly. "Solid, eh?" Johanssen asked, leering pleasantly. "She'll never get out of that. Built like a grand piano."

"I'll say she was," Ollie sighed.

"Who is that man?" Mrs. Bennett asked, squinting at Ollie.

"My assistant," Johanssen said, stumbling over one of the trestles. He shook his head at Mrs. Bennett. "Clumsy old me," he said.

"Have some more shellac," Ollie said.

"Why is that man putting the whisky in his mouth, if he's mixing shellac with it?" Mrs. Bennett asked sharply.

"I warm it in my mouth and then spit it back in the bottle," Ollie explained. "If you warm it on a stove, it blows up. Like Mrs. Fisher. They say when she lit off the explosion broke every window in the house."

"I think you're all drunk," Mrs. Bennett said, her face red.

"No, we ain't, Mrs. Bennett," Johanssen said. "Honest. It's just the shellac. Here, Ollie, show Mrs. Bennett how good it cuts the stuff. Reason we use whisky is because it's cheaper than pure alcohol, Mrs. Bennett."

"Please," Mrs. Quires said, "we'd like to get through and go home. This isn't a very agreeable task, you know."

Mrs. Bennett pointed a finger at Ollie. "Get out, you."

"Go get the old—the remains, Ollie," Johanssen said. "Try to act ceremonious. Mrs. Fisher was a great woman."

"Where shall we put her?" Burt asked.

"Lay her on the floor," Ollie said. "That's where she spent most of her life." He and Burt went into the icebox.

"What a disgusting man," Mrs. Bennett said.

"A great help around the shop, though," Johanssen said, "been with me for seventeen years. I'll make him stay in the icebox, so he won't get in your way." He warmed a little whisky in his mouth. "She's got her nightie on. All you got to do is just shuck her into that dress you got, and we'll plop her right in the old box. I know she'll fit. That is, unless she's swole some." He eyed the casket with a pleased smile. "I don't think she's swole yet, though. She's been in the icebox ever since it happened." He turned a beaming smile on Mrs. Bennett. "Right next to the hogs."

"Oh, God," Mrs. Bennett said.

"You don't mind if I warm some more shellac, do you?" Johanssen said. "Got to give the box one more coat." He went over to Ollie's bottle and putting the neck in his mouth, tossed a slug down his throat. He didn't give a damn for Mrs. Bennett and all her airs.

He had seen too many prominent citizens laid out on a board to be impressed by uppity women.

Ollie and Burt stumbled out, swearing at each other. "She ain't stiff," Burt said.

"She broke," Ollie said.

"No, she ain't broke, and she ain't swole," Johanssen said, scuttling over to them to give them a hand. "She's just let loose, kind of." They swayed and staggered forward with Mrs. Fisher swaying respectably between them. Mrs. Bennett stood with her hands over her face. Never in her life had she expected to see Annie Fisher in such a position.

"Get her butt off the floor, you idiot," Johanssen said to Ollie, "can't you see she's tearing? Here, swing her up on this here board. Madam," he said, turning around as Ollie and Burt swung Annie back and forth, trying to get her higher each time, "Madam, I don't see how you're going to get that gown on her. She weighs a ton."

"Rockabye baby, on the tree top," Ollie sang.

Mrs. Bennett slid to the floor in a dead faint. "Oh, God," Mrs. Quires said.

"Here," Ollie said, dropping his end of Mrs. Fisher and shoving the bottle of whisky at Mrs. Quires. "Give'er a shot of this stuff. Have one yourself." He gave Mrs. Quires a warm, friendly smile.

"All right," Mrs. Quires said, kneeling by her friend, and thinking that Ollie looked something like a gypsy. "I don't mind if I do. She'll never know I did, as long as she's fainted." She put the bottle to her mouth and took a slug. It hit her like a load of birdshot and she began to cough and choke.

"That stuff really hits, don't it?" Ollie said, smiling appreciatively as Mrs. Quires strangled. "Have another."

"Don't mind if I do," Mrs. Quires sobbed, and swallowed.

Ollie stuck the neck of the bottle in Mrs. Bennett's mouth and poured. It slopped out and down her neck, she choked and gurgled. She smiled dreamily. "Gimme another, Alf," she muttered, her eyes still closed.

"Who's Alf?" Ollie said, pouring another slug down Mrs. Bennett's gullet.

"I don't know," Mrs. Quires said. "Mr. Bennett's name is Adenoid. I mean Oddenrad. I mean—oh—Ackroyd." Mrs. Bennett choked and swallowed. Her eyes opened slowly, already blurred.

"Head like a chicken," Ollie said. "Drunk as a skunk."

"Where's Alf?" Mrs. Bennett said again, looking dully around. "Gimme another shot, boys. Need another shot."

"I'll bet you been around Phoenix some," Ollie said, handing her the bottle.

"Mind your own damned business," Mrs. Bennett said, sitting up and lifting the bottle. She stopped and looked at Mrs. Quires. "Let's get that dress on old Annie, kid."

"Get her up on the board, boys," Johanssen said. They went back to swinging Annie.

"Higher," Johanssen said.

"Heave," Burt said.

"*Up* she goes," Johanssen cried.

"Poor, poor Annie," Mrs. Bennett said, lowering the bottle, "I bet she ain't been swung around like that since grammar school."

"All right, *heave*," Ollie said, and Annie flew through the air, up over the board, and landed on the floor on the other side.

"My God," Ollie said, "she like to stove in the whole building. You ever hear such a crash?"

The five of them struggled with her, and finally got her on the board. Annie kept grinning at everyone and nobody.

"If you put her in the coffin now," Mrs. Quires said, "we can put the bottom half of the dress down first, and then put her on top of that, and then put the top half on top and snap her up in it, like a ham sandwich."

"You ought to get a patent," Johanssen said, taking a quick one.

"Human dignity," Mrs. Bennett said. "Have to be damn careful about human dignity."

"Yes, I know," Johanssen said. "Funny thing, all we got is our damn dignity. Funny, ain't it? Take a human being's dignity away and you got nothing but a lousy ape."

"Let's not let Annie down," Mrs. Bennett said.

"What you all talk about dignity," Ollie said, "what is all that? I ain't seen much dignity. Come on, Burt, grab her feet and dump her in and get it over." They put her in and snapped her up in the dress.

"Did you bring the powder and all that, dearie?" Mrs. Bennett asked Mrs. Quires.

"This has got to be very dignified," Ollie said. "Annie was always dignified, no matter how long the lineup."

"I didn't know you knew her," Mrs. Quires said, getting out the powder.

"I knowed her most all my life," Ollie said sadly. "You talk about dignity. Annie was nothing but a damn sow. All her life. Living like a hog."

"Oh, now, Ollie," Mrs. Bennett said, "let bygones be bygones. Everybody's got something to hide. You know how all us people got out West? By running

away from something back East, that's how. Nothing
the matter with a reformed woman, is there?''

"Yeah, but when did Annie reform?'' Ollie said.
"She was still the boss madam of this town, and Buck
was the pimp, running that house down by the river.
They couldn't break the habit. Whatta you talk about
dignity? What's dignity about an old whore? Was she
a saint or something? And look at Buck.''

"Now, don't make me nervous,'' Mrs. Bennett
said, leaning over with the lipstick to fix up Annie's
mouth. Mr. Johanssen stole a peek down the front of
her dress. All he could see was a bunch of old wrinkles.

"That'll cost you two bits, sonny,'' Mrs. Bennett
said complacently, and made a stab at Annie with the
lipstick. She missed the lip and a gob of the rouge got
cut off on Annie's front teeth. She looked like a clown.
Her strangled oyster eyes glared pointlessly out at the
world from far away.

"Ain't she beautiful?'' Burt said.

"Phew,'' Ollie said, "you'd better cover over that
mess with some powder, lady.''

Mrs. Bennett fumbled and dropped the powder
box. Half of it spilled into the coffin.

"Oh, God,'' Mrs. Bennett said, suddenly sobering
with horror as she tried to blow the powder off. She
had come too close to Annie's face and the glaring,
dead, blue eyes. "I got to get out of here. She's like
a fish. A dead fish.'' She turned. "Help, help,'' she
said, blundering toward the door. "Oh, why do I
ever get drunk? Why? Oh, Alf, Alf, where are you?''

She and Mrs. Quires staggered out on the sidewalk
and stumbled out of sight.

"Interesting, interesting,'' Johanssen said, reaching for the bottle. "What you said about human dignity. Peculiar, peculiar.''

"I ain't never been a liar," Ollie said. "You take like tomorrow, the preacher's going to get up and make a big spiel about Mrs. Fisher and her good works. And everybody'll pass by and look down in this wonderful coffin and say what a sweet, good, kind woman she was, and gone to heaven. Why do they have to lie about everything?" He sounded sad. "If I was a liar and a cheater and a briber, I could have been rich like Buck Fisher. But I never could be a pimp. How can a man be so disgusting? But look at Buck. When they bury that son of a bitch, they'll call him a pillar of society, because he's rich. And them two ladies. What about dignity?"

"Peculiar, very peculiar," Johanssen said. "Everybody wants dignity, nobody wants the truth."

"I'll give 'em the goddamn truth," Ollie said, his eyes suddenly sober.

"I'm going home," Johanssen said. "You take that dummy up to Quires, now, and then lock up."

"Yeah," Ollie said sadly. "I should have told you, Mr. Johanssen. I'm leaving town tomorrow."

Johanssen, standing at the door, looked back at him, smiling a little. "Well, goodbye, Ollie." He pulled a five-dollar bill out of his pocket.

"No, thanks," Ollie said. "You know something?" He took another slug. "When I was a kid, in Phoenix, Annie Fisher was supposed to be the most beautiful whore in the world. Anybody went to bed with Annie, he had what you call dignity. And all the time, I would dream of going to bed with Annie, so's I could go home and tell them other kids I'd done it.

"And time after time I went to Buck Fisher's house to get in, dressed up right and with the money in my hand, and you know, that son of a bitch never would let me in. Why not? I had the money. I was clean and sober. So what if I was a kid? I had the money. But he took a dislike to me, or something. I guess it was my teeth. I didn't hardly have no teeth, all little and rotten, and he would laugh at me, standing out there in the street. He's a mean man, Buck Fisher. He could see how hard I wanted to get in, so he just wouldn't. And after a while I had to give up. But not for a long, long time. I used to dream about Annie, and all the time, there was Buck Fisher laughing at me, the way he used to do, standing there in the door with a tray of empty steins in his hand." Ollie's voice died out.

"That's why they made bottles, kid," Johanssen said. "For people like you and me." He shut the door and went off down the street.

It was getting dark outside—a few little yellow lights in the backs of stores, and plenty in the hotel, but the rest of the town kind of empty and lonely. Inside the shop the gloom grew deeper and deeper.

"We better get them cans of powder," Burt said. "Powder, caps and fuse."

"And my teeth," Ollie said. "I can't face that bank without my teeth. I told Maddy to meet us in Cheyenne next month. She and Gracie's taking a buckboard to Silver City tomorrow."

"Where we staying tonight?"

"Right here," Ollie said. "We'll go knock over the hardware store and get my teeth and bring all the stuff here, and sleep here all night. In the morning when they come for the hearse and Annie, we can hide out in the stable in the back with the horses."

"Okay," Burt said. "Let's go. People all at dinner now. We can do it quiet."

Ollie stood up. "We got one more job, after."

"What job?"

"I'm going to leave San Vicente a message, Burt. I'm going to leave 'em a piece of the truth."

He put down the bottle, hitched up his pants, and started for the door.

TWENTY-FIVE

PEPE LAY ON his back and watched the stars through the trees—a far-off, mystic pageant of unknown worlds. Slowly, up there, mute in illimitable distance, a sign and a prophecy was unfolding; it was not there for nothing; God had put it there for a reason.

"Will he come?" he asked his old friend, the priest.

"No," the old man said, "you know he won't." He sat silent, invisible, out in the dark. Pepe would quite often hold these silent, wordless conversations. It was his way of looking at life from a higher point of view than his own. Long ago, Pepe's friend, the priest, who had been jailed, had told him to do this when he needed advice. "Imagine an old man, a wise old man. Ask him your questions, and he will answer you wisely." Pepe had done this, and it always worked. And little by little, the old man of his imagination had taken on the recollected figure of the priest himself, the priest Pepe had loved, his true father.

"Suppose he wants to go off again? And I am not here? What then?"

"You think he will be lost," the priest said, beside him in the dark. "You are the one who is lost. You loved God, and now you are risking your life waiting for a man."

"A child."

"Oh, I know that. I have picked up babies out of the gutters by the dozen," the priest said. "I know all about children. One must let them go. I would still be alive, and you could be my assistant, if you gave up this life. If only you had not had hatred, when they put me in jail. Why did you think jail is so bad? You cannot get out, it is true. Another house, you can get out of, but when you are out, you just go back in, so what is the difference, really? Life itself is a jail. You were so angry. You smeared dog filth on the police door, an act of pride which has led to all your trouble."

"Yes," Pepe said. "Everybody sins, father."

"You must learn to live with what you despise, the evil in men. It would take courage; it might be dangerous, to go back; but it is the solution. Charity."

"Do you remember," Pepe asked, "how I used to go ahead of you with the candle and the bell, when we went to carry Him to the old sick woman? I would go ahead through the dark, with my light, ringing my bell, and you would come behind carrying Him."

"Do you remember how you used to kneel in church, and look up at the tabernacle? You thought he was so little, a Child living in that little house. That was true love. Yes, to serve Him well you do not need much. Certainly not brains. A bell and a candle will do very well. Or even a broom." They sat in silence in the dark, a heavy sadness growing in Pepe's heart. The priest was aware of it.

"You know how it is on the tops of the mountains," Pepe said. "I thought he would be there. You know how I used to build those little altars, piling the stones up."

"Altars to a possible God," the priest said. "Like the pagan altars. It won't do, Pepe. You know where the real God lives, in the tabernacle."

"But if I go back to Mexico—the police."

"Didn't you know, didn't I tell you, that dread is the sign of duty? The police caught God, they killed Him, He permitted it for a reason. But He was not stealing a cow at the time." The priest smiled. "Give up this stealing. If you were killed on the journey home, to serve Him, you would belong to Him forever."

"And Gorham?"

"The Child is the only friend you will ever have, forever. Ah, there is nobody like God; God is everything. He is a child, and has infinite majesty, terrible and gentle. He is the One, Pepe. All other love is merely a shadow of God's love, like waves on the water, shadows of the wind."

Pepe got up and stood there in the dark. All around him lay silence, the sleeping forest.

"You think it will ever really be the same again?" the voice asked. "It's all gone, Pepe. The freedom, the fine times. All good for a little while, that human happiness, but not forever. There is no lasting freedom, Pepe, except in a total slavery like mine. Is that a mystery? No. I am the slave of God, who is infinite, because of love, a total slave infinitely free within that love. And you who have tried to find God in freedom and seeking your own will and profit, you have nothing but the limitations of yourself, a handful of dust. Everything is closing in on you, and there is no solution possible except by love and sacrifice of your-

self, which is your prison. That is the secret I told
you, and you abandoned it. But it is the truth. Look
at the stars, so orderly, so peaceful, set in their final
array by that Child's hand, each one obeying. And
then the others, falling into perdition, because they
will not find their places in the order. Free, yes, but
lost and dying. There is no freedom, Pepe, except by
way of love, and your little human love is all worn
out, no different than the women. Make up your
mind. Choose."

Pepe stood silent.

"Now you can go back down the canyon and take
the road south in the dark. Lawson will be asleep.
That is the easy way. If you wait till the amnesty is
over, tomorrow night, you will have to go out up the
canyon, past the meadows, up the back way through
that pass, the hard way through the mountains. Give
up your son."

"Tomorrow," Pepe said finally, and the old man
was gone. Nothing, now, but the dark night, voice-
less. "A little while, and I will," Pepe said to himself,
or was it to the Child? "I will come back and carry
my bell again for You. Would You like that? I will go
tomorrow as soon as I know Bill does not need me
any more. Is that all right?"

No answer.

"I know now what I should do, that I should go
back and serve You again in some little way, as I used
to do, but just let me wait this one more day. Will
that be all right?"

No answer.

TWENTY-SIX

AT SEVEN O'CLOCK Sunday morning the bugle
sounded in the plaza and Ollie waked up. Burt
snorted, grunted and opened his eyes.

Ollie sat up and almost fell down again. His head
swam, bursting with pain. "What was I drinking?"
he groaned.

"Mostly shellac," Burt said. Burt was red in the
eyes, but not so bad off. Ollie sucked his gums.
"My teeth," he said, looking around. "Where's my
teeth?"

"At the dentist's, I guess," Burt said. "Where else?"

"I got them," Ollie said. "I got them last night.
Don't you remember?"

"No, you didn't," Burt said calmly, sitting up out
of the shavings and brushing himself off.

"But damn it," Ollie cried, "that was the plan, to
get them last night after we got the powder, so we'd
be ready."

Burt looked at him and shrugged. "We didn't get

them," he said placidly. "That's all I know. I guess we forgot."

A sudden cold swept over Ollie and he shivered, sobering. He could still hardly see, but his mind was cooler and more focused. "Son of a bitch," he said. "We'll have to get them now."

He went to the front of the shop and looked out. Down in the plaza, the soldiers were forming up for roll-call.

"Look," Burt said, "if we blew the church and then the bank, everybody'll be looking at that, won't they? Then we can beat it around back of Cameron's place and get them then. If we do it now, we'll get a crowd and ruin the bank job."

Ollie's mind suddenly snapped into focus. "All right," he said. He was dying of thirst. He went through the icebox into the butcher shop and got a long drink of water. He blundered back, grabbing a couple of sausages on the way.

"We better get out of here," he said to Burt, who was already gathering up the two cans of black powder, each about as big as a nail keg. "Let's take all that junk out in the stable with the horses and fix things up right." His eyes lighted on Quires' dummy. "Hell, we forgot to deliver that too."

"That's too damn bad," Burt said.

"Yeah," Ollie said, looking at the dummy and thinking. An idea was coming up out of somewhere. "Where's that half of Annie's dress that didn't get put on her yesterday?"

They found it under the trestle, and Ollie picked up the dummy and carried it out back, with Burt coming behind him with the rest of the things.

In the stable it was safe enough until Johanssen came for the hearse and the horses. There were three old nags, two for the hearse and one for the spare in case one of the others dropped dead.

They filled their belts with cartridges and shoved their rifle magazines full; stuffed what they could in their saddlebags and threw the rest in the oat bin. Burt punched a hole in each powder can, shoved a length of fuse in each hole, and tied them to the cans with old harness straps. He looked at the job admiringly. "There's just one thing," he said. "We ought to set this stuff against the wall and pack it. To make all the blast go in. Like we used to set a charge on a boulder and pack it with mud to drive the blast down. This way, loose, most of the blast is gonna go away from the wall." He thought. "But what the hell are we gonna do about it? We won't have the time to make no pack, even if I could figure how to do it up against a wall like that. No time to bore a hole." He scratched his head. "Hell, I guess twenty-five pounds will do. Ought to break up that wall, blow some kind of a hole loose, anyway."

"I don't need no barn door," Ollie said. "Just enough to crawl through. You forget the matches? You don't want to get caught up at that church with no matches."

"No," Burt said, and showed the matches to prove it. They gathered up all their things and climbed into the loft. Lying in the hay, they began eating the sausages.

"When you think they'll come for Annie?" Burt asked.

"About nine, maybe," Ollie said. "You know what they'll do to us if they catch us busting that bank."

Burt stopped chewing. "What?"

"They'll kill us. You ever think of that?" Without his teeth, his confidence was gone.

Burt looked at him. "We can't quit now. We already told the girls. They're halfway to Silver City already, ain't they? If we don't get that money, what're we going to say?''

''I don't know,'' Ollie said. He felt awful, he bent his head and groaned. If he had had his teeth, he would have felt a lot better, he could have stood it; as it was, he felt like a bagful of skunkbutts.

Burt said, ''If all them people in the plaza thought a woman was being dragged by a runaway horse, they'd all sure as hell chase it, wouldn't they?''

''That was my idea,'' Ollie said, looking at the dummy. ''You reckon any of Johanssen's nags actually can get up into a run?''

At nine, the pallbearers and Johanssen rode into the yard and hitched up the horses. They got the coffin out of the shop and shoved it into the old black hearse, and Johanssen drove it out of the yard with the pallbearers riding slowly after him. Looking down the alley, Ollie caught a glimpse of the procession as it formed up on the main street. The whole town was out, carriages, buckboards, anything they could get. It took half an hour for the line to pass the end of the alley.

''All right,'' Ollie said, hurrying down the ladder. ''Toss me them things.'' His heart was beating hard as he caught the stuff. His belly felt shrunk and his mind felt light, and his heart knocked in his chest like a slow sledge.

They saddled up and got the horses packed for the run into the mountains, gave them a last watering, and then saddled Johanssen's last horse and set the dummy on it. Ollie tied one foot of it in the near stirrup and folded the dummy down. The dummy was a good deal thinner than Annie had been, so the half of a dress went all the way around. They pinned it up the side with horseshoe nails. It was a mess, but dragging along the street, it wouldn't matter. Ollie threw a split sack over it, which hid it well enough for the time being. They rode their horses down to the main street and sat looking around to size things up.

Neither of them had watches, but the clock on the bank said a quarter to ten. Half the soldiers had gone with the funeral procession, to act as a guard of honor. The other half was loafing around the plaza camp. The saloons were closed in honor of Annie.

Ollie drew a deep breath, and the cold, fresh air did him some good. "Okay, Burt," he said, "you walk your horse up to the church and see if it's all clear. We got to be ready at ten."

When Burt came back, he reported the church was empty and even locked. They hung around the north side of the plaza until five minutes to ten, and then Burt ambled off down the street again with the powder can in a sack under his arm.

Ollie, leading the dummy's horse, turned and rode slowly around to the alley behind the bank. There was nobody around, the alley was empty. He could see part of the plaza, down the alley, but there was nobody in the part he could see; they were all down at the lower end. His eyes had clouded with nerves, everything seemed smaller and farther away. His hands shook as he took the can of powder and laid it at the base of the wall. It wouldn't do. He had to get it higher up, at least seven feet high, where it would blow in against the end of the vault. He saw a stick corral down the alley. He ran and yanked one of the poles out of it, and hurried back. He wrapped the fuse around the end of the stick and propped it against the wall, so that the can hung down from the upper end, against the wall. The fuse hung down within easy reach. He stuck his hand in his pocket for a match and froze, his insides turning to ice. Burt had all the matches. He hurried through the rest of his pockets. Nothing.

He ran down the alley to the street and looked up and down. A man was coming along the boardwalk, dressed as though he were going to church.

"You got a match, friend?" Ollie asked, forcing a grin through panic.

The man stopped short. Ollie was appalling enough at any time, but now, with his face a dead gray, covered with the sweat of shellac, and the horrible grin on his mouth, he looked like the walking dead.

The man pulled out a box of matches and held it out impatiently. Ollie took the box. "Thanks," he said, and turning, ran back to the alley.

"Just a minute, my friend," the man said loudly. "Those are my matches."

Ollie ducked out of sight into the alley. The man swore and hurried after him. He turned the corner into the alley and stopped short. Ollie was holding a match to the end of the fuse. The man stood there, his mouth open.

"What are you doing?" he asked.

"I'm lighting a bugging fuse, you idiot," Ollie said. The fuse wouldn't catch, the match burned Ollie's fingers, he cursed and dropped it. One slow step after another, the man came forward, his eyes round, his mouth open. He was a perfectly respectable businessman. He knew black powder when he saw it, but he just couldn't believe what he saw.

"I beg your pardon," he said.

Ollie was going around in a fog.

"I said, what are you doing?"

"Mister, why don't you go away somewhere else?" Ollie said. "Thanks for the matches and all that, but go away."

"Is that black powder?"

"Yes," Ollie said. "It is."

"Are you lighting a fuse?"

"Yes," Ollie said. "Mister, will you stand over there against that wall there? Maybe you'd better just stay with me for a while."

"But that is Fisher's bank," the man said.

"I know it is," Ollie said. "I need money." He scratched another match. He wanted to be ready, when the church went up.

"But you can't do that," the man said. "It's illegal."

"Just a minute," Ollie said, "and I'll explain everything. Just stick around, will you?"

Suddenly the man saw, finally, that he was simply at the wrong place at this particular time. "Sorry," he said, "I have to be off."

"Why can't you stand still and shut up?" Ollie cried, infuriated. "You can't leave now. Get against that wall and shut up." He pulled his pistol. The man swallowed and backed against the wall.

A tremendous explosion boomed out over the town from somewhere across the plaza. All at once Ollie's mind cleared and he laughed.

"Holy God," the man said. Vague shouts rose from the plaza. A man ran down the street past the alley mouth. Ollie put a match flame to the fuse and held it there.

"Stop that," the man cried, and ran at Ollie. He knocked the match out of Ollie's hand. Ollie swung with the pistol and missed.

"Help!" the man shouted. A face appeared at the end of the alley, down toward the plaza. "What's the matter?"

"Nothing," Ollie shouted back, and belted the dummy's horse across the flanks with his pistol. The horse jumped and clattered away down the alley. The dummy in its red dress fell off and dragged, bumping, along the ground.

"Help!" the match man shouted. The horse, frantic with the dummy dragging, jumped and sunfished across into the plaza, and the second man followed it, shouting. The match man dashed after him.

"Stop," Ollie yelled, "stop!" The man kept on running. Ollie swore, lifted the pistol, and fired. The gun roared and bounced, and then, beyond the drifting smoke, he saw in the place of the running figure, the soles of the man's shoes as the man lay on his face in the alley. Ollie swore again, terrified at the thought that he might have killed him.

And then suddenly, he didn't care. Time was flying, Burt would be back any minute. He lighted another match. His hands were shaking. He held the match to the fuse and the fuse suddenly spat a sizzling yellow flame. The flame disappeared up the fuse, and Ollie ran out of the alley, around the corner, and huddled against the wall. The explosion shook the building he was leaning against. Dust billowed out of the alley and then a rain of shattered brick began. Chunks began coming down in all sizes, like red hail. Ollie waited frantically for it to stop. It kept on and on, for an unbelievably long time, and then, suddenly, it stopped. Ollie dashed around the corner and peered through the dust and stinking smoke.

Something was lying on the ground, littered with bits of brick. The carcass of a horse, dead. His horse. He had completely forgotten it.

"Oh, God," Ollie groaned. Silence everywhere. The dust cleared, and then, down the alley, he saw the match man on his hands and knees, crawling slowly away. A sudden anger filled Ollie. Somebody should pay for the dead horse. He raised his gun again, but it was too late, the other had gone around the corner. The cat was out of the bag, a witness was loose, somebody who would describe him.

Above him there was a big black hole in the brick wall. Burt had been right—most of the blast had gone outward. There was a pile of brick rubble in the mouth of the hole, but as he climbed through, he could see that the rest of the vault was clean. He stood peering around. The place was neat as a tomb, just a haze of powder smoke and brick dust hanging in the air.

Nothing. Where there had been sacks of coin yesterday, the place was clean. The neat stacks of bills were gone. The gold was gone. Everything was gone. He ran toward the locked vault door, thinking to beat his way into the bank, and stumbled over something.

On the floor in the middle of the vault, as though waiting for him, and for some freak reason untouched by the blast, was a tray with five steins on it—all empty.

TWENTY-SEVEN

THE FUNERAL PROCESSION creaked slowly along the highway, past Pringle's place, past Nulty's, down to the old Spanish cemetery. It was a fine day, with a high west wind and clouds scudding east, their high tops gleaming gold, their bellies dark gray with rain. The wind was fresh and cool with a scent of fall in it.

Creak, squeak, squawk, crunch, high wheels, low wheels, ground slowly over the gravel; all in a long, slow line, everybody with his best on, everybody digesting his breakfast as well as he could, some of them already wishing they had gone to the can before they left town, a few desperate with hangovers, most of them sober, spick and span. Plop, plop, went the horse turds, falling from uplifted tails with a slow, sedate deliberation. It was strange, the Reverend Lewt thought to himself; here is Annie dead, here we go with all the decorum we can muster to pay our last respects to the wife of the greatest mortgage holder in the history of Grant County and the horses break

285

wind in our faces. Is this the purpose of human life, the end of human destiny, to have horses break wind in our faces? Is that all? The Reverend Lewt's horse replied with another. It was having a terrible time with its breakfast, too.

He watched the slowly heaving rear of the hearse, wobbling in front of him. One of the wheels was warped, and the tire slowly made a figure eight. He wondered what would happen if the wheel fell off. Nothing, probably. There they would sit in the middle of their decorum, while it melted in the sun and slowly spread in a puddle, while eight husky men heaved and puffed in their tight suits, getting some other wheel on, and families, all up and down the line, began to fight. Suppose two wheels fell off? Of course, they could always drag Annie to the grave. Under cover of wiping his large, white nose with his large, white handkerchief, Reverend Lewt took a shot out of his cough-medicine bottle.

His wife and six children were not with him. He always spoke better at public functions when his loved ones were not around to supply their usual tacit condemnation. That was one trouble with being a minister of the gospel and married besides, your family knew you as a man and at your worst. It did no good, on Sunday morning, on your way to church, to see your six-year-old son playing doctor in the front yard, using your cast-off truss as a stethoscope. It did no good for your wife to sit in the front pew, looking at you blankly—you knew perfectly well she was counting up the underwear, while you were coming to the peroration.

The peroration. That was the trouble. Why must there always be a peroration? It didn't really matter what he said in the sermons, as long as he said something—he could just as well have read shopping lists.

He was the decor, the figurehead, which, no matter how the bankers blundered, had to smile and give the appearance of knowing where they were all headed. He was not a priest, a master of the people. No, no. He was rather the sacrifice, the scapegoat. Nobody in San Vicente would ever drive him into the desert; that would have been too expensive. They just kept him tied up in the back yard, ready to be driven in case God should ever actually reach down and smack them across the head. And once a week he bleated, to remind them all that there was such a thing as sin. Or was there?

The fact was, Reverend Lewt had not thought about sin for a long time. He had given it up, because it didn't pay to make one's employers uncomfortable. Nowadays he spent most of his time trying to wrestle the budget around so that it could include both a new truss, biennially, and a decent assortment of fly-tying materials, which he ordered from Boston, to keep him busy through the winter.

There was something satisfying about a funeral, he thought as the procession turned off the highway and headed up the rocky hill to the cemetery. Why was it such an accomplishment to plant a human corpse? Was it simply the ritual? Or was there something else behind it? There was a sort of gastronomic satisfaction about burying people. Why did old people attend so many funerals? Surely not simply because so many of their old friends were going under, whom they felt they had to honor. It was because, each time, they felt a personal victory that they were left alive—something of the same emotion felt by a devout cannibal.

There were a number of gentlemen from Phoenix present. Had they come to honor Annie, or simply to make damn sure she was dead? His mind wandered. He wondered, vaguely, how many copulations Annie had been a party to. The score must be fantastic. And then he wondered, in his wandering, innocent way, how sex could be so interesting to some people. He himself had had no little pleasure from this aspect of Providence; but to devote himself to it exclusively, as Annie had done, would have been boring. Annie would never have had time in bed to learn to tie a fly like, say, the Supervisor.

The hearse lurched to a stop by the grave. A few yards away, the Mexican grave-diggers were sitting on the ground drinking quietly together. The pall-bearers, looking sweaty and dignified, hauled out the casket, and set it on the trestles beside the open grave. There was quite a show of late summer flowers around the hole, covering the pile of dirt and gravel, and Lewt regarded them with interest. He took a final gulp of cough medicine and stepped down from his buckboard. Some dutiful peasant had taken his mare by the bridle. He tripped over a rock, and some other kindly peasant, who no doubt, in his simplicity, still thought of him as a priest rather than as a pet goat, steadied him by the elbow. The Reverend Lewt was nearsighted from tying flies all winter. The cough medicine, of course, did not help much.

He took his place at the head of the casket. The little lid at the head section was propped open. He looked down at Annie, within. He could not make out her features at all clearly, and was not sorry, either. Then he realized that of course Annie was veiled. She had a veil of white gauze, with a little circlet of lilies-of-the-valley around it. Had her nose been burned in the fire? In any case, whoever had put the symbols of childhood innocence on Annie certainly had a fine sense of the totally inappropriate.

He waited, with the wind blowing at his wispy gray beard, while the huge crowd of Fisher's debtors slowly labored out of its vehicles and groaned up the slope. They stood bare-headed in the wind, with the breeze gently lifting a toupee here and there, and the Reverend Lewt had the passing fancy that he probably looked somewhat like Moses addressing the Israelites shortly after Sinai. What would Moses have said about Annie? Lewt had not the slightest doubt, but then, he was not Moses, and Fisher had not had a mortgage on Moses' house, either.

Just what was he going to say? He wished to God he could read off a shopping list or two in an emotional tone, and see what would happen. Nothing, he knew in advance. But something would come. Not for nothing had he been droning on, week after week for thirty years, mumbling sermons to the people of San Vicente. At a certain point in the career of a preacher the problem became not to find something to say, but to keep the clichés in the right order—after years of repetition, they had a tendency to fall out of his mouth like a pile of boards, all helter-skelter—the switches in his head were getting worn, and while he would start out knowing where he wanted to go, presently he would find himself shunting down a strange synapse on a totally unexpected line of associations, and it was difficult to get back on the main track. Not that it mattered much; nobody ever paid much attention to what he said. Church was not so much a place to worship God as a place to build up your credit rating.

"My friends," he began suddenly, as the wind twitched Annie's veil, "my friends, we are gathered here, not so much to honor the departed as to defeat the scurvy of the indefatigable." He paused, wondering what he had said. He tried it over again in his mind, and it sounded wonderful—much better than anything he had said for decades. He decided, on the spur of the moment, to let the synapses lead where they may—he had never, in all his years of floundering around in the decayed vegetation of his own religious ideas, come out with anything very satisfying to anybody, not even himself, but the words that had come flitting out, just now, all by themselves, had a peculiarly satisfying quality. Why not let it go on, for a bit? And see what happened? Perhaps, it occurred to him, he was finally speaking in Tongues. Anyway, his tongue felt good.

"Full score," he began again ("full score" could lead anywhere) "of prime and forty years, imponderable and excoriating as the truth may fly, impotent and diseased in flight, the bird of revelation takes the night. Annie Fisher, God rest her soul, is gone; full weighted in her innocence, her light and joysome spirit, not lightly like the feather, but the solemn ton. Not she who downcast the lively and the oak, but rather, in the perfunctoriness of impenetrable doctrines and her doubled twaddle, she would, time upon time, in spite of all cost and boilsome to herself, trundle the blather to some poor person, bringing light and hope to the disconsolate. Full many a fulsome wretch she gathered to the foil, and galled the intertwine unconscionably." Where was he going? He did not know and he no longer cared, and besides, he had a feeling that he might be imparting some profound truth to his audience. From their faces, they seemed quite impressed. He had their attention, for once. The men stood with feet apart, holding their hats in both hands before them, in unconscious defense of their private parts, trying to look as though they were not there.

"Not so the zero and the hour," the Reverend Lewt went on. He could see the strain beginning to appear on a face here and there. True, the wind was gusty, and batted his words about. "She above all was lofty and flue, and in the midst of society's prankish flaws, she strode intermittently down the path of virtue. How many of us have really known Annie Fisher?" A look of relief passed over the closer members of the crowd—they had finally heard something they clearly understood. The pallbearers brightened and stood up straighter. Fisher, who had been frowning, seemed pleased.

"Such a woman was she! And yet, how many of us can say, in spite of all the badging frail, we have truly known the soul of Annie Fisher? Surely in the impenetrabilities of the totally indoctrinate, the lush vargies of such a situation could not pass unpetherbated. Who shall lay aside the mist from her pure, sterile incontinence? Alas, such spiritual consideration must be given the first bong—" he blew his nose—"whoing, or how to figgelhoit the burse?"

The Reverend Lewt had never been so happy in his life. He was sailing along like a bird in flights of sheer rubbish, and in it he found a profound relief. "Oh, Hound of God! Intransigent and hoidle! In parth the roister dimple in the fay, she who ned garnishoy the bear."

He cleared his throat and looked solemnly, sadly, at those nearby. He could tell by the expression on the faces of the pallbearers that they had long ago decided that they could just as well do without the English language. He blew his nose, and four ladies wiped away a tear. He wiped away a tear, and five gentlemen from Phoenix blew their noses.

He spat into his big, white handkerchief, and took another belt of cough medicine from the bottle held therein.

"But though life is long," he continued, shuffling a handful of old rent receipts as though they were sermon notes, "we must all come to that day when, mortaille and fralingo, we stand before our Judge. But I am firmly convinced that the mention of hellfire in the New Testament is purely a fiction and a gloss." This was the last shred of Lewt's theology—he had eliminated hell for the simple reason that he did not want to go there. "Surely this little one, this tender, tithe-worn, toothsome trollop could not be called to a harsh judgment. Her face was everywhere welcomed as a gentle needle in the sweet entrail, her soothing voice a lull upon the shuddering ear, and everywhere that Annie went, her tail was sure to go." He smiled gently at the ladies.

"Let us not weep for those dear, beloved departed; let us rather weep for those undear, unbeloved, un-departed who still abide here with us, and our underwear. Uplift! Uplift! Let not your conderbains, unparted and bereft, dismail in smoky swamp and lender in the tuilleries, depart the mighty society in which we founder and infurscume.

"She lies here, a fitting tribute to our society, my dear friends. Her life was long, her friends innumerable. A friend to all, without discrimination as to race, color or creed, she never heard a single plea without giving the utmost of herself for the most she could possible get. If she lies here, today, gone beyond recall, it is only because she wore herself out, and could not be re-bushed. Can any of us say that she did not lead a life of heroic effort? She tried so hard to please so many, in as short a time as possible. Who else among us can say that they have given so much, of so little?"

Far down the field, he could see a couple of men skulking behind the rocks and he knew that the flock was again doing battle with the requirements of nature.

"Many of us, I know, have not had an opportunity to take a last view of our dear, beloved friend. So I am inviting all of those who wish to gaze on her beloved face once more, to form a line to the right and come by in single file. Be patient, please, no shoving."

The crowd, pleased with the prospect of a good, fat look at Annie, shuffled and shoved to get into line. Fisher took a place just beyond the casket, where he could see, not Annie, but the people who came by. It was, he knew, a day of tribute, and he had a black book in the back of his mind for anybody who did not come to pay their respects, whore or not. He had not heard half of what Lewt had said, what with the wind and the big words he used, but the words he had caught here and there certainly sounded like the right ones.

The first lady in the line came up, and Lewt, standing at the head of the casket, lifted the veil and laid it back over Annie's forehead.

The first lady passed, sniveling into her handkerchief, and went on. Ten feet beyond, she stopped dead still, and let out a shrill scream. Then she burst into hysterical laughter. Two or three other ladies hurried to take her by the arms and lead her away. All over the crowd, women began to cry, deeply affected by this sign of emotion.

One by one, the ladies paused in front of the casket, and lowered their eyes, brimming with sentiment, to take a last look at Mrs. Fisher.

One or two fainted on the spot and had to be carted off; a few others also burst into screams of laughter, or sobbing, and were carried away. The few men who cared to be seen looking at Annie in public took one glanced and appeared to have been stabbed.

"I can't understand it," Lewt whispered to Murphy. "I have presided at a thousand funerals, and never have I seen such a reaction. Such hysteria, such shock."

A low, hollow boom, like that of a heavy explosion, came rocking down the valley from the direction of San Vicente. Murphy looked up, startled. Fisher and Murphy looked at each other. The crowd turned as one, and gazed in the direction of town. Murphy looked at his watch. It was only half past ten. It couldn't be Ollie and Burt—they weren't going to hit the bank till eleven, at the time of the interment.

Down the highway a wagon came, horses galloping. It whipped into the cemetery yard and the driver came straight up the hill. It was Manuel. "Where is Braun?" he shouted. He pulled up by the hearse. "Where is that son of a bitch butcher?"

The ladies all looked up, shocked to hear in public language they had thought was confined to their homes.

"Shut up," Murphy said, grabbing Manuel and hauling him down from the seat.

"I got to barbecue my dinner," Manuel shouted, wrestling free. "I go to the butcher shop, I get in the box. I get my peeg, I take him home, I open the package. What you think I got? For dinner! Take a look, fat stoff!"

Murphy looked in the back of Manuel's wagon. There lay Annie on her back, neatly wrapped from head to toe in butcher paper, except where her face peered out of the hole Manuel had torn. Her dead blue eyes goggled coyly at Murphy, and his gorge rose. "Oh, God," he said, and turned away to stare fearfully at Fisher. "Where ees my peeg?" Manuel shouted, dancing up and down in a fury. He was full of tequila, as usual. "I got only three hours to cook him in, or I get the hell from the Colonel. Who's got it?''

Murphy went slowly up to the Reverend Lewt.

"What the hell are those bastards down the hill laughing at?" Fisher shouted, pointing to a crowd of men, his face bright red.

Lewt bent lower over the casket, squinting to clear his eyes. How strange, he thought. I never knew Annie had such a long nose. Goodness, what long teeth, too, and she is smiling. Dear me, such a lot of rouge—and such a big mouth.

He got within a foot of it, and started violently. The sow was smiling at him, its lips bright with rouge. Its little eyes seemed to be winking invitingly. Fisher strode around the casket and threw back the whole lid. The pig grinned up at him, with an expression both suggestive and content, smiling with gentle prurience. Fisher stood there, dumbfounded. The expression was Annie's, perfectly, the way she had always looked on a busy night; but it wasn't Annie. A profound confusion settled over his brain. He was looking at his wife; but it wasn't her body.

A second explosion rocked San Vicente. The cemetery cleared of wagons in a hurry. Manuel saw the pig. With a squeal, he grabbed it by the front feet and began to haul it out of the coffin. Fisher went blind.

"Let go of my wife," Fisher shouted, and he, Manuel and the sow fell to the ground, struggling. Dust rose and gravel flew as he and Manuel fought for the carcass.

"Children, children," the Reverend Lewt cried, holding up his hands. "Peace, peace, my dear little children. Should we fight over the dead this way?"

From San Vicente came the rattle of gunfire.

"Fisher," Murphy shouted. "The bank! Come on!"

Fisher didn't hear. His eyes were red with a terrible

rage. Manuel was in a double fury; he hated Fisher to begin with, and now Fisher was trying to take his pig away from him. They rolled and scrabbled in the dirt beside the grave, the pig in its red velvet dress, the circlet of lilies still around its long, white nose.

"Little children," the Reverend Lewt said, taking a quick snort of the cough-medicine bottle, "have you not heard it said, long ago, that we should love one another? Love one another, little children."

Fisher, Manuel and the pig rolled, thrashing, into the grave, where the battle continued, though the noise of it was dimmed.

The three drunken grave-diggers came up. One of them touched Lewt politely on the elbow. "You ready, boss?" he asked.

Lewt peered around, wondering where Fisher and Manuel had gone, and sighed. "Sure, go ahead," Lewt said, swigging again. He was alone. Murphy had gone.

The grave-diggers drove their shovels into the pile of flowers, and began heaving dirt down into the hole, on top of the battle, still raging below.

Fisher and Manuel stood up, shouting curses at the grave-diggers. A shovelful of dirt hit Fisher in the mouth, and the grave-diggers stopped and stood there, staring.

"Get me outta here!" Manuel shouted to his compatriots. They ran forward and seizing him by the arms, dragged him out, and then the pig. Fisher stood in the six-foot hole, his head barely level with the top, and shook his fist at Manuel.

"I'll get you for this, you greasy son of a bitch," Fisher shouted in a rage, scrabbling at the walls of the grave. "I'll burn you all, I'll have you hanged."

The three grave-diggers looked at each other. Manuel shrugged, the grave-diggers shrugged, and

Manuel walked away, dragging the pig to his wagon. Calmly, one of the grave-diggers raised his shovel and hit Fisher over the head. Fisher fell unconscious in the grave.

The grave-diggers glanced at Lewt, who was wringing his hands and trying to find his bottle, which he had dropped. They looked at each other briefly, shrugged some more, sighed, and then went quietly back to work, shoveling dirt into the grave.

Up above them, in the fresh, clear wind, the Reverend Lewt had found his bottle again, and was perorating his last peroration. "For all belie," he sang, transported, the wind blowing his hat off his head, pulling at his tie and beard, as he gazed far out over the lovely valley, "where all belie the purly and the blue, consign the dignity and fall, then casual and fulsome far below, and gainsay venture in the lull. Who can in diner sing a lill? Or finer wail the viner pail in die? No sadder lies the father in the dale, then mother die in burn a little ale."

Gently, his face lifted, he began to weep, smiling at the empty sky.

TWENTY-EIGHT

IN A BURST of fury, Ollie kicked the steins into splinters. There wasn't a dollar in the whole place. Fisher had cleaned it out.

"Ollie!" Burt shouted from outside the hole. "Hurry up, they're coming."

Ollie turned and jumped down into the alley. His rage was gone. There was nothing left now but danger. "We've been crossed up, Burt," he said. "There ain't a dime."

Two men appeared in the end of the alley, down by the plaza. One of them raised a rifle and fired. The bullet cracked past Ollie like a whip. He jumped up behind Burt on Burt's horse and Burt rammed his heels into it. "He seen us," Burt said. "Now they know who we are. Let's get the hell out of town."

"My teeth," Ollie said. "Slow down. We can hide in Cameron's." He slid off. "I got to get my teeth," he said. He was going to cry any minute. Those steins had done it. The tears came up hot inside him. He

turned and ran for the main street. Burt drove the
horse on, across the street, up an alley and around
behind Cameron's. He left the horse hitched in the
back, and went up the back stairs of the old adobe
building, down the long hall past all the wood stacked
up against the wall, toward Cameron's office. He saw
Ollie come up the front flight and turn and kick at
Cameron's door. Together, they crashed through the
inner door and stood facing the plaza through the
front window. There was a man in the street below,
over near Fisher's bank, who was pointing at Cameron's building with one hand, and beckoning to some
other men down the plaza to join him. Ollie drew his
gun, and steadying it against the side of the window
frame, aimed. The gun boomed and the man fell on
his face.

"You idiot, now you done it," Burt yelled.

"I had to stop him, didn't I? He spotted us, didn't
he?"

"So you shot him, you dumb idiot," Burt said. All
the men in the plaza were staring at their window,
and at the dead man in the street. Ollie swore. He
turned and began hunting for his teeth. He pulled
open the top drawer of the cabinet. A million tools
and drills. Then the second, then the third, and sweat
broke out on his face. He pulled open the bottom
drawer. There they were—hundreds of plates, old,
new, broken, white, yellow, pink, pair after pair of
them neatly taped shut, grinning at him.

"Come on," Burt said. Shouts outside, down in
the street.

Ollie crouched there, blinking at the piles of teeth.
He began to cry; and then, furiously, he began to dig,
tears streaming down his face, sobs shaking him, he
dug with shaking hands, picking up one after another

and throwing it away. A shot cracked outside, a bullet smashed through the window pane.

"Dammit," Burt shouted, "come on, or they'll trap us." Ollie got one of the patient-sheets out of a drawer and spread it on the floor. He began loading the teeth into it, in an agony of haste, fumbling and dropping them. Burt was right, he knew—he could sort them out in the woods.

Burt ran out through the office, into the hall. He saw figures down at the rear end, silhouetted against the light from the back yard. They saw him, and opened fire; it was too late. He had left his rifle with his horse; all he had was his handgun. He fired. The figures disappeared. He turned. More figures at the front end of the hall. He fired again, and the figures dodged away. Ollie ran out of the office and stood staring down the hall.

"Too late," Burt said. No resentment any more. A rifle came up over the edge of the back steps and fired, and the bullet knocked adobe out of the wall and ricocheted out the front. Burt grabbed the stack of stovewood piled along the wall and toppled it over. It spilled across the corridor in a deep jumble. Ollie grabbed the stack farther along and dumped that across the hall, making a second barricade toward the front. They lay behind the stovewood and fired at the rifle. It disappeared.

"You stay here," Ollie said, "and hold them off. I got to go back and find my teeth, I don't give a damn what happens."

"What difference does it make now?" Burt said. And then he knew. Ollie at least wanted to die with the teeth in his mouth. "We better give up now," he said. "Before it gets worse."

"Not me," Ollie said. "I had enough. I'll kill every

son of a bitch in San Vicente before I hang. But I got to get my teeth first, is all. That's all.''

Because he knew it, then, he was going to die. The time had come, all of a sudden, and he didn't give a damn. He just didn't give a good big damn any more, since those steins. He couldn't beat Fisher and Fisher's world, and he had had enough.

Silence from the plaza. He went back to the laboratory and looked out the window. Men far down the plaza, conferring. He began searching again. The sweat ran down into his eyes and he rubbed it away. The teeth had to be in the pile somewhere. Out in the hall, Burt let off another warning shot at the men trying to sneak up the stairs. From the plaza, a rifle bullet cracked through the window and went on through the frosted-glass door. A little dust showered down. Ollie sat on the floor, under the window, protected by the heavy adobe wall.

He was suddenly bewildered. How had he got here? It seemed a miracle to him, that he should be sitting here, suddenly hemmed in, suddenly trapped, completely. He hadn't done any harm—busting a bank didn't hurt anybody but Fisher, who hadn't lost a cent. And he hadn't meant to kill that man in the street, he hadn't aimed to kill, just to shut him up. Why hadn't the damn fool minded his own business? He hadn't mean any harm to anyone, all he wanted was a piece of it all for himself. And here he was, surrounded. Only this time it was not the Rurales, but Americans, around him.

Ollie looked out the window. Peace. Sunday. Sun. Dust. Halfway down the plaza, a sprinkling of men, of white moon faces looking up at his window. Blank, faraway faces, wondering, troubled, doubtful. Why wouldn't they just walk away somewhere, and let him and Burt go? Before things got any worse? He could see the Lieutenant talking to Murphy and Moore, and there was Fisher, God rot him, clothes a wreck, dirt from head to foot, he looked as though he had got caught in an avalanche, and barely got out with his life.

A sense of total defeat settled down over Ollie, a vagueness and stupidity. Vaguely he recalled putting the pig in the coffin the night before, but now he could not remember the purpose, and suddenly the room was full of peace. He sat there, limp and exhausted with the confusion of failure. How still, how clear this little room had become; into it, now, stole a mist of recollections. Maybe he wasn't even here, maybe it was a hangover, maybe he was just drunk, maybe those men down there weren't talking about him, Ollie, but about the weather and the cows. There she was, among a slow parade of visions, his mother, and an old tin dishpan they had used once for washing hands and faces, back in east Texas, before they even heard of Phoenix; now, moss hanging from trees, birds on dark boughs, white cranes in the swamps. How dim, how far away.

A shot—Burt, in the hall. He saw the clock on the bank across the street. Half past eleven. And then he understood why nobody was doing anything. They were waiting for the end of the amnesty, at twelve o'clock. Just arguing, hands gesticulating, Murphy, the Lieutenant, Quires and Mora, that bastard Captain that he would have killed if—

With a sudden intensity of anger, Ollie got up on his knees. He carefully laid his pistol barrel across the sill. He was trying to sight in on Mora, that bastard, but in his heart he knew he didn't have a chance, it was eighty yards and the sights were lousy anyway. He let off. Somebody fell, another man, five feet short and to the side of Mora, and lay twisting on the ground. A yell went up from the crowd, and a dozen guns suddenly came up. Bullets whacked into the adobe walls outside and dust and clay showered down from the front of the building. Four or five cracked in through the window, snapping through the opposite wooden partition. Two of them smashed into the dentist's cabinet and the mirror in the back panel was shattered. Tools and instruments flew, bouncing off the wall.

The bastards were trying to kill him, now. Something in him, some hot hurt of bitterness, cried out for justice. He wasn't arguing or reasoning—it was just the whole lousy mess that boiled up in him and yelled. The tin pan of his childhood, the ticks stuffed with moss that they had all slept on, his mother's shoes stolen off a dead nigger, all floated in his mind, and the distant crane, awakened by the confusion, flapped slowly across a pink sky, eastward.

So he picked some farmer standing in the front rank of the thin crowd, to represent his world, and fired again. It had a satisfying jar in it, that forty-five. The world went down, his mouth open, a second hole in his head just above it. Part of the lousy world was dead, anyway.

Another return volley and the crowd was talking it up, now, furious. But they backed off down the plaza, and stood there, and Ollie, grinning with his gums, let them have another six. The sons of bitches, let them fight. He heard sudden, violent shooting in the hall, stumbling and running, and then a man screaming.

"Burt? You hurt?" Ollie yelled.

"No," Burt said, loudly and clearly from the hall, and Ollie felt relieved. As long as Burt could hold the hall and keep the ones in the back from rushing them, he could hold off the ones in the plaza. The screaming of the man kept on. He must have been shot in the guts. Ollie sat on the floor, listening, and as the man screamed again and again, slowing down, his anger faded away. Finally, the man shut up, and Ollie was glad he was dead.

And then, suddenly, Ollie didn't want to kill anybody any more. He sat there by the window, sagging wearily. Three men dead. He had never meant it. For what? Because of an accident. Because he could not find his teeth.

He looked at the clock on the bank. Five minutes to twelve. Murphy was tying a white shirt to a rifle. Moore picked up the truce flag and started up the plaza with it. Bitterness rose in Ollie. Moore, the big, kindly son of a bitch. Why did he have to get mixed up with those bastards like Mora and Murphy? Moore was coming up the grass, not fast, not slow, walking steadily, right toward him. The only one of the lot with guts enough. Just the way Mora had come up the walk to that house in Mexico, with the same flag of truce. Moore stopped in the middle of the street below, and Ollie looked down at him.

"Come on out, Ollie."

"Let us go."

"Impossible," Moore said. "You've killed three men."

"So they'll hang us," Ollie said. "Why surrender?"

"They're going to blow you out of there with the cannon, Ollie. To save lives."

Ollie looked down the plaza at the cannon, where it squatted, as it had squatted for weeks, by the flagpole. He sat there on the floor, looking down at Moore, thinking. "Goodbye, Moore. I'll fight their crummy cannon."

"Goodbye, Ollie," Moore said. He stood looking

up at Ollie for a moment, and then turned away and started back. Ollie took a deep, quivering breath and let it out. His hands were shaking. He felt faint, and shook his head furiously.

"Burt," he said in a loud voice.

"Yeah."

"They're going to blow up the building with that cannon."

"Huh?" Burt said, startled. "They can't do that to a white man."

"You want to give up, Burt?"

"Not to hang. I'd rather take a chance. Going to be a lot of smoke and dust, maybe. Maybe we could get out."

Ollie said nothing. He could see them wheeling out the cannon and getting it ready.

Burt said, "I wonder where the hell the girls are."

"Silver City," Ollie said. "They're going to have a long, long trip, and nothing at the end." He thought. "It'll be winter, then, and Cheyenne is colder than a witch's tit. Poor Maddy."

Long silence, while the soldiers piled up the sacks of powder and the shells, getting ready. It took them a long time to do anything. Ollie could see them, checking shells off a list, counting everything, doing everything twice, stopping for some son of a bitch to roll a cigarette.

"You know something," Ollie said, "whatever it is, it ain't my old woman's fault. If she'd of known what a pile of crap it was, she'd of never of bore me. It wasn't her fault."

She came back to his mind again, gray hair, a lined, firm face, dunking something, the old man's under-wear most likely, up and down in the wash tub—up, down, up, down, wisps of gray hair glistening in the sun. Whatever she said, whatever she did, however many times she would shout at the kids, he never stopped loving her. The one good thing he had ever had.

How many times had he sneaked back in the morning from the chores, with the sun slanting in flat across the big iron bed, and climbed up in there with her? And lay there like a kitten with his head on her breast, looking out the window at the oaks across the far field, while somewhere down there, behind his mule, the old man plowed his weary way around the world.

And the other brats would be out working at chores, and she kept him there, as a special treat. He could remember, now, the feel of her breathing, the soft, slow rise and fall of her breast as she lay quiet. Maybe it was because he was so ugly that she loved him the best. Maybe it was his teeth she loved, those lousy, little pebbly teeth. Her ugly duckling.

The first shell hit the side of the building precisely at noon. A six-foot slab of wall and cornice fell into the street with a thundering crash and a shower of dust and chunks of adobe. Ollie's ears rang, he got numbly to his feet, stood there against the wall, stupidly. The second shell hit the wall and knocked him down. The whole room shook, the instruments danced, his head rang, and scared tears began to come.

The last things in this world he saw were a dishpan and a crane, slowly flapping away, his mother's face, and then his father's old, root-like fingers picking up a fork. The third shot came through the window, exploded on the back wall, and killed him.

Burt died one minute later. The soldiers, not knowing, mechanically kept on, repeating their ant-like movements of loading and firing the cannon, and slowly beat down the whole front of the building, until the rooms were all laid open and they could see Ollie's body. Then Aberforth stopped them.

No sound from the building. No movement. The silence, unbroken by any voice, was too complete, too perfect, to be illusory in any way. They knew that Burt was dead, too, buried in the building.

Murphy was trembling in tiny spasms. He had Ollie's teeth in his pocket still. He didn't know what to do with them. And he was afraid of them.

"Come on," Fisher said as the last of the cannon smoke stank away on the breeze. "It's past twelve, it's time to go to Pringle's. Come on, Aberforth, get your men mounted."

Moore, Aberforth and Mora were standing quiet, looking at the gutted building, still burning feebly, at the men slowly approaching it from the plaza. They were in a kind of trance.

"Come on," Fisher said angrily, his insides twisted up tight into a knot of everlasting fury. Nobody would ever forget the sow in Annie Fisher's coffin, he would never live it down. "The law says twelve o'clock Sunday noon, the hunt begins. Well, the time has come. Come on."

Moore turned slowly, "Yes," he said quietly. He looked at the cannon vaguely for a long moment, his eyes blank. The world had changed too much for him; he was no longer certain. Somewhere in the subsurface of this there was a kind of new crime which defied analysis. It had seemed to him that there was, in the frailty of the human creature, a quality that called for respect. Even in the hanging of a criminal, a certain dignity was maintained. And yet, the hostile cannon, that blind mouth that spewed indiscriminate obliteration, this belied just that human dignity. What they had done had been perfectly justified by law and reason; but for some reason beyond his understanding, the significance of the means now totally over-shadowed the meaning of the end. He turned and went for his horse, and the others followed.

Murphy, following, dropped Ollie's teeth in the gutter. They were stepped on by a horse five minutes later, and by evening had been trampled into nothing.

Simon Shaw had not left town, but had considered it wiser to hole up with friends on the edge of things. When they heard how things were going in the plaza, Shaw got these friends together, and while everybody was watching the execution of Ollie and Burt, they went to Quires' house, where it was said that Harvey Muntin had moved. They found Muntin, with a brand new deputy's badge on his chest, drinking beer with his fiancée. They conducted the young lady to the house of a neighbor, and after taking Harvey out in the back yard, to save Mrs. Quires' rugs, they shot him seven times in the middle of the chest, and left him dead.

After that, while the cannon was firing, they went down to Nulty's. He came to the door with his shotgun, opened fire, and was in turn shot down at the range of seventy yards by rifles; after which, as he was still alive, he was finally dispatched by five rifle shots through the chest. They left him hanging on one of the butchering hooks inside his slaughter-house.

That was how Murphy found him, though not till three days later, when jumping rats had eaten away all his lower limbs. It was a week later that Murphy went mad with fear.

After doing Nulty in, Simon Shaw looked for Shep. But he and his friends did not know that Murphy had sent Shep up to cover the canyon above Lawson's.

As a result, they did not get to Shep until he had come back down. Late Monday night they caught Shep in the outhouse behind the Red Dog, sitting on the hole pleasantly drunk. He opened his mouth in surprise which was cut short by four shots in the middle of his chest, and died in the act of pulling up his pants.

TWENTY-NINE

WHEN MANUEL, AT the Colonel's house, had found
Annie in the wagon, the Colonel had begun to feel
sick of the idea of the barbecue thing because, with
his infallibly fallacious sense of relationships, he could
not help but think of roasting Annie; so that when
Manuel, after a long time, came back, covered with
dirt and bruises, with the dead sow rolling around in
the back of the wagon, the bottom had dropped out
of his humanitarianism, and he had decided to let the
bastards starve. Enough to give them a quick drink,
and have done with it. He ordered Manuel to throw
the sow into the pit and to refill the pit with earth.
After that, Manuel was to go into town and find out
the cause of the explosions.

Manuel, of course, took the pig to town and sold it
to a Mexican butcher. By that time, the shooting was
over, and he came back with five quarts of tequila and
told the Colonel and Bill, who had been standing in

the living room listening to the shooting, what had happened with the cannon.

Bill's drink fell out of his hand, and he did not even notice it. The Colonel glanced at his white face. Bill stood there looking out of the window at the river. "The sons of bitches." There was an intensity of bitterness in his voice that made the Colonel suddenly very depressed.

"Ollie was crazy, Bill. He must have fixed up that pig and Annie, last night. He was working in the shop where she was, you know. And as for the cannon—he killed three men."

Bill sat down and covered his face with his hands. The Colonel had not lived with these men for three years, ridden and run with them. After a moment he took his hands away and sat looking at the floor. "Pepe was right," he said quietly.

Allie came through the doorway, floating and soft, and stopped, looking at Bill.

"There's nothing in the towns," Bill said.

"You have to write Ollie off," the Colonel said deliberately. There was no point trying to soften facts. One stood or fell by the facts. "He chose his own way, and he's through. That's the end of it, Bill, and you may as well sit back and take a deep breath and forget it."

Bill raised his eyes a little, and then saw Allie's foot; no more. Just the foot, small and neat beneath her skirt. An image of gentleness, of patience, and above all, of weakness.

"Pepe's still sitting up there, waiting for me," Bill said. "Suppose I didn't go out with your pompous friends, Colonel." He tried to smile. "Suppose I simply were not here, when they come—the hunting party. Suppose I just went up Lawson's canyon and saw Pepe and said goodbye, and let you all go on your merry way and shoot old Shaw. Would I be missed?''

''If you go with them they will accept you as an equal, they will trust you. If you're not here, they will draw the obvious conclusion that you don't like their company, and that's that.''

Silence.

There was nothing the Colonel could do. He wanted to stop him, hold him in a social attitude, at least for this one critical day—if he failed this particular day, he would have no reason left for succeeding the next. But there was a limit to what any man could do with or for any other man. He stood up. ''A man like you,'' he said in a sober voice, ''hardly ever learns. Because it is too easy for you to get away from the facts; both mentally and physically. You were always too skillful. Too quick a thinker, too good a horseman. Too good a shot. You were always so competent in the least consequential ways, and it has always deceived you. A bedridden idiot has more chance at wisdom than you ever will, intelligent though you are. If you were a cripple, Bill, if you had to sit in a chair and face the facts, you would learn, you would grow up. I am through.'' He turned and left the room. Bill stood up.

Allie looked up at Bill's face, and said, ''You know, everything doesn't have to be decided today, or this week. There's time for everything.'' As he looked down at her, now, she was a continued refreshment, coming into the midst of his own dry turmoils sweet, fresh and new, another world entirely. This was the fact that silently nagged him—that there was a whole silent world, quite apart from his mental world, full of its worn old conflicts—a world of no words, of kisses, love, coolness, freshness of breath and eyes, softness of hair. In this world, busy and silent, many things took place, almost unnoticed—children were born, work was done, houses built, there need hardly be a word spoken. But to live it, he had to turn his back on the other. Possibly there was some more fundamental value than intelligence.

He put his hands to her face, and kissed her softly. "I won't run," he said. "I'll last through the day, I guess."

The first horsemen came down the drive, the hooves of their horses scraping the gravel. With unreasoning fear, Bill stood straight, his smile dying, as the Colonel went outdoors to meet them.

Half an hour later, the big room hummed with talk as the twenty hunters waited for the last to come, Fisher and Murphy. They stood around with glasses in their hands, drinking good brown whisky. The Cannons stood there, big and amiable. Quires was there, a sort of portable court, or traveling warrant bench. The Burnses were there, father and son, trying to look as though they had done this sort of thing before. Mora stood talking with his calm, perennial civility, while Moore stood alone and morose by the Colonel and Bill. Bill stood instinctively by Moore, aware of the fact that, while many eyes were not upon him, thoughts and speculations were; there was a certain over-civil avoidance of glances in his direction, as though he were disfigured in some especially disgusting way, that left him all the more pointedly singled out, elected by indifference, ignored into prominence.

Aberforth stood by the buffet with a sergeant. Not even he knew what would happen in this hunt after old Shaw, the first on the list, and all of them expected almost anything.

Then Fisher entered, in a fresh suit of clothes, and

behind him, Murphy. Murphy was smiling, but Fisher's face was a pasty glower.

"Well," Moore said in the general silence, "it looks like we're ready to go. Which way did old Shaw go, Sheriff?"

Murphy said, "There's been a change of plans."

"Oh?" Moore asked. They were all looking at him, now. There was something funny about Murphy, and then they realized, one by one, that Murphy was scared behind the smile. His breathing was fast.

"What change of plans?" the Colonel asked, all quiet attention.

"Somebody's killed Nulty and that Muntin fellow," Murphy said. "We think it was that Mexican, Pepe. We're going after him, instead."

Dead silence. Bill's vision suddenly clouded and the blood pounded emptily in his head.

"The rest of the gang is dead," Murphy said. "Except for Bill Gorham here, who has come in and doesn't count." He turned back to the crowd again, and said, "It seems that Nulty told on the gang, and so did Muntin, trying to help me. So Pepe shot them. We got an idea where he is, but we ain't sure yet. Bill, can you help us out here?"

Bill was sitting against the table, holding himself up. He knew there was sweat all over his face, dead cold. There was a lot of invisible confusion in the room, a business of glances and head turnings. Moore stood there, appalled, looking at Murphy.

"Can you?" Murphy asked, his voice no louder, but his tone a little sharper. "We could use your help, Gorham. I guess, when you signed the amnesty agreement, you had in mind to help us out."

"Just a minute," Moore said. His voice burst out of control, a harsh roar, and Murphy's eyes popped open with alarm. Immediately, Moore had his voice down again to its usual soft tone. "Just one moment, gentlemen," he said easily, "I think this is a little out of order. I guess Sheriff Murphy doesn't know it, but Bill here and this man Pepe were close friends for many years. I suggest that the Sheriff withdraw his question."

Fisher stepped out in front of Murphy and faced Moore. "When Gorham signed that amnesty contract," Fisher said, his voice dead level, "he agreed to assist the law in every way. We are asking his help, now. How about it, Gorham? You either answer that question, or consider that you have broken the amnesty and are subject to arrest."

Bill opened his mouth. He could say nothing. His stomach was tied up in a knot.

"It's in the amnesty agreement, all right," Moore said, "as a matter of law, but I don't think anybody here is son of a bitch enough to press this man about his old friends. We are trying to make new citizens, not double-crossers and personal traitors. We're not that helpless. We're not that stupid or that mean. We don't need cowards to uphold the law, and we don't have to ask any man, or try to frighten him into doing something that none of us would do. And just to make this absolutely clear to you all, I'll tell you now, that this is nothing but a damned, dirty little piece of revenge cooked up by Fisher and Murphy to get even with Gorham for Gorham punching Fisher in the nose. It's as simple as that, and as far as I am concerned, the whole thing is good only for a laugh." He tried to smile.

The Colonel kept his mouth shut. Three or four men said, "Let's get Shaw, and the hell with this," and similar comments.

Fisher looked around the room. Half the man there owed him money, and expected to need it again. He knew it and they knew it. "The fact is, this is a simple question of law. Gorham, give us a straight answer. Where is this man hiding?"

Bill looked at him. "I don't know," he said, making a large mental reservation. He did not know absolutely. All he had was probable knowledge.

"You're a liar," Fisher said.

Moore put his hand out and took Fisher by the shoulder, held him a moment as though he were going to slug him, and then slowly let him go. He was beginning to lose control of himself. Year after year, it had been his unbroken rule, never to lose his temper. But now his face was red and the veins stuck out in his forehead and neck, and he was beginning to think that violence was justified, and this he knew to be a fatal error. He backed away from Fisher. "You listen to me, Mr. Fisher," he said as formally as possible, "I'm in charge of this as the Governor's representative. You have no means of knowing whether Gorham knows or not, and you have no basis for calling him a liar, and if you do not keep your mouth shut, I will arrest you as a disturber of the peace."

"Go to hell," Fisher said. "I say he is concealing the truth to help a murderer, and that is a felony."

"I said I don't know," Bill said. "I don't."

Fisher moved toward him quietly. "Did you ever know? Did he ever tell you anything about where he was going? I don't ask for certain knowledge. I want knowledge to the best of your ability."

"He said he was going to Wyoming," Bill said. That was a statement of fact, if there ever was one. The sweat was salt on his lip.

Fisher moved closer again. "Do you have any idea where he is now? The least idea?"

Bill stood against the table, fighting for some clarity. He bogged down. Then he looked up past Fisher, at the Cannons, at the other men in the room.

"Listen," he said, having difficulty with his voice. "I came in looking for peace. I signed the amnesty in good faith. I have come over to your side. I have given up. I have made up my mind to live among you in an orderly way, as a friend. Does this mean that you demand that I betray my old friends? Is this what you want of a friend? If I do this, now, what can you expect of me in regard to yourselves, in the future?" He stood silent, looking around at them. "Would any one of you, standing here, answer this man, about one of your own friends?"

"No," Alfred Cannon said, "I wouldn't. Fisher, I want you to withdraw your question. I don't question your right to ask it, but I ask you, as a decent man, a practical man, to withdraw it."

"I refuse," Fisher said. "There is not one of you that can force me. I am in the right here, and you know it."

"Listen," Alfred Cannon said patiently, "you are in the right as far as the law goes, but you are in the wrong as far as people go. I am asking you again, Fisher, to make allowances for human nature and take your question back. I do not think the law was ever intended to be administered as you are trying to have it administered, and the intention of the territorial legislature is certainly a basic point."

Fisher barely smiled. "I am going by what the law actually says. If the law does not mean what it actually says, then it does not mean anything at all—that is surely not the intention of the legislature."

Silence.

"Now you listen to me, Fisher," the other Cannon said. "If half the men in here did not owe you money, you would have been thrown out of here five minutes ago. Let me make myself plain, Fisher. I got a lot of money—probably more than you have, and if I feel like it, I can open a bank here too. Don't you force the issue, Fisher. Let it slide. I'm not trying to sound tough, but I want you to get this clear. If you force this, I'll lend money and undercut your interest rates till I break your back. I can do it, Fisher, and you know it, because all you got is that bank, but I got a hell of a lot more to fall back on. Now do us a favor and withdraw that question."

Fisher smiled, staring with hard, open boldness in Cannon's eyes. "Screw you, son," he said. "Screw you both." He turned back to Bill. "Answer the question. If you don't, I'll take this to the Governor. I'll have Moore wrecked and thrown out of the state for betraying his sworn duty to uphold the law. I'll bring charges in Santa Fe against every man in this room for conspiring to defeat the law of this territory, for assisting a fugitive, and as accessories after the fact in a first degree murder. Now answer my question, if you want to be a friend to these men. Tell us."

The sun was lower in the west; it was about half past two.

"Give me a little time," Bill said. "A little time to think."

Fisher whirled and said to Aberforth, across the room, "Throw a guard around this place. There's a Mexican servant here. There's no telling how many accomplices these people may have. Don't let anybody leave this place. Nobody is to go ahead and take a warning." He turned back to Bill as the sergeant left the room.

"All right, let's have it."

"He told me," Bill said, "that he would be at a certain place to the west of here, across the river."

What difference would it make? If he led them astray, until night, Pepe would get away, and they would never catch him. And as for himself, what difference would it make? He wouldn't give ten thousand of such men for one Pepe, he would not move a hair to stop them if they fell into the pit. "About fifteen miles off."

"Fifteen miles west?" Fisher asked.

"Yes."

"You're lying," Fisher said.

"Why should I be lying?" The accusation, like a slap, stiffened him.

"He isn't west," Fisher said. "He's east."

"You son of a bitch," Moore said, "you couldn't know that unless you already know where he is. You're trying to trap this man into betraying himself. You know where Pepe is and you'll go and get him there, and at the same time, you'll be able to convict Gorham of lying to you and breaking the amnesty. Fisher, you are a rotten bastard. I tell you so to your face, and I ask you to make something of it."

"Not now, not here," Fisher said, his face tight. "All right, I do know. He's up behind Lawson's, at the pool in the canyon. We found out. I have given Gorham his chance, and he failed, and I want him arrested for lying and breaking the amnesty. Arrest him, Murphy."

"Murphy has no jurisdiction yet," Moore said. "I'm still chief here."

"Then you arrest him," Fisher said. "Do you refuse?"

"Certainly not," Moore said. "Gorham, consider yourself under arrest and confined to the borders of New Mexico."

The Cannons smiled. Fisher's face turned red and he stepped toward Moore. "Do you refuse to lead us after this Mexican Pepe?"

Moore looked down at him, and saw the look of victory in Fisher's eyes.

"No, I don't refuse," Moore said. There was nothing he could do. If he refused, he would have to forbid it, and he could not forbid his own duty. "I will lead you."

Bill's hand suddenly grabbed at his sleeve; and then as suddenly let go.

"Then let's get our horses and the dogs," Fisher said, and turned away.

"Listen," Bill said, and his voice made no sound. "Listen," he said again, trying to speak loudly. No sound came out at all. It was as though they were all deaf, or in a dream, turning, coming, going, gathering their things together, unaware that he even existed.

"*Listen!*" They all stopped dead still. "I ask you one favor, give me a chance to talk him into surrendering. Ten minutes."

"You'll just try to help him get away," Fisher said.

"Put Moore on guard, let Moore go with me. He can be a witness. If you start a battle, he'll fight back or run, and if he does either, you'll kill him. Do you want a dead man? Is that what you're after?"

"No," Cannon said. "Take the ten minutes. Moore, you can cover them with a rifle while they talk."

"And let them both go," Fisher said. "I know you, Moore. You're rotten, you're soft."

"No," Moore said, looking steadily at Bill. "If they run, I won't let them go. This is the last chance, Bill."

He went out with Bill and the Colonel, and the rest followed them out to the horses.

Bill stood by his horse, too weak in the knees to mount. "Moore," he said in a low voice. "If you stand there with a gun, how can he run?"

"He can't run," Moore said.

"You can't simply shoot him down," Bill said, "just because he doesn't want to come in."

"That's all past now," Moore said. "I have a duty, I will have to do it."

Bill put his foot up. He couldn't make it. It was as though each movement were bringing him nearer to his own death, as though he had to be dragged.

"Pull yourself together," Moore said. "You've got to talk him into surrendering, Bill. It's up to you."

Bill turned and looked at the sun. Far down, about half past three now. Suppose Pepe surrendered, and Murphy got him in jail? Murphy would simply sell him to Mora.

He saw Allie at an upper window. Her white face looked down like a ghost's for a moment, and then disappeared. She came running out of the door, through the horses, up to Bill, and held something up to him. "Take it with you," she said. "Bill, don't go away. Don't go away again."

He looked at it. A locket. The first thing she had grabbed. Small, gold, heart-shaped. This was love, the idiotic gentleness, the senseless gentleness. He put it in his pocket, and then changed his mind and held it in his hand. She would think it meant something. Looking down at her, he found that his mind was clear again. In him the vague leapings of action were beginning, the stiffenings of alarm were beginning to take some kind of shape into flight, after his long stupor.

"Goodbye, Allie," he said, and turned his horse.

She did not answer. She stood there in the drive,

looking after him, and silently began to cry. It was the way he had said it.

The others followed, strung out. Behind them, the dogs in chains, then the four Papago trackers, and then the platoon of soldiers, mounted. And after them, the Colonel, leading the long train of men, riding quietly.

THIRTY

PEPE COULD HEAR the barking of the dogs from far off, across the country toward San Vicente, but he paid no attention. His bed was rolled and packed, his horse waiting with the cinch loose. In an hour the sun would be gone, and in the starlight, he would take the trail back up the canyon, eastward, and start for home, to find the priest again, in Mexico.

He went on with the leather thong—a piece of latigo he had cut off the cinch and rolled round between his palms. He was tying knots in it, about a quarter of an inch apart. First, ten knots in a row, close together, then a space, and another knot, another space, and then again, ten more knots close together. He was on the third decade now.

He had not seen a rosary for ten years, and he had never used one, but he remembered them well enough from the old days, the everlasting rattle of beads on the prie-dieu, the rattle of the sisters' big side-rosaries. He was amusing himself, he was in-

dulging himself in a way, for he did not know how
to pray, and he did not even want to learn. Not now,
at any rate. Maybe later. He was, in effect, making a
decoration for a new life, something to show the
priest, when he found him, perhaps. He had never
owned a rosary, and as he worked, he began to de-
velop a feeling of pride.

It was peculiar how the sound of dogs advanced so
steadily. A continual yelping and barking, like a hunting pack. Some rancher out after possums or rac-
coons, probably. The dog-voices were closer, a little
clearer, down on the plain.

He turned and looked at San Vicente, which he
would never see again, far away, as it had been that
first evening, when the five of them had camped there
and talked and made vulgar jokes, talking about home
and women. San Vicente, white in the late light of
fading afternoon, a jewel in the hand.

How still the forest was, how empty. He remembered Bill in the silence. How deep was silence, when
a friend had gone, how permanent that emptiness at
the side. When he was younger, he would have
thought, because he was full of dreams, that the forest had a friendly silence; but now he knew that it
was the silence of death.

There was nowhere to go in the mountains. That
was through; the rebellion was over; he knew now
that there was nothing in his solitary life. He had only
one frontier to cross, to go back, into Mexico. Once
across the border, once through the thinly peopled
northern states, once he was down in the crowds of
hotter Mexico, they would never find him.

Who would remember him? Inconspicuous, and
shabby as the rest, working in some parish sweeping
the floors, cleaning the furniture, digging the garden,
and that most perfect of all labors, renewing the can-

dles of the altar, filling the cruets with wine and water, little routine things, day after day, always near his one great Friend. Who would recognize an outlaw and a thief in that small figure? Nobody would care.

He smiled to himself. In the evening, someone would come hurrying in to the rectory, the priest would get on his coat, and take Him from the tabernacle; and Pepe with the candle and the bell would hurry before him through the dark, down the stinking alleys, and his stomach would swell up with joy.

He tied the last knot in the rosary, looked at it with affection, and put it in his shirt pocket, over his heart. All it needed was a crucifix.

A peculiar note entered the sound of the hunting pack, a sudden clarity and direction. To his ear it suddenly had the sharpness of a knife, and internally, it was as though he had been pierced. The dogs were in the canyon below. He could tell by the echoing quality. He sat there, alert, with the sharpness of his instinctive alarm, and listened carefully. The coldness of alarm inside him slowly turned to pressure, as he listened. He went to the boulder, walked out on its brow, where it overhung the canyon below, and listened.

No doubt at all, they were coming up. They had said that they were going to hunt down old Simon Shaw. But if they were following a scent, it could not be Shaw's scent, for Shaw had not come up this trail. Nobody had passed him, except Lawson, the day before, going down. And anybody going up or down would have had to pass him, because below him the canyon was cliffed in on both sides, and again, above, the meadow was cliffed in at the eastern end.

Suddenly he felt sick. There was a possibility that they were hunting him, deliberately. But nobody

knew where he was, except Bill. Then, suddenly the
answer rose complete in his mind. Lawson.

He had thought Lawson had not spoken, as he
passed down through the trees, because Lawson had
not seen him; but now he realized that Lawson had
seen him, and Lawson had not spoken because Lawson was angry with him, and Lawson had told them,
down below.

Through the fear and sickness, a kind of delight
began to dance. He was used to it, it always came
after the first shock, in every crisis, this happened.
This was nothing new. He had escaped far worse sit-
uations than this. The fear remained, of course, but
it was keened up now, and had become alertness and
competence.

He went into the trees, got his horse and tightened
the girth and led it back to the head of the pool, away
from the boulder, ready to go. His roll was tied behind the cantle, his canteen full, his rifle in the boot.

He opened one of the saddle bags and took out a
can of red pepper. He put it in his pocket. Red pepper
had the outstanding quality of ruining a hound's nose
for days. There was plenty of time to run, quietly,
shaking the pepper on the trail, cutting it.

Farewell, Bill, he thought. Farewell, and in his heart
a sort of benediction; peace be to thee, Bill, as though
a wish could descend like a cover over a sleeping
child. One man could not keep another, one man
could not forever guard another, that was not God's
will, Who was the real father. In the end, every man
was to be surrendered to God, in life as well as death,
like a child, and after all, had he not done quite well,
with Bill?

Bill was no longer a school boy getting drunk in
gambling houses. Bill was a man, now, a most competent man, who knew his way around the moun-

tains, who could live where a hundred other men would starve or freeze. Surely he would now become a good father, and bring up other men, his sons.

He squatted on the boulder in the growing dusk, and waited. They could not see him, from below, against the blackness of the trees, but he would be able to see them well enough, in time. The light was going, rising along the mountain sides as darkness filled up the valley below. San Vicente floated, like a pink vision on a violet plain, for a moment, and then turned gray and disappeared.

The pack had stopped, somewhere below, around a bend of the canyon. And then he saw, with troubled surprise, a lantern swing, and a man on a horse, and another on a mule; and then, in the light of the swinging lantern, he saw a piece of white cloth tied to a rifle barrel; and then he saw that the man was Bill. He had his hat off, so that the lantern light would shine clearly on his face. Then, around the bend of the canyon, the rest of the party came, and stopped. They too had lanterns. He could see them, soldiers, brass buttons gleaming faintly, the blue of slanting rifle barrels in the faint light, the paleness of faces.

They stopped and waited, a hundred yards down the canyon, while Bill and the other rider came slowly forward, their mounts' heads bowed as they worked heavily upward over the rocks of the stream bed. The man on the mule was Moore.

He ached with the instinctive knowledge that something was already wrong. Why had they stopped? They were making no effort to surround him, men were not climbing the sides of the canyon, to come up behind him along the spurs, as they should have. True, the sides were steep, the trees too thick for shooting; but they would not have stopped for that.

Then the answer rose, complete and final. He was already surrounded. There must be somebody above him, in the meadow, or in the trees, waiting for him to come up. Nobody had passed him; but somebody could have come around through the mountains from the other side, and taken up a position farther up. If this were so, he was already trapped, completely. If he got out, it would be with a battle, and only with luck.

His mind suffocated for an instant as panic rose, and then the usual anger came up, hardening him. Many traps had been made around him, but none of them yet had proved complete. And perhaps it was not even true. Perhaps this was something else again. The flag of truce was at least a sign of peace.

The white flag came on. Pepe got his rifle and squatted again with the hammer cocked, a cartridge in the chamber. Bill stopped below him and looked up. Moore came up and they got off their mounts and stood quiet, facing up in the lantern light.

THIRTY-ONE

"PEPE," BILL SAID. "I want you to surrender."

"If you don't," Moore said, "they will come up and get you."

"They are welcome to try," Pepe said quietly. "Why should I ever surrender?" A sudden feeling of bitterness rose. Why should a friend ask him to?

"I don't want to see you get killed," Bill said. "That's all."

"Don't you think it is better for me to stay free, Bill," Pepe said quietly, "and get killed, than simply give up like a coward, and be caught? I don't understand you. Why is it better to be in jail, alive, than dead, and free? I have always taken my chances."

"Are you crazy?" Bill said. "Do you want to die?"

Suddenly Pepe laughed, quietly. "That is the one difference between us, Bill. When you are dead, you are dead. When I am dead, I live. I have a God. You don't. My God will lift me up. But you have no God, so you will fall, and all those men down there with you, and in your hearts you know it, so you are afraid of death. They think they can buy me with a life, but I have a life in my hands, that I will live forever. Why should I care if I die? Cowards.'' He looked at the crowd, down the canyon. ''Cowards, trying to frighten me with death and all that. What am I, a dog, that I die, and am dead? No, I am a man with a God, and when I die, I will live. That *is* a big difference.'' He laughed again.

''That is one hell of a big difference,'' Moore said. For some reason, he too felt like laughing, a peculiar elation lifted him out of his own internal hell.

''So I will take my chances,'' Pepe said. ''I can afford to.''

''Where are you going?'' Moore asked.

''Back to Mexico,'' Pepe said gently. ''You remember the time I told you, how I used to carry the light for the sacrament? Well, I am going back. I was a fool to leave, but I didn't know. Be a good man, Bill. Have many children. Be a good father.'' He paused. ''Be as good a father to them, as I was to you.''

''Pepe,'' Bill said. ''If you try to go, I will have to shoot you.'' It was like a child's voice, Bill's, dead with fatigue and bewilderment.

Pepe smiled down at him. ''So you bargained with your new friends, to try to save my life, by selling my freedom. And now you are caught. This is what always happens to those who bargain and haggle with the enemy, fools who call cowardice prudence. But you won't have to shoot me, Bill, I will see to that. Moore, is there anybody up the canyon? Did you trap me in that way?''

''Not that I know of, Pepe. I didn't send anybody. But I have a duty to arrest you. I warn you. I will stop you, Pepe.''

''A duty to what?''

"To the state. I have an oath, you know that."

"An oath is to God. You have a duty, then, to God."

Moore looked at the face of the boulder before him. "That is not what I said," he answered. "I am an officer of the state. Pepe, if you come in, I'll get you free. I can stand off Mora."

"With Murphy? It is Murphy's jail. If I am in there Murphy can do as he likes. Do you really trust Murphy that much?"

Moore said nothing. He had no answer.

"This is so strange," Pepe said. "I have done nothing. But you want to arrest me. There is Fisher down there, the man who struck me in the nose. Is that why you want to arrest me, and have come with all these dogs? Because I committed the crime of standing still while Fisher injured his fist on my nose? I am so sorry, I apologize to your state."

"I am asking you for a favor," Moore said. "You can't win."

"The dogs are always saying that to the foxes, but there are still plenty of foxes. You are both asking me for a favor. Why? So Bill can be happy with his friends, and so you can do your duty to the state. You are so afraid you will have to kill me. Tell me, Moore, who is this state of yours? Is it somebody you know? Someday I would like to meet this state. I would like to shake his hand."

A shout came from below.

"We only have ten minutes," Moore said. "I can't stop them."

"You are in a difficult position," Pepe said. He was smiling gently. "You should be either on the side of the good or the bad, you cannot be on both—God will spit you out of his mouth. If we start shooting, you are between. I must save your faces and your hides.

How strange it is, when the hunters must ask favors from the hunted. Bill, why don't you come away with me? Climb up the path at the side of the boulder here. Moore, you come with me. Come down to Mexico. Eh? What are you living for? To please a pack of blind fools, blundering along through the dark after shadows that are not even there. To please a state which does not even exist except in your imagination, or else as a great throng of thieves in the government. Come with me. Do something decent. We will carry candles for a living God. Brooms instead of guns. What do you think of that? Do you think it is crazy?''

Moore didn't answer. He stared at the rock before him.

"It is crazy to carry God to the dying, you think."

"I am going to have to shoot you, Pepe," Moore said, staring at the rock. "It does no good for you to tell me what is wrong with me. Everything you say is true; but I am going to have to do my duty."

"Sure," Pepe said. "Your duty to the invisible state, which is invisible so logically since it doesn't exist. My God, you see, is invisible because he does exist, a spirit." He smiled in a moment of sublime contentment.

"Let me go talk to him," Bill said to Moore. "Alone. Let me go up there and talk to him privately. I swear I won't cross you up."

"Don't swear lies," Pepe said.

"If we let you go," Bill said, "they will think we betrayed them."

"Oh," Pepe said. "I had not thought of that."

"You give me your word, Bill," Moore said.

"All right," Bill said, and climbed the steep path.

"Don't try to come up, Moore," Pepe said. "I know you are a man of duty. I might have to hurt you. Be careful."

Moore stood alone in the dark, below the rock, full of pain. Pepe was right. But how, how had he come to be serving evil, instead of good? He had failed somewhere, but where? He could hear them talk, above, just barely able to make out the words.

"There is nothing you can say, Bill," Pepe said. "It is useless to come up here, nothing can be done. You have to choose. Either you go with me or try to stop me, and you have given your word to Moore and to those men down there."

"I don't care about Moore," Bill said. "Why didn't you go sooner? Why didn't you go yesterday, the way I said?"

"Yes, why not?" Pepe said. "I thought maybe you would come. A weakness. But I never thought you would come like this. Go on back, Bill, say you could not stop me. I will give them a decent chance to catch me. I will even hit you over the head, to try to deceive them, to let you out. But you cannot expect me to live the life you have chosen. Why should I? To oblige some tiny law of man that those people down there have written down? Some feeble law, full of mistakes and errors? Is this something to sacrifice for? I told you and Moore to come with me, to serve a far better law. But he thinks he has his duty to his invisible state, and now you have given your word, and you cannot go, I wouldn't take you. Go back now, I must be going."

"I'm not going back," Bill said. He threw Allie's locket away, toward the pool. It made a tiny splash, and was gone. "I'm going with you. Where, God knows. Do you think I can see them kill you? Do you think I can live back down there, year after year, knowing I had something to do with your death? Come on, we can both ride your horse tonight, to get away and steal another in the morning. Let's go."

Pepe looked at him. How tired his face was, how white, how drawn, the way it had been when he was sick, five years ago. "Are you going to start drinking again, Bill?" he asked quietly.

"No," Bill said. "I am going with you. Come on."

"Listen," Pepe said. "You are going to have to live down there many years, till you are an old man. Many, many years. It won't be easy. But you cannot come with me. You have given your word to her, you have sworn that agreement, you have promised Moore, just now, to be faithful. You cannot break your promises. You chose. Down below, that is your real life." He looked at Bill for a moment. "You are acting like a coward, Bill. You cannot face it, to shoot me, to do what you have to do. Listen, Bill, you could not stand it in Mexico. I am a servant, a low servant, the lowest of the low. When you come to despise me, then what? Murder, drinking, whoring, ruin. You cannot be a traitor to yourself. And are you going to leave Moore alone, to face others? They will think he was part of your plan, they will accuse him of treachery too. Don't ruin Moore."

"I am going," Bill said, his voice like iron. "Come on. We can get on that horse and go, and be gone ten minutes before they even know it."

"You are not going with me," Pepe said.

Bill started along the edge of the pool, toward the horse. Pepe followed him.

Moore, below, stood lost between two terrible weights, crushed from both sides. There was no time to think any more, and he acted as he had to act. He pulled his rifle out of its boot and scrambled up the steep path beside the boulder. He reached the top, cocking the rifle, and lay forward across the stone. Words, now, were totally useless. He lay there with his sights on Pepe's back, as Pepe and Bill walked away toward the horse.

Bill put his foot in the stirrup and started to mount.

Pepe said, "Wait." There was a note in his voice that made Bill turn and look at him, and when he saw Pepe's face, he took his foot out of the stirrup and turned completely around.

"I found you dying in an alley," Pepe said. "I nursed you back. You are mine. I own you. Do you think I have hated you all this time? You are like my own son, everything I did, I did because it was good for you, to make you grow up, to make you strong, so that you could face your life like a man. And now you are going to betray everything, destroy yourself, and make me ashamed. Listen, don't think. Obey. Bow your head. What good are your reasons? Are you a god? You do not even know why your own bowels move when they do, and yet you try to understand the stars. Don't you know what God said to do? Love. That is all. Love your wife, your children, your friends, and try not to hate your enemies. To whip bad children, that is love. Love is very hard, it sweats and cries. Many men will spit on me when I carry that candle again, many hate God, think it is foolish. But I am His slave, I do not care. I know now what it is to serve. I have tried everything else, I have known everything else, there is no freedom except in this, for me. But your freedom is another kind of slavery, to the world, but you have chosen it. So now love it, serve it. In the end, all of us must serve something, we must bow low, our heads to the ground, blind; the only freedom in our slavery is to love, to serve because of love. That is the secret. I am giving it to you as a law. You are to obey."

Down below, the dogs started yelping in a new

fury, and they suddenly heard the clatter of many hooves on stone.

"Are you coming?" Bill said, his face like stone.

"You are being a bad child," Pepe said. "You are not going."

Bill smiled with sudden cynicism, turned quickly and put his foot in the stirrup.

As he rose, the barrel of Pepe's rifle cut down across the back of his head, and as he fell, Pepe caught him. He lay there on the ground, on his back, unconscious.

There was the beginning of panic in Pepe's face as the sound of dogs rose from below. He stripped Bill's belt and tied his feet. But they would never believe that, it was too obvious. He took the belt off and threw it away. He heard the roaring of the mastiffs as they caught his scent.

Then the panic in his heart died, and his face set. He would have to do the one thing that would solve everything for Bill: shut all mouths, make him stand fast, and give him, finally, peace.

He stood and looked at Bill for a long moment, and then slowly raised the rifle. He sighted it carefully on his son's right knee. It had to be that knee, so that he could still mount a horse, and live usefully. He would be able to walk, but slowly. No more running away, no more fighting, no swift retreats, escapes or sudden turnabouts. He would have to stand fast. It was the only way he would ever learn.

He looked through the sights at the knee, he squeezed the trigger slowly; his belly melted, his brain turned dark; he froze, he prayed, and then he fired. The rifle roared and flamed. For a moment he stood still, and then as the blood came out of the shattered knee, the tears flooded out of his own eyes and blinded him.

He flung his rifle into the pool. He turned and mounted the horse, and quirted it toward the trees, blind.

Moore, still not believing what he had seen, got up and ran, shouting. "Pepe, stop!" He halted, aiming on Pepe's back. "Stop!" he shouted again, desperately.

But Pepe did not stop. The horse was running for the trees, was going into the shadows when Moore pulled the trigger. He saw Pepe sway, grab the horn, the vanish into the darkness.

Down below there was shouting and the roaring of dogs at the base of the boulder. Moore ran into the woods after Pepe.

And onto the meadow above, past where the body of the wild horse lay, Pepe went, swaying in the saddle, riding up where the wild horses had fled, across the open meadow through the last light. He had been right, he knew he had been right, he had had to do it. But he could not stop the tears, he could not see.

He did not see the orange flash or hear the sound of the second rifle from the trees at the end of the meadow, ahead. The pain burst in his chest like enormous red fireworks. He did not even feel himself fall; the horse thundering away. And then he lay quiet, looking up at the evening stars, with blood slowly coming up into his mouth.

Moore heard the shot, and ran out onto the meadow. He stood looking around. Then he saw the horse, galloping away; then he saw the shape of Pepe, darker than the gray-white grass, lying in the middle of the field.

He ran to him, and knelt beside him, and Pepe looked up, or past him. Pepe knew him, and smiled at him, as at a friend, and died.

The dogs burst out of the trees, the two mastiffs

first, roaring and leaping with terrible jaws, with terrible bounds. Moore stood up, his rifle raised, and waited. He waited until the first mastiff was twenty-five yards away, and then calmly shot it as it bounded toward him. He got the other at fifteen yards, and then as the rest of the pack came on, he began cranking bullets into it, scattering the dogs over the field and into the trees.

Then Fisher, Aberforth and Murphy were suddenly on top of him, on their horses, the horses dancing and rearing. Soldiers with lanterns shouted at him. He stood like a stone, in front of the body, waiting, and after a while, as he said nothing, they quieted.

"Who was up there in the woods, waiting?" he asked. "Who killed him here, in the field?"

"Shep," Murphy said. "I sent him."

Moore said nothing.

"I had the right," Murphy cried. "The amnesty is over."

"Go away," Moore said. "He is dead. That is enough."

They began shouting again. Moore quietly reloaded his rifle. The Colonel came up.

"Bill is conscious," he said. "He says that Pepe shot him in the knee. Is that true? I thought they were such friends."

"Yes," Moore said. "Bill went up to talk to him, to try to get him to surrender. And Pepe shot him."

"Ah," the Colonel said, looking around with satisfaction. "Then Bill did his duty." He looked at Fisher.

"I will take care of this body," Moore said calmly, "if you would be so kind as to leave me an extra horse. You go on down, Colonel. I will see you later."

"You should not have shot the dogs," Aberforth suddenly cried, as he stared at Pepe's body, his face ashen. "You should not have destroyed government property."

"Go away," Moore said quietly.

Something in his voice made the Colonel wheel his horse in front of the others, herding them away.

Moore waited until the crowd had moved away again, back down the meadow, out of sight, and out of hearing. Then he picked Pepe up and carried him back down the meadow, down to the deserted pool, and laid him on the ground. There was a horse waiting, an old bell mare from the soldiers' pack train, and beside the horse stood a lantern on the ground, gleaming faintly in the dark. The bell tinkled now and then, the tiny sound alone in the vast silence of the forest.

Moore slowly sat down beside the body and put his face in his hands. Very slowly, unaware, he rocked back and forth, not breathing, not weeping, making no sound, except at long intervals. When he drew a breath, it was a long, dragging sigh. He had told Pepe there had been nobody in the woods above, and Pepe had thought he had betrayed him; and Pepe, dying, had forgiven him, all at one time. Of all the men that Moore had hunted, Pepe was the only one in whom he had never found a reason for pity, the only one he had fully respected. And he had had to kill him. That was the law.

Why was it that in the end, the law of men was made, finally, only to kill? It had to be that way, there was no other way. He remembered Ollie and Burt, dead in the rubble; Harvey, poor, simple Harvey, led away by a cheap dream. They were all his children. Why had he never been able to hate the poor, the miserable, the stupid and the desolate? Why was it that the rich, the proud, and the cruel were the only ones who had ever driven him to anger? All his life he had served the law because he loved peace, and all his life, the law had forced him to jail the weak, the stupid and the poor, while he saw the rich go free, their right hands full of bribes, walking on the faces of the poor. That was his law.

But Pepe had another law, that had no part of judgment. Judgment there must be, but he need not be the judge. He took off his star and sat there looking at it.

He saw, sticking out of Pepe's pocket, the thong he had been working on, where it had fallen. Moore knew what it was. He picked it up and looked at it. Was it possible that this was a superior law? One might not suspect it had much power, and yet Moore shrewdly saw, with newly-opened eyes, that its simplicity was also an immensity. He sat there with the star in his left hand, and the knotted thong in his right, and above him, unseen, the pageant turned, the sign with continual meaning. After a while the answer came, perfectly simple. If he were God, and could do all things, then he might serve both justice and charity, it might be possible both to judge and love. but he was only a man, and in his life there were only a few things he could ever do. If this were the case, if time were his final limitation, should he not better, then, choose to serve the poor as their servant, rather than as a master? For his law was a master, no matter how careful, how kind and wise, and the law bound no wounds; its wretched legalities were full of error and fumbling unwisdom. If he had put a bullet in Pepe's back, as a just master of one law, then there was good reason why he should take his place as the servant of another law; and in due time, with order, sense and moderation, in some place where his abilities could be used to the advantage of such people as Ollie, Burt, Harvey and all the rest, he would find his own way to the place where Pepe had been going.

He stood up. He put the thong in his shirt pocket, where Pepe had had it, and taking his star, he tossed it out over the middle of the pool, and watched it fall and disappear.

He put the body on the pack mare and tied it so that it would not slip, and then, taking the mare by the bridle, and carrying the lantern, he led it down the steep path, letting his own mule follow.

So, through the dark, they went down the long, steep trail, into the deeper dark; down the long mountain, a tiny procession, while up above them in eternal battle, the stars stood in their places, some serene and true, while others fell into oblivion. Slowly, halting, the lantern gleaming like a tiny golden star in the dark, the bell tinkling, gradually fainter and fainter into silence, they went; as, long ago, the candle and the bell had gone before the Child.

AFTERWORD

Many years ago a man wrote me a letter, telling me this story. His letter ended this way:

Sometime, if you go riding through those mountains east of San Vicente, you will find a pool; and if it is a Saturday, you will maybe find Bill, sitting there with his stiff leg. But you know the story now, what he is thinking about: the locket, the rifle and the star, at the bottom of the water. His boys holler in the woods; and down in town, Allie is waiting, old too, with old friends, plenty of money, and good talk.

But there is a stillness up there that holds all the past, all his questions, now muffled down under that terrible patience he has taken on. He can't get away, there is no escape from this earth, no freedom any more, and Pepe, who showed him the way once, is gone. He is lost, but he is patient, hoping that if he waits long enough, somebody will show him the way again. At least Pepe left him something—a duty, and he is doing it.

Now you know how the three things got into the pool, but there is one thing more that only Bill knows, one thing in the mountains that nobody else has ever seen.

One night he went up there, high where the pines are stunted, among the gray boulders, by bright starlight, and found it, almost hidden under an enormous rock, where it rolled down and was caught. It was round and gray too, like the rocks. Round and gray, with short, stubby teeth, one of the front ones big and gold, grinning upward at the starfall, mocking and defiant. The foxes have scattered his bones from where he fell, killed by an old she-bear. Struck down, still he grins forever at heaven, the last of the free men, old Shaw. There he sits, caught forever, grinning at the falling stars, with a stolid defiance and a brutal mirth that nobody today could ever understand.

I stood and looked at Shaw, and after a while I knew this: There's not a lifer left among us that will not say, you were wrong. Shaw; freedom got you nothing but pain and death on a mountain, alone. We all have our holes now, lined comfortably with suppressed agonies, and we all sit by our pools, thinking of what is hidden.

But if you were wrong, then why do I find you grinning at the end? In an eternal, perfect intimacy with the warning above you, sneering, grinning at the starfall. Only Pepe and you had any purity at all, the one of peace, the other of perdition; but Pepe has gone, where I do not know, where I cannot follow; and so I stand here, with the only purity that is left, admiring not your perfidy, but its perfection. And so I will wait, until another Pepe comes along.

Don't miss...

The
Rainbow
Runner

by
John Cunningham

Now available
in hardcover from

Tor Books

SKYE'S WEST
BY RICHARD S. WHEELER

The thrilling saga of a man and the vast Montana wilderness...
SKYE'S WEST
by the author of the 1989 Spur Award-Winning novel *Fool's Coach*

"Among the new wave of western writers, Richard S. Wheeler is a standout performer."
—*El Paso Herald-Post*

☐	51071-2	SKYE'S WEST: BANNACK	$3.95
☐	51072-0		Canada $4.95
☐	51069-0	SKYE'S WEST: THE FAR TRIBES	$3.95
☐	51070-4		Canada $4.95
☐	51073-9	SKYE'S WEST: SUN RIVER	$3.95
☐	51074-7		Canada $4.95
☐	50894-7	SKYE'S WEST: YELLOWSTONE	$3.95
☐			Canada $4.95